IN / THIS / SIGN

ALSO BY JOANNE GREENBERG

The King's Persons
I Never Promised You a Rose Garden
(as Hannah Green)
The Monday Voices
Summering: A Book of Short Stories
In This Sign
Rites of Passage (stories)
Founder's Praise
High Crimes and Misdemeanors (stories)
A Season of Delight
The Far Side of Victory

JOANNE GREENBERG

An Owl Book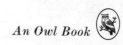

IN

THIS

SIGN

HOLT, RINEHART AND WINSTON
NEW YORK

Library of Congress Cataloging in Publication Data
Greenberg, Joanne.
In this sign.
"An Owl book."
I. Title.
PS3557.R378I5   1984   813'.54   84-6737
ISBN : 0-03-000438-1

First published in hardcover by Holt, Rinehart
and Winston in 1970.

First Owl Book Edition—1984
Designed by Robert Antler
Printed in the United States of America
1 3 5 7 9 10 8 6 4 2

ISBN 0-03-000438-1

TO ALBERT

"The right hand, palm inward, covers the left hand, which rests on the heart."

IN / THIS / SIGN

1

HEY SAT ON THE BENCH AND WAITED. Now and then people walked past them on the mysterious errands of the Law and, as they passed, looked at them sitting there and then looked again with small, quickly hidden smiles. They had been sitting on the bench for almost an hour and slowly Abel had begun to understand why the looks were strange. They were sitting very straight, he and Janice, because they were frightened; it made them stiff in their clothes. The strange looks were because their clothes were not correct for the season. He had felt so free and wise in these same clothes before. They had been beautiful when they were new; he remembered walking proudly out of the store in them, into the carefully portioned light of September, knowing that the last of his great money had gone for them. It was January now, and Janice beside him was still Summer, all summer green and gold and wearing a hat full of flowers.

Maybe it wasn't the right thing for her to wear the thin gauze dress or a hat piled with flowers, but it was her good outfit; it made him remember the summer days and her running down the street toward him, running for joy, the wonderful automobile and the food, all the food, and the tent show they went to in August, and how, in The Summer, what they had and what they hoped for made a shine in their eyes and faces and gave to each of their ways and gestures a special grace.

All of his summers before were nothing but a haze of dust and the smell of dust, tiredness and sweat. That was the farm. Town Summer was different. He thought he had never looked at a tree when the leaves were full, or walked in the night's little wind, or seen the green-moving sun-dapple on someone's face, or felt it on his own. Janice's yellow hair was warm and it smelled of herself and of the sun. He gave her a green jewel ring to keep the sunlight in and he got himself a marvelous watch, fat with numbers, a chain and a fob and a fob charm in the shape of a lion's head with red jewel eyes. The Summer . . .

Janice moved a little. The door of the courtroom had swung open and she was leaning forward to catch a look at the inside. They saw some benches, rows of them, but the door swung closed again and that was all.

A man in a heavy coat came around the corner and toward them. Abel began to raise his hand just a little for Janice, to tell her that this was his boss, Mr. Webendorf. There was another man with him, a thin man, very clean and dressed tightly, a stranger, but before Abel could get up and give his greetings, Mr. Webendorf nodded and went away into the courtroom and the stranger was left standing in front of them.

"Comstock," he spelled out with his fingers, and into their astonishment. "I'm here to interpret for you."

"You deaf?" Abel asked, stuttering because his hands followed his mind.

"Parents," Comstock said. "I work for the Court sometimes. Come on, they're ready for us now." His Sign was quick, educated, a little ugly with impatience. Abel and Janice turned to each other, surprised.

"Let's go, let's go," Comstock said. He swung through the door, and they winced and followed.

A man took them all the way to the front of the courtroom near the Judge, and between the Judge and themselves, Mr. Comstock stood. Everyone swore to tell the truth and then the thing began.

It was, the Judge said, a Hearing. Weren't all of them *Hearing?*—latitude—what was *latitude?*—would be given the respondent in his replies in consideration of his infirmity. The beautiful, unmeaning words that the Judge was saying broke hard through Comstock's fingers. Into the dark wood-and-stone room, an old, shaking sunlight was slowly venturing. Chair by chair it crept the way down the aisle and by the time Mr. Dengel, the automobile dealer, was finished with what he said, the light had slid down and gone to sleep between the front row of chairs and the tables where people talked to the Judge. Abel was happy to watch the light. It was the only thing in the room which was not strange to him.

Mr. Dengel was the man who had sold him the car. This trouble must be about the car, then.

Mr. Dengel talked for a long time, saying everything about the car, about the color and the kind and the different papers that had to be signed because of it. But when he told about the money—what the car cost—Abel had to jump up and tell what was true, because the car did not cost what Mr. Dengel said. That was a lie. Then the Judge was angry and Comstock's hands shot out that anger against Abel and told him that if he did not sit down and wait until he was called, he would be fined for contempt of court. What was *fined?* What was *contempt?* Abel saw then that it was very important to keep them all from anger. He sat down. Mr. Dengel said some more and the Judge asked things and then told Abel that he, too, must tell about the car. He began, trying to see everything clearly in his mind: Town and the shining machine and The Summer.

They came in late spring, he and Janice, from his father's farm. There was a job for him and for Janice. They had a room on Perrer Street and money for their start—the savings his father gave him in a deep, old-fashioned snap-purse. On his way home from the printing shop each night he walked past the place where they sold the automobiles. He always stood for a while, staring. On nice nights the big doors were open and a light was on so people could stop and see the beautiful machines, glowing and smooth. Sometimes the man came out and took someone by the arm and smiled to him to come and sit behind the wheel and notice this thing or that, try the horn, try the lights. Once, Abel was that person. The man motioned to him and he went and sat in the car while the man spoke to him aside, privately, like someone of special fame. He didn't need to hear the words to feel the honor, so he smiled and nodded to show how glad he was because of it. Then the man began to write numbers on a paper. He showed them and Abel nodded under the light. All that time the man was saying and saying things, his mouth moving without rest; smiling, too, because he was telling Abel that for the small savings in the snap-purse, for only the small money which his father gave him—it was true, it was to be his own, his and Janice's, that wonderful car. Then Abel nodded yes, and yes again and signed the papers and the man came all the way around the car and opened the door and shook his hand.

Abel also remembered very clearly, the light trembling in the leaves of those summer evenings. The air was warm and the late light was warm, and more rich, golden light lay all along the streets. In such a light, he came to the room and told Janice about the automobile. She was so excited they left without eating dinner and went back to see it. The streets and stores were dark by then; there was little to see, but they were glad they had gone anyway. They walked home slowly, in silence, because of the dark. The stars here were not spread out on one wide night as it was back on the farm; they were comfortably measured and held between the buildings of the city. Everything they saw, thought and knew had splendor for them; happiness, richness and strength. They looked at everything in a clearer light. How could there be bad in such joy, in any of it?

Tell about the car. The car was blue; very, very smooth to touch. It made the days perfect. Abel tried to describe the silvered fittings gleaming on it and the steadily made fine outlines, red painted around the wheels. A new car; Pierce-Arrow 1919. The Judge was restless in his chair; Comstock told Abel to hurry, so he tried to ask how it was anyone's fault if the joy of the car was short. He was used to handling horses and the need to see far ahead and rule every move of the machine was strange to him. On his first drive he ran the car into a fence; on the second he scared some horses and they kicked at the back of it, and in fear he steered too much, so that the machine tipped over on its side. Also, he did wrong, many times, to use up all the gas, and Janice became too frightened to go in it. She began to nag at him to sell it. For a moment he stopped speaking, his hands caught over a Sign. He was remembering the anger he had felt at Janice then. For a week he did not speak to her, not even giving a greeting night or morning. She was afraid to ride with him. She kept asking him to sell the auto. She cried and told him she was afraid. After many fights and crying and days without speaking, and after two more accidents, he agreed to sell the machine.

He put a sign on the car and sold it to a man who was passing. They wrote out different prices until they agreed. At first Abel was proud because he sold the car for more money than he paid. Then, for a week after, he was sad the way people feel when someone dies. He and Janice walked on Sunday. . . .

"Hurry!" Comstock said. "The Judge does not want to know your feelings."

"I will tell everything. How can he know if I do not tell everything?"

When they walked, he went on, they began to look at the prices of all the beautiful things in the stores and the food in restaurants and they began to see that the car money could give them all these things. That was how they had the idea to have and buy the jewels and clothes. Abel smiled. The pride they had in this richness made them sleep well every night and wake up hungry; and be glad and work all day with quickness. At night they went to restaurants and ate every kind of strange and remarkable food that never was on the farm or in the cold school where they met. On Sunday afternoon the stores were open and Janice began to look carefully at how Town women dressed. He bought her the hat, the one she was wearing. He bought her the ring with the wonderful jewel in it, and his watch, and the chain and fob charm, this lion's head with a jewel eye. When the tent show and fair came in August, they went. They bought a toy monkey on a string, spinning tops, pinwheels, pine-needle pillows and cedar pillows and Chinese burning sticks to smell good and many different kinds of paper flowers. The Summer. He smiled again.

"And what then?" the Judge asked.

"Summer ended then."

One evening after work, Abel and Janice counted all their money. The warm days were gone and the money-joyfulness shriveled. The nights were getting cool for summer clothes. They tried to be cheerful, but soon it was cold at night and the mill girls walked from work in hard-dark, shivering. Then they saw that they could not eat away from the room until payday. All the starting money was gone; all the car money was gone.

Still they weren't angry. Abel didn't tell the Judge about the store windows. The Judge would laugh if he knew that they always used those windows for mirrors, and that in those windows it was still summer. When Abel passed them, he saw a well-dressed man walking, a man raised in a city, not a boy from a stone farm; a man of ways, of things, not a boy of fear; and beside him, smiling and sure, a gold, glowing woman, his wife. They walked together past the windows and people nodded to them and smiled sometimes, not knowing what they really were, taking them for city people surely, successful, rich, unafflicted.

The winter came, Abel said, and all the money was gone. They had to use all the money they made. That was Abel's six dollars a week and Janice's fourteen. She worked in a mill, sewing caps and jackets, and the hours were seven to seven. When she came home, she was angry because of no more dinners out and after the rent and food there was nothing left for extra coal for hot water. They were afraid to buy a gas ring and she couldn't cook, so they had to eat in the room, cold dinners, and be afraid of the landlady.

The Judge was speaking. Comstock said there were questions. "When you bought the car, did you read what was given you to sign?"

"It was about the car. I signed it because it was about the car."

"Why didn't you answer the letters that were sent to you?"

"They were about the car, too, but I sold the car—the car was gone, then. How can it help to read about it?"

"Weren't you aware that you had made only partial payment?"

"What?"

"Didn't you know you made only part of the payment—that you had more to pay?"

"No."

Abel's eyes went from the Judge to Comstock and back again, watching how his own words were taken up, judged and laid aside in the Law. Now the Judge was not speaking, but Comstock's hands were breaking words. "I bet you tried to hide that you were deaf. I'll bet you never told him you were deaf!" Abel looked again at the Judge, but his mouth was not moving.

Abel was afraid. This Comstock knew what no Hearing knew and how to ask it. This Comstock was trying to hurt him with secrets, things that could only be known by a child of their own people.

"Did you tell him you are deaf?"

"The Judge wasn't asking that. I didn't see his mouth move."

"*Did* you?"

"No." Abel's 'no' was almost invisible, quick, hesitating, a barely formed triangle of the hand, and then, "I did not tell him . . . he called me 'sir.' "

Comstock's mouth was moving for the Judge. Abel watched, and because he knew what would be said, he was able to read a little from the side: ". . . man . . . say . . . he was deaf . . . people . . ashamed . . ."

"But why?" Abel could read the words on the Judge's lips because they were few. He looked away. Then sun had awakened from the floor and had gone touching weakly up on the legs of some of the chairs. A little bit reached Janice and climbed on her dress as she sat watching in the third row. She looked like a stranger. The sun went away, tired. Comstock was finished. The Judge looked out at Janice for a moment and Abel saw that she wanted to smile, but was too frightened. Then the Judge began to speak again and Comstock asked; "Did you try to read Mr. Dengel's lips?"

"Yes. I cannot read him. He chews a cigar while he talks."

"But three letters were sent. Didn't you think the letters might be important?"

"I tried to read them, but I didn't understand. Only that they were about the car. I sold the car."

The Judge shook his head and said something and Comstock flipped the words out to Abel in disgust, "Go and sit down."

Abel began to sit, then stopped and said, "Why are you angry?" Comstock's eyes got wider. "*You.* Why are you angry? You don't know us. The Judge is not angry."

Comstock's hands flew with his words; "You damned fool. You'll be out begging in the street before winter is over, with a sign on your shirt!" His Sign was almost too quick to understand. "Hearing will pity you because they're stupid and they pity all Deaf, so you'll beg and all the Deaf will be pitied. Why did you come here and make trouble? People who work hard and never owed a cent will be called Deafie and be laughed at and taken advantage because of you. You're nothing but a damn beggar——"

The Judge moved his mouth and Comstock turned with a smooth gesture to say he was only explaining something. Then Mr. Webendorf was called.

Mr. Webendorf told about Abel. It was strange to hear Comstock's hands saying things about Abel's own life. Yes, he was hired from Apprentice Training at the deaf and dumb school. Yes, he worked well in the big shop, and was a good and responsible second-year apprentice. It was true that most apprentices were only boys, but since the man was deaf . . ."

Then the Judge asked about wages and Mr. Webendorf told about that.

"He gets union scale for second year: six dollars a week to start and last month it was raised to seven." The Judge looked surprised and Mr. Webendorf went on, "In three years he'll be making fourteen dollars and when he's finished his six years, he'll get good money—twenty-eight dollars." Then he stopped and shook his head and said, "I didn't know about the car." Abel felt the same kind of shame as once before when his father had beaten him, but he couldn't look away from the words. "I didn't know anything about the clothes, or—well— the wife, either. The boy came in the same every day, in old clothes. I knew where he stayed—it was a room; I didn't know he had a wife with him. If he'd come to me, I would have told him how bad it was ... all his savings ..."

The Judge moved in his dignity and began to speak. In a strange way, Comstock's hands made his words of a different speaking than Webendorf's. The Judge-words came heavy, loud and full; they swung in strong curves; they waited longer on the air. They were so beautiful that Abel leaned back in awe, watching them. They were so rich that he didn't understand any of them. As deeply aware as the Court had been made of the plight of the respondent, the Judge-words said, the Law was clear. The car had been sold and the respondent, having concealed his infirmity from the complainant, was guilty of what amounted to fraud. (So beautiful, those words! Abel watched them as they moved in their long rhythms. They reminded him of other long-rhythm things: pitching hay, scything. Yet, this infirmity was also a mitigating circumstance, and although the garnishment of the maximum of ten per cent of the respondent's wages was mandatory, the Court was inclined to favor a more lenient approach to the fraud charge than would ordinarily be entertained.

Comstock finished; Abel sat staring at him patiently, waiting for meaning.

"I am going to order payment," the Judge continued, "over the ten-per-cent garnishment, which will cover the fine of one hundred dollars and the additional court costs. The payment will be two dollars a week for the next five months, increasing to three dollars as the apprenticeship wages are raised, and so on by wage-steps until the apprenticeship is finished, and thereafter five dollars a week until the debt is satisfied. The Court hopes that the interest rate will be no more than six per cent.'' The Judge looked at the dealer. ''Although there is no law against usurious practice, the Court hopes that in this case you will modify your present custom.''

Abel's hands moved restlessly for the interpreter. ''I do not understand the words. What did he say? Did I win or lose?''

Comstock made a gesture of disgust and turned to the Judge again.

Abel saw the Judge smile a little. '' 'Lost the case,' the Judge says, 'lost it, ''Comstock's hands said in a pretty way. Then: ''The Court has no choice; the law is clear. The Judge wants me to tell you that it could have been much, much worse.''

Comstock had to begin again to explain to Abel what payments would have to be made and where he was to bring the money each month. It no longer seemed to matter if he understood the words or the complicated, secret balance of the Law. He sat like a suffering animal, too sick to get up, too enduring to fall down. Then Comstock was finished. He said, ''I told you you will be a beggar; no Deaf will speak to you. You——'' Stopped. The winter light of the courtroom had stopped him, coming up in front of him in a bright, dusty band that made him squint to see Abel on the far side of it. The Judge had gotten up and the people were leaving. It was over.

''I will never beg,'' Abel said, but he saw clearly in his mind a picture of himself sitting at a wall, with his hat out, because he was too weak to stand.

''You will ruin everything for all the Deaf around here,'' Comstock said, without knowing if Abel could see his hands. ''I wish you'd stayed out on the farm, hidden away somewhere!'' He began to walk to the doors. There was a sound on the other side of the sun shaft. Abel had put his head down on the table and with both fists, one on either side, was slowly pounding.

2

*T*HEY HAD TO SELL THE RING that kept green sunlight. Abel had paid seventy dollars for it, and after Webendorf wrote about what interest was, he knew there was no choosing now between this hope and that. Janice cried and argued. She made him spend nights adding and adding again numbers that never changed. And in the end, he made her take the sunlight ring off her finger and they went back to the jeweler's with it.

Abel remembered the jeweler who was pleased with them, a happy and friendly man when they had come before. Now he looked at the ring with quick eyes and didn't hold it up to catch the light the same as before. He did not smile now, but was careful and kept his arms close to his body. "Twenty dollars," he said.

A fear came like something falling down inside of Abel. They tried to show the jeweler his mistake. They were careful, trying to make the man remember who they were, that they had bought his ring for seventy dollars. Janice spoke more clearly of the two—they knew this because people seemed less impatient with her than they were with Abel. Their faces did not always harden with dislike when she used her voice— and so she spoke, asking the jeweler if he remembered this ring, the same ring he sold them in the summer. She motioned to the box behind the shining glass. "I' wa' 'ere, 'ere," She pointed again.

Abel remembered how carefully the ring was put in the fold that held it, in the box, how carefully the jeweler reached in and took it and lifted it to feed it with light and then held it out to them. Maybe he did not understand. He motioned to Janice with his eyes to write: "We are people we came in summer and buy this ring seventy dollar. Jewl is very good care. All ways take off before wash."

The jeweler read the note quickly and shook his head. Then he wrote *"Twenty Dollars"* and put a line under it. They didn't give up the ring and they didn't go, but stood stunned and pale in front of him. He took the paper again and wrote: "I am in business. I will give you twenty-five dollars and no more. The ring is used, not new any more. If you can't get a better price for it somewhere else, come back and I will still give you twenty-five."

Janice would never Sign in front of Hearing, but now she turned Abel away and began, in the smallest of Sign, to say what she had to: "I'm afraid. What is happening to them? Why are they doing this to us? What will we do?"

"I don't know. We can't go to the police."

"You are the husband. You must make him take the ring and give us our money."

"He won't do it."

"You must make him do it."

"Go on," he said, "and wait outside. I will talk to him —alone."

She looked away and made a small, quick sign of good-bye, leaving the store. Abel saw she felt better to go.

He picked up the ring from the glass where it was lying and with his left hand, motioned the jeweler to come with him toward the back of the store, darker, where Janice could not see them. Abel began to walk back, his loneliness pulled into a single place that reminded him of a time he could not name. The jeweler did not look at him. Then Abel took from his pocket the marvelous watch and the fob with the golden lion's head and red jewel eye that gleamed even in the dim place. "'ake it." he said. He could see the man's eyes narrowing with bad thoughts at the sound of his voice. The man turned to

: *14* :

him and Abel said, "Uh ring an' wa' an' *ehv-ry'ting*—" and then wrote: "$70." Even then the jeweler didn't look at him; he only turned and struck his money-machine and the drawer ran open. He counted out money fast and put it on the counter and as Abel picked it up, the jeweler swept the wonderful things into his hand like crumbs from a table. How carefully they had come from the cases before—each thing was held like something alive and important. Now, their poorness—his and Janice's—spoiled the jewels; the green stone was unlucky, the watch had given bad hours to count. The jeweler took them to hide them away in shame. An assistant came from the back of the store and was standing too near for comfort. Abel walked with his head up, hoping he wouldn't bump into the door in his pain. He felt the shadows of the two men behind him. He wondered if they were laughing in The Hearing World behind him.

"Did you get the money?"

"Yes."

"All of it?"

"Yes."

They stood by a restaurant window and pretended to look in.

"When the owing is finished, we will buy it back."

"Never. I will never go there again."

"I want to hope for it."

"Never again. He made me ashamed."

There was someone on the other side of the window, watching them, so they turned and went on. As they came to the corner and started across the street, Abel took his hands out of his pockets and said fast into the cold, "This is Outside, Outside. This is where everyone wants to go, everyone runs!" Then he put back his hands and glared. Silence.

Outside was all everyone talked about at school. Their eyes shone when they spoke of it, and down the narrow halls, railed for the blind, they made their Signs sail over the teachers' heads, hide behind books, slip between the desks, and the Signs talked about Outside. For Abel there was never Sign before, on the farm, and no real words. He came to the school mute and deaf to everyone, even to all the others who were as deaf as he. He took the Boys' Program: lipreading, arithmetic, reading and writing and had a choice of three trades: kitchen helper, printer's helper, boilermaker's helper. The Girls' Programs taught lipreading and sewing. These things the school taught. The things the boys and girls learned from one another were the language of Signs, and the dream of Outside. Every day for two hours, candles were blown out to make the letter P and mouths moved to letters and pictures on the blackboard and the students stared at tongues and teeth and lips— dill, till, still, skill—but the words, the real words were behind the outhouse, waiting; the Language given and taken quickly at the fence; the forbidden Signs made their users rich.

After six months at the school, Abel had friends and enemies and Outside. Now he was Outside, and he had the words to lie awake in bed and think of the time in school. It was a bad-smelling place, without color or taste, a dark place (color and light are wasted on the blind; the school served blind as well as deaf and so denied both). It seemed strange to him that in the school's ugliness he had found Janice.

Janice had gold hair, a smile that made him burn and be cold at the same time, a quickness, a slowness, like water going over stones when the sun shines on it. He was pulled by her and changed by her the way the river changed him when he went under the water—it made him another creature in another world. He was shy about being overage in the school; he came for the trades training and after years of trying to understand lipreading and to talk, he had been amazed to find there wére in the world, others of his kind. He was eighteen then, Janice was sixteen. She had grown up in the school and knew almost nothing about Outside. She did know Sign, the forbidden language. How confidently she joked and gossiped and talked behind the backs of the instructors. How busy she was and how wise, with plans and ideas, with friends, angers and the small wars of enemies. To Abel, hand-mute in the mind-silence of his farm and Hearing school, these plans and arguments were so wide a life, that they seemed magic, beyond belief. In three months he learned all the Signs that anyone knew; his finger-spelling was faith alone, but he dared it:

listening, talking, telling, sharing, arguing, wondering. He was made free in a language learned in spite of watchful teachers. Until he began to go with Janice, this language took a part of the places where it was learned. It seemed to smell of standing water, bathrooms, shame, hiddenness and lye-cleaner. Hands that masturbated in the storehouse doorway spoke about it before and after, and the boys Signed in their cold-sweat sleep. When the older ones had the twice-yearly lecture on the Dangers of Self-Abuse, Abel, sitting among them, wondered if the teacher who spoke of touching and rubbing, of fear and release, was referring to speech.

The boys and the girls were seldom together, so he saw Janice many times before they met. After they spoke once or twice, he began to look for her and he found that she had her chore in the kitchen, washing the pots. His wanting to be with her made him learn more than ever. He had to watch the teachers and see what made them forget him so that he could get away. He had to learn the times when there were people busy around the kitchen so Janice could take the chance to be away from her work. There were not many times to slip away from training or meet her as she went to her own class. The need to see her made him watchful and keen and took away some of his innocence. He began to see how Mr. Conroy's habit of a smoke in the afternoon could be used, how his own regular habits, even faults like lateness, began to have a kind of order about them until they were accepted as his way. He met Janice outdoors behind the kitchen, or when it was too cold, in the empty hall outside the dining room. He got cautious, so he stopped going with other boys to hide in the attic over the blind girls' dormitory; he stopped fighting with everyone who said things about his age; and he began, very slowly, to wonder about words and thoughts themselves. Perhaps there were words for things not seen or touched, and for thoughts not as simple as "go" or "stay." It was Janice who first asked him what he thought about the people and things they knew, and then about his wishes and his dreams. The idea came to him that there was a big open place inside him that felt and saw pictures of great meaning for which there were no words, and that someday he might be able to tell her some of the difference he felt between the world he saw and the world that saw him.

Of all the girls, Janice was the one most interested in Outside. When anyone spoke about it, she came alive. The more words Abel learned, the more things had meaning; the more meaning, the more memory. She began to ask him questions: What was his town like? Were there many cars? What kind of clothes did the rich people wear? What did their houses look like? Was it nice on the farm? Was the work hard? She asked more questions about town than about the farm, and even more about the city. City was Outside at its richest. City was everything that was new and joyful and always changing. Janice loved the idea of traveling; she loved all motion, all change, and Abel, who had spent his life in The World, who must have traveled easily from farm to town to city seemed to her and the others, a prince of promise. His smallest memory had the weight of great wisdom.

During his second year, he and Janice were together everywhere, and together they ruined all the attempts the school made to put them out of each other's way. They found forgotten windows and unused storage rooms. Most of all they used their deafness. They were all and completely mute; they understood nothing, they agreed to everything. They nodded and smiled and said yes to everyone, teacher, matron and master; they promised to reform and then went where they wished. In April they ran away together. Outside. They found a Church like one Abel knew at home. When the minister saw what they wanted and that they were deaf, he wrote another man's name on a paper for them and so they were directed finally to a Justice of the Peace, who married them without questions—for four times the usual fee. That Monday morning they presented themselves back at the school to start their week's work as though nothing had happened. The school was afraid of bad talk, so it pretended not to notice them and allowed Janice to graduate with her class. They told her to write to her parents immediately. She put off doing it and in the end, the superintendent wrote to both families and told them of the marriage. When school was over, Janice and Abel went to his parents' farm. Janice's parents had thirteen other children. They sent best wishes in a letter to Janice and no return address. Abel

and Janice took the train. Outside, She opened her eyes wide
to try to see all of it, touch all of it, taste, smell, feel all of
Outside. She gleamed with life. . . .

Now Abel turned in the bed and watched her sleeping.
Sometimes, brushing across his mind too quickly to make words,
was a feeling. It was the beginning of an idea and it was about
the courts and stores and people—that maybe they were not hating or angry at his deafness and Janice's, but that they did
not care. Strangely, the not-caring was worse than hate. Always in school there was talk about hate, the laughter and
cruelty of Hearing people. Some had things they told over
and over again, their faces all stiff with anger, and they told
these things to everyone many times, until everyone knew they
had pleasure telling and a big pride in the pain and laughter
that was put against them. Abel began to feel that Outside's
real cruelness had to do not with hating but with not-caring.
He did not have the words to tell this to Janice, and so the
thought stayed haunting the rims of his mind, almost making
itself plain. He was also sometimes close to another knowledge:
that the world was working against them and that their
ignorance of the world was against them more, much more.
This too was only a sudden running of something across a
place that was lit too late to see by; there were no words to
hold it.

His trouble weighed all night in the close room. Every
night for a week he tried to find a way to stop that money—six
thousand dollars—and more because of what they called Interest. Interest meant liking something. It meant working
well and staying awake. He knew the Sign for it; it was close,
that Sign, to the one for *liking*. Now, by some strange Hearing
law, this good thing was made into money, more money for
Mr. Dengel. It was Mr. Dengel who was staying awake and
interested enough. Janice and Abel could only live on Janice's
fourteen dollars a week, and his own money this second half of
second year of apprenticeship, $7.00 less seventy cents to pay
the debt. If they were careful they could creep past the Court
and the jail. If they were very careful and there was no more
trouble. But there was no money left for hope. Each half-year

there would be more money going to fill the debt. It was all to keep strangers calm; all to keep them from anger. The Hearing are always angry.

One thing they had always told him in school; Keep working. They had begun his trade, they said, because they wanted him kept safe; and working, they said, was safety. Beside him Janice Signed in a dream, vague, unreadable Signs, and she turned in her sleep. Just before The Summer ended, at the top of all the good things, they had met a Deaf man who had told them about a church for Deaf on the other side of the city. Once a week a minister came and had services in Sign. At school it was often said that one part of The Hearing World had time for them—churches. They had made a plan to go as soon as they could, with jobs and nice clothes, the ring, the watch. They wanted to make frinds, to have habits, to invite and be invited. Now the world was cold; ring and watch and money and hope were gone. Even if they could pay the carfare to that church, they wouldn't go. The friends were too expensive now, and the hope too feared for. Abel stirred the bed again, trying to find the right position for sleep, and it came at last, heavy with scattering, gray dreams.

3

SEVERAL TIMES DURING THAT WINTER Janice and Abel
wondered, each secretly to himself, if he was going to
die. There was starving, freezing, or even broken heart,
which Janice had heard of at school. So they waited, watching
for something out of the sides of their eyes. But they did not
die; they only imitated the living and the months went on,
days counted like papers that Abel shuffled and made one
jog in his printer-hands, and then put away.

After the Court, Abel felt a change in Mr. Webendorf. He
was more impatient; he did not smile or wave in a friendly way.
For some weeks Abel was sad and angry, but soon he got used
to it and its hurt was flat; the time passed over it and made the
new way into a habit. Webendorf was Hearing, Abel told
Janice, and Hearing always change. She nodded, but she wasn't
listening to him. She was thinking instead about the mill. There
were two other Deaf girls working in the cap room and she
hadn't told him. Half a room away she had seen them, Signing
quick and secret over their lunches, and slowly, so no one
would look, she had begun to make a way closer to them. It
was better to be careful, not to get attention, and three Deaf
girls together might bring trouble. So she waited and when the
time came, she made Sign, the bare word, fast as thought, a word
without breath, without sound, without motion except the

flicker seen and known only by people whose lives are turned to motion. They gave her understanding with an eye blink, and at lunchtime, without seeming to move, made place along the back wall.

They were always together after that, turning no attention to themselves, but sitting by the damp north wall that no one else would choose for an eating place. They sat close, hands hidden by one another's backs, and they talked, leaving only the last minute or two for the crazy eat-without-chewing before the work bell broke them apart. They hated the bell. It came to Janice as a numbing *thrum* up through the bones of her feet and buttocks and up her spine—counting all the hidden ends and edges, the way a blind man must feel things—into the bones of her face; again and again until her teeth rang and she chewed upon the bell. For Hearing it must be that way always, chewing bells, chewing voices. She wondered how Hearing could stand it—sound. At the bell there was time only for a last swallow, gathering up the greasy papers, brushing crumbs from the lip, the hand-flick good-bye and back to the lighter, smaller chewing of the sound of the roomful of sewing machines.

Janice had been working in the cap room for eight months. Her work was fast. She didn't look at her hands any more; they moved the cloth and took it away without her noticing them. She had found a measuring to her work, regular as a pulse, but faster. After a while it was possible to go for a long time without stopping the machine at all. One hand reached for the new cutout while the other guided the last seams in the cap just finishing under the machine. Now thread came and was fixed with one hand, slowing but not stopping the work and she learned to wind large bobbins tight and full to get more time out of each one. One Saturday she opened her pay envelope and was surprised to find a dollar more in it. It made her frightened. Who was looking for that money, to call her a thief? In the end she had to go to the floor foreman, and he told her the money was "moans," or maybe "pones" or "bones." The fear grew. She pushed a paper and pencil to the man until he wrote it out; "Bonus—more pay. You go over top quota, you get a *bonus*."

"Safe money? Good money?"

"Yes."

She took the envelope and walked away, fast, out of the factory and toward home in the freezing almost-dark. The walk was another of the cold savings for Abel's debt. It meant she had to use all evening in bed trying to get warm, unless there was wash to get out and water to be heated in the basement before midnight. The walking tonight was different, lighter. Halfway home she stopped and stood on the corner, thinking. Now there was money for the streetcar. She decided against it. Abel would be happy with this money. It could mean dinner out, the laundry done, better shoes—they hadn't bought any shoes when they were rich. . . . Then it opened in her mind that if the Law found out about the money, they could take it away from her and throw it into the lost place of Abel's debt. She was Abel's wife—already they had made him come to her and take the green jewel ring away. She stopped again in the middle of walking and everything began to sway between fear and anger. Why the Law hurt them was the Law's secret. Then she must have a secret, too. She made up her mind and moved into a doorway to take the extra money out of her pay envelope and put it in her pocket. It would be hers, not for the Law. If Abel knew, he would only take it for himself and then Law would get it. She must find a way to use it without his knowing; until then it would have to be hidden. She went the rest of the way home slowly, thinking. Bonus is good; only Abel is there to make it bad. . . .

The landlady had told them in the beginning they were not allowed to cook in the room. When they crept in with a small gas ring, she was busy and didn't see them. They kept the gas ring hidden when they weren't using it, but there were cooking smells from the soup or beans or canned stew and they were sure she knew. But she did not speak and they did not speak. In their new poorness there was very little coal, and hot food let them go to bed in the icy room holding a small warmth inside them. They wiped the dishes with newspapers after eating and hurried to bed to keep the warmth. Then they slept or made love and then slept. It was too cold to sew or mend; she saved the work most needed for Sunday. Once a week she went to the basement and washed clothes. It was dark early in the days of the winter. They did not want to burn lights in order to talk about their days; it was talk already old to them, so they went to bed and lay awake in the dark and did not try to spell words into each other's hands. That was a thing of before, a loving thing, when they were just married. When there had been money for lights, when the whole world was golden with light, they had lain after loving and spelled words into each other's palms. Sometimes Janice wondered why she didn't tell Abel about the Deaf girls at work. It must be because of the cold and because of the dark. Once or twice she almost stumbled, but the words stopped at the secret and left only the danger of open space between herself and Abel. Now, with a new secret, the bonus money, she was glad she had not told him.

She had to think of a place to hide the money. All during supper she kept looking with her mind. It had to be a place where Abel and the landlady did not look. She knew the landlady came into their rooms when they were gone; it had never worried her before; she had simply put the cooking things away in the closet so it was possible not to see them. Now there was this money to worry about. She waited until Abel left to go downstairs and out to the privy. Then she went to the closet and got down her suitcase. It was heavy cardboard, painted to look like leather, but it had metal corners and there were strips of wood inside to make it strong. The Deaf girls at school had given it to her as a wedding present. It was her only wedding present. She remembered how she had packed her other dress and underwear in it, getting ready to go with her husband into Outside. Her life was very special then, and the suitcase was important. It was a way of telling an idea. The suitcase was the idea of going someplace, of Outside. It was the Deaf girls speaking to her without words or Sign. She had kept the suitcase very carefully. As she looked at it now, she noticed a new chip of paint off in the front. Inside there were two cloth pockets, one on each side. She put the money into the left side pocket and folded it down shut. Then she closed the suitcase and put it away and hurried back to bed. The secret made her feel safe and good and ashamed only when she thought about not telling Abel. It wasn't lying, really. It was because they didn't have time to talk. . . . It was because of the dark. . .

There was an extra dollar in the pay envelope the next week and the next. Janice had never had any money of her own to spend or keep. She was surprised at how it made her notice different things. For instance, how much Abel was in their room. He was there all the time; she had no chance to hide the money except when he went to the privy. She started work before he did and finished later, and all the rest of the time he was there watching her, in the bed or eating or waiting for dinner or looking out the window. If she didn't tell him about the money, there would have to be excuses and lies for the things she planned to bring home. Maybe she would buy a new skirt, or warm overshoes. They would have to be hidden in some package and put away; she would never get them home before he saw them. He knew all of her clothes, everything she used. . . . And he had said she could never get back the green jewel ring. She would have to get it without his knowing. It was the only thing for which she still had daydreams. They had taken it away, the Court and Abel; poorness had taken the ring away, but it was still hers. She remembered wearing it in The Summer. She remembered it more clearly than what she had eaten last night. It was unfair, unfair.

Before the ring, maybe there should be overshoes. Walking to work in rain or snow made her feet wet and cold all day and then it was worse at night to come home because the wet shoes froze. Overshoes. She tried every way to get out alone when the stores were open, but something always happened. Sometimes Abel wanted to go, too; or he said it was too cold to walk; or he waited for her and sulked until she went with him. Several times the landlady came in to say something or to ask them for the rent, and after these times Abel would be too angry or afraid to do what she planned for him to keep him in. She thought of telling him there was extra work one night or two at the factory, but it was too big a lie. The weeks went on, the pocket at the side of the suitcase was pushing out wide and then it was the beginning of spring and Abel was kept late on a job for three days. In that time, without her knowing how, want-and-want had passed. Suddenly, the terrible need was gone and the bonus money stayed in the suitcase. She decided to keep saving for the green ring. She did not let herself worry about telling Abel when she got it home.

Abel was proud of Janice. She complained, she sulked, she was cold, looking colder to make him feel ashamed, but he had thought in the beginning, after his trouble in the Court, that she would leave him. Did she know how long the debt was going to be? This winter was going to be one of twenty winters of the debt. It was a winter of little more than one meal a day, half heat and no change of the endless same-sameness of work and sleep. He had made the six thousand dollars smaller by three dollars and twenty-five cents. But Janice did not leave. Her light was gone, her laughter and joking, her pride in him, her feminine ways, the softness of her face in the green-leaf sunlight—that part was gone, but still, she did not go. It made him feel thankful and surprised each day when she came in from the dark and nodded to him and turned to the closet to hang up her things. It was spring now. The shadows of the afternoon were not dangerous with ice and there were smells in the air that made him remember springs on the farm. Always before, when he thought of the farm, it was to remember the frightened hurry, the sweat-face, dry-mouth hurry of work from dark to dark. Now he saw again pictures of the times that were warm and yellow with the sun. Some of the pictures were distant, moving like smoke in the no-word shadow-time of his childhood; some were of the spring, only a year ago when he came to the farm with Janice. He had words, then, and a new self, thinking in the words. Janice was so beautiful with all her hope. They took walks together in the hills, going up to the pine-places. They played in the fields, spelling flower names that his mother had written for them. Once they lay down in the flowers to make love, and the rain began. He said he would drive the tame animals home and she started running away. Her hand was spelling bird and animal names behind her. He ran to catch her. She said she would not be called tame animal, and he watched her making the Sign, animal, on her chest. Her saying it made him think again of loving because of the way she made the Sign, and she knew this, too. All moving was the same, was Sign then; kissing was Sign, like talk, but more, and making love was Sign. He could close his eyes and she would spell love-words on his body.

He remembered pictures of distant winters and of those single afternoons when winter changed. It would happen after a long time of cold and rain and feeling hopeless. On one afternoon birds would come. Suddenly there would be a fat bird in winter feathers, not coming to look and eat and fly back to its warm nest. This bird would sit riding the branches; its face not down on its feathers. The horse of winter pasture would still be humble in his thick coat, but suddenly the wind that moved the hair of his tail and forehead could do nothing more than that. It could not make the horse lower its head. A week later, petals would come in the orchard and a green breathing on the big trees near the house and a waste of pollen on all the paths. As Abel tried to make the pictures more clear and more clear in words, there was a filling in his mind. He felt his mind growing big with all his past. He saw the pasture pond; he thought about it, to make it words so he could keep it to see again; and he remembered how thin the water looked and how the mud lay bare around it. Nothing grew near the pond. The sides of it saved the prints of the cows. In spring. In spring his mother opened the windows with a quickness so happy it looked like anger. The wind came into the damp mold-smell house all day, and for everyone who went outside, if for anything, any reason, there would be on his neck and shoulders and against his hair, the happy, good, golden, generous gift of the warm sun.

And sun would be coming here where he and Janice were waiting as poor as other winters of the farm. Soon they would be able to walk home to dinner easily in the late light. Maybe he would go over to the mill and call for her and they could come home together like some couples he saw, arm in arm. He felt good about his work. He was on a big offset press, making handbills and printing the racing sheets for two horse tracks out of town. Lately they were doing more work on a smaller new press. Wages were up and if the Court-money was still eaten and eaten away by the Court-mouth, it was spring and he couldn't stop hoping.

He didn't want to tell this hope to Janice. It could make

her begin to want things again and be impatient. She was always asking, "How much now? What money are they taking now?" as if the money were in her hand and a man came and pulled it away from her. Sometimes he wanted to make her understand Interest and show her all the poor years so she would stop saying, "What after that?" When he tried to talk to her about it, he got too frightened and had to stop. She hadn't left him this winter, but this winter was only one.

"I remembered all the farm today," he said. They were eating, vegetable soup with canned beans poured into it. "I remembered things in springtime."

Janice tossed her head: "Your mother doesn't like me." Her look didn't change; they both knew it was true.

"That was only in the beginning—because of the Signs. She's afraid of Signs. When I was small, teachers told her Signs were bad and made people look funny." He shrugged.

"She doesn't like me because I make her feel all alone."

"She is alone. She's the only Hearing. My father and brother and you and me. . . . Before *she* was Hearing, and then you and I came with Signs, and all of us learned to talk together a little for the first time. It made her be Deaf—see?— when we all talked together."

"She wrote to me once. She told me Signs were dirty, like being naked."

"I think of back home," he said. "I think about it a lot now." She was paying attention, watching, her finger feeling the level of the water in the coffee pot as she filled it. Dinner was always late when they started talking. It made her angry that he would want to keep her from dinner by his talking. Talking never did anything. "I remember days and how things looked," he said, "but not about the people. I never can remember what my mother or my father were thinking or saying, or what they wanted, or what they were like."

"Your mother was against me."

She took away the soup bowls and rinsed them for coffee. It was hard to make words, but to remember things he had to have them. It was the same way that Janice once felt about Outside. And here he sat remembering things before the words. He had stopped eating his bread. It was strange to him that the words seemed to make him remember more and feel more now than he had felt then, when the things were happening. He remembered that his mother was sad. He remembered the smell of lateness and the small cold of outside that always came in with him when he came from school. "She was all alone, my mother," he said to Janice. "When I could not learn in Hearing school, she stopped being angry, but she got sad." And he remembered a little of an ancient weight.

As they waited for the coffee he said, "I think about going to church. There are Deaf there. Maybe we can go. We can take out of the food money to go on the street car. Maybe we can find some friends there. . . ."

He was thinking of the school, the Deaf school, a cold, bad-smelling place where he had found his life and his wife and schoolmates and words.

She shook her head. "We're too poor. Nobody likes poor people. And in church you have to pay. They pass around a basket on a long stick and you have to pay."

"I think only Hearing pay. I remember that. But in school chapel every Sunday we never paid."

"That was different. You have to pay in church. I don't want to go. The others are rich and they won't want to be friends to us there. I remember what that Comstock said to you in the Court, about how Deaf here hate poor people. I want to stay home."

"Oh, he was ashamed. Maybe his parents were no good." Abel remembered the Comstock face, scornful in the court, and the hate flying from his fingers. "Only his hands were Deaf. The rest of him was Hearing."

"The ugly part was Hearing," she said, and they laughed.

When coffee was ready they drank it and rinsed the bowls. The night had silenced their hands. They did not talk about the church again.

Janice had begun to leave for work early to have a few minutes to laugh and talk with Mary and Barbara before the machines began. When she got to her place that day, Mary was waiting for her, but there was no greeting or gossiping, and the Sign was hard. "You get more money. We know you get bonus money. Every week.'' She walked away before Janice had time to answer, and then the bell rang. At lunch break Janice went to where they always sat, but the other girls had already moved farther down and she had to walk the extra way, to mean that she was sorry and wanted to be forgiven. They didn't say anything, but they talk-talked quickly to each other while she sat and ate, her back to the Hearing workroom to protect them. The silence was painful to bear all day and she came home tired and near tears and could not tell Abel why it was. In school she had often done such things to other girls on no more than a whim, and they to her. It was easier in the school where there was always another group to join, new friends, different enemies, wars and truces on a whim. Now a game was everyone, a war, the World. The next day things were the same, and the next after that, and she did not sleep at night. Then the girls got bored with their anger and let her come slowly to the edge of their patience. Afterwards she was slowly forgiven because they needed her and after a week they asked her to show them how she worked.

''My hands aren't fast,'' she told them, but they didn't want to believe her. She showed them how to use the rhythm of the machine to slow but not stop it while work was opened into it and closed away, changing hands. They raised their eyebrows and made unbelieving faces, but she saw their minds moving toward the ways she had shown them, and the idea of the bonus. When the bell rang, they were eager to get back to their machines. The afternoon passed in its own slowing rhythm and the tiredness of the women thickened the air and pulled back the minutes on the clock. Afternoon air was always bad in the shop. Mary said it was from the lunch boxes of the immigrant girls. Barbara said it was everyone sweating with the windows closed, and they all laughed when Mary said, ''That's why the boss walks through in the morning.'' Sometimes in summer, girls fainted during the afternoon because of the heat and the smell. Janice never told Abel how close she came to being sick with it sometimes. When she complained, he didn't do anything but shrug his shoulders. Anyway, there was a rumor that it was worse in the mill than in the power sewing rooms.

The next day at lunch, Barbara said she had a plan for the three of them. She and Mary had tried Janice's way of working and it speeded the caps through the machine like a miracle. Why not get the quota up, all three of them together, and then go and ask to go into the B Section where the workpants and shirts were made. There, they told Janice, a girl worked on a different rate, faster, for more money. Using the new way, Barbara said, they would be able to do better, since the machines were lighter and faster than the ones they had now for the many thicknesses of the caps. Mary didn't seem as sure as Barbara that a change would help them. Janice said nothing, but decided to herself that she would not go with them. Maybe the new place wouldn't give bonus money and besides, the speed was hers, not theirs. The two of them had taken her speed for their own, as their own idea, and even made big plans on it, when it was hers and not theirs at all. She felt almost too angry to speak to them and her face was hard when the bell rang and they all went back to their machines.

At about four, Janice was working against the heaviness of the air and small flickers of a kind of cramping pain she was beginning to get in her shoulders every day. She felt a hand poking at her back. Sometimes the floor foreman stopped a girl. She took her foot off the pedal at the end of a cap and turned to see. It was Mary, and at the other machines the girls were not working and some were standing up, looking toward the other side of the room. They were looking very hard, as if it were more than an interesting thing, as if it were something they needed to see and they would not look away even if someone told them to, or the bell rang. Some of the girls were biting their lips; they were beginning to turn all the way around, watching the main doors. Mary shook a quick B out of her hand—*Barbara*—and Janice stood up and turned too; she got a look of disgust from the girl at the next machine, and she thought it was the first time that girl had seen her at all. There was someone going out and others were making a big crowd around that spot so the person was not seen. Suddenly the people in the crowd looked as if they were all falling and two of them moved away. Janice saw that the person in the middle was Barbara. People were going with her, walking and also carrying, and before they got her out through the door that the floor foreman was holding open, Janice caught a glimpse of part of the dragging dress that was covered with blood.

"What?" She said it quickly, too frightened to hide the Sign.

"She was going too fast," Mary said. "The machine got her hand."

Janice turned away, feeling sick. She tried to say in her mind that Barbara was only stupid and didn't look what she was doing, but there was her own knowing. Every day some part of looking or thinking went away, stopped and slept and did not follow the cloth or the thread or the rhythm. In front of her stood the same machine, blind and hungry, its silver tooth waiting for the joyful rush downward and the bite of more and more, for a hundred thousand yards of cloth. Every day it ate and ate and pushed across the ticking stripes, moving, and if the hand that fed it slipped or was too slow with tiredness, it did not know flesh from cloth. It was just as glad to turn down upon that hand and pull the fingers in and eat them also.

Janice wanted to run away. She looked across the floor. Most of the other girls were back at their machines again and the wheels began to turn as they started up one after another. The floor foreman took three of the girls and they went to get mops and pails and then came back and cleaned up the splattered blood that was on Barbara's machine and trailed out to the aisle and down and out the door. Later he looked over Janice, who was still standing, staring at the door, trembling. He motioned her back to work. Even Mary was at her seat and working again. Janice sat down and began adjusting the stiff cloth under the greedy needle. She knew the other girls were thinking about the blood and the pain and the sick-shock of being hurt, maybe about being crippled and made ugly in their hands. To them hands were only what did ordinary work. In her mind was a picture of hands. It is one of us getting hurt in the hands . . . one of us. To be without hands . . . it means to be dumb; it means never to talk again, like to be dead; one of us, without hands . . .

4

SUMMER CAME and Abel received his increase as a third-
year apprentice. When the money came, Mr. Webendorf
made him sit down and they figured that the debt was
now $5,577.28. If things went all right this year, the debt would
be $5,528. The boss had spent a long time telling Abel about
Interest, and now the Interest seemed more important to him
than the first money and he was careful to keep the Interest
money added, dollar by dollar, in his mind. Mr. Webendorf
wrote a note to him then, and told him that there were things
the Court did not know. Wages had gone up in the printing
trade and Abel, as a third-year apprentice, would be getting
not only his eight dollars a week, but maybe extra money called
Christmas Bonus. Mr. Webendorf told him to save out this
money and not tell the Court. It was not going in his regular
pay, and what the Court didn't know about, it could not claim.
Abel had first thought to tell Janice, to make her happy with
the thought of a dinner out or shoes or a dress, but he was afraid.
If the Court found out, they would send him to jail. If Janice
bought things with that money, maybe the store people would
tell the Court. He could only go on, working his day, waiting.
He tried to keep his thoughts away from the money.

That summer seemed good to Abel, a relief from the cold
and the coal money. Janice complained of the heat as much

as she did of the cold, but Abel liked the long evenings, the golden light that saw him home, the breeze lifting the heavy maple leaves. He remembered the old ladies fanning themselves in the church at home. He did not know what made him think of this. He liked the smell of sun burning the spring sap hard in new wood and the smell of the ground rich with the green leaves that fell and rotted there. After work on Saturday, and all day Sunday, they were able to go walking along the green-leaf streets of those nice sections of town. Large houses were there, sitting like comfortable old women, their cool lawns gathered around them. All day they walked and pretended, arm in arm, silent and wise and there was a new pleasure because of the map.

There had been an order one day for a printing of five thousand city maps to sell at the fairgrounds when the State Fair opened. Abel seldom looked at anything he printed except to check for errors in placement or the strength of the inking, but something about the maps interested him, so instead of throwing away the strike-offs to litter the floor, he brought them home. In the last light he and Janice looked at them. They found their own street and it made Abel feel famous almost —that anyone could look and find where he lived. They found the mill, the printing plant and even the street of wonderful stores where the ring was and the lion with its unclosing eye. They found the court building, too; and then they began to see how much larger than these streets the city was.

"It doesn't matter," she said, "we are too poor."

"You are afraid of friends."

"I am not. I don't like people know we are poor."

"It makes me feel like a man in jail."

"You made me in jail too."

"I know," he said, "but see, it doesn't have to be a small jail—it's bigger than we thought, just work and nothing else. At least in summer, it can be a big and pretty jail."

"A jail, and poor—we are still poor!"

He didn't answer her, but took the map and with his pencil divided it into quarters. "This summer we will walk in this part," he told her, "only in this part."

They put the map on the wall and he had a feeling of pleasure and success; this surprised him because of the new freedom. A year ago, he knew, he could not have been so humble or so patient, putting his pleasure into parts to make it longer, and measuring so closely the movements of their day's freedom.

Each Sunday after that, rain or sunshine, they investigated their section of the summer. To the south they found only mills and factories; to the west the avenue of wonderful stores and busy streets in the newer part of the city; but north and spreading eastward, the workmens' streets, smelling of cabbage and backhouses, led on into a neighborhood of peaceful, treelined streets. The houses were solid and dignified, with large, deep porches and careful white-dress children sitting on slow porch swings, back and forth in the slow noon. No matter which part of the section they saw on their Sundays, they always came back to these streets and, dressed in the still bright clothes of last summer, they strolled up one side and down the other, nodding to the nursemaids and pretending that in just a few more steps they would turn in at their own house and and go up on the wide porch where the rocking chairs were waiting and the cool drinks were set out. They walked silently, their arms linked, but their minds were storing the daydream, changing, improving it, choosing or rejecting parts of other houses on other blocks.

Back in their close, hot room before supper, they found themselves arguing, sometimes bitterly, over the new wishes or the old. Janice wanted a cat; Abel didn't. Janice wanted a nursemaid for the children, a uniformed, starched nurse; Abel didn't. Abel wanted two cars; Janice didn't. Sometimes these arguments took over their fingers and began of themselves to knit the strands of the car and the Court and the debt into these summer dreams. Then their eyes would narrow against each other and then they would pull away their hands, weak with fear, and they wouldn't argue again that day.

At the end of the summer they took down the map and put it away carefully. They planned to leave the far sections for summers when there was money for carfare and small lunches. The section of the Deaf church was the last one on the map. Both of them noticed where it was. Neither mentioned it.

On Thanksgiving, Mary at the mill gave Janice a pound of chestnuts. She took them home, trying not to seem too pleased, and said, "a girl at the mill," and nothing more. Abel was proud and impressed. She must have Hearing friends there. How wonderful she was still, even though the cold and poverty had faded her, and though she seldom smiled. How wonderful the magic that could go so easily into That Other World, gliding by its tricks and confusion, able to be given gifts.

At Christmas they had a letter from Abel's parents at the farm:

My dear son and daughter-in-law. I am taking pen in hand to write to you and tell you we are sorry not to send the things we had been hoping. Things is awful bad here this year all over the Valley and in town, too. The prices has fallen so bad there are people who didn't get nothing this year to get seed, and the ones that had hybrid crops in are just that worse out of luck. People blame the tractors, but I think it was mostly specalaters that done it. Eakers has lost their farm. Yosts, too. They are going out West. Mertens have lost their farm and hire theirselfs out to anyone who can pay them keep and the whole family is broke up. These are not Railroad-siding people, or shiftless people, but neighbors whose folks had land here since anyone can remember and it makes us sad to see such terrible things happen to them. Mr. Pearce down at the store says it isn't only the Valley, but the whole State, and maybe even the whole country, which he means farms. The prices have dropped to nothing. Your father and I don't mean to make you feel bad by this news, and where you are in the city, you don't get hurt by this none. We had a idea to send you some $ and things at Christmas, and with things like they are we will not be able to. We are both glad you got a trade and can make your way in the city and are not caught here like so many of the other boys. We miss you, your father and I both. We are glad you are not having any hard times.

Best wishes for Christmas and we hope you have a good
an easy winter.

Sincerely, your mother,
Sarah, Windom Ryder.

They read the letter twice and then Janice shrugged and
got up. "Why write and say you can't do something?"

Abel put down the letter shaking his head: "I remember,"
he said, "something my father does in spring. We all go with
him and he walks to the end where he owns. He walks around
the whole farm and every field, to the edge. He goes by the
creek to see where it changes its places and to the woods. . . ."

In his mind, he saw his father stopping to look at a fence-
post eaten by some bugs. The picture he had was from the
years before the school and the Words; long before he had
Janice and Words and brought them both back with him. Abel's
father was a Deaf, too; a man without Words. He had no
Sign. He could not show what he meant except by writing
little notes sometimes. Only Abel's mother could understand
his father's speaking. If anyone else understood him, even
Abel, it was because of the straightness of his thinking. He
could point to something or move his hand to show an action,
and by that or by the reason and the need, people could
sometimes see what he meant. Everyone, all the neighbors were
always surprised at how much Matthew noticed on the land.
Now, the letter said, things were bad. The letter worried Abel;
it made him feel afraid.

The next day he went out during his lunch period and
bought a Christmas card with a picture of a table full of good
food and a big fire, and on the back of it he wrote his name and
Janice's also. He did not write about the auto or the Court, but
only Good Wishes, and his name, as he was taught to do at the
school. Then he went to the post office to buy the stamp,
feeling proud at having it to do. People were lined up to the
window with letters and packages, stamping the cold out of
their feet and moving as if to complain with their bodies, at
the line and the waiting. Abel stamped also, and shook his
head and shrugged every once in a while, so as to look impatient as Hearing did.

In the evening, he worked his talk around to say, "I had a long wait today. It was at the post office. I waited a long time because of the importance. I sent best wishes in the mail."

Janice's eyebrows went up and her mouth pulled up in the middle because she didn't want to commit herself by asking questions about it.

"It was to my parents," he said.

She moved her mouth again, in the way she did when she was first married when all her movements were faster and freer. It reminded him with pain of the summertime people they had been and were not any more.

"My parents must have an answer. They had the idea to send me to school to have a trade."

She was lying on the bed, looking at him.

"Did I ever tell you about my school before Deaf school?" he asked.

"No," she said, and picked at a hangnail. She put the side of the nail in her mouth to pull at it.

"Many things happened in those days," he said. "I had no Words in those days."

That day he was early to help his father get water. He worked the pump . . . much swinging. He tried to put his words into that single day, into a place where they had never been. He spoke of it until he was almost there himself, swinging on the pump handle until it came down, then pushing it up, trembling because of the cold of the metal. Down and up, until a cough began that he felt against his body through the handle. Then the water came. All around, the day was blue and bright-cold. It was a day for Woodlot. Soon, he thought, his father would point to the saw and ax and hatchet and then they would go up on the hill into the woods and cut the fallen trees for wood for the fire. There was fast wood and slow wood, big wood; and his work was fast wood, gathering it up, trimming branches, putting it on the sledge. His words made him smell the air, that air, that day. That blue-time day was like a wood day. He tried to tell Janice how the smell of sap is, and to show her the grainy and moist crumbs that dropped from the feeding of the saw. He told her about his father coming toward him, saying, "Oooo" which meant "go" and pointing with his head to the house.

His mother had taken his clothes and set them out by the stove. She motioned him to get dressed. Church clothes, but it isn't church-day. He began to show his mother it was a wood-day, sawing back and forth, the tree-fall. She laughed, but didn't look happy. She made her mouth into something he did not know, a mouth "Uuuuuu." Then Breakfast. After-wards she kissed him, making with her hand: "Outside." And there was the wagon and his father sitting up on it, waiting and making "Uuuuu" with his mouth. Abel also tried "Uuuuu," and they looked at one another until his mother looked away. His mother was a Hearing. He only knew it later. Then he looked down at himself in his nice clothes. But Uuuuuuu is not a church-day.

Not church? They rode away from town, a way only gone when they went to visit the molasses-eating people. His mother was always trying to show or tell him something, but he could never find it. His mother's mouth was always trying to make him do and feel and the things were always mysteries that made him tired and angry. His father did not show with his mouth.

Children were on the road. His father stopped the cart and motioned them: Come up. They did and again and again until there were many. Then Abel had an idea. He was going where they were going. He got frightened. He did not want to keep moving toward that place. They went farther than he ever was, far past the house of the molasses-eating people. They turned in then and stopped at a building with a top made of stone.

A woman came out and there were children running and playing all around. Only children. There was a church bell hung on a slaughtering-frame-thing on the far side. The woman went over and pulled a rope and the bell-feeling went through Abel so that his teeth began to pull themselves inside his head and his face bones shook weak under his skin. The riding children opened their mouths and fell off the cart and every-where they ran and ran, into the building.

His father leaned down and took up an egg box and showed it to him, opened it so that he could see the food inside and gave it to him. Then his father pushed him toward the edge of the seat and nodded and looked toward the building where all the children were swallowed. He made "Uuuuuu," and Abel knew that this was Uuuu. He got down, his face cold and his body feeling stiff and tired. He held the egg box tightly and went to the door. When he was almost there, he turned and looked back. The cart was pulled around and was moving away from him down the road.

Inside was large, and so much with things that for a long time he only stared. There was a sour-yellow smell of damp, cold, old, and bad-boy. The bad-boy reminded him that he needed to go to the backhouse. His stomach hurt with that. But the room held him, and only when he felt the first drops beginning did he turn and run. A girl was coming out of it and he almost ran into her at the door. She said something too fast and ugly-faced him, pointing to *another* backhouse all the way over on the other side of the schoolyard. Now the front of his pants were damp and his teeth were clenched with trying to hold. A long time to the other backhouse and unbutton the big bone buttons that wadded in the double thick of wet cloth. Too late. When he came out of the backhouse, he knew that he was only to be sad, very sad for the wood-day.

There was no one in the schoolyard now. He went back to the big building, opening the door that was closed, as he knew he must.

Everyone was sitting at the row of desks that filled the room, and at the front, facing the wrong way, was the desk at which the woman sat, against the children. Her mouth was speaking and there was something "Aaa." He quickly took off his hat, because he thought he understood "hat," but the whole room rose, big and small. Backs were to him, blocking him from the woman's mouth. Suddenly, they all sat down again. The woman came and took him to one of the desks, pointing into his chest with her finger and then at the seat. His eyes kept her face to make sure. A little nod, a lowering of eye. Yes. He sat.

Time-time. Years. The air got filled, got empty. Children were up and down, went and came back, some with books and some with papers, mouth-mouth, important-too-fast, nothing to follow, so he sat until the things were done for him, or until his seatmate, a tiny, white-haired girl with no eyebrows, jabbed him in the ribs. Often he swept the room for signal. His row he learned, was: Woman's teeth on lip, roll, teeth-smile-top and-bottom. When he saw that lip-thing beginning, he swept the room, hoping to see, to anticipate, to know, to do, quickly, before he should be punished or laughed at.

His seatmate showed him that he must copy from the book, lines, just as they were: A A A A. For a while he was happy at this, doing as the others did. Afterwards the woman spoke to them, but he caught no meaning, not even one word, as he sometimes could catch meaning with his mother. He wondered if he would ever see his mother again. He remembered her as very wonderful. She seemed so long a time dead, she and his father, and the farm. Then the desks yawned suddenly and went down by signals he could not see. Certain children were talking and some raised their arms up and then they got up and then they sat down, and then, without warning, his seatmate flung herself away from him, slamming her book away into her desk as she went, and all of them blew from the room like leaves, spinning from their seats and away out the door.

The woman came over then and sat with him and got him to say her name, or something like it. He remembered that look to the mouth between his mother and his father. She looked at a glass machine that was taken from her pocket. Such a glass machine, large, was on the wall. She waved him out to go with the children. He followed the movements of her eyes and the way her head turned a little toward the door, so he got up and went out slowly. He didn't want to go. He was afraid of the children.

Girls with a clothes rope, mouths gaping all together. His head began to ache with trying to understand. He walked away slowly, moving with great care around the outside of the schoolyard. He didn't want to alert the children to make them notice him.

The yard was a nice place. Children's feet had made its dust fine, fine, soft and smooth as flour. It was warm with sun. If no one was here, he would have made a mound of it, a big, warm pile and then taken off his shoes and walked around in it. There was a swing, too; and beyond that another big slaughtering-frame with the tying ropes hanging down, but the big boys were climbing up on them. Others were running after a boy. They turned and swooped past Abel, the last one pushing him away. Their mouths were busy, busy. How could he follow the mouths of the fast, wild, jumping, turning, over-the-shoulder players, the tar-chewers, the nail-biting head-bent ones? His head was pounding. If only he could stop them, freeze them in play, hold the jump in mid-air and face them front to make them form to his mother's round perfection, their casual, wild, fearful-friendly, sudden-gone.

He felt the bell again with the bones of his face. Everyone stopped then and they all went in. More hands up, hands down and getting up and down. Then they all took out lunches, so he did, too. The sun-square was gone from his desk. The afternoon passed. It went so slowly that by the end of it, he had long forgotten the beginning. The children wrote, the children spoke. He followed and did not follow, too tired and growing impatient at the mouths. They were only quick, passing, not real, the moving of them lost before they made meaning.

He copied a picture with no idea. He cut out a star from paper, eight arms, not six, but no better, and when the others left and the sun was making its window-squares far on the other side of the room, he found himself breathing the dust of it all alone with the woman who was not a mother and whose name he could not imitate.

When he was let go at last from the building, the light was long and golden and sad with its going. He was surprised and confused at the length of the light. Didn't he take all the day's pain with a strong face, never weeping once, never running away? Wasn't that enough, without the day being used away besides? In spite of all he could do, his eyes filled. He looked about, trying to find some secret place where he might creep away and cry. . . .

There was a cart coming toward the place from down the road. He watched the light catch its metal now and then, and once or twice it was overtaken by its own dust. A terrifying hope began. It came up and beat inside his body. His father, dead these long light-passing times, was coming back. His father-mother-farm-life was coming back to take him away, to take him home, to forgive him. He began to run in circles, unable to contain his joy and his gratitude. Then he stood humbly, as a person does at any miracle. Never had his father been so powerful or so straight, never so different and so much the same.

Abel was standing motionless as the cart came on. His father saw him and raised a hand and then smiled at him. They had forgiven him. He got up into the cart before it stopped and they turned and left the bad things behind him. The day of pain was over.

When they came back to the farm, his mother asked him about Uuuuuuu and he smiled and nodded because it was over and he had lived through it and came back into the season of living things, and into their forgiveness again. It was only when his mother set his clothes of that day carefully on the chair again did he realize what his punishment was to be. Tomorrow also. The day after that. He stopped breathing; there was a pushing in his throat.

That night, he lay staring out at the dark sky, unable to cry himself to sleep. In front of the window the maple tree moved. He felt angry that he had been in this bed this morning, knowing so little. Beside him lay his younger brother, sleeping. He began to shake the bed to wake up the little boy who was taking the days so easily. The boy turned and slept on. Once, Abel knew, he had trusted like that. Once, he, too, had been good. For a while he watched the night and the moon in balance on the slender tips of branches.

From that day on, the time, which before had been a long measure, was now hung for him in endless strings of five and two. His mother began to wait for him with pencil and paper, and sometimes he wrote words there, but only the ones he had learned in school. He did not understand what they meant to be, and he never understood her when she tried to make them important to him. She was eager, somehow, and then angry, and finally, only sad. It was his fault, for which he was being punished. Soon she got tired and stopped.

Janice lay sleeping, her head twisted around as she was when she had been awake, watching him. Her hands were loose and quiet on the cotton quilt she had pulled up to warm herself. He shook his head and began to undress. He was eager for the warm bed and no more thinking. All the years he had not thought about the way his father looked sitting up in that wagon on the first day of school. Suddenly, he saw his hands drop the stained shirt they were holding and begin to speak to him. *School.* Yes, it was *school* they were trying to say to him on that first day. *School* was the Uuuuuuu. Only now, years and years away, and with Words in his hands, was it plain to him. He smiled at himself in the weak light and made the Sign for it, shaking his head again. What was the use of it, now he no longer needed it, that knowledge? Still it came back to him again. All the mouths of his years, all the mouth-mouths of the city and the shop had meanings and reasons. Too many. Too many to know or to want to know. It was a strange thing, though, wanting to think backwards. It was too strange even to tell Janice, that his mind, here in another place, was still holding that cart and the school, holding them waiting.

He looked at Janice again and she moved her head away, putting her arm up over her head and then down again. She turned on her side and settled more, and slept. At the Deaf School she was held also, waiting. Then she was all alive, always moving, changing, laughing quickly, scowling and laughing again. She was like the light that changes but is always beautiful, always different, always to wonder at. It was different with her now. Now she was pinched-in and always tired. She would only eat and finish eating, wipe her mouth and crawl into bed and fall asleep with her clothes on.

He looked around the room. The dinner things were there, drying and crusting on the windowsill. He moved around the bed and picked up the coffee bowls. One of them stuck to the sill for a minute. Something on the bottom of it, something that was not washed and dried away. It put a greasy feeling in his mind, a greasy smell in his mind, like mice that died in the seed sacks of the barn. He had found a nest of them once, packed in tight among the sacks, in the close, hot corner where the outgrown, unmended things were put by against some unexpected need. The memory was in his body still. His hair rose along his neck and down under the collar of his underwear.

He took the bowls to the washstand and poured some cold water over them. For a minute he thought about washing the pots, but he was beginning to be too angry with Janice and he put the pots in with the bowls and turned away. It was her job to do that—the wife's job. She was getting away from him and from her jobs every night, going to sleep for the warm, secret dreams where he could not follow. Every night, as soon as she was home and warm with a little food. Tomorrow she would wake up and say she was still not rested, not ready, and she would drag off to work yawning, her face unwashed from the night and blurred with breakfast crumbs.

He muttered, making half-words, one-handed, and without waking her he got undressed, rinsed his mouth and spat the rinsings out the window. Then he pissed into the alley, which saved having to go all the way downstairs and out to the privy, losing all the warmth of his dinner. It was bitter cold. He shut the window fast and got into bed. It was good. She was sleeping still. Her turning had left him a warmed place and he went gratefully into it and took up his own secrets; one special one, to warm his own night. It was a little like making a magic toward sleep: The Christmas Bonus. The Christmas Bonus. . . .

5

*B*ARBARA was back at work in the cap room; her hand was healed, but with a big scar, and her Sign was halting and lame with the tightening of its sinews. She and Mary nodded at Janice's tired look. They said a Sign she didn't understand and then they giggled and pulled joking faces.

"What is it you said?"

They made the Sign again and then touched each other on the shoulder, laughing.

"What is it?"

"You know, pregnant—going to have a baby. Are you sick in the morning? Do you throw up?"

"I feel dizzy in the morning and I am always tired."

"What about the blood. Any blood?"

"What blood?"

"Oh, you are dumb! The *monthly*."

"No, not for a while."

Janice looked away from them because she was blushing. Her eye caught a girl staring at them from the corner near the door. She turned back. "Someone is watching the Deafies," she said. "Eyes are sticking out over a sandwich."

The other two girls looked sideways, seeming not to look.

"She is so interested," Barbara said, "that the filling falls out of the sandwich and the bread is hanging open like her own big mouth."

"A tongue sandwich," Mary said.

"She is very busy," Janice added. "When the buttons come off, she closes her blouse with safety pins." The Sign had become animated, the witness more intent.

"Maybe that's good," Mary said. "Before she learned better she used to do it with chewing gum."

"Before the chewing gum, she used nails."

"Didn't that hurt?"

"Not her; the nails got bent and she had to throw them away."

"Big improvement."

"That's from watching us. If she didn't learn from us, she wouldn't know anything."

Then they laughed and nodded to each other again and the bell rang.

Janice felt tired and heavy in the afternoon air of the room. She got up slowly and the other girls watched her. She knew they sometimes made fun of her because now she was no faster than they were, no more sure. She had been proud of that speed, but since Barbara's accident there wasn't the same hunger in them for speed like hers. They never mentioned more pay or transferring to piece-work section any more. It was all right for Hearing to cut up their hands. Hearing's hands were nothing more than hands; it was different with Deaf.

Janice was afraid that her slowing down would lose her the weekly bonus. What did the monthly bleeding have to do with having a baby? Didn't babies come from a man's Thing? When she asked the girls later, they made a dummy Sign at her. "How can you forget when you bled last? Don't you know enough to remember *that?*"

"Why?"

And they laughed at her again.

She wished she had told Abel about them. Many times she wanted to tell him things Mary and Barbara said or places they went. The bonus came so regularly now that she had come to depend on it. It would not stop no matter what Abel knew. The reason that she had now for keeping the Deaf girls a secret was that it had been a secret before, made with half-lies and trickings that she gave one after the other. The secret had power now because it was thick; the trickings were gone over and over like the machine going again over its own stitches in the holes it had already made for itself.

In the evening she said, "Maybe I am going to have a baby."

"How do you know?"

"People say when a girl gets tired all the time, it is because of a baby. Also about the bleeding." She said that part fast before he could use his mind to catch at any of the words. "The girls in school used to talk about it sometimes, the bleeding."

"Maybe you are sick. Do you think you can be sick?"

"It is mostly about the bleeding."

"What will I do?" His hands had begun to shout at her. He had started suddenly to be very loud, cutting and throwing hard, short words at her and she began to back away from him, afraid that speech would stop and he would strike her.

"You have to stop this baby! Now! Why did you begin to make it? Why did you begin it now?"

"I didn't know." She was beginning to cry. "Maybe it's not——"

"How can it be now? It will want to eat if it comes and is born. We have nothing to feed it. It will die. It will have to die." He turned and left the room, slamming the door to shake the walls around her.

When he came back, he didn't say anything. Janice wondered who might know about a baby without wanting money to tell her.

Days passed and weeks, just the way they did before. The tired feeling went away and Janice was able to stay awake in the evening after she rinsed the dishes, to play checkers with Abel, or mend, or make love. When she got a little fatter, she let out the gathers in her skirt and closed the belt with a safety pin. Then two pins. Three.

It was sometime after that, on an evening when she was undressing in bed, that the horrible thing happened: Her stomach began to move, to poke in and out. She tried to hide the movement whenever it came, to pull in her stomach, and when that didn't work, to turn away so Abel couldn't see it. Soon he did see. She was in a nightdress she made to hide herself, and the stomach suddenly went all the way out on the left side, moving and leaping as if she was hiding a dog in a leather sack. She tried to turn away fast, but it was too late. His face got sick and he ran out of the room, down the stairs and outside, to throw up in the cold privy.

Abel didn't know why it made him sick. On the farm he saw many births and slaughterings, sickness, dying—he never felt ashamed then, never threw up. It was a baby in there really, a live thing. He began to shiver; a cold of dizziness came up inside him and he almost fell. She would never want to kill it. She would never let it die. It would be a growing, needing Other, eating, eating, eating. It would have to be kept warm . . . it would have to have clothes, a place to sleep . . . eating . . . and money he didn't have. What would the Law do then? And Janice . . . Janice will have to stop working. He was breathing too fast, dizzy again. He held hard to the wall of the privy, and the sour smell made him retch again. Need . . . mouths . . . He had the Sign of "need" in his hand and he felt the forefinger hooking, hooking into himself, that need-hook into his flesh, pulling. He began in slow beats to kick at the walls of the privy and at the door and at the bottom of the seat, with a hard, patient pounding.

Soon, in the back of the house, lights went on, which he saw through the crack-places with his eyes but not his mind. People came out. He did not see them, but felt them standing outside the privy, waiting to beat him, talking about him surely. They were waiting for him to do something bad enough so they could beat him and call the law and take more from him. It made the sick pain worse in him. Back and back again he went, side, side, front, back, kicking with his feet and banging with both fists, until the forward force drove him back by its own power.

The ground beneath him began to sink. It went on and on sinking until Abel, almost falling, understood that it was not the earth sinking, but the privy rising; that the men were all around him and were lifting it up, up over him. He could see the hedges at the side of the house, or their shadows, blowing against the dark. The men were like houses, or trees. They were not taking him away from the privy; they were moving the privy away from him. In the dark, he thought, they would not know who he was. The men were lifting the privy up and up until there was nothing to beat against, only the cold and all of them, dark and great in their big coats.

He was afraid to hit at them, although he wanted to so much that his hands shook. If he hit them, they would drop the sidewall of the privy on him and then kill him, or put him in the jail forever. So he bent down and crept slowly out from under the privy and broke through the space between two of the men. He was grinning in the dark. Their hands were busy holding up the privy; there were no hands to stop him. He ran away from them and broke through the hedge between the houses. He could pretend he was not Abel, but some other Deaf. He was grinning more widely, and when he stopped, he began to laugh.

It was very cold. He stood, Signing wide in the blind night, telling himself the joke of it. "I do not like you in my house, lady fat with a baby. If you do not get out of here, I will move my house away and leave you sitting on the stool in your nightclothes." All around him was safe darkness and numbing cold. The cold was so hard it hurt him to breathe and the stars scratched where God put them to help it be night. No one ever told him about what they were made of, stars, or where they were in the daytime. There were, really, people who knew things like that. World things. Hearing knew things like that. *"But"*—he skipped the word off his forefinger, playing—"Hearing do not know how to catch Deafs in privies!"

When he got back to the room, Janice was sleeping. She lay curled over the lump of her middle so it was hidden and she looked almost the same as when they were first married. Her face had some of its old fullness, and there was the uncareful not-mute look she had once. Maybe there would be trouble because of his making noise in the privy. He sighed and began to undress and suddenly found himself blind with tears.

My dear son and daughter-in-law
    This is just to let you know we are holding like we were. The white mare we had when you were home has foaled. We recieved your Christmas greetings which has been put on the mantel. Tarvis Elder come by and seen it. Your father was against me writin this as he feels what is put in words makes a thing come to pass. Everyone says to send greetings to you which I am doing.
Your loving mother.

    Abel said, "We have to write to them to tell them about the baby."
    "I don't want to tell anything now. What if something happens and then we will end up back there on the farm?"
    "We need to tell them soon there will be a baby, but if they know, my mother might come here. She will find out about the Court."
    They decided to write a letter and also to put off writing it for a while, so it was easy to wait until June when Janice came home early one afternoon and lay down, grinding her teeth and groaning, and began to have her baby.
    When Abel came home, the landlady met him in the hall and told him—mouth, gestures, looks, and writing—what had happened. She showed how she had called a midwife (pointing to a sour-face woman at the top of the stairs). Both the women were angry that nothing was done or ready except a few hemmed cloths. They had to use newspapers, they said, which slid. *She* (gesturing to the room) didn't know a thing about having a baby; she fought them and thrashed here and there. She wouldn't open her legs; she wouldn't lie quietly, turning and fighting until they thought she would kill herself. And then . . .
    He ran up the stairs. The room was angry with chaos and the smell of blood—a hanging, animal odor he remembered from the farm—and another smell he remembered but could

not name. Newspapers lay over the bed, and at first he couldn't see anything else.

The two women came in behind him and stood like Law in the corners. Abel looked and looked at the bloody bed until he made out something lying among the papers and ruined sheets. As he went to it, the landlady began to gesture at him, moving her mouth bla-bla-ma-ba-ba, which he couldn't read because of fear.

He turned from her again to the heap and went to it and began to shake it. The midwife got up and pulled at him; the heap moved under his hands, hair falling away from what came to be a face. Eye in the face opened. It was his Janice; she was alive.

The landlady pulled him back then and began again at him, bla-ma-ba. He did not go to the bother of reading it. At last she got a pencil and paper and wrote down what she wanted to tell him: Since the mother was a dummy and had fought them and worn them out, the fee would be fifteen dollars for the midwife and ten dollars for her; the bedclothes, which were ruined, even with all they tried to do, would come to another two and a half dollars. He read the paper, nodding slowly. Only then did he think that he hadn't seen a baby. He made the Sign for baby, and they took him around the bed and showed him where a basket was on the floor.

In the basket was a wrinkled, red puppet, alive, its fists working, its eyes shut tight like any animal just born, world-surprised and disliking. Even as he watched it, it breathed. The midwife raised the edge of one of Janice's hemmed squares to show its swollen female sex and Abel saw the cord-end and the blood-streaked belly.

The landlady was back to writing again. Abel thought that maybe he could give her the baby for all the money it took to get it out of Janice, but he didn't know how to say it, so he just stood and waited until the landlady gave him what she had written. He got dizzy and had to sit down to read it. She wanted all that money now. She wanted them to move, too. The room was not for three. When his wife woke up, the writing said, give her coffee. . . . Yes, she knew they made it in here. . . . Put the baby to the breast when it cried. She wanted the money by tomorrow at the latest; if not, she would get the Law on them.

She and the other one left. He began to make coffee and then he collected the wet and bloody papers and stuffed them in the stove. They would stink to burn, too.

Janice woke up. "I have a baby," she said, and began to look over the mess on the bed for it. He showed her the basket. "Is she all right?"

"Yes, the woman said to give it milk from you."

"I didn't like them. That other one slapped and punched me."

"They want money. They want money tomorrow or they will call the Court and throw us in the jail. And we have to leave here."

"Is the baby all right? Is it going to live?"

"How can I get that money? Maybe I will have to go to Mr. Webendorf, because I don't have that much."

"Is it Hearing?"

"Who hears?"

"Is the baby a Hearing?"

"Sure."

"How do you know?"

"Born in newspaper. Born in all the words."

When it came to be night, Abel turned on the light and and saw the baby was awake. He went to it, but he did not know how to help it, so it scared him and he turned away. Janice was asleep again, but her face still remembered the smile it had had before. Sometimes he wondered what laughing sounded like. In school many people had ideas about how different things sounded, and some of them could hear talk if it was loud enough. Sometimes he wondered about the sounds of things. Anyway, laughing was gone now, and so were the Strangers, Hearing, who had been in the room and had punched Janice when he wasn't there. The old way was gone, too. It was gone with those Hearing. What if this baby they left was Hearing? In his mind he saw it grown, not to a person, but only itself, very big. He thought he could never be able to speak to it. Hearing are the Strangers, Hearing never understand. Then he thought, Maybe it is not a Hearing, anyway. Maybe it is only a Deaf, like us.

As they sat up tired and frightened, Janice told Abel about the money. There were things to get for the baby—diapers and caps and bands—and money was needed for the landlady and the other one who came. Still frightened, she told him it was special Christmas money which she saved to surprise him. Most of his own secret bonus money had already been spent on food—he found he couldn't go on the coffee and bread she gave him for breakfast, and only bread and apple for lunch. On bad days he also took the streetcar home. He had four dollars saved. He was angry that she had not told him about her bonus, had saved it away and not told him and let him worry about where the baby-money was coming from.

The night passed without sleep. Their fear lay open-eyed and watching, its odor heavy in the shadows of the room. They kept a candle lit because they were afraid the baby might cry. Abel tried to doze for a while, but the fear would bristle somewhere in warning and he would shoot up in the bed, sweating and strange, not knowing for a moment where he was. Janice didn't have any milk, only some clear drops from her breast and she was frightened that the child would die before morning.

Abel stayed home the next day because he was too tired to work and because Janice needed to sleep while he watched. The baby was dying of hunger and no milk came. When Janice slept, she saw the baby dying and saw them in the court and in the jail because they did not pay for it. She became so frightened that she woke crying and shaking and would not go back to sleep again until she could have her hand on the baby's body. In the end, it was the way she felt the baby's cry, and they were able to sleep.

Crying shook the baby's body and that shaking brought Janice awake in an instant, full of fear. She kept trying to nurse the child all the time, but there were still only those drops, not clear now, but like the white cord in an egg, and the baby didn't seem to be learning how to suck hard enough.

When Abel was sleeping, Janice got up and went and took out the bonus money from the suitcase. When she gave it to him the next morning, it seemed very much, but the woman wanted twenty-seven dollars and fifty cents, and there was the rent and another place to move to, and in the end it was very little money. All those weeks and weeks of bonus, very little.

They waited until the evening and then Abel took the money to the landlady. While he was gone, Janice began to think of a name for the baby, and she thought it should be called Margaret Ryder. Someone in school once told her that Margaret was a very good name. When Abel came back he said, "She wants us to move away. Baby cries."

"Where? Where can we go?"

"She says we can stay until the end of the month."

"I want to move to Berard Street." (It was where they had walked in the summer, where the white painted houses were, and the porches, big and cool, and the trees that touched branches over the streets.)

"We will move near work," he said. "Moody Street, Bisher, some place around there. Soon; we have to find a place soon. After I gave her the money, she wrote I must give something to Mr. Webendorf and everyone at work. I have to give them cigars."

"You saw her mouth wrong—that can't be right."

"She wrote it. She laughed, but not in the bad way. She is sure."

"Do you think it is true? Maybe it is some joke against us."

"Maybe it is some little law. I think maybe it's a way like Christmas."

"Maybe they will laugh at us for it."

Abel's eyes went away from her face, puzzled; then he smiled and nodded. "Yes, I remember, Pickard on the linotype in the shop—he did it once. You give cigars to others; they shake your hand and laugh."

"How many, then?"

"Seven."

"How much does cigars cost?"

"How much is possible?"

"I don't know . . . for all of them. . . . Is it something you must do?"

"If I don't, it will be too Deaf."

"Tomorrow," she said, "you can use the rest of the money of the suitcase."

He went back to work the next day. He went early, hoping she did not see the relief he felt getting out of the close room and the always-and-everything of baby.

He stopped at a small tobacco shop and was surprised at how much cigars cost. He remembered then that Pickard didn't just hand a cigar to each man; he had held out a full box and allowed each man to take one or more according to his ways. A full box, even the cheapest, cost what a week's dinners cost. Abel stood in the store, trying to get the box and go. He was too angry to do anything but wait for the anger to leave him. The store man stood with hands hovering among the boxes, also waiting. The Law had its rule; the trade its demands. At last, he sighed, went forward and pointed to one of the boxes. The man nodded and wrapped up the bright-colored box with its beautiful foreign lady. Abel found himself sweating a kind of cold inside his coat because of the cost.

Later, at work, when he got up from lunch, he went from man to man as Pickard had done. He made a Sign and found that Hearing understood that cradle-arm Sign for baby. The men hit him on the back and laughed as they had done with Pickard. They took the cigars by ones and twos, sniffing and lighting one up, and putting the other into a pocket for later. As he moved down the floor, the news went ahead of him, and men turned to him smiling. It gave him, to his own surprise, a shy pride.

Janice lay on the bed trying to rest. The room made her nervous because of all the clothes and rags and boxes piled up and the drying things that were hung here and there. The smell of mess in the diapers was strong in the room and the soft rags in the basket were beginning to smell bad. The landlady had given her a bucket to scrub them in, but she would have to carry it down to the washtub in the basement, or outside in the back. She would have to take the baby too, lest it wake alone and cry. She didn't feel strong enough to do this work; even thinking about it made it heavier. She wanted to be walking in the fresh air, away from the bad smell and the tightness in her that made her want to curse the walls.

Before noon the landlady put her head in and told Janice that there was something for which she had to come downstairs. ("Down," jabbing her finger many times for Janice to understand.) It was hard to believe. Janice didn't know if she had understood, since there was no one who knew her, and nothing but work to leave the room for but the landlady kept motioning to come, so she pulled on an old work smock she had taken with her from the school. The careful chainstitch— *State School of Deaf and Blind* on the front—had been as carefully pulled out, but its outline, less faded, still remained.

Janice checked Margaret, sleeping in the basket, looked at her own pale stranger's face in the mirror, gathered her hair and put a string around it, and then picked her way carefully down the stairs.

There was a tall man there. His back was to her as she came into the front room. He was looking at the iris in the yard. They were purple, with fat stems and big flags. She didn't like those flowers. In a minute the man turned around and smiled at her and his mouth said, "Mrs. Janice Ryder?"

She nodded.

". . . ay . . . old . . . . baby."

She nodded, unsure.

"I . . . . for the bill."

"Wha' " she said. "Wha' di eeou 'ay?"

"I . . ame for the bill."

She fainted.

Afterwards, she could not understand coming awake back in the room on the bed. The landlady was sitting on the chair, cleaning her nails. Her look was bad, angry and impatient. When Janice tried to sit up, the woman motioned with her head to something beside her on the pillow and then got up and went out. It was a note:

Dear Mrs. Ryder,

I am sorry if I caused you any trouble or gave you a shock. Your landlady told me you were deaf, which I was not told at the mill. I am from the Union at the mill and I want to help you if you plan to come back to work. We have some help for working mothers. If you are interested, please come to the Union Office at 52 Bisher Street.

At the bottom was his name.

Janice closed her eyes and began to tremble a little. It was *mill* he had said, not *bill*. Maybe. Maybe nothing about a bill. She began to cry without knowing why she was crying or how she could stop. She was still crying when the landlady came in again with a note and as she left, she pointed angrily at the basket. In it the tiny baby was red and bent up with its own howling. It was wet and messed with its greenish-yellow mess pushing from the rims of the small rag-diaper. Janice got up groaning and tended to it. More work for the evening, and Abel's wash and her own.

She put the baby to her breast and felt a small prickling as its mouth began to move there. Something was starting. The baby had begun to pull and at the other breast Janice saw a large, whitish drop forming. It hung on the nipple for a moment and then fell on the faded cloth of the smock. There was another drop and then another. She felt embarrassed, as if someone were watching. She was surprised at the suddenness of it, embarrassed at the plenty, afraid at the waste. She felt a long, slow drawing, low, where the baby had come from and then a tightening of her breasts. They were, in some mysterious way, a part of each other, and this new thing was a part of something more, and she was now in the rhythm, in the rhythm of it as surely as giving cloth to the machine.

Six hours later the baby really began to nurse. Milk flowed, real milk and then the child drank, the womb drew, the rhythm rose in the web of nerves and muscles to make itself known, and the same rhythm spread to the child who lay in it, rapt and held by it, sucking and breathing; the pulses in the little temples and the soft top of the head moved strong and sure in their beat at the limits of the rhythm; she could see that rhythm, touch it. Deaf or not, the echo was sounding in her flesh and in the child.

When the baby was satisfied and lay sleeping, Janice studied the landlady's note:

> I told your husband I couldn't let you stay here no more. Please find yourselfs a place. You can keep the basket and bedding for the baby, but get it washed soon. The Union man carried you up to bed and I don't want none of that around here either so leave by the end of this week.

They had to use their deafness carefully, smiling and misunderstanding, smiling and forgetting and misunderstanding, so that they had an extra week while they looked for a place, climbing dozens of flights of stairs and staring into room after room of dim, sour apartments. At last Abel found a place. It was over an empty store on a long street and it was near the mill. The street was so crowded with business and people that he thought it must be at the very middle of the city. He thought Janice would like the crowds and movement and he was sure she would like the two rooms he had gotten. There were only two other apartments over them.

The street was called Vandalia Street. Abel did not know that to live on Vandalia Street was to be known automatically as an immigrant, one of a howling polyglot swarm that had flowed into the crumbling slums by the river to take up its generation of The Golden Dream. Vandalia Street's lofts seethed with roaches, its corners winked with rats and there wasn't a policeman for a mile. Its houses were firetraps, its rents were high, but Abel was lucky to get rooms so close to the printshop and the mill. There wouldn't be the torment of long walks in the winters, and the landlord seemed pleased when he found out that his new tenants were deaf. "Good.

Deef-and-Dumb won't be no noise, no loud parties. Good.''

But they had no furniture and to pay the rent on the two rooms Janice would have to get back to work very soon. Before she had the baby, the section foreman at the mill had written down that when she was ready to work, she could come back and ask for something called *Home Piecework.* As soon as she was strong enough, she and Abel went to see the nice Union man who tried to help her before.

It surprised them when the Union man showed great anger about this piecework. He told them that it was evil and an explosion of working people. Janice answered, writing back that she was experienced, and a bonus, and knew her machine. She was not going to do evil with it and would run it good and faster than any girl. When he shook his head and waved her paper away, she wrote that she understood his thought. ''I know. I saw many time girl hurt because careless. The electrical of machines sometimes to come with blue sparks, but this is because wire is old. Will be very careful home.''

He tried to tell her about the home-piecework system. He wrote that it was a kind of slavery, with rates set so low that it doomed the worker to two days of work just to pay for the rental of machines. Janice and Abel looked at each other in wonder. That meant five other days, long, full days to earn for themselves alone—and at home, too. She could nurse and care for Margaret and need less money for coats and hats and overshoes. . . . They left the angry Union man and went to the mill where Janice signed her name at the new section. She was pleased to see that there were new machines that they were made without any cords.

She said quickly to Abel, ''Pedals, no electrical. No danger of exploding working people.''

After dark Janice and Abel brought the machine to their new place, wrapped in a blanket to hide what it was. The Union man had been very angry. Suppose the machines were not allowed by some law? Maybe there was something in the law against their using this expensive thing when Abel owed so much money already for something bought-yet-not-bought and sold-but-not-sold. It was better if no one found out about the machine. It stood, gleaming and powerful in the back room, the only piece of furniture there. They moved their clothes and the baby, smiling as they came into the new place again and saw the secret thing that was waiting for them in the second of two rooms.

On the first evening, after supper, Abel stayed sitting on the floor. In front of him was his cigar box with the beautiful foreign lady, and now he was using it to hold his important papers. With the box to lean on, he wrote to his parents: "We have a baby. It is a girl name Margaret Ryder. Now we move 1522 Vandalia St."

He folded the letter and put it in the box until he could get to the post office for a stamp and envelope. He saw the city map in the box, took it out and unfolded it. It was the one he and Janice used for their walks last summer. He thought he would tape it to the wall with some printer's stripping tape, like a picture. Because now they were living in Section 3, near the lower middle of the city. He turned and asked Janice where she wanted to walk this Sunday. Their summer had almost begun.

"Only a little," she said. "I feel tired because of the baby and we will have to carry her."

"Let's go back to where we went last summer. Where the nice houses are. We can take her with us."

"I can't fit into my dress and I don't have anything nice to wear!"

"As soon as we get some money——"

"I can work Sundays now."

"I am starting my fourth year soon, and there will be some extra money——"

"All day Sunday," she said, "to work for the time I have to take with the baby."

"I want to go to many streets and places this summer. In this section——"

"And I can work at night, too," she said. "They still have bonus for work above the quota."

She was staring at the machine and the pile of cut-out caps. She had been looking at it ever since dinner, eager, he saw, to use it; to turn the big, shining wheel; to begin to give thread and cloth to it; to let the feeding take everything into its rhythm until it ate away the great pile in the slow, steady eating. He did the same with jog and jog of paper, filling and emptying, filling and emptying bail and cradle with the spring-wound foot delicately, like a finger made wet on the tongue, pushing paper after paper under the rollers. He knew that the rhythm had a kind of wish to follow itself, a force to repeat nothing more than itself endlessly; and, of course, each layer of the great pile of cut cloth into so many and so many caps was a penny or two or five, adding, adding as the pile was lessened.

He wondered why the Union people were so angry about the piecework. They had made reasons and nonsense-reasons. Hearing had nothing else but reasons. They went blibber-blobber with their mouths all day and the reasons ran out and into the Court and into the Law and it all went running out like blood and you had to go and pay for invisible cars and invisible reasons.

Janice's eyes were on the machine again. He took his finger away from the map, where it was pointing to a little park in the corner of the second section. "Go, work," he said, feeling annoyed with her. "Get it ready to sew if you want."

The mill had even given her a table on which to set the machine and she arranged a cardboard box they had found in an alley to take the flow of work from one side to the other. She tried the fruit crate she had brought up for a chair and then threaded the machine and checked the bobbins, one-handed, while the other hand pulled the first piece under. He stared at her in a slow wonder, never having seen her so wise and serious. She knew everything about the machine—here she tightened, there she eased, her fingers going surely in their swift, clean motions. Then the gleaming wheel was pushed, the patterned piece caught up and in, pleated and folded with a blind hand, the vibration of the machine humming in the floor and up through his bones.

In her basket in a corner Margaret moved. Abel saw the spasm of her movement and went over to see, then back to stand over the machine.

"Baby is crying."

Reluctantly the machine stopped, the hands came up: "I nursed her an hour ago."

"Anyway."

Janice got up and went to the basket: "Not crying now."

Back at the machine, she started the wheel, sucking her cheek, impatient to take up the torn rhythm and seal it once more. The machine began. In the corner the baby kicked and cried and Abel picked it up and brought it closer. It only howled more. He stopped Janice again and she looked up in irritation.

"Someone," Abel said, slowly, and with a kind of empty calm, "someone in this room is hearing everything."

6

THE GROUND TONE of Margaret's childhood was her mother's machine. It was the sound of the family life and it paused only for the few moments necessary to eat or go to the hall bathroom. By its speed and tone Margaret learned her mother's moods, and when a needle broke and had to be replaced, the minutes of waiting rang in the awful silence with terrible length. It was as though a living thing had stopped breathing, and the watchers waited desperately for breath to come again and save it from death. On Sundays, Abel forced the machine to this horrible waiting silence and they all took a walk, Janice grumbling and scowling through the strange, unwilling ritual.

When Bradley was born, the machine stopped for a day and a half, and so awful was the silence then that Margaret banged the floor and cried in terror and went in to the machine again and again to stroke its black metal neck and beg it to save her mother's life. Only when she heard the comforting click-tick monotone whir-whine again was the family safe, the house alive, the world without terror.

They were a closed family, a family of habit, and their habits measured each day and each week without change. Every evening at the same time Margaret's father would come home and go immediately to the sink to use the special pumice soap he kept there. Not even that soap could get all the ink out of the lines of his hands, but every day he scrubbed, rinsed and scrubbed again. Then he would nod in at the back room where Janice nodded a greeting back, the machine not slowing. Then he would sit down and take out his cigarette paper and tobacco and roll himself a cigarette with great care. He smoked slowly with long, fine expressions of leisure, and while he smoked, he did nothing else. By the time the cigarette was finished, the machine would have begun to slow and then it would stop and Janice would come in and begin to put out the dinner things. During this time Abel talked to Margaret, asking her if she had had a nice day. Margaret always answered his questions seriously and with dignity and she always said she enjoyed the day whether she did or not. It was part of the expected gesture of the day and she fitted herself to her place in it.

Sometimes Janice had to go downstairs to the corner where some dark people named Vlamiki owned a little grocery. While she was gone, the father and daughter played. Their Signs made jokes and they laughed often, saying silly things to each other. Margaret's Signs came from Abel and Janice; her fund of meaning was as poor as theirs, but her Signs had the special beauty of her childhood and Abel cherished even the mistakes she made. Sometimes he would tell them to Janice, smiling and shaking his head at the backward brush of a hand that changed a word into another or dissolved the meaning of a sentence before his eyes.

When Janice came, the playing always stopped, without anyone realizing that it had stopped just then. If she brought milk, Abel would wait until she was busy and then, winking at Margaret, he would go to the bottle, untwist the evil and dangerous silver wire holding the pleated top cap. With his still-black thumbnail, he would take off the cap and lift the tongue in the under-cap to pull it up carefully for the undisturbed, thick coating of cream that lay clotted on the underside. This he would hand to Margaret and she would smell the flowers and the clover that the cows had eaten. He would watch her, his lips moving sympathetically as she slowly licked the cream from the waxed lid. With it gathered on her tongue, she would breathe in and out as he had showed her so that she could smell the flowers again from the inside. When Janice turned for the bottle, it was always there on the table, innocently capped, its wire removed, waiting to be opened, and their two faces hanging blandly in her direction. After dinner the comforting mother-hum of the machine would begin again and Margaret and her father would wash up.

Every Saturday the work caps which Janice had finished had to be delivered to the factory and a new stack of cut patterns gotten to take their places on the left side of her work table. After the mill delivery was made, the new work collected, and the money given, they would walk home through the loud, crowded streets thick with people and smells, gaping with the gapes of fish peddlers, pushcart men, sellers of ribbons, cripples, rag collectors and walking hawkers, and the flap mouth on and on: children opening their jaws over carts of salt pretzels and fried cakes, children silent-screaming the food made by their mothers in the rank tenement kitchens. The alleys were always full of children, they seethed in the streets. Some delivered food or supplies in carts; some escaped, some were busy, some idle. On good days the stores turned inside out also and moved their wares out on the streets and there were always children hiding among the racked secondhand coats or among the stacks of pawned featherbeds.

Janice sniffed disgustedly at the filth of the children, even the small ones, sailing shoeboxes in the gutter, but even as she scolded, she knew there was no way to keep Margaret and Bradley away from the streets. They soon learned where the bullies lurked and where there was safety. They were quick to pick out the shadows of Karoli or Bubu from far up the block and to see whipping fragments of feared coats through the crowds of people. Very soon they learned the sound of Rabbit-nose Fanti's voice from a hundred others. They developed the senses of soft-bodied nocturnal creatures, quickly there, quickly gone, disputing no inch of pavement for themselves, vowing no ice-cream penny to ice-cream. They hid what they had; when they could, they hid themselves. When they were caught, they fell fainting in the clutches of the tormentors, dissembled, broke away and ran to hide again, trembling in a stack of coats or behind the wheels of the ice wagon, their pulses beating with the hot, rapid tempo of birds. They spoke to save themselves; no more.

When Bradley was old enough to speak and be understood by The Street, Margaret broke him of Signing there, quickly and with the casual brutality of childhood. When she saw him with another boy, giving with confidence the familiar words he had at home, she pounced on him and beat him up. At seven she could barely remember the first time she had Signed Outside and been ridiculed, told she was crazy, hooted away. Now, as she slapped again and again at Bradley's dumbstruck face she screamed, "Keep your hands in your pockets!" She knew well enough what their True Words seemed to people who could not read them. He had only been wishing aloud to his marble-game friend: "If I had a cookie . . ." His friend had looked at the patterning fingers glassily, uncertain of what he saw, but Margaret knew, though the Sign was half-formed. She broke from her own game and began to beat her brother, hating him for Signing Outside—that crazy string-game without a string, that finger-fumbling drunk-trick picture-making. After a time of confusion, he learned what Margaret had learned, that the True Words, the mother-father words that comforted, spoke and understood were an alien thing, and that in the World, only the risky, half-understood mouth-talk was allowed. The street and the World did not wish to trust or understand in the True and dependable way.

Abel's term of apprenticeship had ended and his journeyman's time was over. He was a master printer. He could do lithography of all kinds, he could work in flat-plate or offset, on a single or double press. His color work was careful and he had mastered the duo-black, a process that gave to photography and art prints the greatest depth and contour, but which few men in the shop took the time and trouble to do. Yet, the debt, reduced by a mountain, was a mountain still. He no longer took pride in the yearly building against principal and erosion of interest. Only gradually did it occur to him that in spite of the debt he could, in a carefully limited way, be free. He was a good printer—that much he knew. He also knew that Mr. Webendorf saw him as a fool and a debtor—

even after all the years. He had stayed with the shop because Mr. Webendorf said that nobody else would take on a deaf worker with a garnishment against him. Lately however, there had been growing in Abel, the small, hard knob of a wish to go out and try. It thrilled and frightened him—the prospect of another time of grappling with the World, with strange Hearing.

Over the years he had seen that Webendorf's did not do the kind of printing that interested him. Once or twice he had gone into bookshops on his way home and had seen fine magazines and picture books in duotone or duo-black. Once there had even been a display of someone's camera pictures magnificently photocopied. He remembered one especially, a group of sand dunes with late sun, the shadows making them seem almost like living bodies. The photographs were printed in duo-black, he was sure, but he was afraid to inquire what the pictures were or where they had been printed. They were fine work, though, he could see that. Someone somewhere was printing in a way that the men in his own shop gestured away with impatience, or made mouths at as if to say it was too good for them. He knew that Mr. Webendorf expected him to stay always, perhaps as foreman later, or doing special jobs that came in; he had expected the same thing himself, but now he had begun to wonder at the number and variety of printed things. With all their talk and endless talk, words of mouth were not enough for Hearing, and the words-words-words flowed onto paper and were to go on and on. He realized as he thought of it that, looking at a picture, he was the equal of a Hearing.

He went back to the bookstore everyday until the pictures were taken down. Looking at them, he thought they could teach him what silence was. He was beginning to hate the grainy work he slammed out for handbills and newspaper ads. Now, on the Sunday walks he took as an act of rebellion, dragging an unwilling wife and two complaining children, he would stop at newspaper kiosks to muse over the fine magazines, admiring the depth and artistry of the work, the richness of the color and the variety those printers knew. Ignoring the cursing kiosk men, he would stand unruffled in their insults studying the smooth pages. When he told his idea to Janice, she could see no sense in it.

"You make thirty-four dollars a month. The debt has to be paid. After that we can go away from the dirty streets and poor people."

"I only want to change to another place," he said.

"Maybe no one will hire you——"

"I will show them my work. It is good."

"They will try to cheat you. Hearing say one thing, but mean another. They will cheat you."

"I think they do now, a little."

"Yes, but in this place you know how they cheat, and how much. In a new place you won't know—it's too much risk."

She was frightened. He looked at her and was amazed. This was his gay, lively Janice, his Janice of the World, of Outside, of travel and motion and newness. Now she stayed in the backroom all day long, feeding mountains of cloth to her machine. Now she was afraid to go out on Sundays, anxious and irritated at the time wasted, money wasted, daylight wasted that could be moving, moving, moving under the needle. It had happened without his noticing; so gradually and so reasonably that he couldn't tell when the anxious avarice had begun or how it had managed to creep into the muscles and fibers of her body and the reaches of her mind and senses to dull and stiffen them. As he looked at his wife, sitting sulking over coffee at the table, he saw that the few, fast years of the machine had hunched her so that her dress pulled over her shoulders and lay loose in front. Her chest was sunken, her breasts shapeless in the dress, and for a moment he hated her for the defeats she had suffered by his debt.

She saw him looking at her and sat up a little, but the neck and shoulders could not be so easily straightened. If anything, her trying made it worse.

"I don't want to talk about this any more," she said, still frightened. "We have the delivery to make today."

On Saturdays they delivered the finished caps to the factory. Janice never saw Barbara or Mary there, but she was still afraid that somehow Abel would find out about them. The untruth, begun in the immediate animal efficiency of self-protection, was now overlaid with years of silence. It could never be explained or forgiven. It did not need to be. The World after all, was Hearing. What was not made into a word did not exist or have a meaning. She knew, for example, that although Abel nodded and accepted the pay envelope she gave him every week, he knew that she was keeping out as much for herself as she thought she could get away with. She kept money out and he knew it, but since the Word had not been made between them, the fact of it did not matter, wasn't there, couldn't hurt them.

Habit shaped the week, and each Saturday, Abel went into the sleeping room and took up the box of completed caps. Their number still surprised him. On the great squat idol they had moved across the single window where Janice worked, from the cloth to cap, and then to a heap of caps, more and more. He could hardly imagine the number of caps that were all the days. Every day of every week of every month of five years. A mountain of caps, a river of caps. For a minute he had a picture of a city in which every man, woman, mother, child, doctor, lawyer, baby at the breast, all wore one of Janice's caps, a piece of stiff cloth that had paused its last moment as cloth along her table and then turned and gone through the needle, turned again and come back as a cap. It made him feel dizzy. He knew the Union was against such work and against the people who did it and for a moment he thought he saw a reason. He had never thought about the Unions or their reasons, but now everything he saw had a kind of doubt for him, asked him questions, changed. He stood waiting with the box, staring ahead, and then he realized that she was Signing him to hurry.

She picked up the slip on which she had written the number of thread spools and bobbins she had used and what she would need for the coming week. The children were downstairs waiting, old in the Saturday routine. Since Abel took Saturdays off to help Janice, Mr. Webendorf let him make up his time by adding an extra half hour each day of the week. He was glad today, to be out, even for the routine walk and the heavy box, and the worry of taking the children with them. They were city children, careless of traffic and distracted by their hearing.

It was a soft, shining day. They walked along, happier than they had been at home. A surprising gift of sun and fresh wind flowing over the carts and people toiling in the street. The usual spring smells, rancid oil, urine from the alleys, damp plaster, poverty and rats had been carried away somewhere, and from miles to the east, the smells of an ocean were being sent over the streets and houses. It came undeserved, like war or idiocy. They turned up the street to the corner and into an alley by the side of Vlamiki's store. Margaret, pulling Bradley after her, went in through the back. By now she didn't have to ask, but waited until she was noticed. The man who saw her did not speak, but turned and cried out to his ancient sister, "Hey, Julia! Duh dummies come fur duh cart!" The woman pushed past her and went and got the little cart. She never spoke to Margaret, whom she assumed to be deaf and dumb also, but she did hold the door open as the girl struggled out with the cart. As Margaret left, she put the rental money neatly and carefully in the middle of the old lady's palm. Then she gave the short smile and thank you she had been taught and pulled the cart through the door. It was good to get out of the dark back of that place and into the day. Abel put his large box into the cart, and Janice her two smaller boxes and they began their walk.

It was eight blocks to the mill, but because of the cart they were afraid to walk on the Avenue, which was crowded with shoppers. Instead they followed the alleys and side streets and soon they had left the tenement blocks and were on streets of warehouses and wholesale businesses, which were now mostly closed for the weekend. Bradley was here and there, sniffing, scouting, peering into darkened windows, listening at dusty grilles and coming away with the sides of his face blackened in a waffled pattern. When Margaret lost patience with him, Janice put him in the handcart, being careful of the boxes and then Abel pushed him along while he crowed for the bumps.

A block from the mill they turned into another alley. This

brought them to a side entrance around the corner from the main gate. They always went in the side door and took the freight elevator to the counting and inspection room. The checkers were busy, unsmiling women, who took the work without greeting or expression. They counted, measuring every fiftieth and close-inspecting every twentieth, their faces set. No rejects this week. There seldom were. Janice took from them the card with her credits. After this they had to go to the other side of the building and down a floor to where the cutting room was.

The floor foreman there, in charge of piecework, checked the request slip and subtracted the machine rental and the new material and thread Janice was going to use from the money to be given from the credits. Then he gave her another slip with the amount she had made for the week. It always included the bonus and he always smiled at her as if he noted her numbers with special pride. She liked his praise. Sometimes when the numbers were a little lower, she felt bad bringing the card to him, and though he never spoke to her, she felt that he alone knew and was interested in her numbers, the work into which all of her days were poured. He nodded now and handed her the card for her to take to the cashier. While he had been figuring, the cart was being packed with the new week's supplies. She noticed that the model was the one with the little tab in back—they paid twenty-five cents more for every ten caps, when there was that little tab in back.

Abel took the cart and they started down the hall to the elevator. They had to pick up the money at the cashier's desk and then they could go back home. This was usually the simplest part of the Saturday, but lately it had become the most difficult of all. For the past five or six weeks, as they got their money from the cashier's office, members of the Union would come up to them, arguing the Union's case, pleading with each pieceworker there to stop taking work home. They would pick at the workers' sleeves, pushing against them, but none of the Unions ever made clear words because their mouths opened so wide and their faces pushed and strained so much. Janice and Abel were frightened because they didn't know what the Unions were saying, but they recoiled from the violence and passion on their faces and they felt shamed for them, making a disgrace like that.

The only way to leave from the cashier's office was by the front gate, and today when they reached the cashier, they saw that there were more of the Unions waiting outside. Without being aware of it, the family tightened in close to one another and came together to the cashier's window. Two policemen were guarding the sour old lady in her henna wig. She took the card quickly and stamped it and began counting out the money. When she handed the envelope through the grille window to Janice, she said something, so the Ryders smiled and nodded up and down, hard, the way Hearing expected, and turned from the window to go.

Outside the front entrance was a little space and then the gate. They went to it slowly, pushing Bradley, wide-eyed and still in the cart where Abel had put him. On either side of them, in a silence muzzy with vibrations that hurt inside their heads, people were pushing in close, their mouths gaping redly. They were past the gate and among the people and fists were being shaken before Janice's face. All around them eyes stared, faces hung, red and white with rage. Some of the women made moves to pull the cart away or to grab the bundles of pieces from it, but others held them back and they clawed and pulled the air in their own crude signs. In the cart, Bradley's face was making a howl of terror. The crazy Unions started to follow them down the street, but someone else had come through the gate and the people forgot them for the new one.

Janice and Abel began to run as fast as they could, the cart flying ahead. When they saw the alley on the other side of the street, they ran into it quickly. From there they went on, crisscrossing the dark web of alleyways, waking the drunks and the rats beneath the wheels of the careening cart. At last they stopped, trembling, and waited for their hearts to be still. Abel picked Bradley up and held him; Janice touched at her hair and straightened her dress. She was sweating and her face was very red.

Her eye found Margaret, almost hidden behind her father's legs. The little girl was gray-white and shuddering uncontrollably. She must have heard—she must know the words. Abel put Bradley down so that he could speak: "You know what they said?" She ran against his leg and held it tightly, burying her face in the dark cloth and sobbing with fear. Above her the parents looked at each other.

"What will we do?"

"I don't know. They are crazy. They want to take the cloth and they don't even know how to sew it."

"What do they want?"

His eye, too, found Margaret. "She knows. She heard." Janice went down on her haunches and began to pull Margaret's arms from around her father's leg; the little girl clung harder, sobbing until she was wrenched free and had to stand to face their questions.

"Tell us what they said."

"I don't know."

"You heard them. Tell us what they said."

Abel took Janice's arm, "Let's go home first. They may still be looking for us. She is frightened. Let's go home."

The handcart was back at the store and the week's pieces were piled in their Saturday order on the table, thread and bobbins in place, but the sound of the machine, the life of the house, was stilled. Instead, Margaret was sitting before her parents in the death-quiet, her mind emptied by fear. They were waiting for her to speak. The words were a kind of magic to them; the words would reveal it all, would solve the mystery, would show them what to do—but what were the words? She searched for them again; they were hating words, unfamiliar words, one woman screaming, "You're taking bread from our children."

"They said we were taking some bread away from them."

"Do they think we have bread in the bundles? Do they think we are stealing the people's lunches?" Abel moved his hands impatiently, muttering.

"Why should they say that?" Janice demanded, her hands confronting Margaret with the difference between those words and the truth.

"I don't know, but I think it's really about the pieces,"

Margaret said, not sure herself now, why the woman had spoken of bread. Not for the first time had she found herself caught in words, unfamiliar and alone, not Deaf, not Hearing, aware vaguely and inexpressibly that the Words, those holy rewards for which her parents were always straining, were at the same time fixed and not fixed, at the same time formed and loose. The same word could mean a real thing in the World or an idea, agreed on in secret, at a meeting to which everyone had been invited but her parents and herself. Armed with the secret laws, people walked the World, confidently sharing their knowledge.

Is bread bread or is it cloth? Janice persisted, "Didn't they know it was pieces? Can you eat pieces? No! Why has that woman said we took bread?"

"I don't know," and Margaret's sign went vague as she lost what little certainty she had.

Abel put his hand on her head and said, "Don't be afraid. It is a nice day today. Today we are not going to stay here and be afraid. Today—now—we all will go on the streetcar. I found out yesterday how to get to Deaf church, and we are going to do it today."

Janice began to argue. There was work to be done. Did he think she could make up today's work tomorrow? What would she wear? What would the children wear that didn't look ragged and make her ashamed? Back and forth the argument went, the two of them breathing hard in the stillness, clicking their teeth and lips, faces red and savage with anger, their hands shouting so loud that Margaret's head began to ache with the unmade noise.

"Don't you see?" Abel was shouting. "Pieces will be too dangerous. Pieces will soon be over and what then? Who will help us? Who will know us? Will you die, then?" With a gesture of bitter disgust he grabbed his wife's arm and began pulling her out the door. She hit out at him, punching at his neck and back and trying to wedge herself in the doorway. He hit her back from the door and then pulled her quickly through it. When she saw he was outside the apartment, she shook free with an ugly Sign, made a face into his hard look and began to slump sulkily down the stairs.

Margaret and Bradley followed, frightened, hand in hand. Their parents' fights sprang up from nothing, were often violent, full of blows and loud, guttural noises, fading quickly into something worse, a steady bitterness, paced deep and slow, the better to last.

7

*T*HE STREETCAR RIDE had three changes. They rolled and shook down street after street of big stores and shops, streets of stone row houses all the same, past a park where they changed and went in another direction, down a long, tree-lined avenue where the houses were all different, some wood, some stucco, some high-faced and thin, some low and squatting like fat old ladies. The family sat prim and still, their hands in their laps, their faces set. They were imitating some other family. As they passed the tree-shaded houses, Margaret wondered where all the people were. She was used to alleys full of wash and windows full of faces, streets surging with people, carts, noise, litter. Nothing hung between these houses; the windows stared emptily and hardly anyone was on the walks. A few children played here and there in what seemed to Margaret a forlorn and purposeless way. Now and then someone would be seen walking carefully from somewhere to somewhere else. In the streets there were cars and trucks but no people, no carts, papers, rubbish, swearing men or fighting children. The uncrowded spaces seemed immense and the great trees stood over them guarding, shading, silencing. The power and grandness of the trees flowed on to the houses and the people. The trees kept the houses secret and mysterious. That must be the difference between rich and poor.

They got down to change cars, waiting on the platform in a band of sunglare. Smells of wonderful singleness hung all around them: warm tar and cool trees. Horses, cars. The smells were not all mingled into one as they were on the street at home. Abel and Janice breathed in deeply; the children imitated them. The World Outside was so quiet and mannerly, so prim and clean.

Their streetcar came and they climbed up and began to move through yet another area of stores and traffic and then past more houses. When they got down again Abel led them across the street and then he looked around and motioned with his head. Up one block and then down another and there was a big building, the church, he said. It was too early for them to go in; they walked slowly by it and back again. Abel seemed delighted with himself and everything he saw. Janice shot him a few sour glances, but he paid no attention.

When the right time came, they went inside to the anteroom; its walls protected them and made them feel freer to talk. Abel noted the sign saying! SATURDAY: 3:00 P.M. MISSION TO THE DEAF. After a while some other people came.

The women were beautifully dressed; they wore soft, clinging dresses, like petals, with patterns of summer flowers, and their handbags, hats and shoes all matched. Some had white dresses and then they wore white shoes and carried white handbags and the white gleamed and shone as they stood talking. Margaret had never seen white shoes; it seemed strange that they should exist. The women were like flowers and their scent made Margaret slightly sick and dizzy. Bradley had wandered away, but she was too fascinated to go and look for him.

The anteroom of the church was filling up now and everyone was busy talking, talking in near perfect stillness. Now and then a laugh or a child's shout broke the loud silence and there was the sound of feet moving and of softly draped bodies brushing against one another; no more.

Margaret had been buried among the flowered backs and hips. When she looked around again she could not see her parents. Slowly she began to push her way toward the front of the room, where she thought they might be. It was like swimming in a heavy, soft sand, yielding, unyielding, and for a moment she was afraid of drowning. Then, suddenly, she saw Janice and Abel standing together almost in front of her, although their faces were turned away they did not see her. The sudden vision of them, unprepared, made her see them as though they were strangers. They were shockingly changed —barely recognizable. Her father looked rough and unkempt in his working clothes, her mother drooping, hard-faced and unpleasant. Of all the people crowding in that place, they alone looked hot, tired and disappointed, like an unwelcome blotch, a mistake in the pattern of freshly washed, flowery women and neat, dignified men. Now and then the parents would get a brief, impersonal greeting—the Sign was decorous and educated—Margaret knew this, though she couldn't quite tell how. There were many Signs she had never seen, and what she had seen half-made and stunted was given here with full-ness and grace.

She felt she had committed a sin, a terrible sin, to have seen her parents that way, as strangers. She went to them and tried to take their hands, asking in that gesture to belong to them, to be "inside" once more and part of them so that she would not have to look at them as a stranger looks. Abel motioned with his head for Bradley and so she had to leave them again dutifully, to look for him.

Suddenly the doors at the back were opened and people began to move into the sanctuary. Its magnificence took Janice's breath away. Rows of polished wooden benches faced the raised place where the minister would come. There were candles burning in great, shining holders there and a gleaming golden cross against a purple velvet curtain. Everything was rich and shining and the light of the candles was pale but steady in the daylight. People were sitting down in familiar places and greeting friends, everyone still talking happily in rich, fluent Sign. She was frightened of going in there, where everyone seemed to know so much and to be so comfortable and familiar in his place. Abel and Janice stared in until Bradley came and began to run ahead of them. His father caught him up and then they all went forward, hesitantly, into the beautiful place. There were many empty benches at the back, and they slipped into one of them, looking around for fear they had made a mistake. They sat, bolt upright, unnaturally alert, watching across the aisle at the talk flying back and forth, the eager, expressive faces, the smiling.

Janice found her attention caught by a young man who was sitting ahead and to one side of her. He was leaning around the corner of the bench to talk to a girl smiling at him across the aisle. Their faces were closed to anything but each other their hands moving in shared rhythm to the most common, daily thoughts. They were in a single daydream together and they spoke a daydream Sign. "My sister got a new coat." "Can you come to the picnic Thursday?" "How is your mother?"

Janice watched them being pulled toward each other by a force as compelling as the need to breathe. It was not God that made them come to this church every Saturday, but their hands, aching and impatient to trade the simplest words in the True and Natural Language. Janice found herself remembering with a dull envy her own days of that insatiable hunger; the waiting and waiting until Abel came to look for her Words; the force that drove her to share all the meaningless, ordinary happenings of the day with him; the understanding, sudden and complete, that lit in his face and eyes and made his newly learned Sign stutter as he answered. Now he sat on the other side of the children, blind to the shame she felt at her poverty and theirs. Even the smell they carried on them was of close, rank places; of being poor. She was ashamed to be with these people, though they were her own kind and speakers of the True Language.

Then a minister came out from a door to the side of the raised place, stood at a high, thin table and began to speak to them. He used a slow and formal Sign, heavy with vowels, nothing left out. It was Sign that had not been picked up in the half-darkness of corners, cloakrooms and bathrooms; it was not for those places or those words. It reminded Janice instead of the Judge-words coming from the interpreter when they had been in the court. She caught a kind of matching, or rhyming of the symbols and a long, swinging rhythm in the rise and fall of the words. The beauty of them left her open-mouthed. She found herself gaping like someone who was simple-minded and her eyes bore in upon him, taking every

motion, each pause and shade of movement. Never had she
seen such beauty in the simple act of speaking. That this was
her language, the language of her affliction, made her weak
with awe. Now he was speaking of what he called The Things
Not Seen. He spoke often of Christ's wishes for mankind and
of mankind's responsibilities. When he was finished, Janice
found herself strained from having leaned forward so. The
minister blessed them all and then everyone prayed, following
his prayer, and Janice trembled, taking from his hands the
full, exquisite Words.

But when the service was over, they were only themselves
again. The congregation filed out talking to one another about
unknown people and different things, looking past the new-
comers in the indecency of their poverty. Janice pulled the
children up quickly and escaped with them, going almost at a
run past the knots of people talking in the front room and
gathered on the steps. Outside in front of the church she looked
around desperately. Abel was nowhere to be seen. More and
more people were coming out to stand talking in the sunlight.
There was nowhere she could go to be lost, nothing to do to
make herself less alone. She began a quick, nervous nagging
to Margaret, and her stuttering made the girl hand-shy and
frightened.

"You didn't want to tell us what those people were saying about us this morning! You are not a help at all! Look at
what happened to Bradley here; he could have gotten lost or
been taken away by someone just because you are too lazy to
see where he is and make him obey!"

Margaret had a half-knowledge that the scolding wasn't
real, only a way of saying something that might bring an
answer from her, but in all of it there was nothing to say, and
her hands only fumbled with nothing, or with bits of answers,
excuses and apologies from other days, remembered without
thinking. As the mother's scolding went on, a slow feeling of
outrage began to rise in Margaret, and she saw it rising in
Janice also. She knew that Janice would not hit her on the
street, and so, because there was nothing else she could do,
she turned her eyes away, seeking distance, a rest from the
looming of Janice's face.

: *81* :

Across the street some children were standing in a row, their fingers idly poking in their noses or twisting strands of hair, hypnotically unconscious of themselves. Their eyes were fixed on these strange adults in their silence, drawing the quick pictures with their fingers, thrusting their hands out this way and that, their faces mobile and expressive, their hands more rapid than the eye could follow. No ordinary adult faces were ever so alive in the public pose of Outside. Margaret saw the children watching; she began staring back, but the children didn't move or notice. They stood rooted at the curb, their stomachs stuck comfortably forward, dresses hiked over their childish potbellies, faces dirty and rapt, eyes unmoving. She wanted to throw something at them, to break their trances.

Bradley was beginning to get restless. He hopped on one leg and then on the other, and announced in his loud voice that he had to go piss. Heads turned around to stare at them, children mostly, the Hearing children of the congregants. Margaret, trembling with embarrassment, took him quickly around the corner. They crept furtively into someone's back yard and Bradley relieved himself against a tree. Then they walked back very slowly. Bradley was happy, stooping to pick up leaves and bugs and empty seed pods from the sidewalk. Margaret dawdled so as to spend as little time as possible at the front of the church.

When they returned, Abel was there and the crowd had thinned. The children across the street were gone also, leaving an emptiness in the place where they had stood, so that Margaret's eye returned there more than once and she was angry at the space, which had, by contact, become unpleasant.

It was easy to see that Abel was happy, pleased with the outing and delighted with himself for thinking of it. Janice seemed more sour than usual. As they walked back toward the trolley line, Margaret saw her mother's hands moving nervously, picking at each other and making tiny unreadable Signs behind the handbag bounding on her arm. She was muttering to herself without realizing it; she hated people to mutter Sign to themselves and had slapped both the children for doing it. Occasionally Janice's lips moved slightly in sympathy with her fingers but never formed a word. As they came to the trolley line, her hands erupted at Abel. "Where were you?"

"I was with a man—talking."

"You left us standing there in front of that place for everyone to stare at. I told you we didn't have the clothes to wear. I know they thought we were beggars. Didn't you see those people staring at us?"

Abel's hands were quiet, but his shoulders were tightened in a way Margaret had never seen before, and when he spoke, his hands hummed in the air.

"I talked. With the minister. There are five people in the congregation who are printers. When I told them things, they knew. I said about wanting to get another shop. He said next week he would introduce me to some of the people there and ask them to tell me what places there are. He is a nice man, the minister. He is not a Deaf. His wife is deaf."

"If he isn't deaf, why would he want to bother with Deaf, if he can hear? Look out that he doesn't try to get any money out of you. I don't like it there. I don't like the people there."

"Well," he said airily, "we are going to come back again next week, anyway. The minister said our clothes didn't matter. I haven't spoken with people since I was in school. I want to have some friends."

They began to argue and when the streetcar came, they forgot to stop. Margaret glued her attention to the sights outside the window as the streetcar rattled and swayed into motion and then picked up speed. The shadows were drawing long and the day was cooling. Beside her Bradley sat, fighting sleep. Across the narrow aisle her parents were spinning out violence, calling names, numbering the bones of old wars, absorbed in themselves and their anger. Margaret thought that perhaps she and Bradley, sitting as they were, would not be taken as the children of those people, but as strangers belonging to some other family, a mother and father beautiful and handsome, happy and Hearing and untroubled.

Bradley had been conquered. His head fell back and then over, against Margaret, who had turned away toward the window facing the streets and houses and drawn shafts of sunlight that poured between them. The sight reminded her of the church, as it was while the service was going on, when people's eyes weren't on them, and when the minister was speaking of God and love with his beautiful hands. She tried to find a word to think that would weigh the beauty of those Hands. "It was," she murmured to herself, "like *it* was love," and after she said it, she couldn't remember if she had formed the words in sound or in Sign.

8

THEY WENT TO CHURCH every week after that, and soon the very regularity of their presence made them familiar enough to be greeted with a half-smile coming or going, or a nod as they were passed in the aisle. When Janice saw that there was no escape from Abel's will she made up her mind to conquer the church as she had conquered the factory, steadily, slowly and relentlessly. She bought outfits for all of them from the money she had saved. Margaret got a white linen dress whose stiffness made her feel like an ancient insect held prisoner in its shell. The dress wrinkled at a look; it was clammy against the body and the unbound inner edges of the waist and collar pricked and itched. There were long white stockings and stiff black shoes, and before they went out each Saturday, Margaret's thick, dark auburn hair was pulled back and braided so tightly that she could scarcely blink her eyes. Bradley had dark knee pants and long stockings also, and under his jacket a soft shirt starched hard and a full ribbon-tie, also starched. Janice wore the kind of summer print dress she had seen the other women wear. It did not go well with her muted coloring and made her look more faded and somehow more threatening than ever. Abel wanted clothes like the ones he had bought in that long dead summer of wealth, but Janice waved him away and ordered a suit as close as she could find to the suits worn by the other men as they stood greeting one another at the church door. She had bought all of their clothes in anger and some of it seemed to cling to the fabric of them, to the way they fit, so that wearing them seemed to make the family uneasy together, quick to anger and sudden quarrelling. They were, however, The Church Clothes, and Church was another enemy; they were armor.

One day, two men came to the apartment, pushed a paper into Janice's hand, walked to the back room and came out carrying the machine and its little table. Janice had Margaret read the paper, which said that the men were from the mill and were taking the machine, as anyone could see for himself. The mother stood behind the terrified girl, pushing and poking at her to make it right, to stop the men with words, to argue or curse until they put down the machine and went away. Without the machine, how would they live? She had paid her rental fee and brought back the pieces every week. Her record of rejects was the lowest at the mill, her work the best. Who had told lies about her to cause this?

The man with the table put it down and pointed at the paper, gesturing and shouting until he finally made Margaret understand: Pieces were not going to be done any more. The Unions wouldn't stand for it and there was no way to protect the pieceworkers from union bullies. If she wanted to work, she would have to sign up at the mill again and do the work as a "regular." The rates were a little higher at the factory, and there wouldn't be machine rental to pay. When Abel came home, Margaret and Janice met him, weeping with fear and rage. When they told the story, he knew there was nothing for Janice to do but to go back to the sewing floor at the factory. The mother-hum of the machine left the heart of the house and then Janice left, going out in the gray-whiteness of early morning and coming home when it was dark. Margaret stayed alone with Bradley in the terrible silence of the vacant-hearted back room.

She was seven then; most of her street friends had gone off to the school, a mysterious and forbidding stained-stone place, bigger than the church. It was four blocks away on Bisher Street, and she learned to tell the time by the flowing of the children. They moved left across the window before nine in the morning; they ran right at a few minutes past twelve; they came dawdling left again at a few minutes before one and they poured thickly, slowly, finally, right to left after three o'clock. On cold days, Margaret and Bradley stayed inside, moving between the rooms, around and around, pushing the time before them. Sometimes they ran up and down the stairs or hid from each other in the hallways until the neighbors threatened them. In January, the empty store on the street floor of the building was rented. Five carts came filled with fantastic treasures, wonders, marvels. Over the window a sign was being painted, and inside a man named Petrakis ran, shouted at the movers and fussed with the display cases of his crowded wonderland. Margaret and Bradley were fascinated by the pawn shop. After a time of staring in at the door and a first, shy meeting, the children stayed in the store most of the time, peering at the piles of old latches, kegs, old screws, musical instruments, clothes, clocks, lamps, jewels, and things for which there were no names. In the beginning they had been frightened of Mr. Petrakis, but he didn't mind having them there. They were silent children. They seldom touched things and never upset them. At first he had thought them feeble-minded, but in their silence there was a preternatural alertness to movement; they seemed to weigh the air for danger; they were like very small old people, grave, polite, and little fearful. He let them stay.

On mild days they went out in the streets, hand in hand, watching. Sometimes they walked past the school, pretending that they went there and had just come out for some reason. When people walked past them standing there, Margaret hoped that they were mistaking her for a schoolchild. Once she thought of carrying some books with her when they went past the school, but there were no books in the house and she didn't know where to get any. Mr. Petrakis didn't have books. In school they gave out books. Everyone came home with them; throwing them in the air and stuffing them with papers on which marvelous thing were written. Sometimes she tried to play with the children after school. She would threaten Bradley until he was too frightened to wander away and then they would venture out together and wait at the edge of some game or other hoping to be included. The games had changed and the children had changed. They had been swept away from her into their new lives. Waiting in the jumping lines, they talked about Mrs.

Dubin and Miss Parks. The range of their friendships had grown without her. Sometimes Mary Catherine or Lila was there to remember Margaret for jump rope or playing jacks, but more and more her friends were off somewhere, streets away, and she would have to go searching for them, dragging a complaining Bradley behind her up Vandalia and over to Moody or Warren or Bisher where other friends, school friends had taken them into other games, private and protected. Margaret and Bradley would stand aside, and so, as audience, they were tolerated while the Elect boasted about their difficulties and the cruelty they knew, and could withstand.

"Mrs. Lettiri, she don't use no ruler to hit you; she got a paddle!"

"Mrs. Dubin she got a paddle, and she could *hit* with it, too!"

"Listen, you know what happened in our class? These two girls they hid in the cloakroom. . . ."

They were so worldly, so powerful and fearless that Margaret was humble beside them, and drew them into talk, when they were willing. She collected and cherished every scrap of the day that they would share with her. Soon they stopped, knowing in their child-wise way, that bare hints and silence were more effective than words. "They had to send a kid home today". . . and then a grim nod and tight, righteous lips and silence, and for days after, Margaret would pass the school and listen for screaming from any casually opened window.

One day in March, Mr. Petrakis called Margaret to come to him, and she walked slowly to the counter where he sat guarding the cash register in his hunched-over way. Looking out from the counter, a person saw only the backs of things; their fronts were facing the window. It gave her an odd feeling.

"Hey," he said. "A man come in today. He said he was a Troont Officer. From the school." He looked at her straight on, a thing Hearing did not often do. She didn't answer. "He told me somebody turned in your name or somethin'. You suppose to be in school?"

"I can't. I have to stay home with my brother."

"Listen, you better tell your folks, then. He's maybe gonna come back, they could get in trouble."

She and Bradley had been on their way out to play, but now, with the world gone suddenly dangerous, she turned pulling Bradley around, and giving Mr. Petrakis a silent nod. They went upstairs again and it was a week before they ventured back into the streets. But the Officer made no other visit and Mr. Petrakis didn't mention it again. Margaret had decided not to tell her parents. She didn't know why she kept it from them; she was eager to go to school; she felt separated, younger, less fit for not going, but she couldn't bring herself to speak of it. For a while the fear lingered that the Officer would come and hold her responsible and maybe put her in jail, where she would be beaten with paddles like those used in the school, but soon it too faded, and then the summer came and released them.

It was a night early in July. The children had been in all day because of the rain, a heavy, plodding, patient rain that drove itself down into the street and lifted the garbage of the gutters to the level of the sidewalk. There was water coming in under the sills and down the sashes, and as the darkness came on early, their boredom turned toward fear. Abel was late. He had never been so late. Janice, having just come in herself looked about, annoyed and frightened, but Margaret and Bradley had borne the slow changes of the day minute by minute and were too nervous to stay in one place. They began to run back and forth between the two rooms, shouting. The streetlights came on, the alleys darkened, and the lights made the streets seem darker outside their small orbits, colder and more lonely. People walked close to the stores, huddling themselves away from the rain. Now and then a man who looked like Abel would move into the rain-threaded light only to go on the street and disappear into some other doorway. Below them the reflection from Mr. Petrakis' store lights went out and the children felt the enemy silence palpable in the room with them. They had stopped their own noise and were waiting in the dark. It frightened Margaret that silence could be frightening as the bully you knew was waiting for you around the corner when you went down with the milk money. In church there was silence too, but it was filled with unsounding voices, with talk, laughter and the greetings of the people. The minister held it also vast and grand in his blessing, when he spread his voice-hands wide —a long, full rhythm of pictures that made of the word *God* a bird or a wing of light flashing cleanly upward. The eye that saw it almost believed an ear was hearing the beating upward of that wing. Yet there was nothing, only silence. And here in the room, peering out the window, they were waiting alone, fragile as Signs, listening to the silence come stalking them. Carts with iron-rimmed wheels clattered past and the night closed over them. Their sound was only a different kind of silence that soon faded. The children didn't speak, and because of the darkness they didn't Sign. When Janice had come home, she had lit the kitchen angrily, impatient that nothing had been done. "Where is your father?"... "Don't know." With quick hands, their faces very white and garish in the yellowed-looking artificial light. "I'll have to get supper," and Janice began, tiredly. She slammed when she was angry, but the children were comforted by the hard sounds of the dishes and forks going down, *rrunk! rrunk!* on the table.

Abel came in at last, soaked and smiling and began to tell them as soon as he closed the door. With his coming-in the light in the room sweetened and eased. "I left Webendorf today. At the book press when I showed my work, yes, yes, the man said, and I was hired. Cotter, his name is, the new boss. The place is nice. Two art magazines, cards also. Duo-black. Good." His hands paused while he tried to show them what the word meant, how much richer and better it would be, how he saw himself working to make a beautiful picture instead of a sheet of advertising or a series of tickets to the nickelodeon like the ones they had just finished at Webendorf's. Bradley began to blubber with relief, and while he was weeping, he wet himself, and then he stood, one shoe in the puddle, while his sobs of relief changed to anxious whining. Janice took down his wet drawers and sopped the puddle, and Margaret went and got his other pair. Before Janice could take them from her, Bradley had run to his sister, seeking the warmth of her neck for comfort while he rubbed his nose dry against her collar. Over his head Margaret caught the sudden sharp look of jealousy on her mother's face and then a slower, duller sadness conquering it. Janice turned and went back to finish setting the table. Able was still talking about the new place, the new press, the new boss, and Margaret nodded her head to show that she was watching, dutifully, and with a certain pity.

At first it looked as though there would be some trouble over the garnishee, which even after the ten years he had paid, still had eleven hundred dollars and interest owing on it, but he was able to show Mr. Cotter that his debt would be no trouble and his work would be worth it. He began to bring home strike-offs of some of the things he did; photographs of women posing in different kinds of clothes, a calendar with marvelous scenes from different parts of the country, some nudes that Janice threw away, though he tried to explain that they were not like women to the people, but like shapes of things, mountains, or boulders or fruit that some people kept in dishes not to eat but only to look at. She told him he was crazy. "Dirty pictures," she said, waving her hand under her chin. "If you save them, your mind will get all dirty. What would someone think to come up here if you will have them?" He didn't remind her that no one ever did come, and she burned the pictures and forgot about it.

Abel had been at work for almost a year when he came home and told them that another deaf printer had been taken on, a young boy from Rhode Island. He was staying with his aunt, a Hearing, and he was very lonely. This was what Abel guessed, he said, because the boy had been raised only to read lips and he had no Sign. It meant that he couldn't talk easily with either Deaf or Hearing. Janice shrugged, but he kept at her, pushing and nagging her to let him invite the boy for dinner one night and to take him to the church with them.

"No, as soon as he learns Sign he will gossip about this place, and our clothes."

"I want him to come. I will bring him soon, whether you want to or not."

"I won't feed him, then, I won't feed anyone who will only go away and tell everyone about us, and even make up stories about us."

He nagged and she sulked, refusing to talk, looking away when he began to talk about it.

The gossip wasn't the thing she feared most, although she

gave fearful descriptions of the lies the boy would carry. What she feared was something she could not give words to, but it had to do with the years of her piecework at the machine at home and now in the field of machines at the factory. Somehow, the time had narrowed all of her life to the safe size of the working table and to the rhythm that flowed without change in her fingers and through her body. So long ago that she could barely remember it, she had wished for more things than a person could count—most of all, she had wished for change. In the deadening routine of school she had yearned for change; she had married Abel to change, to keep changing, to renew with a different place, a different dress, a different street, tree, restaurant, picture, the unchanging, captive self. Now, she could only marvel at that dead girl.

When fear mouthed unreadable words at her mind during the day, she turned away and lost thought in the rhythm of the machine, the routine of the seam-turn-seam-turn-seam-back stitch-turn. The pulse of the machine saved her. In the days when the yearning would have made her spend her money, the rites of the machine had prevailed. Now, the money was being saved—or would be saved, if she didn't have to waste it on Abel's church adventure. Well, even that had become part of the order of the days. A guest was too new a thing, too much change. It was not safe to change unless there was a need for it. She would not change for nothing. When she thought of Abel's wild plans, she sometimes smiled to herself over the machine, knowing how powerful the rhythms were. He tries to change everything, she said in her mind, and the spool thread picked up the bobbin thread: Go on, go and dress and be better and get new work and invite new ones in for supper, if you are so smart! The order of the days and the hours will stop you. I will win in the end. . . . The thread engaged, the needle picked its way and the seam drew its line on and on. . . .

But one day, when she came home, Abel had done it, and the boy was there. There was nothing more to do. She left him smiling uneasily at the kitchen table while she took Abel to the back room. "What did you bring that dummy here for—he can't even talk!"

"He's learning. You know how fast people learn, because

it is so good to talk. Don't you remember how I learned? He makes me remember how I was, when I couldn't talk or listen to anybody, and I learned it all when the teachers weren't looking.''

"What are we going to give him to eat? Now all the stores are closed. Anyway, I would have to have the extra money.''

"Don't we have something in the house?''

"Only the cold sausage from yesterday, and some canned green beans left over.''

"Give us that then, and we can all share.''

She made a Sign of disgust at him and turned back to the kitchen. The boy was still sitting there stolidly, wanting to smoke and not daring.

After dinner the two men sat in the kitchen, talking slowly. The room was hot and stifled with cooking smells, and when Abel leaned over and opened the kitchen door, the boy breathed deeply in spite of himself, although his eyes never left Abel, from whom he was taking the Signs that fed him. The window in the bedroom had been opened before and a pleasant breeze began to move through. Janice stood over the sink, her back to the men. Margaret cleared the table and put the canned milk and leftover dinner in the cupboard. Her mother's back was angry; it wasn't hunched, as it was when she was feeling put upon or sad; it seemed to come and go at odd, hard angles, the hips thrust out, the angle of shoulder and neck oddly belliger-ent. Janice could be very cruel in this mood. Margaret worked quickly and carefully, hoping to forestall any bitterness. When she was through with her clearing, she went to the sink and began to dry the dishes Janice had stacked on the sideboard.

Bradley had found his place with the men and had been amusing himself by standing on their feet and staring into their faces. At first they played with him, raising him up and down on their feet, but after a time, they only patted his head, and he began to be bored. Sometimes Margaret let him play in the soapy water after the dishes were done, but this time she only pushed him away. Janice was careful to raise her eyebrow to Margaret to show she knew that the guest had made extra dishes and tableware. It would take more time to wash it all and put it away. Some guest! As soon as he learned enough, he would be all over, here and there, eating other people's dinners and telling tales about the poverty of the people who had first been kind to him. When Bradley came around again, Janice butted him away lightly with her hip and he went back toward the men, who moved to let him by.

The dishes were almost done. Margaret was reaching for a pot that Janice had begun to hand over from the water because it was too heavy to drain with the other dishes. With the front door open she could hear all the sounds of running up and down the stairs, and from the kitchen above where the voices were loud and strident and other dishes rattled in other washpans. For a moment she was distracted, so that she missed Janice's hand and dropped the pot, watching it bang off the sink-edge and clatter to the floor. Janice glared. A group of boys had come rushing down from the apartment upstairs and very loudly they, too, began to clatter and thump down to the street. Near the door, the two men sat motionless in their still world, listening to each other's hands. Then everything was suddenly very still. It made Margaret turn, and without any conscious meaning in her mind, begin to look for Bradley, calling, and when her mother gave her a question, she only answered ''Bradley?'' (Bradley the letter B, waved a little, so they knew it was a name, and the men looked up at the motion,) ''Where is he?''

They looked, and Margaret called in what was now a terrible silence throughout the house, a silence not heard by the others, who looked easily, tolerantly, in case he should be ripping the quilt to get at the filling again. At last she remembered his having gone past the men, and she went out to the dim landing. Soon the adults were behind her, looking down the long steep flight of stairs into the pale, shocked faces of the boys and the spectators who had begun to crowd in behind them.

9

THE ASSISTANT parted the curtain and looked out briefly. There were three of them, a man and a woman, dressed stiffly and absurdly in cheap summer clothes, and a scrawny little girl with matchstick arms and a tight face. He turned to the Director: "Customers." The Director smoothed his clothing and then opened the curtain, surprising them. He went forward to them with smoothly professional calm. The presence of that child was upsetting. A shame. When the voice came, it came from the child, a hard, dry voice, childishly nasal. It shocked him. "Mister, we come to buy a box offa you."

"I beg your pardon."

Louder: "We come to buy a box offa you, a dead-box."

He looked past the girl in her weirdly gay clothes, appealing to the man behind her. The man only smiled slightly, an apologetic half-smile, nodding toward the girl.

"The deceased?" the Director said, trying to look at no one, least of all the hard-elbowed child, "Who is the deceased?"

"What?" the little girl demanded.

He repeated the question and the woman tapped the child on the shoulder. She turned and began a flurry of gestures. Deaf and dumb!

The Director sucked at a broken tooth snagging at the side of his cheek. Well. . . . "Who is dead?"

"It's my brother, Bradley. He fell down the stairs. All the way down."

The Director felt a bit of his control slipping away. He tried to move her, "Your brother—a terrible tragedy, and I know you want more than just a casket for him; you want a funeral, a lovely funeral. Everyone has a funeral."

The girl turned around again and made gestures. Parents . . . the girl again . . . Parents. . . .

The Director noticed that the father's hands were swollen and bruised and he pushed away the thought that the man might have beaten the child to death. Their fingers snapped with a crisp, objective speed. The girl turned back to him. "Nope," she said. "Just a box."

"How old was he?" the Director asked.

"Four years."

The Director pulled a chair around from its place against the wall. He sat down close to the hard little girl. He started easily, warmly, asking her age and grade in school. Nothing. She went as blank as the Dummies behind her.

"Look," he said, leaning closer. "We could sell you a *coffin*, but that isn't really what you want. You loved your brother. You want to see him taken care of, don't you? Later, you and your poor folks here will want to go to the cemetery and lay fresh flowers on that little grave, and you will want to *know* that you gave that little boy the very best you could give."

The mother's hand had begun to drum on the child's shoulder again, hungry for knowledge. The child turned and flashed hands and the Director had a sudden sense of their minds, of a strange, strong intelligence pouring among them; yet when the girl turned to him again, the light died and left only that oat-gray, stolid face and the dead voice: "We just want the coffin, Mister."

The Director got up and pulled the curtain between the waiting room and the display room. He could feel their expected shock at all the space; then the awe. It affected everyone that way. A small stained-glass window had been set at the back of the room and the sunlight was slowed and softened through it, so that it came gently and broke gently on all the polished wood and against the metal fittings of the caskets. There were so many and they were so big that the three people stood lost in the room and couldn't find the courage to move onto the purple carpet on which the Director stood. He had gone ahead, speaking without realizing it, a routine, low-voiced hum of words from which Margaret could make no sense, and of which the bleak couple behind her were unaware. Janice was bothered about the flowers. She remembered that flowers were part of funerals. Maybe there should be flowers, but they had no money. If they didn't have flowers, would it be wrong to Bradley? Would people laugh at them, and at him too, for being their child?

They all stood until the Director sensed for their presence behind him and not finding them there, turned and saw them still standing where they had been left. He sighed and murmuring, went back to them. They were really deaf after all. How patiently they stood in that mouthlessness, that earlessness. He raised his hand and snapped his fingers summoning them, and to that summons they came, the man still with his nervous half-smile that begged for mercy.

Behind the grouping of top-priced caskets were the children's models. Parents with limited means often spent everything they had to assuage the anguish and guilt they felt at the death of a child. The small caskets were made with all the details poignantly in miniature. Tiny keys for tiny locks, little clasps pointing against softly gleaming wood in perfect scale. Even the carvings at the edges and under the lids were not simplified or changed, but only made smaller so that their monumental themes had the wistful unreality of playthings: small urns, small willows, plinths and pediments, all to fairy scale as if they were only dollhouses in the world they promised.

Janice and Abel walked among the beautiful boxes hungering to touch those carvings; to run the tips of their fingers over the smooth, warm wood; the smoother, warmer silver; to go through touch into the carved gardens, the willow-places and the bower-branches. Margaret's hand also moved for a minute as though it would light on a cluster of ripe-rounded grapes at the corner of one of the coffins, but she raised it again quickly. Mr. Petrakis didn't like her touching the things on his counters; neither there nor here could a touch make any of the things real, so that people might escape into them and out of the crude, hammering sorrow that had caught them up. She kept her arms crossed over her chest, her hands fisted until, they would need to speak.

The Director had turned and was beginning again in the familiar and comforting territory of his trade. He pointed out the features of the casket before him: craftsmanship, quality, durability, the satin lining, garish in an adult model, so much more fitting for a child. How much better the sweet, clear complexion of the young would be, brought out against such a color.

Margaret watched him, even though she did not need her eyes to hear, and her hands picked feebly among the remembered fragments of all the words, the dozens and dozens of words. She had heard very few of the Director's words in her life, and had no Sign for most of them. They had all flown away by now, their meanings trailing out behind them into shadow and loss.

How much was the box? the parents asked.

"This one is two hundred dollars."

In a moment they had read the numbers in Margaret's fingers and their shock needed no translation.

The Director's tone of wounded sensibility missed them. "I can, of course, show you others."

To one hundred. . . . To fifty. . . . To thirty-five.

"One has to expect to spend *some* money!"

To twenty-five. . . . Others, even the Poor, vacillated, picked and wept and picked again, thought and thought better as the love words were re-evoked and the bones of guilt picked clean. These dumb mouths said nothing; they stood, shaking their heads, knitting thoughts off their fingers at one another to the final, stolid refusal, like dumb oxen, to the release of their wills. It angered the Director. It was worse than the snuffling shame of the paupers or the shabby compromises of the new-poor. It angered him so that he lost his temper and threw himself against their dumb wills. "Wasn't the child worth anything?" he shouted at Margaret. "Didn't his life have any value to you?"

Her mind ran his words into her fingers. There was no expression on her face. The Sign would not make the same words that he said; she had to say the nearest thing. "Was the child expensive?"

Then, "Yes," came the toneless answer, "the kid was very expensive. Twenty-five bucks when he was born. You don't have to worry about that debt. You don't have to be scared because it was paid already. We ain't crooks or nothin'. We wouldn't bury a kid we didn't already pay for."

"What kind of people are you?" the Director said.

"Printer," answered Margaret from her father's beaten fingers; proudly, because the word had left his hands proudly. "Her, she works in the mill; sewin'."

The Director was defeated. Against the far wall, standing on end so as to take as little space as possible, were the plain pine boxes. He shrugged and motioned with his head toward that corner. After the smooth, gleaming brown and gold of polished metal and varnished wood, the brilliant satins of ruched and folded lining, these plain boxes, standing on end, looked vaguely obscene. It was a thing he hated doing, giving the mourners "the floor thing" but it was the one that got them all, that made them think. These boxes stood near a back door from which the carpet had been taken up. They were made out of the crudest wood, narrower than the average. Mourners always blanched at the thought of some rough workman's hands having to squeeze and push a little arm, twisting at the shoulder so that the body would fit. The Dumbs took it like everyone else. They stood staring at those boxes, conquered, held by the large dead eyes of knotholes staring out of the unpainted wood.

The Director moved closer to the boxes and surreptitiously kicked one over. The clatter of the wooden coffin on the uncarpeted floor always brought a gasp from a mother and drove even the paupers back onto the carpet. But the Dummies hadn't moved, only the girl. The Director realized that only she had heard the very effective hollow clatter. The kid was back on the carpet, but he could see that he had lost the parents. He looked at the girl bitterly. ''Why don't you tell those freaks?''

''Tell them what?'' Her eyes were dry and incurious.

The man had taken an old-fashioned change purse out of his pocket and was slowly counting out money—fifteen dollars. He put the bills, all ones, on one of the standing coffins, and with no motion wasted, bent down and picked up the lid of the fallen box, placed it on top, took up the box, biting his lip against his pain, and turned to leave.

The Director sprang ahead of him and opened the back door, and then he got out of the way, motioning Abel around and out that door with a toss of his head. The three of them left, disappearing in the heat shimmer of the alley without another word or Sign. Following her father and trying to stay in the shade of the box, Margaret wondered idly what freaks were. Her parents were freaks. Another word for Deaf, probably.

It was only at the cemetery the next day that Margaret began to think of Bradley in his own person, not as a part of herself or as a voice screaming its intrusive will that she come and take him, dress him, lift him, wipe him, feed him, follow him. Sometimes he had seemed to her to be no more a person than his plate at the table, a place where he slept, a weight she must answer for. That morning, still muzzy with sleep, she had reached out toward his cot automatically, forming the words to wake him. Only then was there the shadowing of the thought that something had changed, and only when she saw the cot, still folded against the door, did she remember that he had died, and that his untied shoes had died also, and that she would no longer have to stop her play for his trip to the bathroom. The responsibility of Bradley was as dead as he.

On the day they had brought the coffin home she had had a wild crowding in of possibilities: There would be school now, a freedom to go or stay that was bounded only by the hours her parents worked. For a moment she felt giddy and happy in her weightlessness; she wanted to run down the block, reveling in the unhampered, unimpeded freedom. It didn't matter that he could not follow, that he was lost, that he could no longer pick up something from Mr. Petrakis' bins or racks or touch the things on the counters. All of it was gone, dead.

She stood by the hole in which the coffin was going to be placed, watching the clever way the men used the ropes, and the thought of her new freedom came again; it came in a kind of violence this time, and a picture of it rose in her mind, very simple and frighteningly real. It was a clear, sharp memory of one of Bradley's hands, nothing else. She saw it as it had reached out for her every day, a moist hand with barely visible soft blond hairs on the back and down the backs of the fingers. Bradley had wavering, pudgy fingers and their small nails were always crusted with food and dirt. In the vision of this hand there was a sudden, stunning sense of loss. She stood, staring blindly at the grave, and then at Janice, who had moved around until she was on the other side of the awful hole. Her mother's haunted face was full of the puffiness of unspent sleep, her hair combed too quickly so that single hairs and strands of hair had escaped the pinning, and although she looked back at her daughter over the distance between them, she did not seem to see her.

At Margaret's side Abel was standing. She remembered how he had run down the stairs to where Bradley was lying, how he had scooped him up, shaking the dead body and howling, "'ead! 'ead!" in his unreal voice, a discordant, uncontrolled rage making those sounds no longer something that a person would laugh at, but something he might easily fear. The witnesses, shocked, stared and then moved away, frightened and murmuring as Margaret and her mother came slowly down the stairs. It wasn't sorrow that they saw in Abel's face, but a simple, overwhelming rage. Then one of the men had come and said something about the cops being called, and he and another man took the body from Abel's arms.

Abel, freed of the body he would protect even in death, seemed to go mad. The onlookers stood back staring, amazed at the extravagance noise of his wildness. Everything he could not hear himself was loosed from him. He turned from the group of them and ran to the street door, kicking it closed; he kicked at the wall, pounded it, ran to the stairs and kicked at them, pounding on the rail and then at the steps with his fists; then he ran back to the door and opened it again and smashed it closed; back to the wall to pound and kick, bellowing all the time in his horrible voice. Back and forth he ran from wall to wall while the witnesses stood stiff in the uproar. They did not notice the dead boy now, only the man, as they waited, terrified of what he might do. Soon his voice warped and broke, but his mouth was still open—he didn't know that there was no sound coming. Back again he went to smash at the patient wall, one side then the other, until he was too tired to go on. Then he stood, sweating, breathing loudly, clicking his tongue against the roof of his mouth, impatient to begin the rage again. His hands were swollen, and there were bruises beginning from the beating he had given them. The police had come then, and they had taken statements and made their useless notes.

Above their daughter now, Janice and Abel began to argue about the fare they would need to get home. They wrangled back and forth, their faces thrust forward belligerently, their lips working clicks and half words. Bringing the coffin from their home to the church and then to the cemetery had already come to a great deal of money. Abel's hands were moving from bitterness to bitterness, the raw, cutting words snapping from his damaged hands like blows.

Close to Janice the minister watched, sighing and now and then raising a hand to try to stop them. It was useless. In his embarrassment, his eyes found Margaret, and he smiled shyly at her and ventured the mixed words-and-Sign that he sometimes used with the children of the Deaf. She wondered, as she stood watching him, why he was trying to explain to her that sorrow can make the most loving people argue with each other. Looking at him, she felt a vague knowledge that if she had been his daughter, she would not have had to know that by herself. And there were other things, too. Police faces and witness faces, the coffin-man face, the Union faces and the doctor faces would be kept far away from the white-curtained room in which he would keep her safe and a child. Poor man, she thought suddenly, he doesn't know about—about *anything*.

It was then that she began to think about Bradley again.

She saw his hand, with the same clear, inner vision she had had before. Then she thought of Bradley's voice. To think of Bradley really was to hear him, whining or laughing or crying or making soft imitative sounds into his cupped hands. The sounds Bradley made had sometimes irritated her. Why was she no longer relieved that they were gone? It came to her that this part of Bradley, his sound, was a part known to her alone, annoying to her alone and now missed by her alone. The sound of Bradley's voice had been kept from the two grownups looming over his box. She felt a guilty pleasure in this secret; it seemed deserved, a reward for all the tending, the trailing, the buttoning and unbuttoning.

Abel's tears were falling on her hair. The cold little drops of wetness warmed quickly in the heat and then rolled tickling into her scalp. She was afraid to move, or to move her hand to scratch where the tear was itching. They loved him, but they had never heard his voice, the sounds that were Bradley as much as his hand. Could they know him without knowing his voice? She saw the pudgy hand began to speak; his vague and halting Sign. Margaret felt queasy and weak. She swayed and Abel steadied her, pulling her body back slightly to lean its weight against his own. She fought free of his hand and then began to cry, calling Bradley's name as the coffin was lowered into the hole. It had dawned on her quite suddenly that Bradley, four years old and dead, had taken the sound of a human voice from the house, that after this, it would be she and she alone who would be sent against all the coffin men and the bill collectors and the police and all the words of the greedy mouths of the world forever.

10

*I*T HAD BEEN CALLED *Depression,* a thing Abel saw printed
often now, and there was a Sign for it among the Educated Ones at church. Having seen it as a Sign it was
easier to recognize when it blew through the lips of other men
in the shop, sometimes bitten off angrily. He thought it must
really be bad if Hearing were made frightened by it. He began
to wait for it and to question the new things in his life for
signs of it, but whatever it was, it waited its time with him,
and he went on living as he had.

With Bradley gone there was a hollowing ache in sitting
home after work; even the thought of going home was not the
comfort it had once been, but now he was happy in his work,
so he found reasons for staying in the shop after many of the
others had gone. The other men were decently considerate of
him and respectful of his skill. Now, in the fifteenth year of
his debt, the money taken from his paycheck no longer seemed
to bother him, so when the first pay cut hit the shop, he was
not perturbed. The call for fine work had shrunk. People who
had once ordered engraved invitations now used simple printing; magazines cut their color work and advertisers used and
reused the stock copy instead of changing it each month or
week. There were times when men shook their heads over their
lunchtime coffee in puzzlement. Sometimes Abel felt an actual
fear around him. Then a big job would come in and an almost

reckless gratitude with it, as if it had come from God to save them.

The boss had given Abel parts of a strange picture book to make up. It used the finest paper and the highest quality of processing, yet the pictures, duo-black for depth and contour, brilliantly clear and beautifully edited, were all pictures of poor and ugly people, ruined land, starving children; and of ragged, flat-faced women and groups of idle, burned-out men. What kind of people, he wondered, would want to have such a picture book? He had never questioned the meaning of what he printed, but these photographs seemed such a waste that he was afraid a mistake had been made. He wrote a note to Mr. Cotter about it and went up to the office with some of the photographs to show him. It must be a mistake. The men and women were facing front to the camera and in some of the pictures, the women's clothes were torn, so that it was almost indecent. They looked not at themselves or one another but outward, like the dead, through weather-wrinkled faces; no longer caring enough to smile or brighten themselves, or attempt to please. He felt ashamed of them, whoever they were, and a little frightened.

When Mr. Cotter read Abel's note, he smiled and then took up a piece of scrap and wrote: "This is a book about the Depression. It is a limited edition and very expensive, but it is a classic."

"Classic?"

"That means a great work by somebody famous. See how fine the photographs are. They are by a famous photographer."

"Ugly." Abel wrote back. "Who will buy so ugly?"

"Rich people."

"Rich people very crazy if not to buy flowergarden photograph or nice thing."

The boss shrugged, as though sharing a secret with Abel, and then Abel wrote again: "Pay is less because of Depression. Is Depression try to make all people like this?"

Then Mr. Cotter shouted *no* at him and sent him back to work.

Day after day the staring, suffering people flowed through the various photo-processes, imposing themselves as negatives, positives, red impressions and black impressions on the part of Abel's mind that had to judge them as work. Usually he didn't remember from one week to the next the subject of what he was doing. He remembered the problems conquered or compromised with, the smooth insets that had so resisted being cut round, or the very faint moiré he had allowed himself in the background of an off-center piece of work. Now he dreamed of the faces he was multiplying three thousand times upon the world. They stared from his sleep, their eyes following the sip of water to his lips or the warm coat he put on. And they were silent. Their faces seemed not to be the faces of Hearing people, those with mouths always open to suck and push the word-crammed breath in and out between themselves and the world. These mouths were shut, the lips locked; some of the mouths seemed worn away with locking until they were only ridges, held bitter and straight. In his dreams Janice and Margaret looked out from those pictures in faded cotton-sack clothes and lank hair.

And at church they began to feel the slow, long pull of anxiety as the world closed in upon the Deaf. The watch factory went out of business, and for a while Deaf and Hearing alike turned confidently to doing watch repair at home. But no one came. The body shops and the boiler rooms and the stamping mills and the printshops, the thundering, crashing hub-places of machine production, where the Deaf had found themselves small places of advantage over the noise-tormented Hearing, slowed, slowed and stopped. They learned to spell "layoff" when it was a random misfortune, but misfortune turned in the year of 1933 to a one-tone head-sound, heard through the skull and in the marrow of the bones, nerves or no, so that the Deaf heard it. The Hacker brothers were out walking the streets; Minify and his son sat home. Callendar went to his family and learned to eat little and quickly. The Dawes, all of them, left, and people said they were beggars through the South somewhere, where no one knew them. Nina Alford said, "Why not beg if there is nothing in the house? take a sign—*I Am Deaf*—and sit on the street with it. And her father beat her so that she was out two Sundays from church. Some people dropped church because they didn't have the clothes. Then people lost touch with them and felt ashamed.

When the fall term of school started, the first autumn after Bradley's death Margaret had begun in school. She was nine and a half years old then. At first it was humiliating to be sorted with a class of six-year-olds to learn to read and write, but she found herself not alone. There were many immigrant children on Vandalia Street, and they too came as beginners. The first grade had its own back section of foreign-born. In this polyglot buzz of wild curiosity and brutal, undirected energy that seethed and spat and pummeled and scuffled around her, Margaret sat primly, a foreigner. She hated them. They waved their fingers as their fathers did, bargaining in the street or talking to a neighbor, hand to the listener's lapel as though without the touch one might doubt the speaker's existence. They moved their eyes and their mouths widely, acting and reacting as their mother's did, as though a word by itself might have no meaning. They stank of rotten cheese and spoiled grease; their sounds were ugly, their gestures obscene. Margaret alone sat motionless, keeping her hands quietly in her lap when she was not writing; she alone made no comment with twists of her mouth or raising of her eyebrows in the way of the others. By December the back section had moved into the second-grade room and the combat of *The Cat and the Rat* was given over to *Our Country* and *Our Home*.

The teachers spoke gently to Margaret, praising her neatness and good manners. Her hair, which had darkened to a rich brown was kept in two long braids that now hung below her waist, and she spent her Christmas dime on hair ribbons after having visited every ribbon counter on the Avenue.

Janice was home. She was sitting on a kitchen chair, looking strange because it was still light outside. She had not taken off her coat or hat and everything in the house was as it had been in the morning. Margaret went over to where she sat and touched her shoulder. When she looked up, Margaret said, "What happened—are you sick?"

Janice waved her away impatiently, "The bonus," she said. "The bonus is gone."

Then Margaret sat down too. "Who said?"

"They lowered all the quota and now, if anybody goes over the quota, they won't pay any more. And when a machine breaks, they won't fix it; they'll just fire the girl on it." She came alive suddenly, her sign hard and violent in Margaret's face: "You remember, I made more over quota than any girl in the section! And now they made me the same like any new girl one day working!" She began to weep, hugging her stomach and swaying, the tears running down her face and dropping from the edge of her jaw.

Because Bonus was what bought the clothes they wore to church, Bonus was a special kind of money. Common wages could pay for common food, school dresses hard with sizing, things that kept people but did not change them. Bonus was the power that transformed them the moment they put on their church clothes and left Vandalia Street. Bonus was what made them better than their weekday selves, more deserving of the stained-glass windows, the carpeted floor, the full hieratic Sign of the minister. Bonus made them the elect of his beautiful benediction. What would they do now? What would happen to the sunlight of wide streets? The two of them sat still in their chairs, not touching and not thinking so much as having and losing the meaningless and disjointed pictures that came and left their minds without revealing a purpose or a meaning. When Abel came home, he had to turn on the light by which to see them, sitting there still.

He started to laugh. "Look at the Deaf and Dumb. They want to be perfect; they want to be blind, too!"

Janice began to cry again, so Margaret had to explain it all. Then, for a while the three of them sat still and did not touch one another.

At dinner Abel tried to reassure them. "This place I work is good. I am working almost full time, even now, when many places are finished. Webendorf is finished; did I tell you? A man from there came in today, wanted to work. I remember him from there, and I went over. He told me the whole big place just closed up and everyone is out of a job."

He had spoken to comfort them, without being aware that

he thought about what he was saying. In the middle of his earnest words, a new idea came, quickening in his fingers, and before he could tell more about the shop and the new job that had come in, the idea had conquered his hands and his mind. He began to smile, and the stricken women looked at him dumbly, so that he sat back, smiling more broadly, and when he could go no farther back in his chair, he got up and went to the cupboard and took out his package of cigarettes and selected one of them as though it were a special one, lighting it with a kitchen match and inhaling very fully. Then he sat down again and leaned back, the cigarette in his mouth, blinding his left eye with smoke.

"Today in this country, the United States"—he spoke without skipping vowels or abbreviating his Sign; he spoke with the solemn formality of a visiting bishop—"*Hearing* are out of work. There are today, certain Hearing which are going from shop to shop blub-blubbing with their mouth, *please*, for work. There are today Speaking-Hearing, which are not at all Deaf and Dumb, which are using their hearing only to hear the boss say "*No work.*" *But,* and *Never-The-Less* (the word had been taught him at the school; he had remembered it always because it made no possible sense) "one Deaf is not given those words. One Deaf is not a fail." His pleasure widened and became delight. "I wonder," he continued, his left eye red and weeping, "if there is a bad man, a certain Interpreter, who looks for a new job to tell people they will be a failure in life."

Margaret looked from Abel to Janice and back again. She didn't know what he meant, only that what he was saying pleased him, and that there had been no pleasure in the house since Bradley died. She smiled back at him and he gave her a grin that warmed the room.

In the spring, before Easter vacation, some of the children in the third grade foreigners' row were sent ahead into the fourth. One boy went into fifth. He was a big boy, rude and dirty and he spoke with such a thick accent and used so many bad words that Margaret at first couldn't believe he had succeeded and she had not. How could she have been left behind when her work, all the hard endless, continual days of memorizing the spellings and rules to everything had been done so much more carefully, cleanly and constantly than his? She had been stunned by the announcement and was suddenly tired. Having obeyed all the rules, there was nothing left to fight but a blank hopelessness, a failure that was not in anything she might change, improve, remember, erase more neatly or copy more exactly; it was a failure in something too deep to be changed—herself. Helplessly, through the day she searched over and over in her mind for something she had done or not done to displease the teacher, and when the dismissal bell rang, she found herself staring down at her dress, thinking wildly: Is it torn? Is it dirty, or spotted? Maybe my stockings or my shoes . . .

Miss Lester clapped her hands and the class rose and the lines marched stiffly into the hall. The final bell rang, and the upper grades, burst through the main doors as they did every afternoon. The third grade could hear them as they spun away, screaming, and Margaret felt the line begin to move faster past the teacher, giving its rote, "Good Afternoon, Miss Lester." She found herself looking at Miss Lester as she passed, still hollow with shock, still picking at reasons, sorting and rejecting small, half-forgotten lapses that could explain her failure and leave some small hope behind. The teacher caught her eye. "Margaret, will you stay for a moment, please?" She stepped out of line and the gap closed quickly behind her, faces smug, faces pitying, going past until the line had gone. "Please come back into the classroom. I want to talk to you."

Miss Lester was a chubby woman, a woman of monumental homeliness; her hair was strawlike, a muddy brown; she had small eyes, a large bulbous nose and teeth like the unkempt tombstones in an old cemetery. And she had warts. These warts were of all kinds, rough and smooth, soft plumed with hairs, some shiny. Her chin was large and horselike and she had a heavy underlip. So strong was her homeliness that it made a kind of grandeur all its own; Margaret thought of her sometimes as carved in stone; the figure on the soldiers' monument; another law special and separate, of what someone should look like.

Margaret liked to watch Miss Lester's face, but she understood why her mother could not read the teacher's lips. Janice had once come to school for Margaret, whom she needed to interpret for her at the clinic. Miss Lester had tried to speak to Janice, rejecting the pencil and paper held out to her. Miss Lester's lips were crooked because of her crooked teeth, but she had wanted to speak, Margaret thought, out of vanity. Miss Lester's voice was her only beauty; it was rich, deep and bell-clear. She liked using it, but this attempt had ended in confusion; it was the lips, of course; the lips and the teeth.

"I think you must be wondering," Miss Lester said, "why you weren't promoted with some of the others. . . ."

Margaret was not ready to dare an answer.

"I hope you didn't think that I was not satisfied with the effort you have shown." The teacher took a breath. "You see, we pass the foreign—I mean, the *older* students because their vocabularies—the number of words they can use properly, are great enough, and their reading is as good as that of the children in the new class. Do you understand?"

"Yes'm." She felt it was required. Miss Lester nodded and smiled not widely enough to unveil the wilful teeth.

"Do you remember the test I gave last week—the one where there were groups of words for you to make into sentences?"

"The third-grade children know all these words and can make sentences from them." Miss Lester turned and began to rummage through the papers in a drawer of her desk. Soon she brought up the offending one, a forgotten thing, a thing of the past which was bringing its failure to damn Margaret now, in the innocence of this ruining afternoon. It seemed unfair to be blamed for what had already been done and forgotten as long ago as an hour, a day, a week. "You see here, you have written, 'The lady is tunnel the dishes for us.' Do you know what a tunnel is?"

"No, ma'am."

"Did you ever hear the word used?"

"No, ma'am."

"Could you tell me what word you thought you meant when you wrote, 'The lady is tunnel the dishes'?"

"I forgotten it," she said. Confession was not enough; the wretchedness went on.

"Here you have the word *friendly*," the teacher said, pointing to another red-pencil wound. "You said, 'dog and cat can not make friendly.' We do not use that word in that way."

Again, she tried to explain, and told Margaret a dozen other words all about friend. Why did they need so many words for the same thing? Friendship and friendliness and friendly were only about one thing. They were all one thing, and yet some guessed-at, senseless differences had been enough to put the dirty snot-nosed Lambrinos twins into the fourth grade, ahead of her in spite of everything she had done and been.

"I also wanted to mention your absences," Miss Lester said. "You have been absent quite a few times this year."

"I was out cause of my mother."

"Your parents are the deaf-and-dumb ones, aren't they?"

"Yes'm."

"And they don't hear or speak at all?"

"Yes'm, they could talk, only they don't like to—people don't understand them good."

"Your mother has taken you out of school many times."

"It's for the clinic. She don't like to talk or write it down what she wants. I go see the doctors. Some days you wait so long you only have to come back." She didn't like to say so much at one time to anyone, especially a teacher.

Miss Lester was looking attentively at her, but the look was kind. "Has your mother gotten any help from the clinic?"

"They don't know; she got too much bleedin' up in her—" and Margaret stopped, her face flooding heat to the roots of her hair. She hated to remember the clinic times. The doctors were young; it embarrassed them to have to talk through her about Dirty Things, women's things. She didn't know the words they used and when they couldn't use those words, they hated her and her mother.

Now Miss Lester was looking away, blushing. The back of her neck was red and Margaret wondered if the warts turned red, too—those that were not very dark—or if they stayed the same. After a minute Miss Lester turned back to her, and her face was back to its regular color. So were all the warts. "You mustn't think you are being punished by staying in this class," she said. "If you work hard and study your words, you will pass with the rest. Do you know why Taddeuz went ahead so fast? He reads. That boy reads three or four books a week and so he has learned many of the words that aren't used in ordinary speech"—and then she added in another tone—"*here,* at any rate. Do you read books at home?"

"No, ma'am."

"Strange," the teacher murmured. "I would have thought the Deaf . . ." She shook her head quickly, and it reminded Margaret of a big animal, shaking its fur straight. "In any case, keep studying your spelling and reading books. See how the words are used in the examples and then you will know how to use them yourself. Listen to Miss Follett when she speaks, and to me, and speak as we do. You have often heard me say, someone *has* gone, but not *'he* gone."

Margaret murmured, "Yes'm" and started to pick up her books. As she did so, Miss Lester reached out and touched her arm, stopping her. The freckled hand lay lightly on the sleeve of Margaret's pink sweater she could feel its warmth through the knitted layer. "You know who it is who gives us these afflictions, don't you, Margaret?" Margaret looked up, frightened a little by the intensity in the teacher's tone. "It is God. He does it to test us, to see how well we rise above them. He afflicts the ones He loves, and the harder the affliction, the greater the love. You must always be grateful, Margaret, at this evidence of God's choice." Her voice took on a kind of shade like sun clouding over so that the room went suddenly cooler, too. "There will be times when you will not wish to be grateful to God and cheerful to those who are not His chosen ones. You may wish to be like other children. You may even wish your parents to be like others"—she looked as though she were going to say something more, but then she lifted her hand and patted the sleeve once, gently—"but this is a foolish wish, Margaret, a wish against God's plan. You must always be grateful to receive His special Grace.''

Margaret walked home very slowly, going over the words in her mind and trying to find where that word was, where in the kind, gentle flow of all those words, was the one which was shaming her. If she had been called stupid or a failure, she would have felt less weakened. This weakening was of a kind she did not understand. Miss Lester's hand on her arm had been comforting and gentle and those words which she had understood were praising and not for blame. Even the teacher's expression had been gentle and almost loving. It must have been the words, those secret-keeping, knife-hiding, truth-shadowing, alien words, those cheating enemies. Only they could hurt so deeply, could bury their pain so deeply and mysteriously that no doctor would be able to find the wound which they made or where they still lay, festering in the flesh.

She passed Mr. Petrakis' open door without nodding to him and walked up the stairs to the apartment. The key was around her neck on a string and she kept it safely underneath her dress so that no one could get it. She opened the door and went inside and put down the books and said aloud, ''Just a lot of words.'' And then she sat down and began to cry. If only she could use those words, could have them as her own, could take from them the strange magic and power that even Taddeuz could pull from them, even as they were lying dead on the pages of books! A single word could have a dozen meanings; it could mean the opposite of what it said, and when it was most a game, it was its most serious. The hearing of the words was not enough. Her parents thought that hearing was everything. How could they know that she, with all her hearing, was suffering death by thirst even as she sat in school, lost in a meaningless tide of words?

11

BUT THERE CAME A DAY when she could at least listen, and when listening brought the hard truth that poor people speak differently than rich people. Margaret began to see that the teachers in the school, Mr. Kaplan, the druggist, and old Mr. Golos, who had come to Mr. Petrakis to work behind the back counter, were not really Poor. People like them could have no money and still not be poor. She was thirteen then, large-headed and shy, but she knew that Mr. Protheroe, her teacher, liked her, and one day she asked him about the difference. How did he and the other teachers learn to talk the way they did? He said many things and she didn't understand all of them, but she understood when he said that anyone could learn to speak the right way, and that it happened by listening to educated people and using words as they used them. If that were true, she decided, it might be possible for her to learn to speak well and so to stop being poor. In that stubborn and single-minded way, Margaret began to listen. At first she didn't know how to begin. She stayed late in the drugstore when Mr. Kaplan was talking to his slow-witted delivery boy, and she hung back to hear the casual conversations between teachers stopping in the hall. She spent time waiting at the back of the Pawnshop for old Golos to say something. In the end, a teacher appeared. It was a radio. Mr. Golos had rigged up a creaking makeshift set from the broken parts of three others. From this radio came the language of her freeing, a never-ending stream of language.

Mr. Golos had wanted music. He was a wizened old man, a distant relative of Mr. Petrakis and had been taken in because of the Depression. He had proven to be quick and skillful at fixing electrical and mechanical things, but he was a bitter person and he had fixed up the radio, he said, to drown out the world and not to bring it all in on him. For a few days Margaret had stayed away from the store, going past it and up the steps to the apartment without any more than a wave at Mr. Petrakis. He must have said something to Golos because one Friday when she came home from school, Mr. Petrakis was standing in the doorway of the store and he motioned to her as she went past. She went into the crowded, cluttered pawnshop and the air was heavy with the elegant serial passions of *Our Gal Sunday.*

After that she spent all her afternoons sitting behind the counter where the lamps and wilted lace and hand-painted china sets were kept. She didn't do her homework or read, or even sew; she listened. Every word was taken with an almost savage intensity; the endlessly repeated slogans of commercials, and the declarations of love and jealousy of every daytime drama were made into the web of absolute laws by which she would succeed in life. She had no interest in the characters or plots of the stories or in the subjects of the interview programs, or in the news. It was the phrases themselves and how they were spoken that would save her. How sure and wise the heroines all sounded, how full of success were all announcers!

At night there was time to sit at the kitchen table and do homework, and in the very early morning she read her assignments in the English books, trying with humorless, stubborn will to force every word to make a meaning for her.

That was the December that Mr. Cotter cut wages in the printshop. Abel shrugged and didn't complain, and in the shop there was trouble with the Union. Janice shook her head and predicted that he would soon be out of work. She hated Unions since the one at the mill had stopped her piecework. They missed the bonus, but Janice's lay-off days were full. A new clinic had opened on Bisher Street, and there she and

Margaret often waited out the time, doomed and glassy-eyed until their turn came. The neck . . . the back . . . tired . . . The pains, low, urine . . . bowels. . . . Sometimes I can't breathe. . . . The blood . . . the bones . . . a cough. It hurts here . . . here. . . . Sometimes Margaret got frightened for the hand-whining, sad-eyed woman, and she would ask a doctor, "Is my mother very sick?"

He would answer in the madhouse game which Hearing played, and for which no thousand afternoons of *Stella Dallas* could prepare her: "It's nothing that a Florida vacation and a small fortune won't cure. Have this prescription filled and tell her to take these pills."

The doctor must have known they could never get a fortune or go to Florida. He didn't seem to know the rules of the radio, but she didn't know any other, and so she had to say, "Thank you, Doctor. We owe you a debt that can never be repaid," and then they would go and he would stare after them.

Outside the clinic, the wounded, hopeless look would leave Janice's face and her body would straighten. All the way home, her mouth would make its small, bitter, chewing movements, her fingers mumbling half-talk endlessly.

In the spring, Abel's wages were raised back. With many printshops out of business, Cotter got the pick-up jobs for time-card printings and calendars, schedules and movie tickets and the desperate handbills of small businesses dying. Some of these went bankrupt before the handbills were paid for and then Abel would bring them home for Margaret to use as scratch paper. She began to take them to school: a five-hundred-sheet jog of Delany's Glass & China 20% off, and she passed them out to friends. The stock was good; you could hardly see the printing on the other side. After Delany's was used up, Kaminsky's Fabrics closed and their flyers had women wearing Easter dresses made of dotted swiss and artificial silk. The younger girls used them for cutouts. As the years and years of Depression went on, Margaret found herself among the better-off families on Vandalia Street. The man of her family had steady work. Very very slowly, she began to be asked to walk home with this girl, to go down the avenue with that.

When her father did calendar pictures and they weren't indecent, he always brought his strike-offs home and Margaret
passed them out to her schoolmates. They made good book
covers and sometimes were hung up at home. The girls in her
class began to copy some of her ways; the subtly aggressive
neatness, the surface acquiescence, the silence.

She had expected high school to be frightening, but
it was only somewhat lonely and it made time pass with the
pressures of daily work and deadlines for work. Although
she made few real friends, the girls in the class were pleasant
and friendly to her. Many of them were no more eager than she
to invite guests home. Everyone knew that her parents were
Deaf and Dumb but Margaret had a strange fear of any meet-
ings between the hearing and the deaf parts of her life. Sometimes she perceived that other Vandalia Street girls were no
different. They too had separate selves at home, where mothers
presided over strange customs in outlandish clothes and spoke
in half-understood, barbaric-sounding tongues. All the girls
wanted to be like Jean Arthur or Ginger Rogers or Irene
Dunne. They swung their arms when they walked; they talked
about sex and virginity, money and drinking and men with the
bright, brassy, cold independence that was Hollywood's idea of
New York women. Their speech click-clacked in the fashionable,
fast, witty way, and Margaret, who still tortured and misused
her shabby-genteel soap-opera phrases, gasped with wonder at
the short-skirted, fast-talking girls who cracked their chewing
gum with such sophistication. They needed her awe, and so
she was welcome on the fringes of some of the popular cliques.
The boys were attracted to her safe, shy silence, but she almost
never went out.

At church, Abel and Janice found themselves in the kind
of standing which Abel had once tried to imitate in The Summer of the Clothes and the Ring and the Car. Half of the Deaf
congregation were unable to get steady work and most of the
rest were working far below their skills. Abel's wages had
been cut for a total of six months, but he had never been out of
work, and now, in 1938 he had more work and was better paid
than ever. He found himself being looked up to as someone
whose wisdom and foresight had accomplished these things.

He was in the nineteenth year of his debt. In another year, everything would be paid; interest and all. No one at church knew about the debt or the Court trouble. The car dealer had long ago gone bankrupt himself and had moved away. Abel, looking older than his thirty-nine years, cultivated every sign of age with care. Sometimes he practiced in front of the mirror, standing with his stomach out to give himself a more solid look. Now, when they came into church, they were greeted by everyone and Janice found even her faults being praised to her face. At first she had been suspicious. "They want you to get jobs for all of them." But she took extra care in dressing, and Abel noticed that some of the symptoms of her illnesses began to ease.

In April, Mr. Maartens, the minister, came for dinner, bringing his wife, a tiny woman who had been deafened by a fall from a streetcar early in their marriage. It was an act of God, he often said. It had given him his vocation. For their guests, the first they had had since Bradley's death, Janice and Abel bought the new, larger table and they cleared the kitchen of things that had been lying around and unused for so long that they had stopped noticing them. Janice put out every plate and dish they had and she had sought advice from the most silent and discreet of the church ladies.

After dinner the Reverend Mr. Maartens sat back and began to explain to them why he had suggested this informal visit. Janice and Abel pretended to relax, but their eyes were sharp, their hands ready. They knew that the poverty of the neighborhood and the bareness of their apartment had surprised him at first. When the minister had asked to come, Abel had insisted it be for dinner, but they both wondered why he should want to visit. Perhaps he had found out about the debt. He had preached often on debt; perhaps the whole Deaf community knew. The minister kept speaking, his Sign quiet and scholarly. Our Deaf community, he was saying, is not a large one here. Other cities, cities like Rochester, with its important Deaf School, were natural drawing places for the Deaf, and now, with work so scarce, deaf communities all over America were breaking up as people went from place to place looking for work. Janice's face began to harden. What was he asking for? Margaret, hoping to stop him before he could hurt them, tried to offer tea, coffee, another cookie. . . . The minister didn't seem to notice. The Deaf here had to have something to keep them, to encourage them to stay until things got better. He had been thinking, he said, about something to take people's minds off their troubles. He had been thinking, he said, about the movies.

The movies? Janice sat, looking stunned. Abel had a strange squirrel-look, a puzzled look, part guilt, part fear. The movies? Suddenly, Margaret began to laugh, and Janice and Abel let their breath go, so that it rushed out in a sharp, hard cackle of laughter that they could "hear" in the bones of their faces. The Reverend Mr. Maartens' face went through some swift changes, and each of these only sharpened the edge of the joke. His wife was next; a smile wavered across her face for a moment and then broke. She had not been born deaf; she had heard the sound of laughter and knew how it was made, and she let loose an infectious paroxysm of it that broke the Hearing into the same wild gale in spite of themselves. At last they could only sit gasping and clutching their sides, the laughter fading and being reawakened without anyone really knowing why.

Then it was over. They sat flushed and the men were sweating easily without self-consciousness. When they finally got to the minister's explanation, he made it casually without his usual "amen-hands." He had been sitting at the movies one evening and the thought had come to him that since theaters were trying to interest people with offers of free dishes and raffles, perhaps the theater near the church might lower its prices for groups of deaf people and might permit a translator to stand to one side, in a lighted place and help with those parts which were not obvious by action or lipreading. He had spoken to the theater manager and the manager had said he would think it over.

Abel agreed it was a good idea. He and Janice had gone to the movies once or twice, and although they had liked the action (the show was about some criminals in the West), the main characters all spoke without moving their lips and they had missed much of the story. It might be a nice outing if many Deaf could go together.

"Maybe you could talk to people on Saturday," Mr. Maartens said, "and find out how many of them are interested."

Abel agreed and they spent the rest of the evening talking about what could be done for the older members and the younger and gossiping (more gently than usual because of the minister) about the congregation.

Abel was pleased with the evening. "I think the Reverend respects me. Did you see how he asked for my advice?" Janice started to move the new table back against the wall. Margaret was running wash water to heat on the stove. "Maybe I am getting important at the church."

"It will only make more people come to you to try and get a job."

"Because I have a respect there."

Janice began to imitate the minister. "If your Honor does not be disturbed, be so correct, please as to uplift your big shoes from this place because your place, your small part of the floor under the table has more crumbs on it than all the number of crumbs in any other part."

"The minister," Abel said, exaggerating Mr. Maartens' amen-hands, "and the wife of the minister were busy all the time kicking their crumbs into my part of the floor. They are messy, but they want to hide the mess because we may tell about it in the church."

"The minister and his wife eat bread plain. You eat your bread with lard. Please study these crumbs. They are greasy crumbs. They are lard-crumbs. How can you explain this?"

"The minister's wife is clever. While we are eating, looking away because we are innocent, she picks up a little lard with her spoon, throws it under the table and stirs it with her foot."

Margaret watched them playing together. Her mother looked younger than she had ever seen her; her father quieter, more sure. She stood by the sink, not moving so as not to move the moment onward. Her school friends were embarrassed when they mentioned the Old World ceremonies or customs to which their lives at home still bound them, but sometimes, as they spoke, the fashionable scorn would not quite reach to their eyes and Margaret would see a moment's yearning or sorrow or love in Lyuba, who was Lilly in school, before her own particular version of Ginger Rogers' breeziness came up to hide it again. This was the reason, this love pouring back and forth in the silence. The words meant little; they were healing the pain that each of them felt in being known in all his moods, habits, lies, and shame. But the words themselves were invisible. Kati (Kathy, in school) said that the words of her parents' rituals were in another language which she didn't understand. Margaret sometimes wondered if perhaps, in the most secret times of the night, Irene Dunne, sleeping her bright and eager sleep, didn't once dream in some rare and beautiful Sign, and did not, maybe just once, Sign back to it.

Everyone was interested in the movie and even people who had no jobs said they would try to get the money from somewhere. The Reverend Mr. Maartens told Abel that there might be some free tickets now and then. The owner of the theater was impressed, the minister said, when he had learned that most of this group of people were strangers to moving pictures, and would probably make it their only theater if there was Sign. Neither of them mentioned that their group were people of habit, and that they depended, much as the blind must, on the continuity of people and things. The minister did not say it because he was Hearing; Abel did not because he was a little ashamed of it. They both knew that if the movie habit began, Deaf would come from all over town, and many from towns nearby. The manager's Sign nights would be well attended no matter what the movie was.

The minister went over his main points as they walked together toward the theater. He had made another appointment to talk to the manager and this time, he said, he wanted Abel to come along. The two wives and Margaret were following, looking out the corners of their eyes at the houses they were passing and the people.

It was April, but two weeks of warm spring weather

had been ridden down by one night's blackening frost. Budded bushes lay back beaten in the yards and the small edging beds of flowers that lined the walks to the houses had all been conquered. The frost itself had dried away, but there was a cold wind beating between the houses, and it caught the walkers breathless with surprise. As they turned onto Melotte Road the wind left them and they walked more easily then, past some stores toward the big overhead thing where the name of the movie was. The women hung back a little while the men walked to the entrance doors, found one open and went in. All around the ticket place, and all around the doors were bright, thrilling painted scenes and photographs from the movie, and the woman looked at these carefully, going from one to the other, and trying not to seem to be looking, because the scenes seemed so private, like looking in somebody's window. The movie-women were in very bad trouble, the men angry. Margaret had not seen this movie, but she knew enough not to be taken in by the promise of drama in each of the pictures. She liked the movies because no one on the screen was really puzzled or confused by what was told to him; he knew what he was supposed to do, and if he was good, he did it. People might be tricked, but soon everything was explained and everyone was satisfied. Janice could not keep her eyes from the pictures of the people suffering inside their marvelous rooms. It did not seem real to her that anyone who sat on such furniture could be truly unhappy. Even hidden behind glass, the photographs were smooth and shiny and the suffering women beautiful. In one of the pictures a poor man was standing at the door, trying to explain something and the colored maid was pointing a spoon at him. Janice decided that if there were poor people in the movies, she would not go. Even the minister's wife looked at the pictures. None of the women spoke. Their hands in clean white gloves were held low, empty and fashionably limp.

When the men came out, they were smiling and the Reverend Mr. Maartens asked Abel if they would come to his house for lunch. His wife bit her lip quickly and tried to make the offer also, but Janice understood her and said no quickly, in the middle of Abel's acceptance. They separated and waved good-bye, the minister and his wife going back toward the windy corner. Abel was feeling too good to go home. He motioned Janice on down the street, and they strolled past shops and restaurants, looking idly in the windows as they went. It was a long time until Saturday Services. The Reverend Mr. Maartens would surely mention Abel's advice and help when he announced the beginning of weekly movies with a special rate for Deaf.

Janice was impatient to find out who was going to be approached as interpreter. Everyone had his favorites, but Janice felt it was her right to demand the job for Margaret. She wanted to begin on Abel before church started. Of course he could never speak in public. . . . They walked on, looking at the stores, and finally they stopped at a coffee shop and had coffee and a plate of doughnuts. They sat eating, watching people pass the plate-glass window, their coats pulled close because of the wind. A man went by and stopped on the other side of the window; they could still see part of his coat at the edge of the glass, coming and going in the wind. People walked by in front of him. Perhaps he was waiting for someone, a hard thing to do on such a windy day. When the Ryders were through eating, Abel paid and Janice pulled her coat tight around her, ready to go out. Abel opened the door, and they turned left toward the car-line going past the waiting man. As they went by, they turned to look at him. He was a short man in a gray tweed coat which was too large for him. He had a worn plaid cap. Then, they saw that the white front of him was not a shirt, but a sign: I AM DEAF. He had his hand out and in the hand was another cap with money. They stopped, all of them, and the man turned to them with eyes that looked and did not look. Abel took a step toward the man. "Where are you from?" His Sign was abrupt.

"Go away," the man answered. "This block is mine."

"Get out," Abel said. "Deafs have no work here. People will think we are all like you."

"Go screw yourself."

"Go away from here, to a big place," Abel pleaded. "There are Deafs here who cannot get jobs!"

"Hearing see you talking to me and they know you're Deaf, too." The beggar grinned and made a funnel of his second hat and the money poured neatly into one of the big pockets of his coat. Abel's body began to pull him forward, his hands came to be fists. Janice and Margaret were looking at each other and then Janice put her hand on Abel's shoulder so that he turned away and began to walk back toward the corner. They were always a surprise, those beggars, and they all looked the same.

That spring Margaret saw the beggars often on street corners, and after they had exhausted charity and gone north, she found them settled with mocking permanence in the unguarded streets of her nightmares.

12

DURING HER FIRST TWO SUMMERS in high school Margaret worked in the pawnshop for Mr. Petrakis. He paid almost no wages, but with a slow, patient thoroughness, he taught her how to keep books, do inventory and separate the various categories of merchandise. Early in the first year, Mr. Golos left the store after a bitter and ambiguous argument with Mr. Petrakis. He went, he said, to live "a life without servile gratitude," and maybe, Margaret guessed, without envy. They missed him for so short a time that Margaret felt ashamed and forced herself to automatic remembrance whenever a toaster or broken iron came in. Mr. Petrakis would nod automatically at the automatic words, and before she had finished speaking, their attention would be somewhere else.

She liked working with numbers; there was a logic to them, and no matter how intricate they were, their parts could be fitted together to form a kind of landscape by which it was possible to read one's way. A mistake in a small addition could cause an ugly, spreading error, but it was possible, as it never was with words, to go back and find the cause and make it right again. She liked the way the numbers fit and the definite, absolute reality they represented. She liked the order and cleanliness of the work; even in a dusty and cluttered pawnshop numbers could be lined straight and made to give the same reality that they gave in New York or Paris. Space by space, number by number, they came together to match one another; balanced, agreed, final. After the first summer, when she was back at school, she realized that the work had given her certain advantages. There was no academic section in the high school. The students with ambition or special talents went into the commercial course and the rest studied for work in trades or domestic science. Margaret's teachers began to suggest that she switch from the domestic science to the commerical course. It was difficult and a little frightening at first. Her English was still poor, her grammar sketchy, but in changing to the commercial program, she joined the elite of the school, a group whose teachers were better, whose classes were more exciting, and whose ideas and activities were models for the rest of the school. The girls in Commercial seldom spoke of marriage. When a few left in the second and third years to get married, the others whispered patronizingly that they must have gotten into trouble and had to have shotgun weddings. Why else would any girl tie herself to a mop and washtub and a roomful of squalling brats? How could anyone be so dumb? Margaret would only nod in agreement, amazed at how close she had come to that tragedy and defeat. In another two years, the girls all agreed, they would be out in the Business World, Ginger Rogers' world, and they studied the movies they went to, so as to know when the time came, the smart suit to wear and the smart brush-off to give the fresh wolves in the Advertising Department.

Margaret had to study without letup, mastering her English grammar by rote. She was at the library until late in the evening and right after dinner would Sign a half-formed reason and a half-made promise and disappear behind other books. Abel was proud of his daughter, and of her quick, competent movements as she gathered up the schoolbooks, full of the World's things, and of her delicacy, the intent, self-renewing, feminine care she took with her makeup and hair, and of the postures conscious and unconscious of her body. He chided her, only half joking, that he knew her only from the top of her head as he looked out the window. Janice was less happy and often bitter. More than once she waited outside the high school, hoping to find Margaret in the groups coming out for their lunch hour. There was hope of getting seen early sometimes at the clinic, but time after time, Margaret wouldn't be there and Janice would find herself surrounded by strangers, all the mouths moving, all the lips reddened and the eyes hard as they passed by.

"She knows I am sick; she knows I need her," Janice complained to Abel. "She means to stay away, to leave me standing alone. I think she knows I am waiting; she can see from the window, and she leaves me there with those girls that paint their lips like movie women. It is forbidden to paint lips in school, so out they go, each noon, and run back late rubbing the red off!"

"You know the high school is not like the other school. If you take her to the clinic so she does not come back in time, they can throw her out of the school. She told you she must go to the clinic after school."

"The school stops at four."

"I will tell her. I will talk to her."

But he couldn't. He couldn't even ask for himself the things that he wanted. They were not useful things, daily things any more. When he became a deacon at the church and went slowly to the altar each Saturday with the collection basket, he stopped feeling afraid of the World, and did not want to keep apart from it because of an interpreter. When he needed to write, he could write to those who did not understand. What he needed from Margaret was another kind of silence; he wanted her to sit very still until he could find words for the questions and ideas for which he had no words. He knew many things. Some of them were about what his life was like far back when he was a boy, and also, what it was like now. He had never told her how it was when he was young, when he met Janice and what had happened to them after, and how it changed them. He knew that Janice did not talk about these things either and this made him sad. It was part of the knowing he most wanted to share with his daughter, but even when he tried—waiting for her to come in from the library, or sitting by until she finished a book for school—he never could break the quick, hard outside of her life; he never could make her stop and wait until he was blessed, made partner in God's mysterious sacrament, the clear, chosen, fitting, flowing, unfolding words.

During her junior year, the last of her high school summers Margaret worked in a small printshop. Her father had gotten her the job through someone in the Union and she hated it from the first moment on. The job itself was as typist and bookkeeper, but Mr. Harger, a bald, harried man, starting again from the dry ruin of a shop in Rochester, saw nothing but the looming of ruin here as well and worked her with a desperation verging on madness. Every idle moment roused the specter of collapse and caused it to turn its eye in his direction. Margaret hated the dirt of the shop, the inky rags and gummy printing solutions that rubbed against her white starched blouses as she brushed by any of the tables or work places, the litter on the floor and the incessant noise—a clatter in a different key and rate for each of the three small presses in the shop. All summer, her proud, new, white blouses went damp and rumpled in the stifling single room with the clatter-pound, clatter-pound grind of the presses. She typed, took orders, set up copy, added and subtracted rows of figures, ordered materials, faced down or lied away bill collectors. When the day was over and there was quiet, she went home and slept, a stuporous, gray sleep from which it became harder and harder to wake again, eat and go back to the shop. She began to think of the place as though it were something else. In dreams she saw it as a torture chamber or a locomotive with the presses as boilers into which the coal-black greasy rags and papers were flung, into which they flung everything at last so that the machines would not eat *them*. Each week she took the pay envelope that Harger gave grudgingly and brought it home unopened. Janice and Abel were happy for the extra money. She knew this and for a few weeks it gave her a brief, dim comfort. They bought some more chairs and an electric iron and Janice was looking to get an electric refrigerator, but after a time Margaret stopped caring what was being spent and what was hoped for. There were only the dragging gray sleeps and the daytime hell of noise, heat, dirt and anger. When at last it was September, Margaret felt like a drifting castaway who finds himself washed up on a beach and lies still, naked and unashamed in the same sun and weeps with gratitude. At school she would lift her head in the moment's perfect, enchanted silence, and wonder at it. Stillness. No-sound. How beautiful it was!

Her schoolmates were impressed with her job. ''Margaret worked in publishing.''

''No, I didn't. I said I worked at a printer's.'' ''Anyway, She was Girl Friday at a printing company.''

She wanted to tell them that it wasn't so, but they had their own hopes to protect and wouldn't listen.

''You were more than a bookkeeper, weren't you?''

''Yes——''

''Well, then. You were a Girl Friday. Did the fresh salesman try to get a date?''

They had all seen Jean Arthur and Ann Sheridan, chic, smart and efficient, orchestrating intercom and typewriter and without missing a word or a stroke, poniarding the greasy-smooth and feral men who tried to get past them, in to see the boss.

For a while Margaret argued, against her schoolmates' version of things, but their hopes were too urgent, too real and well defended in the world of a thousand cities on the screen and after a while even she herself found the bleak reality softened, compromised by what the others said. By words alone, Mr. Harger, sick with despair and defeat was changed, recast as The Cantankerous Boss, a joke, harmless and symbolic that welded the Office Staff into one joyfully complaining whole. Even while Margaret knew and remembered that she had been all alone at the shop except for Harger himself, the words prevailed. Somehow against all the realities, the words endured; her own pictures faded, and the witty, pretty secretary vs. The Cantankerous Boss merged into their shadows.

When she submitted to the dream at last she felt better for it. It was nice to remember having been a Girl Friday and now, in her senior year, she, too, felt close to the mythical offices in the happy, rich, romantic parts of the city. Typing and shorthand and lectures on grooming, dress and manners made the glamorous world seem closer and more real than ever. The Business World. The girls talked about it all the time.

Some of their teachers talked about war, a war with Germany. Margaret knew about the bombing of Britain, and the parts of the war in Europe that came to them between the double features of the movies. She had seen the Japanese impale Chinese babies on their bayonets and had hated them for it, but no longer than the images lasted on the screen. What remained was a puzzled sorrow at the World Outside. Some of the boys in classes before hers had not been able to get jobs after they graduated and now they were in the army. It was something to be thankful for. Soon the countries in Europe would know this and they would leave America alone.

So when the Bund Marchers came up Vandalia on their way to one of their rallies, it surprised Margaret that some of the boys on the streets should want to throw firecrackers under their feet. Mr. Petrakis told her about it when she came home from school. There had been a fight, he said, and quite a few of the boys had been taken in. The street was very quiet that evening but the windows were full of faces. As the evening passed, people emerged from one house or another, mothers and fathers, some with baskets of food. Everyone knew where they were going.

The next day at school, Margaret read in a newspaper an account of the fight. It was only a small article, but a phrase in it stopped her eye and froze her mind for a moment. ''Young toughs from the tenement district . . .'' it said. She sat in the mellow western light of the Business Machines Room reading the phrase over and over again. ''The tenement district.'' It sounded ugly and ominous, savage, corrupt, foreign. Vandalia Street was poor and crowded, smelly, dirty and familiar; it was hers. But the newspaper had given words to it and the words made Vandalia Street seem worse than poor; they seemed to make the poverty final, immutable. Vera, beside her, was pointing to Charlie Caz' name. ''I never knew he was *Casimir Czolkowzci*!'' And she laughed. ''I saw his old lady go out last night, 'cause she came over on our block to get Charlie's married sister. I wonder what the police are going to do with them kids.''

"I don't know," Margaret said absently, "but after I leave here . . . when I'm out in the business world . . . I never want to see any of them again.''

Later Vera said, "Karen knows what her folks are getting her for graduation!" The teacher looked up and Vera went quickly back to work. Margaret knew that Vera would tell her everything, that there was no distance between them on this one subject. For the last two months everyone had been living from hope to hope, hint to hint. Jocelyn knew she would get the last two pearls and the clasp on her add-a-pearl necklace. Some of the others were getting family things, bar pins or heirloom earrings. The Italian girls would take off the small childhood hoop earrings they wore and get larger ones, or rings with stones to show that they were ready to go out with boys. Margaret didn't dare to say what she wanted, except in her mind, but she wanted it more than anything she had ever seen or known of. It was in Ostrander's, on the Avenue, and she had taken Abel and Janice past it a dozen times, stopping for long looks at it before she walked on. It wasn't the latest model radio, but it was new all the same; it had never belonged to anyone. The fine wood of its box was molded like the outside of a church; it was small, but solid-looking, and she could carry it wherever she wanted. One day she had gotten up the courage and gone into the store and had the man turn it on so she could hear the tone. It was beautiful—its voices were so real and so deep and natural they seemed to be coming from the room itself.

This radio was nothing like the tinny, squeaking one that had taught her not to say "he gone" and "them wasn't," in a thousand afternoons under Mr. Petrakis' stacks of fringed shawls. The thing had finally fallen apart and high-school work had swallowed her then. This one, this *radio* was nothing like the ones she had heard before. You didn't have to guess about the stations either and they didn't drift away in the middle of the program. At Ostrander's they wanted thirty dollars for it. She had never dreamed it would be that much. The salesman told her that while the model was not new, these sets here had never been purchased because of the Depression and that when they first come out they had sold for fifty-two fifty. At thirty then, the set was really a steal.

In the afternoon she followed Vera, who followed Karen, who was the center of the crowd of girls and was telling them all the details of the hints she had given and the hope against hope—now that her dad had a job—of finding the box put away behind the pile of winter bedclothes. Margaret followed each word, rapt and intense, living as they all were the same moments of hope, disappointment, hope again. They clung to each word as if there was magic in it, to make what had been true for Karen be true for them also. Some of the girls were lying; they all knew who. Even in the business course there were many girls who had no hope of a gift this year and more than a few who had never had a gift in their lives, something given to them that was intended for them from the first clean, store-smelling moment of its newness. Those girls pretended; they caught on to some fashionable wish, a fur scarf or a pearl ring or a wristwatch and pretended to yearn, hint, hope for it. But their words were only echoes; they gave no detail to those lies for fear of being convinced by their own pretense and paying a price in disappointment.

No one doubted Margaret and although she would not tell them what she was hoping for, they all knew her as practical enough to set her dreams on a level that could be reached without too much stretching. Her father had a good trade and had worked at it all through the years when everyone else was being laid off. She was an only child, and people had seen them on their Saturdays and knew that she had nice clothes. Sometimes they said that her mother was sour and suspicious, but they could not know what Margaret knew—that her father was splendidly, wildly proud of her. The girls took her up sometimes, showed interest in her problem, planned for her the kind of hints to use so that she would get what she wanted; the grounds of her good fortune bordered on their own.

How subtle, how much too subtle those hints were. Margaret knew they would be lost on Janice and Abel. Abel wouldn't understand them and Janice didn't wish to. So after days of figuring she sat down at the table one evening and waited until they were finished and looking around for the evening things to do.

"All the girls and boys who graduate are going to get presents from their parents. They are all waiting to see what the things will be."

Abel smiled at her, his fingers confident with words, "A plan is already made. Money is already put aside. When it is all ready, it will be a big surprise."

"Please tell me what is is."

"It is something electrical," he answered, "something to be proud."

"For everyone? For Hearing?"

"Only for Hearing," he said.

He must have seen then, and understood her stopping in front of Ostrander's week after week, to stare at the radio and say, "Isn't that beautiful?" She wanted to thank him, to thank them both. It came to her suddenly, how much they must love her after all, to give her the radio, a mark of her difference from them, an acknowledgement, made sadly and proudly, of the separation that was thrusting her toward the World and away from them. The radio was senseless and useless to them; its value was only for her, but that alone made it valuable enough. How could she thank them before they gave the gift, so that they might know for how much more than the thing itself she was thanking them?

They had looked away from her and were speaking about a wedding being held at church on Saturday after the service. They planned to spend most of the afternoon and early evening there, gossiping and joking with friends and meeting the groom, a Rochester boy, who was said to be gifted and brilliant and whose Sign was supposed to be better than the minister's. She sat and watched them, their faces intent and enthralled over the quick, urgent, beguiling, passionate Signs. How hungrily they waited for their Saturdays now. Her mother lip-read well and could speak and usually be understood, but the Tongue, the True Tongue was Sign and the true communion was a communion of Signs. She watched, loving, understanding, saying nothing.

On Saturday they were on their way to the car stop, bound for church. As they started to pass Ostrander's window Margaret went over in her mind what she wanted to say. She wanted to be ready when they all stopped again before the wonderful radio in its polished wood and its reverent oval shape, like the church windows. When the three of them walked past the window that Saturday the thick glass caught them in their first spring clothes, passing modestly by, with dignity; Janice and Margaret in soft pastel dresses, like flowers with petals overlapping to form their short sleeves; Abel with his starched white shirt, pinstripe suit and soft hat, newly cleaned and brushed for the season. They stopped and for a moment stood looking at the window, at themselves in it, people of dignity and strength and Margaret between them, lovely and graceful. For a moment they just stood there, recognizing and not recognizing themselves. People of importance, Abel thought, and smiled as he adjusted his hat. We look like people from the other side of the Avenue, Janice thought, and smoothed her dress.

"I know how much it costs," Margaret said carefully, her Sign small because they were in public, "but I wanted to tell you how glad I am, to thank you . . ." Margaret said. Janice and Abel smiled at her, and from the window their smiles came also, and Margaret looked at the image in the window and then at them. Still smiling, they all walked toward the car stop. During the ride their minds were full of their own pictures, fat, rich and random.

Very suddenly, it was June and the interviews for jobs, the yearbook picture, the money for a graduation dress, the hundred fees and rites and decisions bloomed all at once. Mr. Harger, still starving and enduring wanted Margaret back. She snatched herself away from the re-forming memories of being a Girl Friday and said no.

"These are bad times," he warned. "It won't be easy, getting work, an inexperienced girl like you."

The seniors bought autograph books and found themselves writing overblown, sentimental verses in them; suddenly frightened of the long awaited "business world." They went out together constantly, feeling strong and proud nowhere but in one another's company. Margaret learned that her mother had gotten permission to stay late at the factory and that during lunch hours she was using the machine to make a graduation dress. It was horrifying. She thought of herself appearing in an over-large ticking-cap dress like a long work jacket. But the dress finished well; it was soft muslin and the large stitches showed only when it was inside out and the seams were visible.

On graduation evening the streets were mellow with first twilight. Doors were opening and from building after building white-dressed girls and blue-suited boys were coming, families following, as they led the way up Vandalia and walked catty-corner over to Bisher and then down Bisher to Seventeenth and over the bridge, catching and calling to friends along the way. Their movements were stiff and self-conscious and their voices were artificial as they greeted one another and introduced the mothers and fathers behind them, dressed soberly as suicides for the occasion. Old lady Ebinger, who had the fish market and was known by everyone, passed unrecognized without her blood-stained apron, and neither old nor sour, walking beside her tall, blond son.

Margaret had gone ahead to arrange something at the school, she said. Janice and Abel followed the others down the streets and watched the white girls glimmering along. Sometimes people nodded to them and they nodded back and smiled. The light was almost gone. Nobody asked them anything or bothered them with words, but they were greeted as belonging to the neighborhood and part of the proud evening.

Soon the lips of the other greeters and answerers of greetings were no longer to be seen and Abel and Janice walked on in the warm purpling light in a joy so keen that it was almost painful. The streetlights came on suddenly, as they crossed Bisher and without plan they turned and smiled at each other and took hands. At so proud an hour to be moving toward the same place and in the same rhythm as all these others, and to be known and greeted as a sharer in this event was a moment they had not foreseen. Abel spelled into Janice's hand, a word which she did not understand, but he didn't repeat it. The silence was better. They crossed the bridge below which ran no water, but a dozen braiding and unbraiding sets of railroad tracks and the dark shapes of warehouses and loading platforms of the railhead. Ahead of them was the high school, all lit and wide at the doors in welcome. For a moment, only a moment, they hung back, not wanting to leave the darkness and their sharing for the old, familiar, enemy World of the Hearing in which they were strangers.

The graduates had made their procession, looking young and beautiful; the speeches had been made in Hearing's endless love for talk-talk; prizes had been given and accepted—to Margaret honors two times, although for what things they were unable to understand. It was enough that, with only three or four others, she rose to be applauded by everyone. At last the graduates were released to their families to return, now through the nighttime streets to kitchens where cake and wine waited on the sideboards and tables were covered with cloths as for a wedding.

Margaret met her parents in the hall outside the auditorium. As she came through the crowding relatives and flushed graduates, she saw they were standing together, very tall and proud in a far corner, waiting for her. When she was close they motioned her closer where they could talk without being seen. Abel was grinning. "See," he said. He had some kind of machine attached to him. There was a twisted black cord running from behind his ear and going into his collar. In his ear there was a large, smooth, black bulb, like a box for a typewriter ribbon.

"What is that?"

"I got it for your present; it is the present I told you about."

"What is it for?"

"It is electrical. It is a hearing machine."

"Then you *hear*? You can *hear* . . . ?"

His smile faded and his hands faltered for a moment. "I had to shut it off. Terrible sounds. Sound makes a bad, bad pain in all the face and inside my head. When I cough or sneeze, I—I weep because of pain. It is like the sun breaking apart in my head. I have to turn it off."

"Then you can't hear with it?"

"It is not for Deafs, it is for Hearing, like I told you. It is for you, this, like I told you before. It makes me—— To Hearing—to you and your friends—I will not look so deaf."

13

A YEAR IN THE 'BUSINESS WORLD' and Margaret could
hardly remember what daydreams she and the girls
in shorthand class had hatched and nurtured over
their system books. In the year's time she had worked in a small
office on Perrer Street and in a big hive on Miller Avenue.
There had been temporary filing and typing jobs in many
places where the work load was seasonal and where notices from
closures, invitations, sales promotions deficits and inventories
ripened each in its own summer, like fruit. For a week or two,
there would be a harvesting and then the offices would fall
still and the reapers would move on. She was always thanked,
and always praised: "We like your work. We hire our permanent people in the fall." Then they said it was after Christmas
that the work would pick up; then spring. The permanent
jobs come in the spring. By spring the want ads began to shrink
again. She always left her name at the good jobs, giving Mr.
Petrakis' number, and when she came home, she always stopped
and checked with him before going upstairs. Sometimes there
would be a call, but she stopped mostly because she liked talking to Mr. Petrakis. He was the only person who could tell how
she was feeling by her face and manner. If the work was dull
or the people unpleasant, he would shake his head and say,
"Ah, look how they make you tired . . ." Some of the offices
were like small forests, alive with predators, and these baffled

and exhausted her. Only he knew when she was working in such a place and he would make a clumsy, comforting joke about it. "If this bunch calls you afterwards, I tell 'em, nothin' doin'! I am *her* seccatary an she ain't workin for no bums!"

"But she's the best bookkeeper we ever had," she would say.

"So, she got a little job now, typin' up letters for the President of the U.S.A. an when she gets through with that, she'll let you know, but don't start hopin', because you are on the end of the list."

It pleased her that he knew the places and remembered each change and was sorry with her when one of the good ones was over and it was time to look again. When she said good night and went into the narrow vestibule and up the stairs, she always felt better than she had before. She would help Janice get supper and do the dishes afterward, although there was seldom much to do. Janice took fierce pride in her own routine of work. Sometimes Margaret took in a movie with some school friends who were working or looking for work; and sometimes there was an engagement party or a wedding for one of the girls from school, but usually she would finish in the kitchen and then sit down to her radio and listen while she mended, or rolled up her hair.

Mr. Petrakis had given her the radio. It was an old set; the tone was scratchy and the mahogany veneer on the cabinet was cracked and had peeled out from under the rim where he had tried to glue it. He had given it to her on the night of her graduation when she had come home too disappointed to go or to explain about going to the graduation party. Abel had worn that hearing aid twice since graduation night, both times without the batteries. Sometimes when she looked at the bulky thing squatting on its little table, she remembered that first look at her father with his 'machine.' She had been too angry and disappointed to do anything but stand there. Later, when they came back home together, Mr. Petrakis had been standing in his doorway, holding something bulky that he had wrapped in an old blanket. They smiled at him and began to walk by. "Hey," he said, and stepped out in front of them. There was an apologetic smile wavering on his face. He thrust the thing at Margaret and said, "You're a good girl." It looked like a dead dog, wrapped up in the blanket that way. "Congratulations." She took it and felt sides and corners under the blanket, while Janice and Abel stood by, smiling and nodding and waiting for meaning. She said "Thank you," and went upstairs. In the morning she put a letter under his door to thank him and she made note of all the fixing he must have done on it to get it into such good condition. She tried to be grateful; she tried to want nothing better.

Rarely did the Lone Ranger ride without her, or the Creaking Door open. She broke into a thousand deserted farmhouses with the G-men and sat with the Green Hornet as he squealed on thrilling rims around the desperate corners of the night. There had been nothing in her education by the soap operas to match the excitement of the nighttime programs, which she had never heard before. She listened to every mystery and adventure program, drama and comedy. She didn't like the famous comedians; their wit seemed to elude her. Words meant-did-not-mean and the laughter of the audience came so fast that it made her feel ashamed to be caught unready, still sorting among the words. She liked the dramas best; clear, simple dramas where people could make choices that they understood. She never read books, but would sit rapt and half-smiling, uplifted, despairing and terrified as the heroes and heroines died or married in voices of unusual beauty.

It took her a long time to realize that Janice and Abel were jealous of the radio. They treated the set with casual carelessness and Margaret was always replacing the plug or mending the cord after finding it wrenched from the socket during Janice's cleaning. Abel piled packages against it until it was pushed to the edge of the little table, and Margaret sometimes saw them looking at it as though they were trying to make it fall by an act of will. Sometimes they made jokes about her as she sat listening, leaning forward, her head tilted toward the silence from which silence came, her sudden smiling, sudden weeping, tension and release of tension for nothing and no one.

"Look at the Margaret-show," Abel would say. Then, without Sign, using only his expressive face, he would proceed to suffer a dozen changes of emotion. Once he enacted a savage murder, killing as joyfully as he died, both villain and victim. Once he went mad and took to drink and joined the vaudeville.

Margaret knew he was ridiculing her world, the stories and plays of which he had never been told. But she couldn't take her eyes from him; he was her father, yet he could be young and old in a minute; his face and body could perform acts of separation from his true self that were almost fearsome; all in the service of his game. Although it was ridicule and sad because Abel was jealous; and although the ridicule was poignant because he was lonely, the unplotted and outlandish imitations had flashes of breathtaking reality. Sometimes Margaret found herself waiting for his jealousies to burst into these inventions and she would watch intently, above a smile or a grimace meant to mask her interest.

Abel himself seemed to enjoy his game. He lost husband-father-printer, even Deaf. He was none of those things when he played, but was reborn into a life un-Deaf, un-Hearing. He liked being a policeman with a dead robber at his feet. Then he saw the robber. He saw the money in the robber's hand. He would not take the money . . . he would not take all of it, but maybe just one bill, just one that could be lost in the spaces between crime and justice. And his policeman-face showed these things and his policeman-body showed them in the way it bent to pick up that single bill. Margaret always marveled at this sudden melting of faces and bodies between policeman and robber, victor and victim. Every time he played the game against her, he used another life. Margaret laughed and pretended to wave him away, but the laughter was a laughter of wonder and she would go back to the radio more slowly and listen with a grave face.

Margaret had never thought of her parents as being perceptive. They mistook the motives of other people, Hearing and Deaf; and they always credited everyone with the worst of motives. They kept grievances for years like family pets and filled themselves with gossip. Now she saw how closely Abel could watch, and with what accuracy he recorded the momentary hesitation of a hand or the turning of a head, things that spoke apart from language and sometimes made liars of the words that were spoken with them.

The radio made Abel sad; Janice hated it, and Abel's playing made things no better. When they were alone, she mocked him with her own cruel skill, saying he was afraid to stop Margaret from doing anything she wanted to do.

"When she is here, she is not with us; she's sitting with her ear against that mouth, listening, listening, all the time!"

"They like to listen; it's like a movie to them."

"What does she listen to that is so important, night after night. All that makes her tired, makes her old. Too much knowing makes people troubled in their mind. Look at them all, how impatient they are, how smart at hurting people. She is getting like them more and more!"

Abel, driven against his own wishes, to defend, began his usual defense, but Janice waved his hands away. Why didn't Margaret go out with them any more to the social hours at church? She didn't make friends with any of the sons or daughters of the people there; she didn't want to go shopping. She didn't have time to go to the clinic or the dentist or the bank man or the plumber or the salesgirl, or the tax man. She only had time to keep secrets with the Wooden Mouth.

Abel looked at her and then shrugged. There was no way to change things. Now the debt was paid, paid at last and over, and they had money and freedom at last to spend and save and share and enjoy—after twenty years. And now it was too late. The hunger, the wanting, the joy in which Janice had once run into the world were gone. The piecework had finished it. The piecework had taught her that every moment away from the machine was a moment that made no money. Now, when the piecework was gone, she measured her life by a thousand other tiny, miser's measures. Now that the growing time was over, it was too late to give Margaret sunlight through shade-trees as a memory. Now that the debt was paid, it seemed that no one was left alive. Abel saw Bradley in his mind. He had not thought of Bradley for many years except to push the thought away when any small bit of it appeared. Who is alive any more? Then he thought, simply: I am alive.

"Janice . . ." He seldom used her name even in abbreviation; it surprised her in the middle of her argument, and made her stop with a stunned look on her face. "I want to buy a house. On a street with trees. With a place in back. Green. With a tree."

She looked at him for a long time, without blinking or breathing. All her time had stopped because of shock. Then it broke in violent, soundless rage. Words flew out, stuttered, her fingers unable to follow her mind. Gestures were mixed with words, her hands as twisted as her face, her lips framing formless things. Abel, with one simply made "Stop," turned and walked away. She seized the bedside lamp and raised it to throw to break against the wall, but the piecework had given its punishment too well. The lamp had been bought with money, and so it had a value. To break it would be to break the time it cost, the work, the money, the reality. It was like breaking a part of her own body. She put the lamp back and lay down and beat the bed and kicked at the wall until she could weep.

The two of them waged bitter war from that time on, and Margaret wandered vaguely through the skirmish mornings and the battle nights. Sometimes her mind seethed with the silent wrangles, fingers in ambush, bruised arms, revenges. Both of them tried for her allegiance, and failing, seized her as hostage to the other.

Their quarrel was about a house, she knew. She wanted a house; but wanted it too much to let herself think about it. At work she tried to clear the struggle from her mind.

It was one of the nicer jobs and looked as though it might last, for once. She had started as a temporary typist, but when the partners learned about her bookkeeping, they found some extra work for her to do; and when the regular secretary was out, she took over the desk and did some of the simpler billing as well. Margaret worked hardest when she was worried or unhappy. Bustling and business took her mind off other things. So the battles that Janice and Abel inflicted on each other were causing the filing system at Patman and Rulliger to be overhauled while the secretary was home with what Margaret suspected was morning sickness.

One day a man came in to see Mr. Rulliger and when he

gave his name, Margaret looked up at him a little surprised. He said, "Is something wrong?"

"No," she said. "I'm sorry. Mr. Rulliger will be with you in a moment."

She had not wanted to tell him that she had taken some of his calls and that from his voice on the telephone she had thought him a much older man. He sat down to wait and she went back to the files, which were in a small room off the office. The door was open and occasionally she glanced at him as he waited. What drew her attention was his stillness. Most people waiting, no matter where, or for whom, made waiting as much an action as walking. They fidgeted, picked their nails, took magazines up and did not read them, looking up every two or three minutes to the door by which they would be delivered from their waiting. This man was reading a book he had brought with him and he seemed completely interested in it; he didn't pace the room with his eyes and wasn't caught off poise when Mr. Rulliger came out to greet him. When Margaret went back to the desk, she noticed a valise set carefully in the corner near where he had been sitting. It was one of the cardboard kind, the cheapest that the five and dime had, and very new.

When the man came out, he asked if he could leave it and come back for it later—at around five. He was leaving for the army, he explained; his good-byes had been said and the winding up of the rest of his affairs had taken less time than he thought. She smiled and said, "Certainly."

He was back at two minutes of five and then he asked her if she would have a cup of coffee with him. He asked simply, seriously, without affectation, and she agreed. Her directness seemed to surprise and please him. When they were drinking their coffee in one of the small, pleasant restaurants on Lamarr, she began to have the feeling that he wanted to ask her something else, but couldn't. He was not a talkative man; his gestures were made very small and with great subtlety, they seldom went outward from his body which was also compact, his arms and legs kept close. She had the feeling that even his tightly curled black hair hugged his head closely out of a kind of neat, objective reserve. What he wanted was being said by his hand, or by one finger of it that moved up and down on the outside of the cup as he spoke about going away. The gesture was not like him, not like the way his hands seemed to speak. She saw then that he was afraid and could not admit it; that he wanted some kind of comfort. Then it was hard not to smile. To cover the reason for it she asked him if he would like her to see him off, just to have someone who would go down to the bus terminal with him. His eyes widened and he smiled. He was not conscious of his finger moving on the cup, nor of its stopping. He was busy explaining to her why there was no one else. She said she understood.

So they went to the bus terminal where they waited again. He asked her for her address and copied it neatly in a small book. When the bus began to load, they got up and shook hands and she stayed until it left, waving him out of sight. She knew she would probably never hear from him again, but it had been a relief to take a rest from the argument at home.

Miraculously, when she did get home, she found that the fight was over. Janice was sitting defiantly at the table among the dirty dishes, Abel smoking in cool triumph by the window. When Margaret came in, Janice motioned to the stove where a plate was being kept warm. The food was too spicy and over-salted. They must still have been arguing while Janice cooked; Margaret could see her stirring with short, hard strokes, Signing back, then shaking in the salt and pepper with savage motions. She ate as much as she could and dumped the rest out while Janice sat staring and pretending not to notice anything.

"Now," said Abel, enjoying himself, "we are going to buy a house. What do you think of the idea?"

"I think it is a good idea," Margaret said.

Janice's hands moved as though they did not belong to her body. "He will have the Law on us. He will have us in Court again, another shame."

Always during their arguments that thing came up about the Law and the Court, and whenever Margaret had tried to ask about it, neither of them would tell her. At first she had thought it must have something to do with Bradley's death because of the police coming, but since it came up in this way again and again in their latest battles over the house, Margaret got the feeling that it was something older and more bitter; a deep trouble, a humiliation. Apparently it had been Abel's doing, Abel's blame, but Janice had been the one punished for it, because it was always Janice who spoke of it, throwing it as a last weapon, the one to wound most deeply. Now Margaret could see that it had been used once too often. It no longer carried so far or hurt so sharply. Abel only shrugged and told Margaret to call some real estate men and to tell them this: He took a paper out of his pocket on which were the features he wanted in a house and the amount of money he could pay.

She looked at the paper and was moved. How long and carefully he must have figured it all. He must have asked many people at work and at church where there were nice sections to live with houses that were modest but well built, places with lawns and backyards, not too far from church or from the car line to work. The details had all been lovingly assembled and when Janice looked up again, Margaret took the paper to her to show the care in it. "Flowers, Mother. Trees. A little garden, maybe." Janice only sighed and looked away.

The next day, on her lunch hour, Margaret called a realtor for whom she had done some extra work. He didn't remember her but sounded pleased with the exactness of the specifications she gave. Since there were many houses possible, he suggested calling for them at their home and taking them from place to place in his car. She talked him out of meeting them at their home, suggesting that his office would be better. She hung up the phone without allowing herself a smile or a picture for her mind of a house, any house. It was better not to think of how much she wanted a house, a place to belong; a past, even if it were a fiction, for her to remember having grown from. Something might happen; it often did. Maybe they would not be able to agree on a price. Janice would find some other way to wage her battle; something would happen. So Margaret went back to work and that evening told Abel and Janice the arrangements she had made. She did not mention that there would be a car. Her only worry was that she had not told the realtor her parents were deaf and that he would be doing business through her.

The meeting was stiff and somewhat embarrassing. It was a chilly day with a winter rawness in it and a fitful wind that blew in sharp gusts down the Sunday-empty business streets. The office had looked closed, but Margaret insisted that they try the door. It was open and the realtor was inside waiting for them in his coat and hat. Margaret introduced them and explained about her parents, giving him a moment to understand but not long enough to worry. As he led them to the car, he said to her, "I never had anyone—like that—before. Can they sign contracts? Legally, I mean."

"Oh, yes," she said, and did not add the word of sarcasm that was suddenly in her mind.

Janice and Abel had stopped before the car and the realtor motioned them in, relieved when they understood and stepped back for him to open the door. Abel noticed a change in his wife's face as they seated themselves in the back. Margaret was up in front with the man whose mouth was going on and on beneath a face that had a set, closed look; but Janice's closedness was gone. She was trying not to show it. Her lips were pulled together and her head was held in the righteous-hurt way she used, but Abel saw that she was only imitating herself. Something was changed in her, and had touched the subtle lines in her face of which she had no knowledge. He saw it in her cheeks, her chin, her hands, spread a very little as they waited in her lap: Janice was having fun. As secretly as a child hiding his candy, Janice was trying to hide the enjoyment that threatened to break upon her face at any moment. It was the car. Of course. Abel smiled himself then. In all the arguments, in the ugly words they threw at each other, in the times of begging, in the times of stubborn anger, she had always managed to include that car that he had bought and lost; that car that had been his own selfish, vain need; that chained them in the end to debt and poverty for twenty years and shamed them before the Speaking and the Deaf. Now she was being driven around, like a rich person, in the back seat, in a fine new car with ashtrays in each arm rest and a lap robe in case of cold. Very slowly and secretly, her hand moved down to the thick, scratchy-new mohair cloth on the seat and she began to feel it a little, feeling for the grain of it this way and that, until she found it and then in a hidden way she began to stroke it in the way a person strokes a cat.

A terrifying thought suddenly came to him and he lifted her hands quickly, so that she had to look at him and then he said, "You won't do a bad thing—you won't let him take us around all day and say 'no' and 'no' to all the houses just to have the ride?"

She pulled her hand away and went back to stroking, with only the thumb now, back and back on the smooth track of the mohair. He could see a pulling at the corners of her mouth, very small, as though she were just about to smile. But Janice was too many years away from playing, and the mouth only pulled downward and her palms turned up. She shrugged one shoulder. "You have the money—you have the choice. You are the one who buys the cars and the ruby rings and takes them away again——" Then she set her eyes straight ahead and her thumb crept back to stroke, stroke over the mohair seat.

The first two houses were not right, although they fitted the careful demands that Abel had written. There was some mysterious lack in them and in the neighborhoods, and he was unhappy because he was not able, even in Sign to Margaret, to explain his dislike. He was also afraid of the realtor's displeasure, but to his surprise the man was not angry or even annoyed. He gave Margaret some facts, which she told them, about the heating or the foundations, the roof, the water, but when Abel showed his disinterest, the man stopped what he was saying and took them right back to the car.

The third house was a little better and they tried dutifully as he suggested, to see themselves living in it, with familiar furniture here and there, or as they hoped to furnish it later, with nice things. Still it wasn't right and the realtor could see them beginning to tire with the effort of giving their imaginations into the rooms and the yard and the corners.

"Your folks are getting a little tired," he said to the girl. "They aren't used to this kind of thing, up and down steps, in and out. It tires some people out quick."

"No," she said, but then was unable to say more. Coming

stolidly behind, Abel and Janice walked with heads ringing. They ached with the effort of filling rooms with invisible furniture, seeing and unseeing, making and unmaking the invisible lives of their invisible wish-selves. The realtor looked at Margaret to explain, and when she didn't, shrugged and looked at the next house on his list. Many people had housedreaming as a Sunday recreation and he had to make sure that no one just did the rounds without the intention of buying. He suggested they stop for lunch and then continue down the list. The relief on their faces was evident without the easing Sign.

They got into the car and Margaret said to him, "I hope you won't take us to a big place—I mean fancy." She paused and added, "It embarrasses them."

He looked at her and answered pleasantly, "Okay." He smiled when he said it, and the look and smile seemed too frank to her, as though he were judging her in some way. Where does she fit in; what's in this for her? She turned away only to feel Janice's forefinger poking her shoulder, an annoying reminder that Janice used when she felt left out of something and wanted the words of it.

"I told him to pick a little place, because we didn't want anything expensive to eat. He said he would."

"I don't know where we will get the money for all this —buying houses, eating out, riding around in cars. You said this can take weeks and weeks, before we find a place. And all that time, lunches out, maybe dinners too. It all costs money, all of it." She sat back, vindicated.

"I had a grandmother who was hard of hearing," the realtor said. "She had one of those black ear trumpets, you know, and I'd have to go up close and yell into it for her to hear me. But you could open up the cupboard door way in the next room, and she'd call out, 'Get me a piece of that candied fruit you're taking!' " He laughed, a short, sudden laugh and then turned quickly to accept Margaret's laughter and when he saw there was none, that her face had not changed, said, "No offense meant; your folks back there just reminded me of her, that's all. My granny, she used to poke me all the time just like your mother there, to try to get me to tell her what everyone was saying.'' He shook his head. ''She was a dilly, though, my granny. Died last spring.''

''Oh,'' Margaret said, ''that's too bad.''

''Well, I think she really wanted to go. She was way up in the years, and at the end there, she was deaf as a post. I really think she was glad to go.'' He chuckled a little and shook his head, his hands and feet working smoothly at the mechanisms of the car.

Janice and Abel sitting in the back, had begun to speak in a very small language, brief, impersonal 'public' thoughts. Both were amazed at the ease and grace with which the realtor drove his car. It humbled them that Speaking could have the kind of closeness with their machines that Deaf did. Janice did not need seam guides but could ''see'' a seam straight, could feed to and from that making seam, naturally, in any rhythm of her machine's own speed . . . Abel could feel faults in the press even before the printed sheets came through . . . and the man in front of them knew to drive without looking, to move the stick and wheel and to push the pedals without conscious thought to do so and without looking at his hands or feet. Often he would not be looking at the road at all, but into the little mirror put up over the front window to provide communion with those in the back. Considerately, they moved closer together and into his angle of vision so that he might be able to see both of them at the same time.

They stopped for sandwiches and coffee at a strange place with a long name, Deli—— (twelve letters, and sss somewhere). The food was foreign and unfamiliar, but it was very good, filling and not too expensive. They were refreshed when they started again. The realtor, feeling more comfortable, ventured a joke, which Margaret Signed small to them. He was halfway through when he realized it was a play on words and that the Signs might not render it. He struggled on to the end and they all laughed anyway. As they got into the car, he caught a glimpse of Margaret trying to explain it to them.

While they were at lunch, the sun had come and had taken possession. They walked into noon brightness which wind had

cleaned to an autumnal purity. Of course, the trees were bare
—it was already December, but the smells, the flavor of the air
were the smells and flavors of late last harvests.

"It doesn't feel like winter at all," the realtor said. "It's
real football weather."

"Oh?"

"Sure is. Say, I was going to listen to the game today.
The Giants are playing Brooklyn."

"Baseball? But I thought——"

"Football. The football teams. I thought maybe the game
might get called on account of snow, but look at it now. Great,
just great." They got into the car again. The realtor's face was
the business-face again. "I'm going to another part of town,
an older neighborhood. I have a nice one there. The houses
aren't as new, but they're built well and they have more ground
with them. The house I'm going to show you is a real little
honey."

Margaret told her parents and they nodded and the car
went its smooth, instinctive way over and across and through
street after street, turning right, left, north, east until Margaret's head spun. They had come around, though in a wide
half-circle, and she recognized some of the streets as being not
far from Vandalia. Only now, they were south of where Vandalia began in its filthy boxed-in end of river and railroad
yards and where the city folded over and crowded in upon
itself. As they rode on, Abel's fingers began to move in faint
half-formed Sign. He was murmuring to himself, "This is
that place, that summer place, this is the old one, the old number one where . . . This is the summer . . ."

"What are you saying?" Janice poked his arm in irritation. Abel didn't know it, but sometimes he Signed in his sleep,
and when he was dreaming he often had the bits and ends of
words in his hands. There was something about these vaguely
waving gestures, spoken without mind or presence that were
terrifying to Janice. She also remembered the school lectures
on self-abuse and its badness, and groped at the ideas behind
the flap-flap minister's mouth, words written on the board to
make sure that everyone understood. Fingering one's self.
Play with private parts. The school people said that fingering

to one's self was dirty and playing with the secret parts was a sign of madness. Wasn't it so, that insane people always gesture and make wild signs, their fingers picking and seeing here and there, moving not of their owners' moving will? Abel must know how much she hated that muttering of his. He was only doing it to annoy her.

"What is it?" she insisted. "What are you talking about?"

"Only—I was only remembering that we used to live near here and we walked near here sometimes, on Sundays . . . in the summer."

"I remember," she said, and her face moved toward sorrow. "We couldn't afford anything else but walking."

"But don't you remember how happy . . ." and he stopped because it was silly to try to tell someone of her own past happiness. Janice had changed, and in changing, had made over all the memories behind her. He felt lonely, suddenly, and when they passed the place where they once lived and where Margaret had been born, he did not look at his wife or touch his daughter to show her where it was. He sat back and said nothing.

They went then into a neighborhood of generous houses where huge trees touched branches over the street. Hedges, arbors and shrubbery waited in the fine-boned fragility of their dormancy, and brown lawns spread in the laps of the houses. Toward the middle of the block the car slowed down and then pulled to a stop along the curb. The house was quite a bit smaller than the others on the block. It looked as though it might once have been part of the house that stood to the right of it; a house for some married relative whose needs were simpler. The house was white and square but with bow windows on both floors and a small porch on which one could sit in the summer and look out over the neat front lawn to the great trees.

They went up the walk with the solemn, self-conscious caution of visitors in a hospital. At the bottom of the steps Abel touched the tips of one of the naked hedges, his face rapt and silent. The realtor began to explain some of the features of the house and Margaret translated quickly, almost clinically. No word was said nor questions asked. With the docility of sleepwalkers, they allowed themselves to be led up the stairs and inside.

"It is an older house," the realtor was saying so as to give them no cause to complain when they came to themselves. "It needs repairs. Until you get the roof insulated a little better, you are going to have to pay a pretty heavy heating bill, and some of the plumbing is a bit old and leaky. . . ."

They went from room to room, the realtor almost pulling them on as he noted and pointed out the necessary details. When they had been shown the upstairs and the attic and the kitchen and backyard, they came into the parlor again and stood in the middle of the dusty, empty room whose floor was streaked and squared with branch-hatched sunlight. Margaret watched her parents standing there motionlessly, so close to each other that their clothing touched. They looked old and fragile and lost in all the empty space of the room.

The realtor bustled forward and raised and lowered the windows several times to show them how easily they worked. The sight of his car at the curb seemed to give him a sudden idea. "Say"—and he turned to Margaret—"would your folks mind if I hopped out to the car for a minute? I want to get the score on that game."

She said it would be all right because she wanted to speak to her parents quickly before he came back. They had been too awed and unquestioning, too deeply found, too homed. There were faults in the house, questions to be answered. The realtor might make the price high because he had seen what she had seen; how homed they were, how numbed at the miracle of it.

"Well, you just look around," he said. "Anything you want to know . . ." He waved a bit and the door closed and Margaret saw him through the window going down the walk.

Janice and Abel came to themselves in a panic. "What is wrong? Why is he leaving?"

Margaret comforted them and was about to go into the problems of the house when she noticed that the realtor was behaving in a strange way. He had opened the passenger door and left it open while he sat inside to listen. Then he had gotten out of the car, leaving the door still open and he was standing on the sidewalk, his head turning right and left as though watching for someone with great urgency. His hands were moving slightly, his eyes looked blank and his face was dazed. In a slow, dreamlike rhythm, he began to walk back up to the house, bumping against the front gate which he did not seem to see. Behind him the car gaped. Margaret found herself coldly alert, fearing. She moved between the dreamers and the door through which the man—frightened or angry, or suffering some kind of madness—might come. She heard the door open and then saw him. He was ill; his face was strange and very pale. He gestured weakly toward the outside, the car.

"On the radio," he said, "breaking in on the game"— Janice and Abel had turned and were staring at him and Margaret felt the familiar jab—"they said—they said the Japanese just bombed Pearl Harbor."

"Where is that?" Margaret said, and moved out of Janice's reach.

"Hawaii, I think. I think it's in Hawaii."

"But that can't be . . . It must be some kind of joke. The *Japanese?*" She tried to laugh. It was as fantastic as Finland or Paraguay declaring war.

"Come on out and listen," he said.

So they went together and when they came back to the house, Margaret told her parents, who were still standing in the floating dust-mote-sunshine of the dreaming room: "The Japanese have made—explosions—from airplanes. In Hawaii." Their faces were open, interested.

"Why?" Abel asked. "Did the airplanes crash?"

"They have made these explosions—to start a war."

"Mistake, bad and wrong!" Janice said. "We must tell them that we do not want it."

They turned back toward the window and then Janice motioned to the wall where a sofa must be and a small table, with flowers or ivy growing, just the way it was at the minister's house. Two or three times they asked Margaret about the necessity for a rug, but she seemed suddenly to have lost her interest in the house. She and the realtor were just standing there, staring at each other. Then without a word they both went back to the car and sat in it listening and listening to that blind, invisible mouth.

14

A T FIRST it was difficult to understand how the bombing of a place that was not even in America was war, but through the week everyone came to the minister's house, seeking information because of the strange new times. Everyone needed the reassurance of friends. One could tell by the day he came, how much contact a person had with the Hearing-Speaking. The minister had it all to explain over and over.

Janice and Abel had been among the first to know, but they were not the first to believe, and after the words had been given and taken, they drew together and waited for the armies of invasion.

"Everyone will hear the shooting and the bombs!" Janice cried wildly to Margaret. "Everyone will run away and be safe. You will be at work, and how will we know where to go and what people to trust?"

Abel, standing in the light, was losing his words in its glare. When he saw that he couldn't be understood, he moved away, momentarily annoyed that it took so much work to try to comfort Janice. "Margaret will tell us; she will know."

"She will leave!" Janice attacked. "She gets letters from that army place from a man there. She will leave us alone in the war when the soldiers come!"

The days passed and Janice and Abel scented the air and watched into the sun for signs and then scuttled off to work and when the day was over came straight home, not daring to stop for the eggs or the cigarettes, lest they be caught unguarded and defenseless in the streets. Had they not seen Margaret going to work each day, they would have stayed away themselves, the door barricaded, the carving knife sharp and ready on the kitchen table.

But the days went by, days that were full of changes, fears and frantic rumors, and yet the war did not come and the country was not invaded. After some weeks Janice and Abel began to grow puzzled about this War where there was no fighting on their streets. Margaret tried to convince them that they should go ahead and buy the house as they had planned. They argued and stalled a dozen times, having pictured it destroyed,—bombed, burned, looted. Margaret kept calling, putting off the realtor and trying to get him to wait.

Since Margaret had met William Anglin at the office, and had seen him off to the Army, she had been corresponding with him regularly. Janice raised her eyebrows when she handed his letters to Margaret, but she didn't know how to ask about the man behind the precise, closely written numbers on the envelope.

William wrote from camp that confusion and rumor were the main products of the war so far. Thousands of men were pouring into camps that were unready and unsupplied. The weapons on which they trained were broken and outdated; they had to be passed from man to man and then demonstrated before the group. Men might go into battle, he said, without actually having fired the guns they would, hopefully, be given. They sighted down wooden weapons and practiced the slow squeeze on a rigid wooden trigger. The only thing plentiful was gossip and a slow, equalizing fear. He wrote again that they might soon be going overseas and that he expected to get home again before leaving. If it was possible, he would come. The trains were overcrowded, the buses impossible; he would do everything he could. He signed the letter, "All my love."

There seemed to be a frantic and fevered quality to the days. People hurried, work doubled; any action was better than none. The greetings that Abel exchanged yearly with his parents did not include the usual message: "We are all well . . ." There did not seem to be time to say such things.

The excitement burned against the winter and made the spring pass dizzily as if from too much breathing. There were air-raid drills and blackout drills. Janice objected to the special curtains that had to be fitted to the windows to keep in all the light. At church Abel heard about plans for rationing and there were rumors of people hoarding the foods that would soon be rare. The people spoke recklessly, their Sign too big, too loud—even the reserved and comfortable people, the rich, well-educated few, the leaders among the Deaf, spoke with a nervous haste, part patriotism and part fear, that raced in the eyes, hands, faces, bodies. Nothing seemed normal. The streets were suddenly full of men in uniform and there were girls with them, very hard-faced, open-mouthed girls, Janice said, and they came walking four abreast, filling the sidewalk and letting no one by; a person had to step off into the street, and she nodded slowly with a grave, pinch-mouth. As the months went on, Margaret also noticed a hardness in the laughter of the sailors and the girls, out late at night looking for something to do along the Avenue. Some of the hard laughter was the giddiness of exhaustion. Many of her friends were working on two jobs, a daytime job and a late shift at one of the defense plants that had sprung up on the other side of the railroad yards. Suddenly there was work everywhere. Amalia Cibelli, whose father had been too poor to die last year, went to work and got himself a set of dentures, and Amalia dyed her hair red and had it permanent-waved.

In June, Janice came home, her fingers wide and stuttering with pride and told them that she had been made Section Supervisor. Her pay was doubled, and she had learned to understand "time-and-a-half." The mill now was making fatigue hats and jackets for the army, and a man—some kind of government foreman, she thought—had come to her machine and stopped and watched her for a long time and then went away nodding and now she was going to be Section Supervisor and her way of end-begin without stopping the machine was going to become The Way, the factory standard.

Even in Janice and Abel there was some of the wild rest-
lessness of Hearing in those times, an unease in which wild
elation was as common as terror and grief. Janice's first day
in her new position was a blend of fear and pride kept to such
point-closeness that she thought she might be going insane.
Always in the past her accurate, fast methods had been thought
too dangerous and her skill was feared by the other girls on
the floor. Now it was all changed. The Union people didn't pick
on her and the girls at the machines looked on in awe as she
demonstrated for the new ones. She began by sitting down with
slow, forbidding dignity, her deafness and silence thundering
in the minds of the watching girls (no charm would put her
off, no excuses would do, no promises would reach her). Then
she leaned forward, the machine started, the cloth began to flow
and there came that steady, magical growing, growing of
quantities of finished work on the side table. She could see,
looking without seeming to, the awe on their faces, sometimes
the fear. Many of the girls who went back to try her way at
their own machines had fingers chewed under the needles, but
now there was no sympathy for them, only impatience because
they had been inattentive.

Abel was also beginning to find himself rediscovered at
his work. A few of the young men had left immediately for the
army and their places were not filled. Suddenly, orders had
begun to pour in from everywhere; there were instructional
leaflets for new and part-time employees; posters, signs and
booklets to urge, explain and teach quickly, quickly, those
leaving and those staying—all in new and urgent language.
Everyone was trying to get the attention of people dizzied
with change. The shop was drowning in a pour of printed
words when news came, first by rumor and then from the government that paper would soon be in short supply and would
eventually be placed on the list of war commodities and ra-
tioned. There were frantic rules and frantic changes of the
rules for other rules, and Abel, his fears now less than his
fellows, only different, worked on in his own long rhythm. The
months went on and the idea of America's having been attacked was replaced by a belief that the attack was a fluke,
and that a few months would see it all avenged. This belief

died in the fall of more islands and cities, and soon, only the realities of supply, need, production and tactic remained. When a machine broke down, there would be no replacement parts. It was as simple as that.

Abel knew that the men in the shop thought he had the power of "hearing" his press. He also knew, fleetingly and ambiguously, far below words that his deafness and the isolation it forced on him made his co-workers see in him a strange kind of strength, a spirituality and virtue, as though his silence, ear and mouth, made him a mystical communicant with things deeper in the world than speech—than people. Now, when nothing broken could be fixed, it became important for them that there be magic. Abel did partly "hear" his machine. Its vibration sang up through the floor, through his shoes and into his bones. The note had a steadiness, like a heartbeat, divided into stronger and weaker pulses, different in weight but the same in "tone." Over the years he had learned many of the signs of wear or carelessness that could be shown by differences in the weight or constancy of these vibrations. He had learned to detect other things by putting his fingers or his palms on the machine and letting the vibrations sound through his hands. He had, a few times, suddenly stopped his press and begun to take it down, and always a worn bearing had been found, or some part beginning to loosen, or friction that oil had not eased. Now, with the war shortages making a burnt-out motor or frozen roller-bearings a catastrophe, Abel also found himself a kind of talisman presence in the shop, and other men often came to ask him to come, please, and "listen" to their machines. Sometimes the trouble was to be seen immediately: overheating, sticking, even smoke! How gravely they would watch as he touched for the humming tone, or, in a press like his own, the double beat. They watched as though he were a kind of priest.

Margaret had kept fighting them in their success-bemusement, to make up their minds about the house. In the first weeks of fear they had told her to call up the realtor and cancel their plans. Margaret had called him, but begged for time. She had kept on begging for time, which the realtor said he would give until another buyer came along. There were rumors that all wages and prices would soon be frozen, and speculators were buying up what they could before the markets froze. Scarcity would soon make any house unavailable. With her usual unwavering persistence, Margaret worked on at Janice and Abel about the house. Her reasons, the deepest ones, were kept from them and they never seemed to suspect a connection in her motives between the need for a house and her growing correspondence with William. They merely shrugged, after a comment or two about the letters that she was getting from ''different places.'' To Margaret herself there were many parts to the single reason of 'William.'

She and William had been writing steadily to each other and from camp to camp their native reserve and caution had yielded to the overwhelming force of loneliness. Their letters had become longer and more self-revealing. They kept the tone of them general, as careful people would: conditions at the camps and at home, descriptions of places and people, but she was able to read need and fear as well as pleasure in his unveiling of a dry humor. It was almost ''Deaf'' humor; not wit that enjoyed plays on words or surprising ideas; but a humor that came from observation and connection. ''The C.O.'s tie does not show beneath his collar in back and his belt is not notched so tightly. I think his wife must be home from Cleveland. . . . The sergeant asked us where we went on pass and no one would say the library, even though that's the only place besides the churches that the town leaves open to us. The younger men make things up, and the older ones say they hung around or went here and there. Here-and-there is never the library. I saw eight or nine soldiers each time I was there. We are not deeply loved in the town.''

In March he had been made a lieutenant and was transferred and she sent him a small sewing kit with which to sew on successive stripes, bars and badges. He sent back a picture of himself standing in front of the barracks, and when he came home on leave before going overseas, she had dinner twice with his family, the second time with aunts and a sister and the formal, fearful hollowness in the air that marked the occasion as ''serious.'' It was too soon, too far in too short a time. She felt she had had no chance to tell William about Janice and

Abel or to do anything more than give a lame excuse to his family when no invitation from them was forthcoming after William went back to camp. That was when she had begun to nag them about getting the house.

The letters stopped. There had been one from Seattle and then nothing, and William's mother had called Margaret twice at work to ask if there was any news. They had lunch together one day and noticed in the careful, subtle measuring they did that they were very much alike in temperament. Time was getting short. In her next letter, Margaret decided, she would have to tell William why she had never let him take her home and why her parents had not invited him to dinner. If only they would move away from Vandalia street *now*. If only they could do it before William and his family would be forced to visit. In that lovely and quiet, tree-lined movie-American neighborhood, Janice and Abel's deafness would seem less like part of an overwhelming difference. They could seem like the other people of the street, dignified and capable. It was almost impossible to write simple facts. While she waited for the words to arrange themselves in her mind, she brooded over William's few moments of confusion when during the furlough, she had made excuses and not let him see her home. It had happened many times and she had used many excuses. It was too far; it was too late; he was tired; but the reasons had sounded false and had left him with a look of puzzled disappointment.

Now, every day that she went home, she saw the street as if for the first time, as though through William's eyes. It was noisy, crowded, shouting, raucous, but a deaf street all the same. How could she have grown up in such a strange, uncomprehending, deaf street? How could she still live there; still, with the mysterious parents whom he had never seen? This new vision of the street was sudden, complete and appalling. She had been to his house and had come back home still bathed in its gentility and quiet order. His house—all the houses on his street—lay in the same decorous, drawn-curtain stillness. Vandalia was like a canyon from which the walls rose overhead, hollowed with a thousand caves and pockets all sprouting the unmade heads of frowsy women, gap-mouthed and bawling.

The pushcart criers and children in the gutter screamed back
at them. The sidewalks were heaped with refuse; obscenity
covered the walls of the buildings, and from every alley and
side window, bank on bank, the washlines lifted flapping,
ragged scarecrows of the week's wearings. It was everyone's
private history, day and night, size and condition, blown lewdly
overfull by the wind.

As she walked closer to her own doorway, the vision was
sharpened in spite of a shame so great that she had to stop
sometimes, afraid of being sick on the street. There was the
pawnshop, and no memories of safety or sanctuary or learning
or affection could save it from the relentless judgment of the
new eyes, William's eyes. She began to wonder how many
times she had brushed by the pale, trembling, hopeless ghosts
that were always coming or going through their shared front
door. Customers. Here they would stand for a moment, out of
the wind, stinking of coal oil, sweat, urine, vomit and bad
whiskey, trying to remember how to make themselves invisible
again. They came to pawn things or to wait in the little vestibule, and sometimes Mr. Petrakis would find them sleeping
there and would have to wake them up and send them away.
Did the years of those old men and their failures hang on her?
Only in a strange way, disembodied and removed, could Margaret remember how she had once seen the dusty mandolins
and trays of junk as priceless and exotic treasures, tests of
every ounce of strength she had not to touch and fondle them
in wonder. And Mr. Petrakis himself—a loud, gesticulating
old man in sour, dirty clothing—dealing in all the ugliness and
failure of the street. Even the little on the street that shone
and was heroic was cheapened in the end and came to him. She
had seen, on the second shelf of the cabinet under the cash
register, a small tray of medals. On any other street, in any
other place such things would have been family treasures, kept
reverently under the pictures of honored dead. Not on Vandalia
Street.

Past the pawnshop door were the stairs that led up to her
"home." William, loving or not, would notice how the hall
stank and that the stairs were dark and that a hand on the
railing would come away greasy or sticky. If she could get her

father and mother out of the bemused daze of their success and into the new house in time, she might be able to pretend to herself that they had always lived there. And they could entertain. . . .

Her next letter to William was written and rewritten until the casual mention of her parents' deafness and the explanation for her odd behavior sounded stiff and artificial. His answer, a month later from an unnamed place in the Pacific was gentle and puzzled. He didn't see why she had kept this from him. Had they been blind, crippled in some way, it would have been easier to understand. Blindness is so total a thing, she might have been afraid of his pity, but with the stupidities being let loose in the world these days, being deaf was an advantage. There were many times here when he had wished to be deaf, he said.

The letter went on, giving what news it could and speaking of the boredom that was afflicting everyone and in which combat was only an interlude, one, by the way, in which there was less fear than in the waiting. One of the men on patrol had shot himself in the foot and for a week there were bets riding on every feature of his recovery. Many parts of the letter were blanked out by the censors, but these were about the times he had been in combat. He signed the letter "fondly."

She read it through, feeling a coldness in it in spite of the "fondly." She read it a third time and was angry, and only after waiting two days and reading it again did it become clear to her that William didn't know what deafness was; that he had never stopped to think what it must be like never to have words that were truly carriers of thought, or to have possession of the means to understand ideas which were not concrete or direct. He had thought that Deaf meant only unable to hear. It couldn't be explained. She was Hearing, Speaking and did not have the words herself, or the imagination to encompass it.

In July, Abel and Janice bought the house and by September the first few pieces of furniture were moved into the parlor to huddle into the corners like timid strangers. Margaret invited Mrs. Anglin out to lunch again and broached the idea of a return invitation to the dinner she had had with William.

"We've been moving, you see, and with both of my parents working extra shifts there hasn't been any time for the things . . . we would like."

The older woman smiled a bit stiffly. "The war has changed a great many things. I imagine you and William consider yourselves engaged, and yet you have never seen each other in an ordinary daily situation. I think that must bother you, doesn't it?"

"William and I"—she had never used their names together and regretted having caused the quick, involuntary widening of Mrs. Anglin's eyes—"I'm not the kind of a person who is happy in loud, quick places—wartime places. It isn't the war, only. I like to wait and plan. I'm not a very daring person."

"We are alike in that," Mrs. Anglin said, and her mouth was a little easier.

Margaret was warmed and encouraged. She began to speak more naturally and soon she began to hope, a vague, formless elation that overrode the fear curling its edges. Like a drunk, she found herself saying things she had not said to anyone: ". . . Sometimes I think about a girl I know—I just see her standing there, and I don't know why, but it frightens me. We weren't friends, but she worked in the next office and we sometimes had lunch together. She quit to go to work in the tube mill. I heard things about her: that she was bored there, and then that she had been fired for trying to set up a black market. When I saw her, she was with some sailors and she was drunk and so were they. She didn't see me. They were all talking about going swimming in the canal. . . ."

"The war confuses many young people. The first war was the same," Mrs. Anglin said. "I suppose that people's moral fiber isn't so strong as they think."

"It wasn't the moral part that scared me," Margaret said. "It was that she was so—so *unprotected*. When I think about her I wonder—what if they did go swimming and she got drowned—nobody would miss her or worry. She goes from place to place, but none of them is hers. She works at different jobs and meets different people, but none of them is hers. She learns different things, but none of the jobs or the learning is hers—she doesn't *belong* anywhere.''

Mrs. Anglin sighed. ''I think you are right when you say that you and William cannot be happy in times like these. There are people who are, you know. War brings change and some people enjoy change. It brings a kind of excitement to everything and makes it seem important and makes them seem more alive. People think they feel more deeply in war.''

Margaret sensed that something had been said against her, a slur made in that muffled, Hearing way, that seemed innocent enough, yet caused such dull, and lingering pain, such delayed pain. Where was the criminal word? Where was it hiding?

''How could people think that,'' she said, ''when men are being sent away, are in combat and maybe——''

Before she had finished speaking, she realized what she had done. Mrs. Anglin had anticipated her thought and had probably given it a picture: William lying dead somewhere. . . . So subtle and dangerous were simple words.

She was flustered now, and confused and she hurried away from that thought, too quickly, too recklessly, into what she had been avoiding at all costs, the monster at the center of the maze: ''I don't really think that people are excited at the thought of men having to fight, I'm thinking about the excitement of average people, not people like my mother and father, who had to have a war to——''

She had eluded that last turn in the maze for years to be defeated not by years, but by a single, simple minute of abandonment. A single minute of groping for poise, such a small and modest thing, this minute lapse of guarded consciousness. Mrs. Anglin was looking quizzically at her, waiting.

''You see,'' Margaret said, a sweat hot and cold together beginning at the neckband of her dress, ''it's because they are Deaf, my parents—deaf-mutes.''

''But I thought you said they worked in a war plant.''

''My mother works in a mill, making army clothes. My father is a printer.''

"Do you mean that they couldn't get work before the war?"

"No—it's just that now they're needed, really needed and people are glad to go to the extra trouble of understanding them. They're happier now than they've ever been and they're proud and people are proud of them, too." It sounded like an unforgivable reproach, a profanation of all loyalty. Had they been present and had she spit in their faces, the effect would have been no more shocking. Mrs. Anglin looked away for a minute and recovered her poise by taking time to put on both of her elegant kid gloves. Then she opened her purse to look for the embroidered handkerchief that was in it. Margaret stared in awe at the almost ritual motions of it all. She liked the way William's mother dressed—gloves, purse, hat and shoes all matching. She was a small, dainty woman with tiny feet and a face that looked stern even in repose. She must have known this, because her hats were never severe but always very neat and always worn with the softening bit of veiling. Looking up from the purse she said, "I hope that your parents' handicap will not keep us from becoming acquainted. I would like to meet and get to know them." Numbly, Margaret assured her that there would be a meeting, dinner, of course.

"We are simple people, plain people; we don't need anything like that." Abel said.

"Your father is right. I don't want someone coming around and looking down her nose at us. Besides, the parlor is empty; there is hardly any furniture in it."

"But I'm almost engaged to this boy, don't you understand? It's his family and they have to come—its the way people act."

"It's the way *Speaking* act, like moving-picture people."

"It's the way Deaf act! When Harlean Thomas was going with that boy, didn't the families go to dinner, meet each other, go out together? They were close—the families were brought close because of the marriage."

"There were Deaf in both families. Harlean's husband was raised with Deaf; his father and two of his brothers. The whole Deaf community knows them; they've always been part."

"You have to invite William's parents. It's your responsibility."

"I don't have the clothes or the time. And what do I want to meet them for? It is you, not me, who wants to go into that family."

"It is the bride's family who has the responsibility of making the wedding. You will have to meet them sometimes."

"They wouldn't have anything to say to us. They don't even *know* any Deaf!"

"Hearing need things too." Margaret was near tears. "You are always complaining that people judge you as Deaf first and a person later; that they say you are stupid because they don't understand your speech. You're Deaf when it suits you—and you're different when it suits you! Before William comes home—if he comes home—I want you to ask the Anglins to dinner: Mrs. Anglin and her daughter and son-in-law."

She saw the fear in their faces. It was a fear she had seen before; not sudden or violent, but slow, deep, abiding, and it flowed between them without gesture or glance. Outside had come in upon them again and there was no need for each to ask how the other felt about it. Very slowly and deliberately, Margaret faced her parents and closed her eyes.

15

BEFORE ANYTHING COULD BE DECIDED, William wrote that he was coming "home." He had wangled a trip back and three days in San Francisco, if Margaret could meet him there, if only she would meet him, please. . . .

Janice and Abel argued against it, but she went all the same. They couldn't keep her from the mysterious machine-like will of The War. She sent letters from many places on the way, saying that the train had been too crowded or that she had had to detour and take buses or that she had had to stop until another train came. She was gone for sixteen days and she came back drawn and exhausted—and she was married.

"Why?" and the hand shook down from its touch to the forehead in the Sign. Janice's hand shook because the world had shaken and was shaking out of control—war, money, death, bad-things. There were starving pregnant girls of thirteen and fourteen, pale and sick and frightened, trembling over the machines now. They seldom talked to each other—they were like some Deaf who never learned Sign and to whom the world was full of enemies.

"It was all the killing and dying, and the waiting and being afraid," Margaret answered. "He wanted to."

"I wonder," Abel said when he and Janice were alone, "if they married the way we did." It really was a cold thing he remembered, in spite of all their show of freedom. Words were taken and given, strange, inexplicable things in the harried impatience of a bored justice whose chin still had the shine of grease from his dinner.

Janice gave a numbed Sign. "Maybe."

"We'll have to invite those people to dinner now, and spend the evening. All the evening."

"She went and came back," Janice said, "without a word more than telling us."

"Margaret will be here. We will write things until we see if they are made angry or ashamed by Sign. I will wear my hearing aid."

Janice wasn't paying attention. She was seeing a memory of the green trees and sun-spattered days of a summer so far away it seemed to be imagined more than remembered. In this new house there were trees outside the window of the bedroom. If she turned off the light and drew the curtain, she could see their branch ends, too many to count, and a little frightening, they whipped so stiffly in the cold. How strange it felt to have so sharp a picture of summer that the winter night and its branches outside this window seemed the dream and the unreal thing. Now the wind seemed to move in summer branches of wide-webbed maple leaves, and sun-dots waved and spun, dotting her and the man beside her with circles and squares of light, cool for the shadows. What time was that, and why was she remembering it now, after years whose summers were only stale sweat and machine oil baking together in the noon-hours and the tired heat of evening? It was That Summer, that single summer when she had not been afraid. She looked around at the room. It was a miracle that it should belong to them—such a room, such a house, on such a street. Why didn't the fear go away, then, after they had come so far; when they owned what they had once only dreamed of? The summer day evaporated, the sun-dapples and the warmth sank and Janice shivered and crossed her arms over her breasts, hugging the cold away, now certain of winter.

The guests: three of them. Three strangers. Three Hearing. In twenty-four years of married life, Janice had never entertained any more than two people, and never any Hearing, not of the Deaf world at all. Every night Margaret would come home and there would be another round of doubts and complaints. Together they would re-plan the dinner and the moves involved in serving, an elaborate dance of time passing : cold things warming and warm things cooling, and Margaret would go to work the next day and greet Janice in the evening with a complete reversal of the plans. They must be changed, begun all over again, because of some insignificant possibility they had not foreseen that morning. When the furniture had been rearranged four or five times, the dinner plans set and topics of conversation gone over for their suitability, there was a three-day discussion of what to wear. Gray or colors, severe or frilly, the beads or no beads? Into this discussion Abel came also, choosing and re-choosing each of his three ties over and over.

But no one could hold the night away, and in the end, it came and everyone sat against the walls like guards, set to defend one another's smiling. They smiled continually, relentlessly, between dry lips, their eyes lonely above the smiling. Janice had finally decided on her good black dress, but it had a shabby look beside the neat faille outfit set off in white that Mrs. Anglin wore, and Margaret felt strange when her sister-in-law called her Mrs. Anglin also. She knew that William's urgency in marrying her was impersonal, really, and not connected with love so much as it was with fear. His life had been so changed that he felt himself being lost, melted into another element, and he was struggling to make sure of any one or anything by which he could mark his way. In endless boredom (he had called it "waiting for the war") imagination ate vast, unnatural canyons into reality. Dreams became tyrants, hopes talismans against the wasting months. And the upshot of it all was that here she stood alone with the congratulations and gifts and this unwilling wedding dinner, without a groom. Margaret was beginning to have her own fears of the unnatural reality. If only Janice would stop smiling and say something—even if it wasn't easily said or the answer mistakenly heard; even if it had to be written out. . . . She had a sudden horrifying picture of that smile of her mother's, enduring, hopeless and inopportune, frozen, while age came and death and the flesh melted and the delicate bones fell inward and the skeleton went to dust—the teeth, smiling on alone. She shivered and felt sick. It was bad, evil to have such thoughts. Once again she threw herself resolutely into conversation like a suicide off a cliff. They had done with the winter, the weather, the war and William (now in the Aleutians), the quality of army jackets and the progress of the printing trade.

A brief light was struck when the brother-in-law made a pleasant comment about the parlor, but after a moment of more smiling and nodding that light flickered and was gone.

There had been a terrible argument about the language they would use. Janice had stated flatly that she would not Sign. Abel had wanted to, but wanted to lip-read the Anglins, using Margaret as interpreter for his side of the conversation. Margaret had begged for a natural flow of Sign and words, such as they often used with the mixed group at church, in which Sign gave an additional clue to their difficult words and a grace to the ugliness of their sound. Janice would not be changed. "At church everyone has Deaf in the family——"

"But now the Anglins have Deaf in the family, too."

"Not the same thing, not at all. We know how Hearing are ashamed of the Deaf in their families." It was too old an argument, too deep a reservation, too much now.

"Not all of them are," Margaret said. "Not all of the Deafness of the . . ." She could not go on; she had no words for the feeling.

So Janice sat, bolt upright, grinning and on the edge of hysteria. Mrs. Anglin had come in so solidly, so forcefully, so fronted—a gray feathered hat and little gray purse and gray gloves with tiny buttons. Behind her the lesser in-laws with measuring eyes. No sooner did Mrs. Anglin begin to speak than Janice knew the thing was hopeless. The woman moved her lips with ladylike gentility, which meant that she moved them barely at all. Often, a modest, well-manicured hand would rise and discreetly cover the hard-looking lines of her mouth. Beside her, Abel was succeeding a bit better and it was to him and to Margaret that the sister and brother-in-law were trying to speak. When Janice at last had the excuse to break free, she left for the kitchen, visibly relieved. Behind the door she humored himself with a rapid muttering of dissatisfaction. Why didn't Margaret see how foolish it was to make this thing? Yes, even if it was the correct thing—Abel was always asking his friends at church about that—now, just the word from Margaret that this was to be done and off he went to his high friends. He was always asking opinions of the people he respected, big-word people, the educated ones, who had Hearing friends and made their way easily in that world. And, what had it all come to? She turned disgustedly to her work. She was getting as bad as Abel, talking to herself. The minister had a joke that made her smile: "Deaf women are nice, and Deaf men stay out of trouble because they can't gossip while they work." It wasn't true, and everyone knew it; it was a Joke on Hearing, who thought it was true. It was a Joke on those Talking ones out in the parlor.

She would have to go out soon—it was too long to stay away, safe in the kitchen. She had not felt so deaf in many years. All the time of her working, Margaret's growing up, all the times of the clinics and the doctors, she had gone somehow protected. Only now, with those Hearing out in the other room did she realize how well she and Abel had protected themselves from that world of Strangers. She had taken ridicule as an ordinary worker on the sewing floor. People sometimes laughed or made jokes, but she had never bothered trying to read what they said and she had made herself mind-deaf to their existence and their jokes. As supervisor, her quickness at the machine put her above the laughter and comments of the girls. She even sat above them now, on a raised place so that she could look out over the floor and spot trouble. What good was it now, all of that, and the clothes and house and freedom from the shame of the Court? There were other judges now, sitting out in the parlor, saying, "No one is alone who does not deserve to be alone. No one is alone who is not unfit. You are stupid and your minds are deaf." She sighed and picked up her tray reluctantly, to bring the food into the dining room.

Dinner began with agonizing formality. The in-laws wished to speak, but feeling it excluded the Ryders, grew shy and stopped. Janice and Abel, long trained to see the hints of half-formed movements and unconscious expressions, kept up a continual, subtle, surveillance of the table and the passage of food and plates. It banked the need for speech. It betrayed the Hearing. By the end of the meal the silence was growing cold and sour in Margaret's ears and the gestures subtle but disturbing. The Anglins, needing the quiet, random, formless communion of the Hearing, found themselves staring grimly at these stunted strangers. Margaret, who seemed unable to do anything but watch, found herself staring at the scene with a kind of frozen awe. Janice had disappeared into the kitchen again and out of the corner of her eye Margaret saw Abel beginning to get up. Dessert and coffee had still to be served.

She asked a question, something silly, and barely heard the answer. In the unsounded sigh of polite relief from the Anglins she talked on, asked and answered questions, defending the lone outpost at the table which her parents had left to her. Hoping they would come out of the kitchen before their absence became unbearable, Margaret's eyes kept straying toward the mirror on the opposite wall. The kitchen door was open and she could look into the mirror, and see a few feet inside. She saw her parents come forward into the mirror. They had been fighting in there. Almost at the door, they went on, eyes wild, bodies tense, and a bitterly angry spate of words thrown back and forth. The words were loud, screaming even, and Margaret's head began to ache with the clamor in the kitchen and the loudly hostile silence of the dining room. There was no sound anywhere. In that silence she waited for the pushes, the slaps, the blows. Their world, Janice's and Abel's, was concrete and physical; their anger not less so. The slaps would sound like cannon, the blows like earthquakes in this terrible Dumb-Supper.

Then their movement in the mirror caught Mrs. Anglin's eye, even as Margaret was struggling to pull her glance away from it. The in-laws on the other side of the table saw where the attention had wandered and turned to look directly into the kitchen. Everyone knew that it was a violation of manners and even of decency to do this, but their strangeness and frustration made the manners seem unreal, as unreal as the situation and the grinning, mindless, Deaf people who had brought it all on them. Now they sat staring, enchanted, aware for the first time of Janice and Abel as living beings, totally alive and as real as they were themselves. Face to face they stood, dancing at each other, eyes, lips, fingers, bodies, all impatience and anger.

At last Mrs. Anglin recovered herself and turned from the mirror. "Margaret, is there something we can do to help?" Her harsh face had softened, the brow wrinkled with concern, and Margaret felt a memory of the ease she had had for only one moment before in the presence of William's mother. It had been a very costly moment, that lunch time of confiding and she was frightened for another. The first had caused this miserable evening and forced it on all of them, unaware, unready.

She turned to her mother-in-law and her voice was low and careful: "It is a family disagreement, but part of it has to do with drinks. They—my parents don't know if they can ask you to have something to drink." Quickly, she chose among the sharp, broken pieces of the argument. "Our church is generally against alcohol; my mother doesn't drink at all, but my father likes to have something after dinner on special occasions."

"A drink would be fine," Mrs. Anglin whispered, "just fine." She spoke comfortingly, placating the fury of the gestures. Margaret was deeply grateful that they had understood none of what Janice and Abel had said. The argument had raked over every fault in the Anglins that trained eyes could find. She excused herself and disappeared into the kitchen, sweeping Janice and Abel out of the mirror with her.

In a moment Abel was hurried into the dining room with a bottle of brandy and his small special glass. He went back for four fruit-juice glasses which he then set down before the silent guests. Everyone sat perfectly still and looked straight ahead. Nothing was said.

Abel poured one inch of brandy into the juice glasses and filled his special glass full. This he gave to Mrs. Anglin and was handing the others around when Janice, her eyes lowered, her mouth crimped defensively, came in with a tray and began to clear the dishes from the table. Out of habit, Mrs. Anglin and her daughter gathered themselves to rise, but Janice shook her head at them, hard, and they subsided into their places. Margaret saw and tried to catch her mother's eye. The Anglins were looking a little terrified. Abel had not sat down and now he was signaling to Margaret. She read his meaning and the knot of anxiety tightened down again. "My father wants to make a toast . . ."

All the faces turned at once, the expressions suddenly keen and alert. There was a minute of waiting and then he began to speak to them, his Sign slow, balanced and precise. Margaret watched in amazement, translating automatically but unable to convey the difference between the butchered and debased Sign that was his ordinary speech and this haunting and evocative flow of language. The Signs were formal and complete, and they had a grace and subtlety that she had never seen even in the minister's hands; there was also a rhythm, a long, slow measuring made not in beats but in turnings, small lifts and lowerings of the hand in the way that the Deaf Signed songs or poetry. For whom was this being made, all this secret eloquence if not for her alone?

"My father wishes to say—he says—he has heard that on important holidays it is correct for a man to say over his drink what he wishes for the people who are close to him— who are in his thoughts. He says he wants—to—observe all the things that are necessary and correct." She found that her face was contorted with the effort of trying to bring to them the cadence of his words and their quality of yearning. "When Hearing have a child and she grows to be a woman and is married, father—mother—the parents cry at the wedding because she is leaving them and they know they will be lonely for her. When Deaf have such a child, a Hearing child, she grows up in the Hearing world, and when she is married, mother and father do not cry. When the Hearing child leaves the house of the Deaf, their mouths also are taken away from them and their ears are taken away and the child also, whom they love. For this, tears are not enough. So they sit in the darkness because"—the words stopped abruptly, and then began again—"I meant . . . my father says he meant to say something else, to say what was correct for this occasion which is of so great importance. He has asked many people about what is proper and has looked in different books to find out the custom. He did not understand these sayings and did not want to say anything that he did not understand. Instead, he says he will tell you something he does understand and that will make you happy and not being afraid. His wife was made deaf when she was born because of measles her mother had. He is deaf inherited from his father, but because both of his children were born Hearing, the doctors say there is very little chance of more Deafs in the family. He says he wrote letters to make sure of these things to tell you because Hearing are afraid, and you must not be afraid when the young p-people have ch-children . . ." She hesitated, beginning to stammer. The Anglins smiled and then chuckled as the heat of blood went up, reddening Margaret's face from throat to scalp.

Abel, seeing laughter, looked about him quickly, trying to sense the mood of it, but when he saw Margaret, now almost purple, he laughed himself and said, "Don't *you* be afraid." When Margaret had stumbled in translating his Signs, everyone laughed aloud and when they were quiet again, they found themselves looking not at a deaf man and his interpreter but at a father and daughter.

"My father wants to say now that he hopes for everyone here to have everything for a good life always: food and their family and work to do and peace and also he wishes these things to William."

Abel raised his glass and drank, and everyone murmured something and drank also. They had been moved by Abel's words and by the poetry and beauty of his Signs and they wanted to show him that they were comfortable now in his presence. The women leaned back a bit in their corsets as though to relax and they offered Margaret small, delicate observations to translate—the easy-seeming but still careful small talk of the measuring time. Margaret was busy with translation; so busy that when Mrs. Anglin asked her opinion on what they were discussing, she had to admit that among all the speakers she hadn't had time to decide what she thought. It proved to be the easing thing—the sister-in-law laughed and said she didn't wonder, and the women sipped their brandies again and unconsciously drew a little away from the men to be more at ease talking among themselves. Janice had come back and sat down with them, having brought in the coffee and served it and they asked her about her work at the plant and her plans for the garden in back of the house. She answered in quick, restrained snatches, tinily, tinily fingered, so as to make as little movement as possible. After Abel's full grandeur her shyness-of-hand seemed charming and feminine, old-fashioned in these new days, and so, lovable.

When everyone was finished with the coffee, Janice got up and this time the other women got up with her and waved away her head-shaking and began to help clear away the remaining dishes and the coffee things. They went back and forth from the kitchen, working in the slow, relaxed pace of after dinner, the Anglin women murmuring to each other in comfortable half-heard tones, the unnecessary, reassuring undertone of women working: "I'll just take this platter." "Uhmm. These are nice shakers. I lost one of the set I had." "Oh, did you?" "Do you want to put these napkins down there?" "Uhmnn."

Whenever they were ready with a load of platters or dishes, they waited for Janice to go back into the kitchen. They were not yet so comfortable in her house that they would enter her kitchen alone.

Mrs. Anglin had two cups and saucers and she picked up the coffeepot with her free hand and began to move forward. Janice had stopped and half-turned and Mrs. Anglin cried, "Watch out—this is still hot!" The movement of Janice's arm did not stop. Mrs. Anglin found herself blocked by the table; she couldn't move back. Janice's arm was still moving around with her turning. "Get back, look out, you'll get burned!"

Margaret, coming from the kitchen heard her mother-in-law cry out and looked up too late to see anything but her expression of irritation giving way to one of fascinated horror. Janice's upper arm was stopped firmly against the hot side of the coffeepot. With a strangle-sound she pulled away violently and cutlery scattered from the plate she was still holding. The reflex movement had turned her around and she was facing Mrs. Anglin with a wounded vulnerable expression, like a child beaten for no reason. She touched the arm gingerly. The flesh had gone white and then red and even now an angry red blotch was coming out plainly. Mrs. Anglin's voice sounded pettish. She felt guilty and was also perhaps at the end of her patience with the evening.

"I told you . . . I called out and you—well, you just *stood* there!" Her face had lost all its softness again. "Why didn't you get out of the way? I *told* you——"

Margaret had come around to Mrs. Anglin's side and was Signing gently to Janice: "She told you to get out of the way, but you didn't hear her." Janice opened a slow, half-frightened smile, and said in her tiny Sign, "I'm sorry—it's not a bad burn. It only startled me."

Mrs. Anglin looked around in wonder and then her hand came up to her face. "How could I have done that? You told me she was deaf—that both your parents were deaf. I saw your father making the Signs but somehow, somehow I didn't *believe*—I didn't really *believe* it could be. Is it possible, really possible that a person can not *hear* at all?"

"Yes," Margaret said, "it is possible."

"And there's just silence, nothing but dead silence always?"

"I don't know," Margaret said, "but I know that when people talk my parents only see mouths moving. Sometimes they see a word here and there, or recognize a sentence or two, but those words are not real to them. Not the way Sign is real."

Mrs. Anglin shook her head and the hand went in its habit before her mouth. "You poor girl," she said to Margaret. "You poor, poor girl."

16

PEOPLE HAD GOTTEN USED TO the wide swings of expectation and anguish, rumors, propaganda posters, their dead, war movies and pleasures as hectic as an orgy of prisoners. When William came home, it was to a country at two removes from the one he had left. He had been wounded by shrapnel, some of which was still buried in his back and shoulders. He spoke of the wounding in a matter-of-fact almost bored way, which surprised Margaret, to whom a diet of movie heroes had offered no preparation. It was a "ticket home," he said, the wound everyone prayed for and a few got—serious enough to mean no more combat and not so serious as to maim the body or shatter the mind. That didn't sound like the war movies or like William, and Margaret didn't know what to answer to it.

For a long time after he left the hospital he stayed at his mother's house, "resting," and there was an aura of remoteness and hopeless weariness about him. Margaret made a habit of going to see him after work and there they would sit formally opposite each other at the kitchen table. After the first embraces, cautiously, because of his still painful injuries, he had not touched her and when she tried reaching toward him, he seemed to shrink away. He felt unreal, he said; the war seemed unreal and he had been unreal in it, fighting and waiting and running and waiting again, more bored than frightened, more like a shadow than a person. Once or twice he had had the sensation of having stumbled into someone else's life and of having to keep it inhabited by his shadow until the real owner should come back to claim it. Now that he was home and in his own life again, he seemed to find himself a stranger here as well. Sometimes he would wander the city and would stop in at Patman & Rulliger to see Margaret. If she had lunch with him, he would look around and drum his fingers in a perpetual restless impatience. Thinking back, she could hardly remember what he had been like before the war.

The War. She didn't need to be told that war was savage. She had thought William might come back a savage man; she had been a little afraid of that, having seen in newsreels the rows of men at bayonet practice, over and over, the narrator said, until killing became natural and instinctive.

Collie Beatty at the office had been told never to come up quietly behind her brother; to keep him from sudden loud noises, to move slowly in his presence. Collie's brother had been discharged with what were called "war nerves," but the symbol of him seemed true for them all—someone who might hear a door slam or a dish fall and revert to the death-trained savage of the newsreels, a blooded killer, wary and primitive on the forest trails.

Margaret had been prepared for anything but the subtly provoking invalidism she found in William. Sometimes in the evenings she would read his letters over, letters written from many places at all times of the day and night, but always the same. In every one there was talk of plans for the future, for "home." She would read them all and then put them away, shaking her head incredulously. This *was* home, now *was* the the future, and he seemed unable even to remember the plans that had taken up so much of his thoughts. Having to make any choice or decision upset him. With an almost cavalier indifference he would leave everything up to her, growing balky and miserable when her ideas did not please him.

It was not hard for her parents to show sympathy, to tell her to be patient. They themselves felt patient; Margaret was still at home. The parting that Janice and Abel feared in the blackout nights and in all their vague and haunting half-sleep thoughts had been put off. The time had gone by so delicately that it was not even mentioned. They felt clever not to mention it, to let the days grow and grow until it was possible, now, to hope that William would leave Margaret alone and go back to his cold mother.

Abel said that it would be all right if William came to live with them, although they had barely seen him since his homecoming. It was a hope to which he hesitated to put words; a lame, orphan hope, wandering aimlessly across the mind. It came and then came again, and when it came for the third time, it was not alone: William will come to live with us. He will learn Sign and soon he will come and be in the printshop, and there he will see the reasons for the great respect I have—all the men asking me to put my hands to their machines. Margaret will stay and keep the house when Janice works and on Saturday and Sunday we will be together and soon they will join the church and when they come home from church with us, we will walk again, in the four sections of the city. So pleasant. It will be so pleasant to sit on the porch in afternoons that seem always like summer. Until it is dark and we can no longer see to gossip. . . . In four years or five there will be a little baby and then all the time to love it, that we did not have before. That baby will not fall down; it will be protected always by people with enough ease never to be impatient or too tired or making mistakes. . . .

As soon as the details of the future took on form and became peopled and real, Margaret began, with the perverse cruelty of Hearing, to remind them of her own present difficulties. When they criticized her for visiting at William's house instead of having him come to see her (How will he come to stay if she does not help him to see that he must come?), she told them that he was too restless to be a good visitor. Once or twice he did come and he tried to learn one or two Signs, but now he had no concentration and no real interest in it, and his way of speaking, like his mother's, made him almost impossible to lip-read. Sometimes Abel saw Margaret with swollen eyes that meant she had been crying and then he tried to tell her that this was foolish and that soon, so soon, the problems would go away and be over. During these times she would twist her wedding ring on her finger and say that she wanted to be a wife, but that William did not want a wife, and that he saw her now as a responsibility, a weight he could not carry. She had never wanted it to be like this, she said. Then she would shake her head and twist her ring and move back into her room to the mysterious spell of the radio.

Then, one day there was a note. It said something about William, and some government thing and some college, so that she wouldn't be home for supper. That was simple. The next day another note about student housing, but that, too, was only that she wouldn't be home for supper. On the third day she was gone; her clothes, her radio, carried away eagerly, eagerly into a car that came from magic and was driven by a friend (shake hands; how you do? . . . nod-and-smile, and the mouth going-going) who backed down the steps and went into the car and she was all gone, waving and smiling from the front seat with William and his friend, all so fast it was almost leaving painted lines of wind like in the funny papers. Gone. Forty miles to the college. Another country. Forever.

The days began to cover over that car and that waving hand, although Abel often looked at the place where it had stood parked while Margaret ran up and got her packages and bundle of clothes. The memory of it lay dull and heavy, waiting for the time before Janice and Abel went to sleep and the time they woke up. They never spoke of it, or of the hope they had had before, but one day at the dinner table, Janice suddenly cried out at him, "She was out all night, all night with him!"

"But they were married. If she was with him, there is nothing wrong——"

"She says they are married, but I never saw a marriage. She had that paper and a ring, but anyone can make a paper and anyone can buy a ring!"

"William is going to the college. She told us that. She has to go with him—she is his wife."

"I don't like him. He has no feelings. She will be pregnant and then he will go and be a soldier again and be killing people."

"Margaret said he will go and be in college. That way she

will be with the fine people, educated people and she will learn things. Maybe she will have important families as her friends. . . ."

"How can that be, when she is your daughter and my daughter?"

They got letters. The letters were like sparks by which they tried to warm themselves. Margaret and William had found a place to live. They were lucky in this, Margaret said, because now that the colleges were accepting men under the GI Bill of Rights, many soldiers were coming to the campuses and with the war still on, nothing was being built for them. She had found a job as a secretary in a bank, she said. It was very dull, but something better might come along.

Margaret's letters always seemed quickly written and cheerful and a little hard; letters that were all about what she and William did, as though describing their movements was covering up something else, a sin in what they had become. The words were being used to hide them. Perhaps it was the fault of the writing itself; written words never held the meaning that Sign did; a person could not really trust the reality in the written thing. That was why the letters were only a phantom comfort. The loneliness of Janice and Abel increased instead of diminishing into habit.

One Saturday, Abel woke early and when Janice opened her eyes, she found him sitting up in bed, studying a folded sheet of paper. She twitched the bottom of it to get his attention: "What is that?"

"Schedule for the buses. I went to the depot yesterday and got it."

"Where do you want to go?"

"I want to go and see Margaret."

Because of the War there was no Sunday bus to many places, but there was one from downtown to the University. "Here," he said. "See—it runs in the morning—seven fifty-five—and comes back in the night." He read the times of departure and arrival with a look of satisfaction, as though he had created it years ago for his own pleasure and was now sitting back to reap the benefits of his forethought. "The bus makes seven stops, and comes to University at nine twenty-five.''

"Sunday?"

"Yes, here it says Sunday. I want to go tomorrow."

Janice began to fuss. When could they eat breakfast, if they had to go so early? The streetcars were far apart on Sunday morning and it would take longer to get downtown. What about lunch and supper? What would the University be like, and how would they be able to find Margaret and William in that strange place? Maybe there were rules or manners that they did not know—hadn't they been careful over the years to learn to avoid those bad things? Had he forgotten so soon the disappointments and embarrassments of such bad times? Had he forgotten Margaret's dinner party? Didn't that prove how dangerous things could be that looked so simple? And what about——

At last he waved her hands away and said shortly, "I'm going. You can come or not."

Sunday was bright and crack-cold. They had ridden down to the bus depot in the winter's darkness, having set the alarm for five. Since Margaret's leaving they had tried many different ways of waking up on time, finally settling on an extremely cheap alarm clock which they put into the bed, near the foot. When the clock was ready, the vibration caused it to flip itself and buzz against any part of their bodies that it touched. They had been so nerved for the early waking that as soon as the bone-ringing buzz touched Abel's shin and then Janice's toe, both of them leapt from the bed in shock, having forgotten where they were or who, and knowing only the dim guilt of not knowing. When they came to themselves, they began to dress quickly in the dark. Janice wanted to warn about the weather, but it was not yet light enough for speech, nor would it be until they were on their way downtown. She was afraid of all of it and quickly, unseen, cursed the bus that was going to take them away, head-on into that wall of strangeness. In the near dark, she could feel her face getting stiff and tight with resentment. She wanted him to see it, but he couldn't, and even later, when they sat in the kitchen for a quick cup of coffee, he seemed determined not to notice any of the loud Signs of her discontent.

They left the house quickly and walked the way to the car tracks in light that was still not yet day. It gave them a feeling of awe, as though they had been admitted to a place beyond darkness and daylight, where the day was still waiting to take up its rhythm.

The bus to the University was old but lively. There were some young people going back early from weekends at home, and servicemen, some hefting great bulging duffel bags on their shoulders. There were one or two salesmen with battered sample cases and an old lady who seemed to be carrying all the possessions of a long lifetime. She moved and fretted among a dozen falling parcels.

At eight the bus began to move. Soon it was going swiftly through the empty streets of the city, turning north two blocks from the mill and crossing the bridge over the railroad yards. Abel jostled Janice's elbow and motioned with his head to the high school where Margaret had gone and which the bus was passing as quickly as if it were no more important than any other building. It looked smaller than Janice had remembered it, and dirtier. The days when Margaret had been there seemed so far in the past that it was hard to recall them at all and Janice felt a strange relief in passing the school and going on beyond the familiar streets to a road which they had never traveled. She liked looking out at the starved, bare trees and the frozen ground, patched with gray snow. She liked it because she was sitting well dressed and warm in the bone-sound of the vibrating motor. The floor of the bus was thin and the heat from the motor pounded up through some vent under the seat, while the cold only moved sluggishly and sullenly along the floor. The mood of the people on the bus was cheerful. Janice and Abel could see them smiling and talking to one another and as the time went on, the bus stopped for many farm people dressed in their Sunday outfits. She saw Abel looking at them and understood that he must be remembering his own farm days. "They're going to church," he said, very small and from his lap, so as not to be seen. "Someone will drive them back in a car, afterwards, maybe, but they don't want to impose anyone to bring them.''

"Impose?'' she spelled it *in*pose.

"It's like depend.'' He had wanted to say "make responsible,'' but responsible was a Sign on the shoulder and he didn't want to draw attention by it. Besides, he wasn't too sure himself. The minister had used it once or twice and he had thought he understood. Now he wasn't sure. Janice looked at the farm people as they sat prim and apart from the soldiers and the collegers. The women leaned over and spoke now and then among themselves, but there was no laughter. The clothes they wore seemed strange and fantastic to her, ancient styles that had been mismade even when they were in the fashion, their lines and details jarring because they had been copied but not understood. She remembered suddenly a talk the new minister had given when he first came to take over the Deaf church. Like Mr. Maartens before him, he was a Hearing and had learned his Sign not from Deaf, but from a school. Sometimes he made mistakes and gave the wrong Signs and once his hands had moved toward and not away from one another in a Sign and it was a dirty Sign, which he had never seen. All the Deaf knew what he was trying to say, and no one laughed, but now three years later, Janice was remembering that mismade Sign, like the mismade clothes that were not understood, and thinking again how hard some of the Deaf worked to fight against their faces not to laugh, she began to laugh, trembling beside Abel, her face breaking all its hardened lines, her eyes filling with tears.

"What?'' he asked, as her head went down. He saw she could not see his Sign; she was weeping beyond help, onto her dress, shaking again as new things came to her, or as she imagined the different holy looks on the minister's face. The bus stopped for more people and Janice tried to stop her thoughts, wiping her eyes and blowing her nose. Abel kept asking what had been so funny and she was not able to tell him, so that when the bus started again they were sitting as stiffly as they had been before.

The University was the last stop of all, and everyone got out. Janice and Abel stood and watched everyone walking away to different places; the people all seemed sure of where they were going and what they would find. Abel looked but could not see the University or any building that seemed so important. After a while the bus turned around and began to go away and they still stood.

"Let's walk at least, try somewhere," Abel said. So they began to walk, keeping close together, looking for any sign or clue, even a wise-looking person in a flowing robe, whom they might follow.

After turning many ways, first north and then east, they came to a large park, all snowy, but with paved ways shoveled clean. There were great trees in this park and some houses and other buildings. When they looked on to the end of the park and saw a great building with white columns, and stone designs on the roof and many low steps, Abel smiled knowingly: "This, this here is the University and we came into it and did not know."

Janice looked around. It still looked like a park, a big park. They stood looking at the long, shoveled walkways and the buildings. It was surely a favored place. These buildings, all around, were churches of the mind. On the walkways between them scholars walked, full of knowledge and power.

They began to follow the path themselves, toward the great column-building at the end, and as they went, the ways parted and they saw other buildings to the right and left, buildings like big courts or post offices. They walked on with care, holding each other's arms in case the power that had been gathered in the walkways from the thousands of scholars might overwhelm them. Only a few young people were walking here and there, and none passed them. At last Janice and Abel had no choice but to show the address on Margaret's letter, and so they did, catching up with a tall boy in a leather flyer's cap with sheepskin ears. He talked to them and pointed and then saw that they were not able to understand him. Abel let him take the precious slip of paper, thinking that he was going to write something on it, but when the boy gave it back they saw that he had drawn a little map for them. This map showed them that the place where Margaret and William lived was not in the University at all.

They began to walk again, following the awful truth of the map, away from where Margaret had promised, and into the lie she had told. William did not live at the University; he lived at another place; blocks away from its wisdom and power. That young man had been in the army like William. Like William he had seen evil things and ugliness, but *he* was in the University, and William had lied, only lied.

There was nothing else to do but to follow the little map. They walked out of the University grounds and up a street that looked like any ordinary street and was lined with stores and offices. At the end of the block they turned again and walked the four blocks that were shown on the map. There were large old houses on the side streets, some of them had strange marks over the doors but as Janice and Abel walked on, the houses seemed less well kept and many of the backyards had other houses, small ones growing in them, or trailer and sheds that had been pulled up behind and in which there seemed to be people living also. There were long strings of washlines back of the houses, and the lines made Janice think of Vandalia Street. She shuddered as they went on. At the corner of the block they turned left again and there was the name: South McKinley.

The first house they came to had the number 313. There was a whole gathering of baby carriages, bicycles and wagons cluttering the small front porch, and a woman coming out to shake a rug over the porch railing looked at them suspiciously from under a writhing mass of curlers that pinched her forehead white. Slowly Abel and Janice went up the walk; she held the rug like a bullfighter, against them, because they were enemies and were attacking. When they came to the porch railing, they showed the little card that they had written with William's name on it. The woman swept the card with her eyes and not taking her hands from the rug, jerked her head around like a nervous horse. She was chewing gum, so they did not know whether or not she had spoken also, but after a moment standing in the hard light of her stare, they realized she must have meant them to go around to the back of the house. How cold it was today! The University was no more than five or six blocks away, and yet it was not so cold there—only brisk and refreshing. Here it was cold, bitter cold. They huddled inside their coats and began to walk across the frozen, littered front-yard path around to the back of the house.

Margaret had awakened early to the room's accustomed blackness and a jarring cold. Damn it, the window again! She would have to struggle out from her place between William and the wall and go to the end of the bed. It was two steps across the freezing floor to the other side of the room where the slack and stubborn window gaped open. She hated that window. It was a cunning, malicious window, leering or playing blind or staring, dropped vacantly, with an idiot's false innocence while the wind rode down on them from the unprotected north. During the day it let in so little light that they had to keep a lamp on even when the sun was bright outside. It stuck when they needed it open and fell apart on cold nights to leave them to the winter. Margaret's teeth were chattering as she wrestled the warped frame up, and put the propping stick against it, wedging it back hard with the heel of her hand. Then she had raced for the bed again and the fugitive warmth she had remembered leaving there. It was almost gone. Curled up and shivering, waiting to fall asleep again, she thought about this "place" of theirs. What an awful hole it was! What a dismal, squalid place, and how lucky they had been to get it!

Betty Schilling and her husband had a bigger one, but they and their clothes and everything they possessed carried a faint but penetrating aura of wet feathers and chicken dung which no amount of sanding, painting or washing could remove from the walls and floors. . . . The kids at the stable couldn't even eat in their thinly partitioned "apartments." They, too, had a special, identifying hint of odor about them, especially in wet weather. They had a communal kitchen shack downwind and their privacy was almost nonexistent because of the way in which the stalls had been placed. Each stall was now a "bedroom," which somehow commanded the going price as an "apartment." William had worked so hard to get this shack. It was dark, dank and somber and there was no water—

you had to go to the "big house" to bathe or wash—but they had a fair amount of quiet for William to study in and they didn't feel embarrassed to go to a movie when it was raining. William had nailed some old boards over the bad places in the roof and except for the continual darkness . . . She was pulled away, into sleep.

Then there was a pounding. They heard it as an addition to their separate half-waking dreams. Finally its crude persistence pulled them away from sleep. William called out for it to wait a minute, but it only kept on. He groaned, turned in the dark and fumbled for the string that lit the overhead bulb. "Jesus——!" He stopped. He had to make a conscious effort at times to get out of the habit of using the universal modifiers of army life. "It's ten thirty, Marge. Someone——"

At that moment the door, a makeshift of scrap wood and salvaged nails gave at one of its panels and sent a piece of wood bouncing across the floor, a cut of light following after it.

"What the hell——" The door was next to the bed and William leaned out and opened it.

There stood the Ryders in their elaborate Sunday care, new hats and faces of frozen disbelief. Margaret was sitting up by now, clutching the blanket around her for warmth. "Your parents," William said very quietly, "seem to be paying us a visit."

"I'll take care of them. You'd better get up and fix the door."

He muttered something which she did not hear and got out of bed. He had been used to sleeping in his underwear in the army. As he began quickly but matter-of-factly to get into shoes and socks, he saw an even further narrowing of the visitors' faces. The room was tiny. The bed and table and two chairs filled it almost entirely and with Janice and Abel now inside the door, there was a feeling of terrible crowding. William went to the "kitchen"—a shelf on the other side of the room where an electric hot plate stood beside the random assortment of plates and cups and the two dishpans. On the floor were the buckets of water each with a delicate aureole of ice at its edges.

Margaret put on the coat, which she kept at the foot of the bed, trying to keep her shivering unobtrusive as parts of her body touched the icy lining.

"Please sit down—over there by the table. . . ."

The twin stares moved away to the two chairs, found them and returned to her. William had finished dressing and put some water up to heat for coffee.

"Marge"—he looked boyish and a little lost—"I'd better go fix the door, huh?"

"I think so."

"Everything okay?"

She nodded and he went past the judges on tiptoe as though his footfall, even unheard, might somehow offend. Because he had been offended and he was angry, too. Margaret saw it without knowing how. It wasn't in any action or expression but it was there all the same—anger and hurt pride, and with it all, a desire deeper than momentary anger, to be respected, seen as a man. She sighed. Her husband was a toughened, competent fighter who had learned a dozen kinds of patience, had passed through horrors and kept his mind whole, had endured the terrors of war and the pain of wounds, and yet, confronted with these scary Sunday guests in the best married-students' quarters in town, he fell back into a boyish resentment and confusion.

"We were sleeping late," Margaret said to her parents. "We had a late night last night."

They sat still, their faces set.

William came back with a hammer and some nails and a piece of board. "Tell them we don't always lie around like this. . . ."

Margaret translated dutifully and they nodded. The words were betraying her again. The Sign made it look as though he had meant not always, but often, usually.

"What happened to him?" Abel's hands were tight.

"Nothing—we're fine."

"You told us he was going to the University."

"He is."

"College people do not live like this. We know. We have been to the College. This morning."

"You don't understand," Margaret said. "The problem is not money; it is that there are no places for married students, for all the people who are now able to go to college on the Government's plan."

"I don't like this place," Janice said, looking around. "This place is too small, and you surely have mice here and roaches, too. College people don't live in places like this."

The old stubbornness was hardening her face. Margaret noticed that she had put on weight in the last few months. It made her seem taller and more formidable. Janice's section had won two production pennants from the Government. She saw a picture of her mother, still more of a stranger on her little raised platform, scanning the work floor relentlessly to catch the girl who was stealing thread or slacking off or spending too much time in the new lounge.

"He is lying to you," Janice said. "Or you are lying to us because of him. This is a bad place." She looked all around again, confirming, with her supervisor's eye. William had turned from the half-fixed door to watch them. How intense they seemed. He turned to the work again, relieved for it.

"Don't you see?" Margaret said. "Things are this way for all the married students. Because of the War there aren't any new houses. This is one of the best places, really."

She wanted to show them in some way that she and William both felt—wanted to feel—that this was starting place for them—although who could be sure? Who could really be sure? "You and father weren't rich or successful when you began. . . ." She had hoped to waken understanding, memory, communion. Hadn't they been poor, and in the best possible way—in the past? Wouldn't they remember that poverty now as a challenge through which they had come as conquerors?

The force of Abel's rage was almost palpable in the tiny room. His hands hurled words so violently against the small space that her head rang.

"Do you compare yourselves to us? You are not like us. Never! Deafs in the bad school we went to—Deaf and Dumb and not even can learn our own language in the school so that we learn nothing and anyone can cheat us and take our money and make the Court come against us! You are *Hearing*. So is

he, that lying, lazy pig who says he is a college man. *Hearing!*
He hears *everything.* I tell you, I tell you, you sit here in
this cockroach house that is worse than any place we lived.
How can you come away from our nice place—trees, your
room, warm, everything nice—and live in this—this beggar-
place and take money from the Government like beggars,
beggars!''

And he made that Sign, to her. Even Janice, stony beside
his rage, pulled in her breath. William, knowing that something awful was happening, was kept from action by his
ignorance of what it was, and helpless in the silence, he watched
his wife begin to weep.

17

ABEL began to wonder if he was getting sick. For a time—it felt like a long time—the world seemed to lose the sharpness of its outlines for him. The life of the Speaking, all the war news, his work, his travel to and from it, the faces of people passing on the street, his own house, resting its weight on the little throne of lawn and shrubbery, became vague to him. Even church and the people of real existence, the Deaf community, in whose respect he had always taken such pride, went into a kind of shadow, darkening, chilling and becoming unreal even as he stood talking with them after church.

Janice was more bitterly unhappy. She went over and over the visit they had made, blaming him for what Margaret had done, blaming him also, he thought, for showing it all to her when they could have stayed home and been innocent and gone on receiving the bright, quick, lying letters from Margaret. At first her anger was ugly and desperate, as though, if he took the blame, she would be saved by it. Night after night it went on until the attacks and defenses were habits and the anger was weary, dogged and routine, like tired feet that still keep walking.

Once he went to the minister to see if there was a way, some kind of medicine, law, wisdom, some special healing that was not for the pains of the body but would ease Janice's anger. The minister spoke to her twice and failed; there was no one else, nothing for the Deaf, although the minister said there were special doctors for such things among the Hearing. In the end, Janice's anger became a habit, among the others and took its place at its set time, and Abel found defense to it.

Rumors were starting at church that the War was going to end tomorrow or next week. Prayers were said at every service and Abel's wishes for its end moved guiltily among his fears of what would happen at work when the men came back and new machines came with them. Those men were heroes and he was not a hero, but only a deaf man and getting older. He worried for Janice, who defended her position and herself to him every day, with more and more reasons why she would not be fired after the War.

The Union men were against her and they had told her so. They had even sent an interpreter down to talk to her: "The Union thinks that your ways are unsafe. They are not going to argue about changes now because of the War, but as soon as the War is over . . ."

She had waved him away and then turned her face so as not to hear him. Ever since the days of home piecework she had hated the Union and had told all her friends at church that they were out to get the Deaf.

She had told Abel the Union's words were only Speaking-gabble, but he thought of it often afterwards and worried for her. Who knew what they could do? Some complicated secret legal thing for which there was no weapon known to him. He had heard that in places like New York City and Washington D.C. there were lawyers who could Sign and who understood Deaf people. What money would it take to get one of those lawyers? No, he told Janice wearily, if the Union made trouble, it would be better not to fight. Let the thing happen and wait and then try to creep in somewhere, and make a place in some hidden or forgotten little fold. Deaf people who were noticed were lost. It was better not to be noticed.

This led, as every thought must, to Margaret again, and Janice mounted the theme and rode him down upon it. If he had fought, Margaret would be home with them now. If he had stood against that College Soldier, Margaret would not be having to live and believe in his lie this moment, "College

Man!'' Of course she didn't really believe William's lie; she knew, and only thought it was easy to lie to them, to keep them Deaf and Dumb and out of the way!

The time went on in shadow. They lived it with great caution, fearful of any change and peering at everything as though for the first time. Rumors about the War came and went and went again until no one listened to them any more, and then, very suddenly, as suddenly as it had begun, the War was over. Janice and Abel waited as they had waited for the invasion, and like the invasion, the great surprise was that no surprise came. At the mill there was talk about some new thing. Janice didn't even try to make sense of the mouths any more, and when they handed her notice of another change, she took it home only because she didn't want to throw it away at the plant or on the street. She showed it to Abel before she threw it away.

''They are closing the spinning and weaving sections,'' he said. ''It says here that they are closing that whole part.''

''How can that be? How can you sew without cloth?''

''It says that U.S.A. cotton is less profitable and now that foreign cloth will soon be coming, they are closing the two sections and will only make the clothes from ready-woven cloth.''

''That's trouble for the weaving girls, not for me.''

''What is strange is that they say that in order to close down, they have to expand . . .''

At the printing shop orders increased and new machines were promised. All of a sudden it seemed that everyone wanted color, all the color he could have.

''The boss keeps giving me notes: wide margins, lots of space, lots of color and contrast, he says, like before the War. Before the War. Everything, every day they say, make it like before the War. It was paradise then.'' And he showed her Heaven in a Sign vast to burlesque, so that she laughed.

''Hearing always dream.'' She went to put up coffee.

''Hearing dream,'' he said to himself. ''They tell themselves the dreams are true, but then they make a law and everyone believes in it and it is true after all. And if you say—if anyone says—it is a dream they put him in the jail.''

She came back and shot a hard look at him and his hands dropped. "I got another letter from *her* today."

"What does it say?"

"Nothing."

The letters from the dreamer continued to come steadily, once a month. They were always the same and always had bits of news about William which Abel didn't understand and the evidence of which Janice tried not to believe: "William's Inorganic Chemistry didn't prepare him for Organic, really, and it's been a strain." "William has passed his finals." "William has a three-point average this semester."

Sometimes Abel looked at Janice over a letter and when she caught his eye, said, "Do you really think he is lying?"

She always said, "Yes."

"But you know he is really in the College, don't you? I mean, really."

"Yes, I know."

"Then why do you say he is lying?"

"I don't know. I know he's lying, though."

"About what?"

"I don't know. He is, that's all." And she wouldn't say any more.

As far as they could tell, Margaret and William still lived in the awful cockroach-house, which Margaret said had been "fixed up" during the vacation. Janice and Abel never answered the letters; writing was a strange and artificial game to them. They did not try another visit. On birthdays and holidays they sent a card, and by this Margaret was to know that they were only waiting for her to take the blame.

After the summer, another subject was introduced. "The Government has *finally* decided that something has to be done and the school is getting money to start building soon, I can't wait for the new married-student bungalows. The need is getting urgent."

"What does that mean?"

"It means they are ashamed," Abel said. "That place shamed them and they are admitting it now."

Janice thought it was saying something else, but she didn't know what. Hearing were never ashamed.

"The Government should hurry with that housing. The army is willing to give surplus Quonset huts and there are barracks which are standing idle and could be moved."

Margaret wrote of overcrowding in all university towns because of returning soldiers and praised William again for getting their "place." In September she mentioned that William had gone to the owners of the big house to see if an addition could be built onto it.

Janice and Abel wondered why they would want to add anything to that disgusting shack. It was horrible that Margaret would write such a thing; it hinted at permanency and at accommodation to ugliness and poverty. For what had they worked? Why had they moved, if not to raise her from it!

Abel read the letter over, hoping that the periods or commas or one of the words was lying to him and that, given the proper way to read it, the words would come right. When he saw that there was no hope of this, he wrote to Margaret and told her to come home for a visit. After a delay, she answered. It would have to be over a weekend, she said, and it should be soon. The week after next would be fine. She could take the four-o'clock bus on Friday and this would get her in at five thirty. She would have to leave on the Sunday morning bus, though, because the evening one would get her back too late to get ready for work on Monday. There were chores to do around the house. They would have Friday night, though and all day Saturday and she looked forward, she said, to seeing them.

Abel was exultant. She had forgotten how wonderful the house was, how clean and airy her own room was, which she had left on a whim over a year ago. Now that she had agreed to come back, she would see all the things that she had left behind. She would no longer want to stay with that liar and warm his lie for him. For the whole week he had Janice running back and forth, cooking and cleaning and buying new curtains until she began to protest that she would not be a servant in her own house. On that Friday he took a suitcase to work so that he could change at the end of the day and he got time off to be down at the depot for Margaret's bus. In his eagerness, he left too early and had to endure waiting at the depot in an impatience that was like pain.

At last the bus came. He saw the people begin to get off one by one and then the driver got off and began to help someone down. He saw a pale face and shock of brown hair pulled back. It couldn't be . . . it was some older woman there, sick possibly, because of the way the driver helped her. He found himself sweating, staring at the bus, unable to go forward and find his child. Then he saw that it was she the bus man was helping. It was Margaret, and there she stood, waiting for her suitcase which was being handed out by someone. She was bare-legged, and his Margaret had always worn hose, of which she had been so very careful. She was standing strangely, with her feet a little apart, like the farm women he had known long ago, women who were used to carrying . . . She turned and he saw her looking around for him. He stood up, but was unable to move and she came toward him smiling, carrying her suitcase and the big belly stuck out in front of her, pushing through the light coat which she had had to open. He was faint and sick and he had to sit down because he was afraid of falling. When she was standing in front of him he got up again, quickly, so as not to have that terrible belly before him. As he looked at her, a pity for her rose in him and at the same time such a deadly hatred for William that he could scarcely contain it. Those two, William and Margaret together, had killed his daughter, his glowing, loving girl, and had given this stranger, this tall, cool woman her place and her name.

"Are you glad to see me?"

"Yes." He couldn't see himself make the Sign because his eyes had tears in them.

"Are we going?" She stopped, realizing that he couldn't see her Sign clearly either. She had put the suitcase down and after a minute he picked it up and they went out to the car line. It was light outside, springtime. He suddenly wished it was winter and dark now so that wouldn't have to look at her. She said, "I'm happy," speaking quickly. Her purse bumped against her arm as she spoke. She was large now and clumsy.

He shook his head. There was a terrible noise in his head, a beat like a great press running hard and slow, slowed down to forty-five copies a minute and each beat of the press made a pain behind his eyes. He was glad he was carrying the suitcase so he didn't have to speak to her.

They got on the D car and took their transfers and moved to the back of the car. They sat side by side and stared outward, blankly into the afternoon.

Janice saw her daughter with no comment but a shake of the head. Her eyes had gone small as with too much light, and then she had blinked, shaken her head and motioned Margaret in, leaving her to stand in the mud-mat place while Janice hurried away to set out the celebration. At supper she ate and drank and passed the platter to Abel and Margaret as though nothing had happened. Abel picked about at his food and ate almost none of it.

Margaret, more disappointed and angry than if they had shouted at her, sat and stared from her plate to her father's. There was so much she had wanted to say to them and to be told. She knew they did not think her brave and resolute to go with William when his own doubts had been so great. This year in the miserable house had shown on her, not without awe, the measure of her tenacity, but she was pregnant now, and there were terrors in this which she could never tell William because he would take them as a reproach. She had known that Janice would have no comfort for her, no pride in her strength. It was Abel, Abel on whom she had counted.

In the kitchen after dinner Janice was more at ease and after a while she asked a few laconic questions.

"When will the baby come?"

"In May."

"You have things for it?"

"Some."

"Are you going to have it in that *place*?" She made the Sign look obscene.

"No, in the hospital. William was in the army, you know. There are certain benefits I can get as a dependent. They call it 'dependent,' of a serviceman."

"You don't depend on him. You work, don't you?"

"I will quit next week. They don't like pregnant women teetering around at the bank. You have to quit when you get too big."

"What do you live on, his Government begging?"

"It is not"—and then Margaret sighed and gave a half-shrug—"yes, on that."

In the front room she heard Abel slamming things around and then he went upstairs banging as hard as he could on each step and pounding on the banister. Upstairs he went from room to room, kicking the doors open and slamming them shut in his futile quest for noise. Janice, aware of no more than a few vibrations from the shivering doorframes stood stolidly at the sink.

"Why is he so angry?" Margaret asked, and Janice looked irritated and did not take her hands from the suds. They did the dishes and cleaned up the kitchen mechanically, and Margaret, humbled, said no more until they were finished and the last dish and cup put away. Then again, as they began to leave the kitchen: "Why is he so angry?"

Janice shrugged and went on past Margaret, going widely with a cruel fastidiousness that would very purposely avoid the great belly.

On Saturday they allowed Margaret to make the excuse that she needed to shop for baby things. She didn't come home until late, and when she did come back, her face looked so drawn that they were both frightened. "You all right? You look sick."

"I am a little—not sick, but sad. I went back"—she started to say "home," but changed the Sign quickly—"back to Vandalia Street, where we used to live. I guess I wanted to say hello to some of the girls I went to school with. The store downstairs was empty. Mr. Petrakis died. He died last year, and we didn't even know. The people at the store told me. I needed . . . I wanted to see him so much and he isn't there any more. It made me so sad that I didn't know."

She couldn't tell them that her first emotion had been fear and not sorrow.

Abel sat back relieved. He had felt ashamed of the way they treated Margaret, and even though it still sickened him to look at her, so blatantly pregnant with that beggar's child, he knew it would be wrong to offer no help. "You don't have to go and buy things at that pawnshop any more. When it's time, you can get a new thing, a baby bed or what you need and we will pay for it.''

"I didn't want to buy anything, just to see him.''

"He was always dirty,'' Janice said. "The wrists of his shirts were always black with dirt.''

"I wanted to tell him about William and the way things are, and the GI Bill and what we are doing now, and the baby. I wanted to show off about the baby, and to tell him about how they've opened a laundromat near us so now I won't have to haggle and fight over the washer at the big house that no one takes care of. I wanted to tell him——''

"You went all the way back there to talk about *laundry*?''

"He was always so nice to me. I wanted to write so many times, but it seemed strange without some special occasion, and working over Christmas there wasn't time.'' She was beginning to cry so she made an excuse and went up to her bedroom.

The big advantage in being in that room in that house was not that it was lighter, prettier or bigger than the room in which she and William lived, but that she might lie on the bed at night and sob aloud against all the need and the fear and the things lost to her and not be held to account for it. With William sleeping beside her, there could only be the long, slow, silent grieving, which dare not even alter breath. She realized as she lay back and wailed, that it was for this reason that she had come.

In the living room Janice and Abel sat facing each other and it was Janice's turn for shock. "I worked and worked to keep them clean when they were children.'' It was the first time she had spoken of Bradley, even indirectly, and for a moment Abel wasn't sure of her meaning. "All the time they were growing up, I tried to separate them from the dirtiness and the poor people there. Margaret had a clean dress every day, not like the rest. And now, at the first thing, off falls the college ways, off comes the University, off comes the job at a bank and back she goes to Vandalia Street, pregnant, a woman who has to pay her husband's house and food.''

Abel, numb, retreated into the newspaper.

The newspaper had been an affectation at first, and a defense against having to stare at people on the bus, but since he had come to be a leader in the Deaf community and someone to be consulted, he had come to know the few well-educated Deaf, in the city, people who spelled more than they Signed because their needs and knowledges exceeded the Signs that were used for the basic things of living. More and more he felt himself needing to grow into these new words. How complicated they were! How minutely subtle the differences they could express! As he watched these Deaf he began to understand dimly some of the joy they felt in their arrival at the perfect meaning, the exact word, the shade of difference between "discipline" and "punishment," between "respectful" and "respectable." He had begun to try to read the newspaper and later had even bought a dictionary by which he hoped to be made able to understand it. Janice had laughed at him and accused him of trying to make himself more than he was, and later of using his reading to close away her advice. Both of these things were true, but it was also true that over the years, Abel's world had widened more than hers and that now he knew a few of the Two-World Deaf, the rare, beautifully Signing, well-educated Deaf who did not consider reading an activity for Hearing alone. He began to wonder if he might be able to reach their worldliness.

Nevertheless, although he did not admit it to Janice, the dictionary had been a mistake. It embarrassed him even while he blundered and stumbled over the words that were supposed to explain the other words—when he was through, the words had sieved all meaning and left him with nothing. Somewhere, somewhere it was hiding; and he was not quick enough; it escaped. This evening he was glad to be free of his house and vanish into the hunt. He settled back in his chair with that dictionary and the *National News*.

Mr. Truman had made a statement about his position on an arms treaty. Abel sighed. *Position.* He had struggled with *arms* in the newspaper before. There were times, Mr. Walker from Church had told him, that *arms* did not really mean arms, but guns and cannons, bombs—things that neither looked, worked nor acted like arms, and were not part of a man's body. Nevertheless. *Treaty.* The word was under *treat* and right under *treatment.* "The act of treating or negotiating for the adjustment of differences." None of the words but *treating* and *difference* meant anything, and the *s* on the end of difference made him suspicious of it. The President was talking like a doctor about treating, so the arms must be body-arms after all.

Abel read to the end and found little to understand. The work done, he turned with relief to the local and sports news and the story of a little girl who had fallen into the river and been pulled out by a heroic boy. The words were much simpler here and the ideas were real to him. It was so good when people helped one another—when they could help and understand one another. He thought he would cut out this article and show it to the men at work. Sometimes he saw one man with a news-paper point out something to another as they sat eating lunch. The second man would nod and maybe smile, showing his ap-preciation of being included. Occasionally there would be argu-ments, no more than half serious, about something in the paper and the men then began to motion at one another, freely and happily, a gesture Hearing could use that was sometimes vul-gar Sign. Yes, he decided he would take the paper in tomorrow and show it to the new man, Doran. Maybe something was the matter with President Truman's arms. The article had said *position*—that meant which way you were standing. Maybe his arms . . . It was better, the other article, the one about the little girl. At least he would not have to conquer his pride enough to ask. Who was there who would not laugh at him?

And he remembered with a sudden shock that Margaret was home. He had been so bereft at the loss of her and had put the thought of her help so far out of his mind that he had forgotten its possibility even when she was right upstairs. Mar-garet had never seen him with a newspaper. He had begun to feel this need since her leaving and now he could go up to her room right away with President Truman's troubles and ask her to explain them, and also he could share the part about the little girl pulled out of the river. She would be proud of him and of his wish to join in the things that the whole world shared. His eyes lost the words he was trying to read and his mind drifted away. Only after a long time did something pull against a thought and snap his eyes back to the present world. Once he could have gone to her and asked, but no more. She had never told him she was sorry for leaving them, or for denying all their years of work, or for giving them the terrible suffering of their uncomprehension as they stood in that horrible shack. Now she had come home, overwhelming in her pregnancy and had made him feel more deaf and more mute than he had ever felt in his life.

He put down the paper and was relieved to see that Janice had gone away. If he banged the doors again or stamped or broke things, Margaret would hear him and know what awful power she had over him. He felt so deaf that he stumbled into the banister when he went to go upstairs, up to his own safe room.

18

MARGARET left early the next morning. Her parents didn't see her go and they didn't talk any more about the visit. After a while there was a letter from her that the baby had come. It was a boy. Named Marshall. There was also something about plans to move, but Abel said it was only her lies to save William. He often forgot that William wasn't lying.

Janice grumbled through the dozen false springs until warm weather and then began to worry him about making another visit: "I want to see the baby."

"It will be the same as it was before, only more crowded."

"We have responsibility. It is not nice if we don't go."

Abel flipped a hand at her, but he was only pretending to be irritated. Whenever Janice talked about responsibility, it meant she did not want to do something and could be told that the responsibility was too great. "You got things for the baby; that's enough. You can send them in the mail," he said. Her face eased.

And then they got a letter from the In-law, Mrs. Anglin, and they thought it was sent by mistake. The careful handwriting was full of congratulating words for them, and insisted that they be happy and that they be proud.

"This is for Margaret, this letter," Janice said. "It's the mother and father that have all the shake-hands and cigars."

Abel had a sudden sharp memory of the box of cigars he had bought when Margaret was born, not long ago.

"She is going there, his mother," Janice said, reading on, "this Sunday." They stared at each other.

"Is she going so soon?"

Janice nodded. He could see her fear, the closing of her face against it. In the strange way of its spreading, he found he felt it too, a fear, and he hated being afraid. Janice said, "I wonder if she goes up there all this time."

"No," he said, the fear growing in him. "Margaret would tell us that."

"Margaret!" And she scowled. "Margaret keeps secrets like any Hearing and they have the telephone to talk with and make their plans. I think that woman goes up there all the time and brings presents and sees that baby."

"Well," he said, "we have a right to go, too, when we want to."

"I want to go on Sunday then, when she goes. This time I will write to Margaret and she will know we are coming. We are the grandparents more than his mother is."

Still, the fear. . . .

The day was measured with an exacting, ceremonial equality. The baby was given gifts precisely timed and admired precisely and they all went out for lunch, which Abel insisted on helping to pay for. Mrs. Anglin's brother, who had driven her to the University for the visit and had to be back early, offered the Ryders a ride in his car. They declined triumphantly, and Margaret let Mrs. Anglin hold the baby all the time they were riding to someplace William had insisted on showing them. In the end, it turned out to be nothing but a flattened strip of land behind the backs of the University buildings, even behind a dump of cinders which had been mounded and washed down into banks and gullies over the years. The piece of land had been stripped of weeds and soil and stood raw and yellow-ugly, wavering small fingers of heat in the afternoon sun.

"Buildings, for the married students," Margaret explained. Janice and Abel stood and looked and ventured nothing into Margaret's busy fingers. Even her Sign was like a Hearing now, full of unsaid things to make them afraid. She went on, "They are going to bring in some army barracks and set them here and they'll be painted and fixed up and walls put in between the apartments and each one will have its own door and at least one window on each end, and there will be regular heat and light and water . . ." She went on, full of excitement.

Janice and Abel looked at the bare place stretching before them and back at the Anglins and back at the bare place again. Somehow Margaret's words didn't seem so wild or false with Mrs. Anglin's eye moving over the scene and her brother making some comment or asking a question now and then. William's own family treated him with smiling and respect. Even his uncle noted his words and didn't wave them aside. And to Margaret, who was only a beggar's wife, carrying their water in buckets, they gave a deference which made Abel look at them in wonder.

He tried to study William more carefully. In the long months of separation and the betrayal of their hopes, they had taken all of his remembered features and twisted them into uglinesses that could not now describe him. Here he stood open in the daylight before them. The pinched and bitter look of his early times with Margaret was gone. It was not possible now to remember him as a person who had known war and the pain of wounds.

As they were leaving, Abel asked how long it was going to be before the new houses were made. William spoke and Margaret told them that by summer they had been promised. Then William said something more, but Margaret did not translate. He still had the same closeness of mouth as his mother and there was not one word that Abel could read. But Janice asked, insisting, until Margaret, embarrassed, told them what William had said. "He said he will be relieved to get out of the trap we are in." Then she went on herself, speaking in his defense. If they could only see what other married students had had to do, if only they could know the persistence and steadiness it had taken . . .

Abel nodded, but he was no longer really paying attention. That William at least knew that the place he had taken Margaret was miserable. . . . It was some sign of hope. Before they left on the afternoon bus, Abel asked William his opinion of President Truman.

Abel could not trace in his mind how that visit came to be made again, or how it grew into a monthly event, but it was they—he and Janice—and not the Anglins who arrived to help when Margaret and William moved into the Veterans' Housing, and it was they who brought the carriage and took Marshall for his first ride in it.

After a while Margaret asked them if they wouldn't stay with Marshall sometimes so that she and William could go out together. They were always careful to come back in plenty of time to take the Ryders to the bus and see them off, and once, as a Christmas treat, William and Margaret came in to the city for the weekend and, dressed in their best, appeared at church on Saturday afternoon with Abel and Janice. There they gave Marshall to his grandfather to be paraded in his arms before the congregation.

It was because of that visit that Abel was forced to try to talk to William. The people at church, even the few Special Ones had been impressed with William and had made pleased comments about Margaret. What was he studying in college? they asked, and Abel could not answer. The next time the Ryders went for a visit, Abel made Margaret sit down with him as he greeted William. He wanted to hear from William and not from Margaret about the work that William hoped to do.

It was something, they told him, called Human Engineering.

"How can you build people like bridges? Maybe you make those false people they have in the stores to be shown wearing clothes . . ."

He didn't like to think about those false people; he had always felt uneasy looking at the bodiless feet and hands that some stores showed, put into the shoes and gloves they wished to sell. These cut-off stockinged legs and severed heads with lovely hair showed the Hearing world at its most merciless and savage. Just for convenience, for the single part that interested them, they would hack away the rest of a body as though nothing had importance but that shoe, that glove, that hat. Such things had to be built, no doubt. He shook his head.

The young people began to explain. They blew huge mouthfuls of words, hands groping and spilling names and letters: prosthetic engineering, visual field, eye-hand co-ordination. In the end Abel had to be content with being told that it was a new trade, a whole new work where engineering and psychology met, and he was too embarrassed to tell Margaret and William that he did not know what psychology was. He nodded and smiled in the usual way, buying them silent with his smile and closing them away because they were a danger. Yet, this time, he saw that if he really wished to know what they were trying to tell him, there might be ways by which he could come to it. This was a responsibility he had never known before. To learn would be a long search with no real reward at the end of it; not to learn would be to remain mind-deaf, and mind-deaf by his own choice. For a moment then he wondered if Hearing had such choices . . . but how could they? They heard . . . a person could not choose to be deaf. . . . When Janice, bored by the talk, changed the subject, he felt relieved.

That winter, suddenly, William graduated and the school was finished. Margaret told them that he was going to work for a company that seemed to Abel very much like the cut-off-head company. William's company made legs and arms and eyes for people who had lost them. Margaret told him that the job was only temporary because as soon as they had enough money William wanted to go back to school again. In school? Not in school? Engineer, but not an engineer? Then she told him that they were going to leave for Chicago and Abel almost fell, so stunned was he, so unable and unfit to ask the reason for it.

They stayed a year in Chicago and then a year in California. They seemed to go like . . . like . . . He tried to picture with his hands the quick, bright, aimless, scattering way they went. Their way would be like a butterfly Sign, if butterflies were made of wire and steel. Their ways would be like a butterfly Sign, if butterflies were eagles. And he laughed at the picture he had made in his mind. They had more freedom than eagles and less plan, those two, because eagles at least are bound to the laws of daylight and night and the commands of seasons.

He found himself missing his daughter with a terrible yearning, as though she and William were dead and he would never see them again. From their high and terrible distance they sent pictures of the stranger Marshall had become—a little boy. And then, when he and Janice had let them go forever and had made a fragile peace in loss, they came again, blown back by chance. William's work had changed. He was no longer making different arms and legs, but doing something Margaret explained—or tried to explain—as "How Much and How Many." It seemed to be about the numbers of things a quality control worker could check at once, and what kind of things could be checked together. Oh, if the young people were like eagle-butterfly, their trades were like the wind.

"Thank God," Abel said to Janice, "that there are still people in the world who cause clothes to be sewn and books to be printed. Clothes and books can be seen and touched and used and thrown away, but *his* job is words! Words and wind. It comes and goes and no one ever sees anything of it."

Janice shrugged, "Marshall has gotten big. And he doesn't know me. I wonder how long they will stay."

"With a job like wind, I don't know." Abel frowned, uncomfortable with his comparison because he realized that a bird makes its home in the wind.

But they did stay. Later, Abel found out that when William was still at his first job, he had made certain changes at the factory, and had spoken once or twice at industrial conferences about what were called Human Factors in Assembly-line Production. He had also been called in on consultations. In the two years he had been away, interest in his ideas had grown and other supervisors had had a chance to see what he had done. When he came back, he had called at the plants and found that people there were more ready for his services. Marshall was not a baby any more; soon he would be starting school, and Margaret had never had a real place to live. She never spoke of it, but Abel saw that there was something in her that longed for a house, a place, a neighborhood and a few friends. The traveling had always been for better jobs; she had told him this herself. But friends at church said that any move meant a financial loss, at least in the beginning, and when he mentioned this to her, he could see that it was so. Margaret did not make friends easily. She was still enough of a Deaf for that.

Typically, when William made his decision to stay, he didn't tell Margaret until he was sure, and typically, she agreed with neither eagerness nor argument. He was used to this quality of reserve in her. Some of his business friends' wives wrote her off as spiritless and flat, and it was a joke among them that getting Margaret to commit herelf on whether she wanted to go to a movie or stay in and play cards was a study in futility. Sometimes William, too, was a little saddened by the lack of spontaneity in her. Margaret did what was right and only once or twice, long afterward, did he realize that there must have been a price paid.

Things could be different now. Margaret would realize that now there was time for preferences, for choices. He wished she could learn to be less afraid, to risk her wishes. She was so cautious when she approached any of his successes. It was annoying to stand against her cool approval arguing, "But is that really what *you* want?" It did no good to remember how recently this acquiescence and reserve of hers had been her greatest strength, the virtue without which his recovery from the despair of war and his long, hard way through college would have been impossible. Only now . . . It was fine, she said, fine, and he had to be content with that.

They bought a small house in one of the raw new tracts west of the river. The earth had been stripped and skinned for the houses and the dust rose from its dry wounds and danced in the driveways noon after glaring noon. Janice and Abel went to visit them there, but they were uncomfortable on the bare, raw patio and frightened of the continual flow of running dogs and strange children. Three or four times during the visit curious neighbors walked in and had to be introduced, and the process by which they might be understood explained to them. Janice and Abel did not like the small, cramped house, the openness, the children, the raw ground, the dust, the loneliness that kept the neighborhood at continual flow from house to house, the mannerless intrusions and the gape-mouths shouting at them with a silent force that made their heads ache. Margaret got into the habit of visiting them, taking Marshall with her when she went shopping on Saturdays "in town." She would come in and talk for a while and then leave for the shopping while Marshall stayed with his grandparents. They took him to church with them and bribed his boredom quiet with toys and candy. He was a bright, alert little boy, reckless, loving and inquisitive. Margaret never failed to be astounded by his power over her parents.

She had come by to pick him up one afternoon, and not seeing him waiting, had parked in front of the house and gone up the walk to call to him. Lying on the porch were two dead bodies. They lay ecstatically, grandly dead, draping their heads and arms over the porch furniture . . . "What are you doing?" . . . But their eyes were closed and so they did not answer her.

Around the corner of the house, face red with effort, eyes narrowed, head hunched, keeping low in the saddle, guns blazing in the hail of lead willy-nilly for the just and the unjust, came Marshall Ryder Anglin, a sombrero on his head, rowled spurs and black boots and not a stitch of anything else on. He pounded up the stairs, alerting the waiting dead, and they gave him a fine long moment to enjoy the work of his hand before coming to life again. "Hello" (both sheepishly, seeing Margaret).

"Where are his clothes?"

"We did not expect you so soon."

"Where are his clothes?"

"It was so hot—we were giving him a shower with the hose in the backyard. He wanted to shoot, so . . ."

Marshall always sulked when she came to take him away. When he was half sick with popcorn and candy, he sulked; and he sulked now as she held his clothes out to him. He had had to take the boots and spurs off to get into his ordinary pants. The clothes were damp and dirty and stained. Ice cream. They had taken him out after church again and filled him full of ice cream and bought him everything he had pointed to. His stomach would be upset tonight and he wouldn't be able to eat his dinner at all. She sighed. "Come on. It will soon be dark —it's getting late."

"We have to say good-bye," he muttered. "We have to wave bye-bye to the Deafies."

Margaret's mouth went dry, but she didn't realize it until she tried to speak and found it impossible to make a sound. She had borne these very wounds, as sudden and more bitter, at the age of five, six, seven. Children bear great wounds with less consciousness, and so more easily. Now she had trouble breathing and she wanted to slap the insolent, innocent pouting mouth. She had forgotten that she was capable of being hurt so deeply. Hurting and being hurt are childhood occupations; she had grown out of practice. Her hand trembled, but she did not slap him. Instead she helped him into his clothes and, frozen-faced, carried the boots and six-guns to the car.

As they were driving home, she asked him, "Where did you hear that word, the thing you called Grandpa and Grandma?"

"Oh, Deafies," he said, maybe knowing that he had struck her again with it, "The ice-cream man says it all the time, and the kids, sometimes when we walk home."

Speaking very slowly and calmly, she tried to explain to him their difference. The words seemed sterile.

"Don't people like grandma and grampa?" he asked.

She answered the rote by rote, the kind of answer that child-care books preach when children ask where babies come from; a kindly, humane, patient answer, rootless and sterile. There was nothing to be said that he would understand. Because she was afraid of marking him as she had been marked, she was careful, book-careful, and the words were purged of meaning. He went on with his questions in something like glee, although she tried not to think so, until she had to tell him to hush.

The next Saturday, she debated taking him. He had learned some Signs which he used effortlessly, naturally and unquestioningly with his grandparents. At the appearance of each new one, he had received such wild praise from them that he had come to use them a little like virtuoso pieces for which an artist must be begged and cajoled. When he had used Signs to the Hearing, they had drawn no notice. What had any of this to do with a revelation of cruelty that he might see? She couldn't tell him about it; she couldn't even give any reason not to take him back to the grandparents who were so eager to die from his bullets, and so she took him and left him as usual and went off to the shopping.

It was late when she came back, almost six. Besides the groceries she had done a good deal of bargain-hunting around town and the back of the car had boxes of towels and things for the bathroom, some fall things for herself and the wardrobe of new clothes with which Marshall would be starting school. It was only kindergarten, and many of the mothers on the block didn't think it was worth the bother, driving back and forth twice a day just for finger painting and something the "educators" called "socialization." They shook their heads, elaborate with pin curls and put down their coffee cups: "Listen, who's got the time, right? With two other kids at home, I got more so-ciali-zation than I can stand right now!"

Margaret, comfortable only in the background, welcomed as a neighbor but too reserved to be a friend, felt an obscure guilt for her own opinions and her single child. She had wanted sometimes, to tell someone how stunted she felt, how frightened for Marshall. William's work came and went and he still had to work nights and weekends proving its value. Acceptance wasn't easy and there were times when plans had been sabotaged by juniors who resented an outsider being called into the firm as consultant. Often when he was home, he was working on a plan and only half alive to his family. Marshall had been left to her, a stunted woman who could not open the world to him. She was humble and grateful to the teachers and the schools for seeing her lack and for understanding how deeply she wanted him to go beyond all the limitations with which she had had to make peace. He would be in school early, from the very beginning, nurtured in all the ways of expression, comfortable with humor and tragedy, art, music; deaf nowhere in any part of his mind.

And yet there had to be these Saturdays also, and a shame to be born in him, perhaps for being with the "Deafies." Was a person always to be divided by other people's needs? . . . Lord, it was late. They would have to hurry to be home in time to start supper before William came.

As she pulled up in front of the house, she noticed again how settled and peaceful it looked. Abel and Janice had taken good care of it, the porch and yard were scrupulously neat, the walk always swept, but it was the big trees that gave the house its feeling of strength and peace. They quieted the noise, softened the heat and glare of the day, blurred the hard lines of brick, stone and wood. It was nice here; she felt like sitting a long time in the cool, listening to the sheltering sound of the leaves as they moved and watching the slow lines of sunshine going rich against the afternoon shadow.

The door of the house opened and Margaret sighed and began to get out of the car. Marshall came out and Janice and Abel followed him, smiling. The child stopped at the edge of the porch steps and turned to face them, his hands moving. He would be using it now, his mother thought, a new Sign. As she walked around the car, she kept looking at the grandparents' faces, softened with love and glowing in the late light and she saw the little boy begin to step back as a master does, to admire his work. One foot was out behind him, his weight thrown back, trusting for the floor where there was none, and the grandparents' eyes only on his face, his eager eyes, his hands, working the new Sign. Margaret found herself running, tearing up the walk and up the steps to catch him, screaming. "Bradley! Bradley!, Don't fall! Bradley, don't fall!"

19

MARSHALL had been born against Abel's and Janice's wishes; he had been taken away and returned at the whim of his father whose strangeness they still feared, but never had any friends' lips or hands, no books or newspapers led them to imagine what blinding light he would carry with him into their house.

They forgot that, at first, Margaret had brought him dutifully and automatically, and that they had kept watch over the privileged days only so that the other grandmother would not take more than her share. The little boy shone, he warmed the room; the simplest of his smiles tore at them with something like anguish and he gave his joy and wonder to them with a total openness such as they had never known to exist. They soon learned to give him whatever he wanted; when he was hurt or denied, his sorrow could put a shadow against the sun.

When Marshall was seven, the second child, Ellen was born. Then he came to them dazed and shocked by the power of his own envy, and the Saturdays grew ripe and golden for them, staying home from church to bake cookies or to play his games until he was healed by them. He had never learned much Sign—he seemed to be eased by their silence—it was a house without prohibitions or commands, yet Abel taught him to play checkers and gin rummy and later all of them remembered it and were puzzled at how it had been done by half-Sign and gestures and half-read words. When he outgrew their total attention, they sometimes took him to church. There, he would fidget and stare, bored but not unhappy, waiting as they did for afterward and the short greeting with the minister and the friends to whom he was presented newly each time as though it were the first. They were modest as they brought him forward; a modesty in no way false; one is always humble in the presence of miracles. Sometimes in the evenings after he had gone, Janice and Abel would sit together and feel the creeping-in of new fears to threaten their too obvious and abundant joy. The Other One had means and a world to lure their grandchild away. She would soon be taking him to baseball games and picture shows and speaking to him in a grown-up way. When he was ten and eleven and twelve, he sometimes did go with his other grandmother on Sundays and then Abel and Janice would work around the house in a nervous, restless haste, their minds full of pictures of him waving and laughing ecstatically, and for that moment they would hate that Other Grandmother and all her matching bags and gloves and knowledge of the world. But Marshall always came back, and if they asked how he had liked the ball game or the museum trip, he would shrug and nod and offer no details, slipping down again on the couch with his comic books. Margaret and his father didn't like him to read them and he kept a large stack of them under the living-room couch in their house. It was a rare week that they didn't add one or two to the pile, usually mystery or adventure ones with many different flying and running men in fantastic clothes. They had stopped getting animal ones when he said those were too young.

There was another baby, Matthew, and Marshall moved into the crowded Junior High on Kirkwall Avenue, where there were fights almost daily for months. By that time he had a bike and he would ride over by himself on Saturday mornings, do an errand or two for Janice and then sit down to draw or read, or putter in the yard, or play idly, watching the day spread itself wide and then wind itself up before his eyes. The knowledge that he had come at no prompting but his own filled the grandparents with awe. They did not dare to ask him why he came for fear of spoiling it all, but once as they sat prolonging the cold cuts and potato salad of one long, idle Saturday lunch, Abel wrote a note to Marshall: "Maybe hard leaving all good toy you get Christmas come here."

Marshall shrugged, but then he took up the paper and wrote: "Ma makes me clean up all the time so there's no time to play. She gets mad about stuff on the table or dirt on your hands. She's always cleaning or sewing up something that shows."

And Abel ventured timorously from his fingers, "We are glad you like to come here."

Again Marshall answered with the paper, "Sometimes they all treat you like a bunch of doctors listening for your heart to have some kind of disease. It's nice where they don't test you and measure your faults all the time."

Then they all sat back and did not talk. The boy ate and made patterns on the tablecloth with his fork and the grandparents watched him, dumb struck with pride and love, and waited for their hearts to slow.

At the mill Janice had been given a strange sort of death, a death only Hearing could give, a death hiding in something else. When the retooling had been done and the expansion was over, she had been promoted to Assistant Manager of Quality Control. The job paid more and it was Management, so the Union would not be able to hurt her, but they had taken her away from the big room and the girls and the rows of machines. Instead there was only a little room off the sewing floor and she was only to be called when a piece came through inspection that showed one of the machines was faulty. Then she was supposed to trace down the machine from the girl's pile number and find out if the fault could be corrected by hand or if the machine needed to be seen by the Repair Team.

At first she had been proud of her new job. Day after day she waited for someone to come to the doorway of the little room and beckon with a finger to call her to catastrophe, breakdown, the thread-stuck bobbin or the stitch drawn too loose-too tight, the sign of a girl using poor rhythm. For days and weeks nothing came and no one. When she had been on the floor, there were always arms being raised to wag for her to come: a new girl wondering why the bobbin bound, an old machine needing to be gentled back in a rhythm, Janice's own complete, heartbreaking rhythm. Now she waited like a beggar at that door, hoping to be admitted to some crowded, busy place where, in a time no one now remembered, she had been single, regal and indispensable.

After a month of anguish, she and Abel wrote a letter to the president of the company. The letter took them a week to write. Each word had to be selected with great care by newspaper and dictionary. In doubtful cases they used several words in brackets, the better to be understood. After a long beginning in praise of Janice and the company, the problem was brought forth. It was done as Hearing liked it, weighed up with words, intricate, indirect and important with punctuation marks. When they finally mailed it, Janice felt a pulse or two of the power that words can bring. They had now a matter spoken of in writing, official as Law, urgent. The man would look to his mill. But weeks went by and no word came back to them. Then, at last, a mysterious printed note appeared on her table. It said that her communication had been received and contents duly noted and that appropriate action would be taken at the earliest possible opportunity. They spent three evenings making this meaning plain. During the next inspection the vice-presidents and section heads and secretaries paused to smile into the bare cubicle where Janice sat waiting and when they had gone, she went after them and managed to get one of the following, lesser ones who wouldn't be missed, to stop and write for her what had been said. "Our back-up girl," the note said. "We have to have a back-up girl. This worker has been with us for a long time." She thought she had lip-read something like "pack up and go," but perhaps it had been back-up girl after all. And then, too, there had been the smiling. She went home with the note. Abel could not find 'back-up' in the dictionary. Hearing played games and she was trying to play them as well as Abel, but Hearing have no meaning to their lives, no need for meaning. Under this "back-up" there was a lie. She felt it in the smiling somewhere. It was a lie, and how clever they were, lifting and locking and lying and dropping the secret again, fingers to lips, to take it up again without her knowing. There was nothing to do but smile back at them and nod, yes, yes, and stop caring about them.

One evening Abel put down his paper and began to do some figuring with a pencil. Janice watched him from the kitchen. He was sitting at the table and when he finished, he looked up into the mirror on the other wall, staring at it, and then shaking his head. It wasn't long since the death of Abel's father. Abel went alone to the funeral and to help his mother move into a small house in the town. Since then, Janice sometimes came upon him staring at the wall or his dinner plate, thinking of some other place and time. She sighed and came in from the kitchen, drying her hands on her apron. She saw that he was staring at her, not at her directly, but into the mirror, at the person who was there. It made her angry for some reason, so she said, through the mirror, "What is it?" quickly, in annoyance. He looked away from the image and came back to her. "Next month is our anniversary."

"So?"

"We will be married forty years then."

"That can't be."

"Yes, I figured it out."

Words might lie, but numbers never. A decade of piece-work had ground the numbers deep. She went over to his paper and figured the dates. Then they both stood for a long time and peered unbelievingly into the mirror.

Janice had written carefully: "What is *back-up* girl?"

Marshall took the paper, thought, looked again, thought again. Then he wrote: "It could be different things. It depends on how they meant it."

The more he tried to explain the more involved and fantastic it seemed. Because it was Marshall, Janice allowed herself only a flash of suspicion that he was hiding something, that it was one of Hearing's eternal game-jokes to mean-and-not-to-mean, by which the Deaf were always asked to pay the highest price and to wait the longest. In the end Janice and

Abel let themselves be reassured by him that it meant no insult or danger and wasn't a bad thing to be called. With this worry out of the way, they began to plan their yearly trip to the circus. Marshall, now almost fifteen, had gotten too old to enjoy it as he once did, but he was afraid of hurting them. In the last few years, he had lost the ways of telling them any of the subtle things: all of his Signs were gone long ago and lately, he couldn't even read what they spelled to him on their fingers. When he had anything special to say, he used writing, but he depended more on their reading of his moods.

Today he seemed worried—no, annoyed—as he tried to explain things to them and then he wrote: "I'm supposed to keep this secret, but Ma and Pa have plans to get something for you." It was hard for them to take seriously what he had written. Writing was and was not what it seemed to be but because it was something that was making him unhappy, they told him they would speak to his parents about it. He shook his head violently and told them not to think about it any more.

It was supposed to be a TV set. Margaret had been saving to get a set as an anniversary present for Janice and Abel. William hadn't seen any sense in it. What was the point of watching TV when there couldn't be any sound? She only nodded in her quiet, accepting way and kept on saving until William told her it was ridiculous—two dollars a week; he would get the set. If nothing else, her parents could watch the cigarette boxes dancing and the puppets. Wrestling and roller derbies needed no speech and charades were often lettered out for the audiences to read. The Firm had had a good year. "Stop saving the household money. Start buying ribs and steaks again. I'll get the set!"

Margaret studied the buying of the set; she attacked it, she conquered it, the way she did everything else, by wearing it down, by outliving it. She seemed to think of nothing but the TV set, and Marshall hated it. Every night his mother came home from another store, with another report on another model to be worried over and compared. He didn't want a set in the grandparents' house. He wasn't sure why. He watched TV whenever he could at home and argued for his choices with the other kids, but he had a vague feeling that the old people would be changed, betrayed in some way, by so much contact with the rude, cheap, bright part of the world. It made him uncomfortable to think of them side by side on the couch staring at the box flickering white-gray in the darkened room. There were people in the world, certain people, who were separated, like priests and nuns and cripples and midgets. They were holy people, they were very special in the world. The Deaf were like that, special, separated, like holy people. He hated to think of them looking at TV.

When his mother was finally ready with her plan, he made one of his own. She was going to have the men install the set while Janice and Abel were at work. Then the whole family would go over in the evening with a cake. Marshall decided that he wouldn't be there. Maybe he could get Rob Jefferson to ask him over for the night. He didn't want the old people to have him there, watching their shame and embarrassment because of that gift of his mother's. He didn't want to see them stumble over their honesty and their holiness as they thanked his father. Sometimes he barely felt himself his mother's child; she was always so busy fussing over the surfaces of things— she had no time to think what life should be like.

Janice knew that the people at the mill wanted her to go. Somehow she knew that the manager would not come down and point her away. Instead they had taken her *up*, unsuspecting, high above the safe places of work that could be seen and measured, and now they would wait until she did a wrong thing or complained or died of the height, the cold and the loneliness. She was afraid to be absent too much from the useless, workless Quality Control office, lest there be a note there or a final slip in her pay envelope.

"All the War!" She cried out night after night. Abel looked up to catch a word or two and then turned again to his food. "All the war, E on the flag outside and thanks from all the Government and the army!"

"You're still quick, still good. Why don't you ask to go back to the machines? It's all right if we don't have so much money."

"You never listen to me. They don't *do* the pieces any

more on the machines. When they changed the factory, they took out all the old machines and put in new ones and the work goes from girl to girl. One does one flat seam, and another one turns the work and it goes on and other girls over-seam. If a person is too fast, it's bad because it breaks the running of the line. I went in there and saw. The cloth goes by them and comes out hemmed, and that hides where they didn't back-over. I don't know anything about fixing *those* machines, and they know it. Anyway, they don't let anyone fix *those* machines. They have a Scientific Man, so much, it took him three different colleges, and you wait for the machine to break and then *he* comes and fixes it. . . .''

Abel had heard it all before, but now he knew why it annoyed him to have her begin the whole thing again every night. It was because he couldn't help her. The changes were happening slowly in his own trade, too; machines that eased the work and put out more of it. Each new machine was a blessing, but only last year he had noticed that there were fewer men in the shop, and some were there who did barely any work at all. The machines worked. There was no help for this and no way he could comfort her. He shook his head and waved a bit with his left hand, as though to interrupt himself and not her. "Go and finish the dishes, and I'll play you a game of checkers after.''

"For what?'' she said, taking him up as though she had not just been sorrowing over the ending of her life.

"Twenty-five moves—a dollar.''

She rushed to get ready.

He had discovered that gambler's streak in her. She played with the Silent Bridge Group over at the church one night a week, but could barely stand the other players, she said, who were afraid of every bid, and wouldn't risk a nickel unless they had all the cards. She had, because of this, invented a new idea—new, at least for the Deaf Community: the side bet. It was lucky, he sometimes thought, that they were not rich. The very, very small amounts won and lost enabled Janice to play with mad abandon, and he had given in to betting in their checker games the number of moves it would take him to win. Until she had discovered this risk, she had waved away the Silent Bridge, Silent Bingo, and Canasta nights as childish and a waste of time. Now, she could spend hours crouched over a card table or checkerboard of an evening if a quarter or fifty cents was at stake. He used the gambling sometimes to jolly her out of a bad mood, making absurd boasts that she couldn't resist. Shaking his head, he got up and began to get the board and set up the pieces. Janice came in to finish clearing the table.

"You need to play with Marshall again," Abel said. "He is getting better all the time."

It made her smile. Any mention of Marshall's name lightened her. They only used an initial for him, with a special little flip of the hand after it as though the hand would say 'beautiful' very quickly. Margaret's name was a stiff M, a correct M, and nothing bloomed near it.

"You remember that college, when we went to visit Margaret-William?" (The M.W. of their joined names was formal and austere, like the monograms Mrs. Anglin had put on the bathroom towels they had seen in Margaret's house. Did Hearing forget their own names that they had to be so reminded?)

"I remember the college," Janice said. "Marshall should go to college, too. It was a nice place, where we were, where the students were walking under the trees."

"He should go to the best college," Abel said.

"A college is the same as the other colleges, isn't it?"

"Oh, no. Remember what Mr. Durove said about choosing the right college for his son?"

"*Heaven* won't be good enough for that family—they are so stuck up."

"He is smart, Mr. Durove. He spent a year at Gallaudet, and if his father——"

"He never forgets about that year at Gallaudet either, or about his father. Marcella told me she heard they threw him out, and his father died after that just because he was disgusted!"

Abel shook his head and waved her away, but he was laughing all the same. "Never mind about Marshall. Marshall won't go to Gallaudet. He can go to some big college—any famous and great one."

"You know," she said, "sometimes I dream that he does

—go to Gallaudet. In that dream I see him Signing so beautifully and he always comes back here afterward and speaks in
the church and everybody gets so wise they are never afraid
again, and they know how to do all the things, and the Law and
the Court can never come against them.''

He had finished setting up the checkers. ''It's a stupid
dream,'' he said. ''Why should Marshall waste his time teaching a bunch of Deafies?''

During the Second World War, the factories had invented something called sick leave. Janice had never used it,
because of fear and pride, and during the War she had heaped
silent scorn on any of her floor girls who helped Hitler by
staying out sick. After the War she had wanted to keep up her
record, but now, slowly, and with the delicacy of a thread test-
ing through the needle's eye, she began to sick-leave.

She began with a careful note left in the afternoon, a
pained face coming late in the morning. Then, the next month
there was a whole day out, then two. In the winter, she had
three days, then, late in the spring, three together. She had
always had pains, headaches and backaches, and wondered
some mornings if she could drag to work. She had always made
it, feeling barely fit to move, and somehow in the course of the
day, the flow of the cloth would take the pain away with it,
and by evening it would be forgotten with the memory of the
first cap or jacket or the first empty bobbin. Now she indulged
the pains and humored them and so they remembered her.

One Monday, a gang of painters came and began to paint
the second floor halls and workrooms and the fumes of the
paint had made her head pound. After lunch she left a short
note and started home. This absence was really the company's
fault. Surely the smell would be no better tomorrow. She decided to stay out until Wednesday and see how her head felt.

When she got out on the street, her headache cleared immediately, and a kind of tricking gladness made her feel light
and irresponsible. She took the bus home. As it passed the
streets of beautiful and interesting stores, she had a sudden
desire to get off and look in all of the windows, but habit carried her on and she sat back and stared out the window.

A warm May rain had fallen and stopped; the streets breathed a little fog around the ankles of the shoppers and the wheels of the cars and trucks. The bus was warm, smelling of the wetness of coats and wool and people. Outside the bus— she was kept from it only by a window—the world had become clearer. All the colors she saw in the windows, the stoplights and store signs, the people walking, seemed to be richer, the lines and planes sharper and more distinct, as though without the sun, the day itself was glowing. There was an excitement about coming home at an odd time. Now the bus was almost empty, and instead of the tired, pushing, rush-hour people, there were only some placid shoppers, a few students coming from their morning classes and the patient salesmen, shining at the elbows and giving up their weight to the seats with a relief that made the others smile. Then the bus turned off the crowded avenue and it was time to get up.

Janice waited for her stop near the door by habit. She had a fear of being caught in the doors and when they opened at her stop, she always dashed down the step and out as though she were on fire. When the bus was full and there were people to push past, it was much worse, but this time at her stop she was able to step down and leave the bus almost gracefully.

The three-block walk was full of new sights. Small children were out riding tricycles, and a few people were weeding or thinning plants since the soil had been loosened by the rain. Usually, when she came home, people were inside. Sometimes other workers would hurry along past her and turn up this walk or that, but now she stopped and stopped again, fascinated by the different signs and small activities going on around the houses and on the walkways. The mailman passed her and nodded; a car pulled up to him and stopped and a woman's head poked out of the window. After a minute Janice saw him pointing back in the direction the car had come. She went on.

When she was in sight of her own house, she quickened a little by habit and then stopped. It was not a trick of the light. She moved forward and stopped again. The door of her house was open. The front door was open. Her heart began to pound. Then a man came out. He walked as easily and naturally as though the house were his own. Then she noticed that there was a truck parked at the curb; a blue-green color, not large. She was trembling; she tried to stop by clenching her teeth, but the fear came and grew inside her, bursting in the trembling and then beginning again. The man went to the truck and opened the back. He was a long time there where she could not see what he was doing. If she could know how long he would stay, she might run around to the back of the house and inside through the back door and she would get the ice pick, and the big bread knife——. Another man came out of the doorway and seemed to be calling something. The truck-back one was bringing some kind of building thing up the walk. When he got close to the house, he put it down and began to work with it on the lawn. She saw, too late. It was a kind of ladder. The man did not go into the house. Instead he started to climb the ladder that he had put together. He was on the roof when she turned and ran.

At the corner lived Mrs. Nibling, who had helped Janice once during very bad weather. She ran up the walk and pounded on the door. Nothing happened. She pounded until her hands were sore and then she ran around the corner and saw a man working in the yard. She would be clear, clear, and she tried with her voice to get the man to understand: "Bow-leet-mmann! Gaww bow-leet! Gaww bow-leet!" The man rose, looked at her, going gabble-baggle with his mouth, which she was too anguished to read. She tried putting her head back and crying "He——p!" but when she looked again the man had left the garden, tools and all and gone into the house and there was the door going closed behind him.

Then she remembered her purse. There were writing things in it for times when she had wanted to say, "Have you got it in green, size thirty-four?" to someone. She wrote: "I am deaf. Robs house. Call police." Garden-man wouldn't open the door. She ran on, crying in dry sobs, her hair flying from the re-strain pins, her mouth forming over and over as the school had taught, "Gaww bow-leet, gaw bow-leet!" There was a cramp forming in her stomach and a dry stitch in her side. . . . At last there was someone, a man. He was moving toward her slowly, an older man, out for a walk. She ran up to him and showed him and he read, following word, word, word with his finger and she nodded and nodded at each word: It is true. Hear it, please hear it. Bow-*leet*, yes, yes, forming the pictures of the sounds with her lips as she had been taught. The man nodded and turned in at a house, gesturing to her: Follow. When they reached the door, there was the knocking and waiting and ram-gabble-ram-gabble while the criminals tore and harried black visions in her mind. All the furniture was going, piece by piece into that truck. All the careful years and years. She wanted to beat the walls, to slam and beat at everything. The man and the woman had decided to use the telephone. The man was picking it up and as he spoke into it the woman stood back away from her, measuring with a moon-dead stare. After the man spoke for a little while, he closed the phone and they motioned for her to sit down.

The waiting was almost worse than the running. She had no idea of what the man had said or even if he had understood her. Perhaps they had called up the crazy house men to come and take her away to be a madwoman. As they waited a few words went between the man and the woman. The woman seemed to be offering coffee. Janice began to practice-think the words she wanted to say: "Sah-owr-ee truu-bl eeyow," to the people, and "eeyow kum naoww ma 'ou," to the police. She thought the words over and formed them, going very carefully in her mind and then she realized that her face had been moving with them and the people were staring, appalled at her, and so she stopped and put her head down for the time to wash over and they waited.

The police came and the words fled. She could only nod to the people and pull the policemen along by the hand as an angry mother pulls a willful child. She dared not get into the car with them lest they take her to the jail, so she and one dazed officer pulled and struggled around the corner and up the block while the squad car followed them with its magical, inexorable dignity.

The criminals were still there. The ladder was still against the house, the truck still at the curb. As Janice and the policeman came up, the front door opened again and one of the men came out. Her policeman, breathless and red-faced disengaged himself and went forward to speak to the man. The car stopped and the other patrolman got out. They went to the house and then to the truck and back to the house again. Janice stood and waited, trembling from time to time, ready to run or, if shot, to fall. Then someone else appeared at the door and Janice looked and then looked again. Margaret! It was Margaret there. They stood looking at each other, no words forming in the hands or in the mind. They stood that way for a long minute and then Margaret very slowly raised her hands and said, "Your anniversary. We got you a TV. Look around now."

Janice saw that all around her were doors and windows. There were a hundred doors and a hundred windows and all the doors and windows were full of the heads of people, looking. Could there be so many people home, all home in the middle of the day? Some had come out on to their walks to see better, standing with heads half planted in curlers, some clutching dustrags or wet-handed from the dishes. And knee-length, at their pastel pants, were a band of the wide, wounded stares of children. All the eyes moved with her as she went the miles from the corner of the lot to the front walk and up the walk to the steps and up the steps to the porch and across the porch to the doorway. The doorway was empty. Margaret had shaken her head and gone to wait out her shame alone.

20

*T*HE DOCTOR ASSURED THEM that it had been a small, a very small attack, but when Abel had recovered and was able to go out, he went to his friends and asked all of them if they had had such sicknesses and what their doctors had said. Since he had never been sick before, the functions and failings of the body had been of no particular interest to him. Janice had always been the sick one and now he shared with her the hypnotic round of symptoms and signals and doctors' offices.

Sometimes he thought that the attack had saved Janice from a terrible sickness of the mind. For a week after The Strange Day she had done nothing but sit in the house and stare out of the window. He had never thought of her growing old. She had been old nearly forty years ago. He had never imagined her changing any more than she had changed in the first bitter seasons of their debt.

The Strange Day had been meant to be called The Happy Day, or The Proud Day, but there had been part of it that had gone on after Happy and Good, so that whenever he remembered it, he could not tell where the Good had ended and the Strange began. It had started with a letter addressed to him from an office at Janice's factory. It was called Public Relations office and it asked if the man might come to see him at work.

The man had come and brought another man with him

from the Deaf school to interpret. Janice, they told him, had been working for 45 years. She had been longer at the factory than any one else, even the president, who had retired five years ago and given control to a son. Loyalty like that was very rare these days, they told him, and must be rewarded. They wanted to have a big party in which she would be guest of honor. She would be given many gifts and would sit next to the president at the luncheon and have her picture taken with him and with the old president and there would be speeches and champagne. Abel had looked blankly back at them: "What do I have to do?"

They told him that he would have to do nothing but keep the secret, and be sure she came on the day of the party, with him. She must not come in the morning, but at noon, and he must try to get off work and come and be with her. He would have a seat at the head table also. Were there any pictures of her when she was younger, when she had started work? Were there any funny or interesting stories that the family remembered about those early days? Were there children or grandchildren who might wish to be present? The man left a card and told Abel to write down the things as he thought of them and send them to the address that was on it. The party should be on the very day that Janice had started to work, and that was only two weeks away. It left them very little time to work to get everything planned. Then the men left and Abel stood and looked at the card in his hand.

Had it not been for Margaret, he couldn't have done it at all. She had remembered where some of the old pictures were. He had forgotten that in that single, ancient Summer of the car and the clothes and the food and the dappled sunshine, Janice and he had also posed for photographs. There was Janice, standing in front of a backdrop at the State Fair. The dress of which she had been so proud had changed by magic, and now it had a misfitting, drooping look, and the shoes were wrong. Under the too-large straw hat, half hidden, was that incomparable face whose smile cut him so that he had to look away from it. He had handed it back to Margaret: "This is the right picture." Margaret looked at it and he thought her expression had wonder in it.

"Let's get one of both of you," she said. He protested, but she was already turning through the small pile, "Here." The car. He had forgotten who had taken it or when, but there they stood, preening and squinting beside it with pathetic pride, their clothes ridiculous, their faces too handsome and empty to be real. The picture made him ashamed somehow and Margaret laughed at him until he gave it back to her.

For two days they met downtown for lunch and combed their minds for stories that would interest and amuse. "Bradley was the funny one; he was always getting into trouble," Abel said. "Remember when we went to pick up the week's pieces once and we got everything loaded and we left the mill and we forgot Bradley there and we walked two blocks without him?"

Margaret shook her head, "I don't think it would be right to tell a story about Bradley. People would ask where he was. It would make them uncomfortable."

"Remember when the Union people were against us and we kept trying to find ways of getting the pieces out?"

"I don't think they would want that to be remembered——"

"But, about how they said we were taking bread out of their children's mouths, and we thought——"

"I don't think they would want to hear about those things."

"You could tell about the thread. Once—I think it was soon after she started the pieces at home—once they gave her the wrong color thread. The pieces were dark blue—for work clothes, you know—and the thread they gave her was pink. She got so scared she didn't know what to do, so I took the thread to work and dipped it in the printing ink. There were seven or eight spools of it, and the ink is very greasy, so then we had to dry all the thread out. We dried it out in the oven and then we put it in hot water to get the grease out and dried it again. It came out black, but every time a person rubbed his hand on it, it was sooty and the color came off on his hand. She did all the pieces and when we took them back the people were counting them and your mother just stood there with her eyes closed until they were all finished because she was so afraid someone would run his hand over one of the seams and have it come off black.''

"We can't tell that story either. It sounds so—it's so *desperate*."

"Then you think of one."

"I can't. I don't remember any good times there."

"We had!" he said, and was angry. "Many times! You never knew cold or hunger, or studied the money in your hand for a meal!"

She seemed on the edge of an answer, but thought better of it and pursed her mouth and dropped her hands in her lap. She looked so neat and cold sitting before him. Her outfits always reminded Abel of Mrs. Anglin's—everything matched, everything was too carefully made to match; it gave her a false, glazed look. Her hair, which was a fine shade of brown, was still rich and thick, but it had been styled in a hard, elaborate way so that it looked glued in its mass and no strand or single hair escaped that mass to give witness to her humanity.

He knew that she disliked to Sign in public and usually refused; he had asked her to come early and had taken time off to be at the restaurant and get the booth farthest back and to the left. No one would be able to see them Signing. Even then, she hesitated, using a Sign that was barely differentiated from casual gesture. She had come in precisely on time, and had walked back to the booths and his first sight of her was the same as it had been for years, a mixture of pride and sadness. She was such a straight, handsome, dignified woman, so smart, tight and invulnerable. "They are trying to honor your mother. They only want some little thing," he said.

"I know that. I was trying to think of something."

"How is Marshall?"

"Fine. He likes college, but we miss him."

"Do you think he will be able to come in for the party?"

"I've written to him about it, but I don't know. Of course the other children are anxious to come."

Mention of the other children always made Abel a little uncomfortable. "I know they are," he said vaguely. He had never been close to the others, and now with Marshall gone, he regretted that he and Janice had been Marshall's allies against them, all of them, when they were born.

The Happy Day was like a shining banner alive in the wind. Margaret, with her usual, frightening cleverness, had worked Janice around to visiting a beauty parlor and had briefed Abel on the strategies of delay that would keep her from going to work in the morning. Abel feigned sickness, and at eleven-thirty feigned sleep. At eleven-forty-five Margaret and the children came by, demanded that Janice change into her good dress and go out to the park with them to take pictures. Abel, suddenly recovered, was persuaded to join them.

Once in the car, Margaret remembered that they had forgotten the camera, and that since Abel was now well, they would be able to take Janice to work. The children began to demand to see the place where Grandma worked. Janice's objections were not answered and the car kept on. She began to plead with Abel—she had stayed out to nurse him and yet now she was coming in all dressed up. He only turned away. Margaret was busy driving and Abel's eyes were on the road. The children did not Sign. In the back seat beside Janice the youngest one was giggling.

Instead of parking on the side street, Margaret drove the car right up to the main gate, turned in and went right into the plant grounds. There was one other car there and they pulled in behind it, right at the main door of the plant. Janice was arguing unnoticed in the back seat, "They'll take the car away. Nobody is allowed to put cars here. Maybe they will call the police! I don't feel like working today. Let's come again some other time. I want to go home now." Abel turned to comfort her. He told her that Margaret knew what she was doing, and to go and do as Margaret said. Janice subsided, muttering lips and fingers among the children who were bearing their secret compressed almost to eruption.

Margaret had taken a small mirror from her handbag and was reassuring herself that her hair and makeup were perfect. She looked at the children. "Matthew, your tie is crooked. . . . Ellen, you have a smudge—no, now its fine."

It was so hard to talk to her, Abel thought. She was always so busy with plans. Sometimes it seemed to him that she put the plans in front of her to keep him away; the plans were like the way she wore her clothes, like an armor. He remembered Marshall saying something like it once, but the words had long gone; they were only a puzzle anyway, meaning without meaning.

He turned and said to Janice, "Do you remember how we all used to come here with the cart, and we took the pieces out this door . . . ?" Janice waved him away, so he touched Margaret on the arm and she had to turn her eyes from the little mirror and the perfect hair. "Do you remember how we all used to come. . . ."

Margaret looked down at her hands. "Yes," she said. "But it seems so much smaller. The way I remembered it, it was as big as a whole city block." Then she looked away again.

She had driven so as not to come past the streets of the old neighborhood, and she hoped that no one would think to ask her where they had lived, or to take them past it. Then she shook it all away and said, "It's time," and they all got out of the car.

Janice, defeated and hopeless, offered no resistance, but let herself be led in through the main floor and past the new reception desk. It had replaced the old line of cages which Margaret remembered and had steeled herself against seeing. A secretary caught her eye: "Are you the family—uh—Ryder?"

"Mrs. Ryder, yes."

"It's the second floor. Go right up. I'll buzz them and let them know you're here."

They went up in a little elevator and a man met them as they got off. He was smiling and perspiring, busy even as he stood there, eyes darting, fingers plucking and smoothing his clothes or the air. "Come, this way!" He shouted because they were deaf. Margaret flinched. They went down the corridor to a set of double doors. This had once been part of the mill side of the plant and Janice didn't know what it was used for now. She worked on the other side and had automatically turned down the corridor to go the other way before she had been guided back by the unhappy man. The doors were opened. She thought she head-heard machines. There were vibrations as of many machines, but then she stepped into the room and saw all the people, a whole roomful sitting at long tables and. turned toward her, their mouths still and no machines. Their hands were blurred with motion. Quickly, Janice turned away to hide the Sign, "What is it?" to Margaret.

"It's an honor, for you."

"Not a trial?"

"A party."

As Janice stood between doubt and comprehension, a series of flaming white explosions were hurled into her face. She cowered back unable to see, afraid that they had set her on fire. Abel held her while the murderous white darkness blinded her from this side and that. He was trying to spell into her hand, "Photograph," but she clutched at him, too frightened to read his word.

When the blinding was over, they led her dizzily past a large board from which, blown up to nearly life size, a familiar, dead stranger, trapped in a ridiculous dress, was staring back at her. In large letters it said 1918-1963.

Janice was introduced to the president at a raised table and then someone else spoke for a minute or two while they all stood still. Then everyone sat down and began to eat. Janice struggled with the food. There were too many people, too much movement of hands, fingers, faces so that she found herself distracted, and couldn't turn her face to her food. She kept up a restless survey of the room, lest some signal be given which she should not miss or the explosions come again, which they did, from here and there during the meal. It seemed odd that everyone should stop work on an anniversary day and crowd into a room to blind her and then watch her shake hands with the president while red dots from the blinding pulsed all over him and then all sit down to watch her drop crumbs on her front for half an hour.

When the dishes were cleared away a man came up to the table and sat next to her. There were to be speeches, he said, and he had been called in to interpret. Janice made tiny signs in her lap. "In front of all these people?"

"They will be saying things about you, to honor you, and you will want to thank them."

"I don't want to. I am too embarrassed."

"I'll be very quiet. No one will notice."

He was a young man and he looked at her with gentle, Deaf eyes. She decided to do him the favor. "Are you from the Deaf school?"

"Yes, I teach there."

"How do you know Sign? You speak like an educated person."

"My parents were Deaf."

"And they taught you to Sign like that?"

"Yes."

"When we were young," she said, "it was a shame to Sign. Are they teaching children better now, because the world is so modern?"

"Nothing has changed," he said. "Nothing has changed for the Deaf since long before you were born. A few schools, a few lucky ones. For the rest, no difference."

"But everyone says that the world is so modern. . . ."

"It only looks modern, and only to the people who aren't somehow between."

"I am a very ignorant person," she said. "I don't know how to speak like you do."

"Nuts!" It was a wide, local hand, and she had seen it in church from some of the young people. They both laughed.

There were introductions. People introduced others, who introduced still others and they all praised Janice and themselves to each other. Sometimes the interpreter explained when a little joke was made, so that she could laugh along with everyone and she was grateful for this. Now and then she would look past the strangers and toward the end of the table where Margaret was sitting, straight and motionless, her eyes brushing the children for crumbs. Next to her was Abel, kept from the words. Never until this moment had Janice seen how embarrassed Margaret was at her deafness and Abel's. How was it that this young man beside her could be so different, so free and joyful in his Sign?

The speaker was talking about the old days and the hard

conditions, all long changed, all so long changed, which the old-timers could still remember. "Perhaps through her interpreter," he was saying, "our anniversary girl will share with us her memories of those old times . . ." It came to her that the man himself did not know that he was going to say this thing, that it had come to him in his own fear or good feeling after the long lunch and the other people talking. She did not want to say anything, and for long moments she and the young man stood up together, locked in the light, while from the front and side the white explosions flashed and left blacker holes in the burnt-out daytime. The young man was trying hard to help her and time was going by, and the faces of the whole world waited and readied their displeasure.

"You must remember some little thing that happened when you first went to work," he said. Her mind was without a picture. She felt as though she was going to die. "Anything? Do you remember the hours that you worked—your wages when you started?"

"Oh, yes," she said, and told him, hating her hands, and he told the faces, "I made fourteen dollars a week, she says, before the bonus." While he said this to the people, she stole a cautious look at them, all the table-faces turned toward her. They were interested and approving. "We worked from eight in the morning to seven at night," she told them, "and if the machine got your finger, you didn't get any sick-leave." The people were smiling as the boy said these things, their heads and hands and bodies were still, but leaning slightly forward, as people do who are interested. As she looked at them, she knew that they were not her enemies, and then she knew exactly what she wanted to say. It was this moment that they had given her, this moment that she deserved for her forty-five years of work, and they were waiting to hear it, not with impatience but with pleasure, as sharers. Her hands made the words more surely, and with a dignity she did not know she possessed. In her mind there was no conflicting picture, nothing else to think of but the words she was making and the gratitude she felt that she had been privileged to ascend to this day.

"I did pieces. Nine or ten years I did pieces before the

Union stopped it. I don't know why the Union stopped the pieces, but I do not hate them any more and I am not angry at them now. Now I want to tell the Unions and everybody, all the people here, that I never stole food, anyone's food, and that my husband and children never stole anyone's lunch or his food ever.''

The interpreter had stopped, his hands frozen at the end of a Sign. His face had a hurt look. He said to her quickly, "I don't think this is clear. Can you explain it a little?"

She smiled at him and nodded yes. It must seem long ago to such a young person; Margaret was only a little girl when the pieces stopped. She went on, "The strike-people said we were stealing. It had to do with the pieces. . . ." The young man looked at her hopelessly while he spoke to them and managed an almost invisible shake of the head. "You see, I had to do pieces because I had two children and I couldn't leave them, but I never stole or took food from any child. I never stole from any child or anybody. It was around 1930— my daughter there, and my husband, they remember it. It was a long time ago, but some people might remember the bad things those Unions said, and think those things were true, and I thank you to give me the chance to say, no, I did not take bread from anyone, and to tell my innocence.'' And then she sat down.

Afterward they gave her a plaque and a corsage and she shook hands again with the president and others and talked some more with the young man. Looking around, she could tell that her words had been needed, because they all looked tired. Margaret was very pale, and Abel too, and even the young interpreter had a wandering, glassy look to his eyes, such as people get when they have studied a thing as deeply as it can be studied. She realized that she, too, was tired, but there was one thing more. She said to them, "I want to show you my little room, and also the workroom that was where I used to be, and also where the raised place was where I was supervisor.''

The young man said he was expected back at the school so she shook his hand for good-bye. It embarrassed her to find that she had been sweating. Her hand was sticky, and she could smell herself faintly but unmistakably over the cool blue smell of the corsage. Perhaps that was why they gave corsages. . . .

"Come on," she said to the others. She used the Sign widely, eagerly; she was no longer afraid of being laughed at because of Sign. Her years had also entitled her to The Language, and she had not been ridiculed. She took the grandchildren by the hands and led them back to the corridor and then down the hall to the right. Margaret and Abel were following more slowly, and she began to wish they would hurry. Never had she imagined that she would be so eager to show anyone where all the years had been sewn up and sent away. She began to walk quickly, by habit and not with her eyes. The smell of cloth and lint and machine oil and very slightly, of the burning of metal in friction. There was also the smell of the age of the floors and of floor cleaner, and still, of sweat and many people. "Come on!" she said, turning to hurry them. They moved a little faster.

When she got to the large double doors that opened on to the workroom, she found that they were locked. She tried to push through them, almost desperately, but they would not move open as they always had. Surely all the years should have given them that habit, surely now, when it was so needed. But the doors did not move. She had to turn and tell them, "It's closed. Maybe some girls didn't know . . ." She was, for some reason she did not understand, suddenly close to tears. "Well, come on and see this side—my place, my room. It has no door; it is against the wall on the other side; you have to turn this corner. My table is there where I can examine the things they bring me, and where you go in it has my sign; Assistant Director of Quality Control."

She turned the corner and stood very still while they all came up and looked and waited, their eyes gliding across the place and then away. The little room, the table and chair, the sign . . . They must have been taken away, all of them, because there was nothing there, only the wall. On the wall were two thin bands a shade lighter than the rest to show where the Office of the Assistant Director of Quality Control had been.

21

ABEL was sitting in a corner of the porch with the sun's redness captive under his closed lids. It was warm for June and although it was only ten in the morning, the heat was making him groggy. Janice had argued against his going outside while he still had symptoms and had been so sick, and every few minutes she came out and poked him up to watch her glower, or went stamping across the porch making the floor communicate. Abel heard and was comforted. Janice in despair had been a stranger, too frightening to remember. Janice angry was only Janice. He hoped that Margaret's visit would not bring back any of the frightening part, Janice dead-faced and shut against their Signs staring through windows as though they were walls and at walls as though they were windows. Margaret had been over almost every day until Abel's slight stroke had brought Janice back to herself to nurse him. Now that he was recovering, he hoped it would not leave her with nothing to do. He had forgotten how often anger had saved Janice in the past. She was too frugal to waste so valuable a thing.

Margaret was also thinking of Janice and her anger, and this morning she dreaded it more than ever. She guessed that the bitterness would not fall on Marshall but on herself, and though she had tried to keep the fact of her growing vulnerability a secret, her fingers jumped a little as she arranged her hat, and she caught a nail, snagged and broke it against the cloth of her white glove as she put it on. She had taken longer to dress than usual, checking and rechecking the angle of her hat and the condition of her bag, gloves and shoes. If there was to be a battle, she wanted to present herself as invulnerable. Pearl necklace, one strand, matching earrings— full armor.

As she drove to the old house, she was bothered again by how much the neighborhood had gone down. Ten years ago no one had divided the big old houses into apartments or had signs in the windows for transient rooms. Occasionally there might be a very small, genteel notice of "piano lessons" or "alterations"—apologetic whispered calls from hard-pressed windows or spinster-ladies. Now the neighborhood was filling as people crowded into the "apartments" of the divided buildings and the cries of out-of-work men were louder. WELDING—ALL KINDS in a sign three feet high in front of one porch. *Knives & Scissors sharpened, mower blades, cutters* in front of another. WE FIXIT, down the block and a dozen "For Rent" and "Room to Let" signs between. The trees still reached over the street, large, rich and leafy, but the houses beneath them had lost the ample, settled look they had once had. In front gardens and on lawns lay dead and brown, the weeds of last season catching at ragged bits of paper that had blown and come to rest there, short cuts crisscrossed the grounds. Here and there a kind of fierce determination seized some two or three houses together. Neighboring ones would be painted in harsh, fresh color; the lawns and flower beds laid out straight as the laws of science, the porches gleaming and bare of furniture. One felt the rage in it all, and a beginning of hopelessness. It made the unkempt houses look that much worse. The block on which Janice and Abel lived had been no more than brushed as yet, but Margaret could see it was only a matter of time. She sighed. With everything that was happening she didn't know if she had the energy to look around for some new houses to argue and harangue and cajole over. She pulled up to the curb, turned off the motor and went through the unconscious series of checkings and straightenings that were now habitual with her. She patted her hat, smoothed her hair, her hands moving down to brush and smooth her clothes as her face erased from its surface any sign of emotion. As she got out of the car, she looked up and saw Abel sunning on the porch. The front door opened and Janice came out, saw her and stopped for a moment to adjust her own face. Margaret took a deep breath and went purposefully up the walk.

"Did you have a nice weekend?"

"Yes, fine."

She gained time by asking about it. Abel was moving his chair around so that he could see his daughter. There was a tension moving thickly all around them. He remembered the children in the Blind Section of school, who played their fingers over the faces of strangers. "Dad, how were you over the weekend? You look a lot better today." He gained time by telling her about it.

Then at last, "Why didn't Marshall write?" It was Janice, loudly, sloppily, and Margaret almost had to smile. What amazing instincts her mother had.

"I don't know, Mother. I told him what the Company was going to do for you, and that a telegram delivered to the mill would be nice. I suppose he got involved in something at school and it just slipped his mind."

"He has not written to us for a long time," Abel said. "I miss the letters he sent at the beginning. He writes to you. What does he say?"

"He says he is fine. He mentions the work, his classes and what he is taking up—"

"Then why doesn't he write to us? Why doesn't he talk to us also in those letters?" Janice demanded. "If he can't come and if he won't write to us . . ."

The letter was in Margaret's purse and her fingers rose over the clasp, waiting, and then she made a decision, opened the purse and took out his letter. Maybe she could read part of it, maybe she could fix it and read some of it. She opened the letter and skimmed it quickly:

Dear Mother,

I didn't write or send a telegram to Grandma because
I couldn't have said anything that wouldn't have been
hypocritical and dishonest. After exploiting her and denying her her human dignity for 50 years, they cooked up a
cheap publicity stunt to advertise their own good works
through her. I don't see how you could have allowed it to
happen. . . .

"He says he's fine," Margaret said.

I got the clippings you sent from the *Herald* and that
trade paper . . .

"He got the clippers I sent—of the pictures. He says he
was very glad to have them."

. . . and I thought they were a real study.

"He gave them a lot of study."

How horrified Grandma looks at being used like that.
How marvelously she seems to rise above what they tried
to do to her. They could give her that curly hair and pin
that corsage on her, but she never could or would fit into
any of it. How much more honest if she had gone there in
a simple housedress and let them all know that Deaf or
not, she knew what this Society does to its misfits.

"He says that was no work dress you were wearing."

I have definitely decided to go with *We Shall Overcome*
this summer. Where, exactly, we don't know, but it will
be somewhere in the Rural South and we will live in the
poverty that this country imposes on so many.

"He talks about his summer plans . . ." and with the letter
lying in her lap, she noticed a slight stutter in her hands.

Janice and Abel opened their words together. Each knew immediately that his own forgivable greed would be shaping itself in the other one's mind. "Where is he going for the summer? What does he plan to do?"

"He isn't sure," Margaret lied, wondering where her gifts had gone. Years of dissembling for one's self came to weakness and stuttering when it was needed most, in defense of someone loved more than one's self. "There is a group of young people at the University—a group which is interest——" The Sign made no distinction between interested and interesting—and there she hid gratefully in the cleft of the difference. She needed the moment's cover and a chance to peer out at the pursuers. "William and I know that he must work very closely with the people at the University while he is there." Up again and gone.

But Janice and Abel were not to be outrun. They came on paced with the slow, inexorable logic of their need. She must write to him and tell him to spend the holiday with them. If he had friends, he could leave them for a while. He had not been to the house since he had left for college; he had heard almost nothing of his grandmother's Honor-Day. He had forgotten all his Sign, but they would write things to him; at least they could see him, and now that his grandfather was going to retire, there would be time to share all of the things they had promised themselves. There would be time for him to learn Sign again, to help them as that wonderful young man had helped Janice.

"I know he would be glad to hear from *you*," Margaret said, beating backward toward another hiding place. Then she saw that their eyes had moved from her.

There was a woman coming up the walk, a quick woman, moving in a businesslike way, but with small gestures of unease. She had tried to dress well, but something was missing and she looked uncomfortable in the clothes. She was holding a paper of some sort. Selling something, Margaret thought, or trying to. The parents sat still, deferring to her as they always did: Margaret would send the person away without the need for embarrassment. They settled back, their faces dead-ened. When they looked again, however, the woman was still there and in another moment, Margaret was speaking to them. At her side the woman stood, braced, trying not to stare.

"This is a neighbor of yours," Margaret said hastily, her Sign stubbed and small and a little angry because she was conscious of having done this for so many years without having lost the sense of shame. "She has a petition for you to sign." Together their lips formed the word petition and then Abel turned to Janice and explained it.

"There's a house on the next block that's up for sale, and there's a certain group that is trying to buy it." The woman spoke to Margaret and she mumbled, being ashamed to use her voice. Margaret took her words dutifully. "The group is a group of drug addicts."

Addict. Drug. It had first come out as "people who use too much medicine," and so Margaret had to explain again, and then to explain drug addiction. She had begun to perspire heavily now. Beneath its makeup she felt her skin melting in the heat. Abel suddenly came alight, "Oh, yes, I know what it is!" He made a quick Sign to show her, but the Sign was new. "The young people call it this. The minister at church was telling us about it. Also" (and he spelled) "a-c-i-d—h-e-a-d." The neighbor was beginning to feel beyond her depth and the heat was beginning to glaze her eyes. Margaret saw her glance quickly to the house, no doubt longing for the dark, cool recesses of the rooms inside, but then her face closed and she pulled her eyes away because she did not wish to incur any small debt to these people. Margaret fought back the desire to ask her in and so force the refusal from her, but Janice and Abel were both talking together, upset and frightened.

"Now, are these dopers going to get a house?"

"They have to be in jail!"

"Yes, what about putting them in jail?" Janice cried. "Dope is against the law and if they have it and people know, they will call the police and the dopers will have to go to jail!"

Even before Margaret was finished giving the words the woman was ready. "The police can't be there all the time. These people call themselves recovered addicts and they say they need a Rehabilitation Center for others. They call it a halfway house. Halfway to what, is what I would like to know. Our streets will be full of dope fiends and police, people won't be able to go out at night. Those people will get to know who goes in and who goes out and what women are left alone nights. Every one of these people has just come out of jail. You know the kind of people they are, a criminal element, the lowest kind of criminals—people who are *diseased.*"

Margaret translated dutifully, but it came flat against the echo of the woman's long-drawn, venomous whisper. It sounded ridiculous as she reframed it in her fingers, the woman's hysterical picture of the streets overflowing with crime, a dope fiend hiding in wait behind every tree. She would have Janice and Abel sign the petition, of course, but not for this woman's reasons. They were all looking toward Margaret now, Janice and Abel waiting for her to give them the under-meanings of the Hearing, the Difference, that unbridgeable Difference. She excused herself to the neighbor—who lapsed, melting and staring, into her own mind—and addressed herself to the two old people.

"I'm not afraid for your safety," she said slowly, "but if we let these people come in it will mean that the neighborhood has given up——"

"I don't understand," Abel said.

"It has to do with losing something, with having something that makes your life worth living, and then losing it. Has that ever happened to you?"

Janice and Abel looked at each other with what Margaret could have sworn was guilt.

"Yes," Abel said, "it happened once."

"Well," Margaret went on, "if the neighborhood gives up and lets these people in, poverty will follow and you won't have escaped Vandalia Street at all. You'll be no different from the ones that come and you'll have to make the same awful decisions that they have to make." She wondered if it was Vandalia Street he had meant, and then remembered dimly, the arguments about some money, some ancient, long forgotten money owed somewhere. Abel nodded and reached for the petition and he and Janice signed and the woman thanked them and left.

They looked forlorn when she left them. They were standing very close to each other as she had seen children do who are playing in a strange place in which there might be sudden corners that were unfriendly. For some reason she too felt sad, very sad and very tired. As she drove home, she thought how tired and confused Janice and Abel must have been. Janice had forgotten to take up the argument over Marshall.

22

*M*ARSHALL'S new letter lay where his mother had filed it meticulously for answering.

We are all to blame for conditions which have produced such poverty. How can I tell the people here that we didn't know what was happening to them, that no one I ever knew had lived with fear, with despair; that I had to come down here and see before I could believe? I feel guilty and ashamed because of all the things I had—the comfort and the luxury that dulled me, that dulls my family to the whole world crying outside my safe and sheltered little neighborhood. If it hadn't been for that Black Activist coming up to talk to us at school, I would have gone on thinking that Justice in America had been bought out by the middle-class forever—that no Blacks wanted our help . . .

William had raged over the letter for half an hour. "I'm sorry I dulled his sensibilities with luxury—it's a mistake I can remedy. Who the hell does he think he is!" Because Margaret had only been hurt and was not angry, she had tried to placate William, and in the end she had gotten him to laugh a little at the picture that Marshall had sent in the letter. There he stood in the field. He was facing the camera, his shirt off, his hand raised to shield his eyes from the murderous sun.

Around him was something growing—it looked like cotton—
and he was holding an ancient hoe. In the background on a
little rise was a wretched, crumbling cabin.

"Hoein' cotton," William said and sucked his tongue.
"I had to hire a man to help me with the yard work because
he could never find the time . . ."

It was Marshall's letter to Janice and Abel that brought
Margaret to rage. Abel handed it to her without comment
when she came by to take Janice to the doctor, and she took
the letter carefully from him, studying his face as she did, for
clues. Janice had come up and had begun to say something,
but Abel had stopped her and the two of them had just stood,
waiting, "posing as Deaf" and let her see nothing. She hated
this Deaf-role they took when they were hurt. Surely over forty
years of giving had entitled her to more.

Marshall's hand was hurried and irregular, a young hand;
the character in the letters was still forming; the lines of letters were now loose, now crabbed, now slashing and now hesi-
tant:

> Well, here I am in the Ole South. It's like another world.
> I suppose Mother has told you why I am down here and
> and what we are doing. In setting up the Freedom
> Schools and giving assistance and advice to the small
> local Black Churches, we are hoping to bring these for-
> gotten people into modern society. These Beautiful peo-
> ple have been silent for too long. Now they are crying
> out, and America must be taught to heed them.

Margaret's eyes slipped down the page to be stopped near the
end.

> So I know you will be glad for me, and will have greater
> sympathy for this work than the average middle-class
> person. Sharing your problems and humiliations has made
> me sensitive to suffering. . . .

The letter began to tremble in her hand and her face
began to suffuse with blood. Janice was watching it redden,

watching the tremor in the paper. Margaret began to speak, but the words were too quick. Janice only saw something that looked like "humiliation," but the look of Margaret was too angry for it to have been that word, which was a church word. Then she just stood and tapped the paper with her finger because she was angry. Janice could no longer control herself.

"You sent him away! You sent him away into that poor-place with all those dirty people? Look at them!"

Another picture. This one was Marshall, tall, smiling and golden, standing on a precarious porch and flanked by young people, black and white, all of whom were wearing clothes that looked as though they had never been new. "Our Staff," he had written on the back of the picture. It would have been comic had their faces not been so open and young and full of so obvious a pride.

"I . . ." Margaret put the picture face down on the coffee table and took her purse off her arm. She suddenly had a picture of Marshall on the night before he had left. He had stood in the living room arguing with them. He had called them hypocrites. It must have been satisfying for him to have done this; he hadn't yet spent half a lifetime defending out of love things of which he didn't approve. "He wasn't sent, Mother; he went because he wanted to go. Of course we wanted him to stay and do something closer to home."

"What are you saying about this boy?" Abel's face darkened. "How can it be true that he would choose such a thing? I think his father has punished him. I think that William is angry because of something he has done and will not forgive him, but only sends him down there to be poor and hungry and a disgrace!"

It was getting difficult for Abel to speak, the words were halting and stiff as though he spoke in pain.

"It is better to whip him. Whip him and then he will cry and it will hurt him and he will be ashamed, but he will take this in his own house and not with the whole world to laugh at him. William has sent him down there to make the people down there do to him what a father should do in his own house."

"You don't understand," Margaret said and gritted her

teeth a little. "This is Marshall's idea. He said he felt a call to go, just like a minister or a doctor does, and there was a group going from the University, so he went with them."

"To do what?" Abel demanded. "What will he *do* for those people?"

"I don't know, really; I know he wants to help them, to—he says in his letters he is going to 'bear witness.' "

"They are going to Court, then, to jail those people?" Janice cried.

"No, Mother," and the tightness ground tighter in Margaret's chest. Her jaws were aching. "He means to tell people, to see for himself the—conditions down there and then to tell others."

"Is it a secret that there are poor farmers? I always knew that. My father knew it too, and that is why they sent me away to learn a trade. Tell him to come home now; I can tell him all the things about being poor and then he won't have to be so dirty and hungry and he won't have to live in a cockroach house, bad with rats, bad with rain that comes in on the bed. Tell him his grandfather knows all these things."

"But, Father, I think he'll say that he wants to work with the poor, to help them because they need so many things . . ."

"So the poor *need!*" Abel said, "Then"—the hand trembled and then cut like a curse—"*I am the poor! I need!* Do you tell him to look far away, to see with his good eyes all the way to—to—" and he broke the Indian name of the town to pieces in his hands—"when Poor is *here! We* are the Poor!"

Janice's own hands came up but not to speak. She was biting a knuckle, her eyes widened and locked at the word. Then she began to argue: "That isn't *now,* that was before, in——"

Abel waved her idea away. "Not poor in money, I know it, I know it, not in money—poor in—in World-thing, to do, to say, to know! In the World!"

Janice began to cry. For a minute her husband and daughter stood back, embarrassed. She could not see if they were speaking or not, so she spoke herself,

"I wish Marshall was like that nice man they had at the party. Deaf have Hearing for children. That can't be helped.

But the Hearing go away and only a few stay not-Deaf-not-Hearing, to try to make a way in the danger-places where the Deaf have to cross over. You should be ashamed to let him go with the poor and dirty strangers. You took him away from us and you never even taught him Sign. If you made him learn Sign, he can be ready to help us, and be with us and all the Deafs who are not helped in the school where people just want them to look like Hearing!''

''Yes,'' Abel said, and she saw him and stopped. ''Now he is down there, and he will learn all things, a hundred other things to work and make for strangers he will never know again.''

Janice shook her head and there was a trace of a hook in the fingers she held up to speak. ''He said we were humiliated.''

An echo, from Abel: ''Yes, he said that. In the letter, he said it. This is not true. Our family is good and we are proud and we were never humiliated and never made a problem. Who told him this? Who told him we were humiliated? Who told him we made a problem?''

''You were never a problem,'' Margaret said tightly, ''not for him.''

''And you—you, too. You had a happy life, too. No problems were in it.'' There was an icy-cold moment of remove as Margaret watched her hands speaking and suddenly they were speaking as they must have in childhood, without any sound in her head, without any consciousness of words before the True Sign,

''Have you forgotten a girl arguing with a coffin-maker? Wasn't there a young girl telling her mother's female troubles to a strange doctor, and didn't she have to explain his answers without truly knowing what they meant? Wasn't it every day——'' She stopped, and suddenly her face went pale with shock. Then she shook her head quickly as though she had been hit by something, ''I'm *sorry*, very sorry.'' The ''sorry'' thumb trembled. ''I never, never meant to say that. Forgive me, please excuse me, I'm just tired and upset today. . . . I'm sorry.''

She sat in the car and listened to herself breathing like a runner after losing a race. As desperately as she wanted to start the car and get away, she was afraid to drive just now. Her hands and mind were being pulled and thrown in spasms of anger and shame, all independent of her will. She tried to think, at least to see into her own feelings and recognize the thoughts, but all that came to her had already been repeated over and over all down the walkway and into the street and around the car to open the front door: What have I said, what have I said, what have I said? She knew she would have to drive away. Janice and Abel would be looking out the window because her leaving had been so hurried and confused. If they saw her sitting in the car, just sitting, they would be down the walk in a minute to find out what was wrong. Carefully she took off the emergency brake and eased the car out, and slowly, slowly on down the street.

If only there was someplace to go, now, with this lovely new car that William had bought for her. If there was only someone, some psychiatrist or minister or friend or husband or mother or father to whom she could tell what she had done and who would understand—not forgive, not advise, only listen and understand. Her own minister had gone to the easier side long ago. No doubt he was this minute in the church rec-reation hall organizing some teen-age seminar or other in which earnest, angry young people would declaim about their generation's rejection of values it had never sounded. He was a popular minister. And why not be on the winning side? Marshall's friends were so unwounded it must be a relief to deal with them. If she told the popular young minister about her parents, he would quote the New Morality: ''You have to live your life—if they can't adjust, well, that's their prob-lem.'' How easy it would be for him to tell her to sacrifice that in which he recognized no value.

Her mind paused briefly and then passed over the Deaf-minister. Abel was too well known at church and his position meant too much to him. News of a visit would surely get around and there would be questions. Deaf communities might form in cities, but they were still each a small town in itself with all the small-town time to pick threads and knot and em-broider rumor, and moves to feel again and again at the knotted underside of feuds and wrongs and jealousies. There was nobody, really, and if someone existed for her, all wise and uninvolved, what would she say after all?

She came out on Webster Avenue and for no particular reason found herself crossing Webster and turning down toward Vandalia Street. She continued to follow Vandalia until she was back in the old neighborhood. She had no idea why she continued to drive on and on toward ever-more-familiar streets, or what she intended to do when she finally came to "her" street, "their" street. But she was aware that her hands no longer trembled on the steering wheel and that she had lost the feeling of panicky urgency at the stoplights where she had waited her time with the civilized, patient trust of the city driver. She crossed Carver Avenue, but it was barely recognizable. Familiar stores were gone. The huge furniture store in which she had always looked so longingly on her way to school and back, was gone, and in its place were many small stores all jammed together with a dumpy, hopeless look to them. And there were Negroes, only Negroes all around. She crossed over, continuing down Vandalia slowly. It was all the same; it was all changed. It was the way a dream would change things, strange eyes staring from a familiar face.

The street was absolutely bare of commerce. There were no pushcarts, sidewalk merchants, pretzel men, peddlars, beggars, paper boys with loaded wagons, hand-bill passers, sidewalk preachers or women in sag-hem housedresses haggling the evening meal. A few cars were parked at various places along the street, a few children were out running among the alleys and women were at the windows for whatever breeze might have lost itself on its way from the river. And they were black, women, children, old men scattering the stoops—all black. How long had it been since she had seen this street? Where had all the other people gone? She began to count the years in disbelief. (I was pregnant with . . . yes, with Marshall; it's almost twenty years since I came here last.) It gave her a hollow feeling, that she had lived in this city for so many years and had never come this way, had never had a single errand nearby that would have taken her—and then she remembered Janice's Honoring Day. They could have come back and seen all these streets and this, where she had spent the first twenty years of her life. It wasn't fitting, not on that day —it wasn't fitting any day—to revisit places where you have been wronged or shamed or unhappy. She had argued with Marshall about it during the vacation, his preoccupation with misery,

"Doesn't it make you feel guilty that a family in Vietnam could live on the food we throw away?"

"I've told you all to clean your plates. It isn't your father and I who waste the food in this house."

"You're missing the whole point—the fact of our over-consumption, gorging ourselves while others are starving!"

"I thought the point was that we should be grateful for the food we have and proud of your father because he has been able to give it to us, and thankful that our country is rich enough to feed its people."

"Do you know how many of our people are hungry?"

"Does it help the poor when we have dissension at our table?"

That had made him so angry that he had stalked out. William had begun to call him back but had changed his mind, and only looked at Margaret and shook his head.

"He wants me to say I'm guilty and at fault," she said. "I know that he wants me to take the blame for something and unless I do, he will continue to go on like this. He says, 'Be honest and take the blame,' but if I am honest, I can't see any to take. Next time, I'll just say I did it, whatever it is and maybe we'll have a peaceful meal."

"You know better than that," William said. "He wants to be a saint, and we are not the kind of parents saints have. We would be better if we were—uh—*afflicted*."

Abel had said, "We are the Poor," and now Margaret thought; *I* am the afflicted.

She had ridden past the place. She turned at the next corner, hoping the old eyesore would be where she had left it so gladly when she had left the neighborhood. She turned the corner again and there it was, as ugly, squat and foreign, as out of place as ever; almost abandoned. St. Casimir Catholic

Church. The sign was gone, of course, it had been gone in her day and everybody knew it only as The Polack Church. She pulled up beside it and sat in the car for a long time, feeling stupid and self-conscious. She had thought at first of going to the place where Mr. Petrakis had once had his pawnshop, but it had been broken up into two stores and both were strange. Other people lived in her old apartment, the school was closed, the school grounds locked. This place was familiar, remembered, but now that she was here, what should she do— sit and stare at it?

At last she got out of the car and locked it, and went up to the church, and then slowly up the narrow ridged set of steps and in through the peeling archway to the door. The church façade was stucco of some kind, with wooden columns and the archway and entry painted to look like stone. It hadn't looked like stone when the church was new; it looked now like a closed booth at a carnival. She tried the door; it opened, and she went warily inside. The air there was rank and fetid, but images were still in the niches and a picture of the Virgin hung on the side wall. She looked gingerly into the holy-water font. There was about a half-inch of water in it. She thought: *Now*, I feel guilty, and her mind summoned Marshall again. *"Now,"* she said to his image, "you can be proud of me at last." It made her smile.

She sat down at the back of the church, alert for any movement or sound from some "legitimate" congregant who would discover her, a trespasser. There was no sound. She waited, wondering why she had come and what she would do now. The minutes went on. It occurred to her that she had come here to speak her piece, to be understood without being answered. "It's a foreign place," she said. She spoke in Sign, a pinched, crabbed Sign that mirrored her reticence, even to herself. She began again, self-consciously, her ear still tuned for a footstep, a cough, a door opening. "I want you to know something." She got up and moved closer to the picture of the Virgin. It was a poor picture, simultaneously crude and senti-mental, but the hands were in a gesture as though the Virgin too was Signing. "I want to tell you about my father," she said. "My father is proud and dignified and unselfish. He wants to share in the World, to read and learn and grow. And all of these things that he is, he became too late for me. His accomplishments are all spread out in front of me and instead of comforting, they only confuse me. To whom can I go and say; 'Help me. My father has learned and grown and improved, and in his changing, buried the truth of my past from himself and from me and from my son.' " The words exploded. "You wouldn't write!" she cried. "You were too proud to write and I ended up arguing with the police when Bradley was lying on the floor and I—I am alone to remember the coffin-maker and the things I dream about after all these years. You went and changed and Marshall never knew I had a brother whose memory haunts me along with the stench of the tenements!"

She felt herself getting so angry that the words were almost out of control. Her hands were working in her lap as though so eager to use themselves that if she paused a moment to regain her calm they would begin to fight each other. She closed her eyes tightly until the anger passed a little and when she opened them, she saw Marshall in her mind and was angry all over again. "You fool! Your humility has an arroga . . . , a pride that makes me sick!" (She used the "proud" Sign widely, the manicured nail raking up the buttons of her dress.) "You watch someone's despair and think you share it. You watch someone's poverty and think you see it. If you want guilt, you spoiled, pampered, beautiful, beloved boy, you will have to stand without one single one of those crutch convictions of yours—no virtue, no single saving grace—and watch the ones you live with and will love for a lifetime cheapened and made ugly and even in your own eyes. You want praise that you can afford, your false poverty and false guilt and false humiliation. Your life, freely and gladly given for the fashionable cause, the visible cause, or what is dying worth? How dare you sacrifice without asking me? You are so sure that your life is all yours to give, and that we have no claim on it!"

She was too angry. The fingers began to scramble at the words leaving one unfinished for the next. She felt she must have been running somehow; there was suddenly not enough breath in her lungs, not enough air in the church. She let her hands fall into her lap. This thing she had done had come to nothing; it was only a lunatic departure from the normal, decent day of a normal, decent woman.

Margaret got up and smoothed her clothes, turning to leave. There in the back of the church was an ancient, black-clothed creature, sitting huddled against the wall and staring at her with frank, unfeigned fascination. She couldn't tell if this witness was male or female and this disturbed her almost as much as the fact of its watching. In the toothless, caved and wrinkled face, the eyes, unnaturally bright, did not blink. They followed her with pitiless and disinterested amusement all the long way back, step by step of it, to the door and out of the church.

The street was still and the backs of the tenements empty. Windows gaped, but there was no one sitting in them, and the buildings had a closed look, nursing their own grievances. Margaret walked down the steps and went to the car. It lay dying quietly at the curb, the tires slashed, the doors opened slightly, to invite a look inside at the eviscerated upholstery. From underneath there was a slow drip-drip of some life-fluid or other. It ran into small, dark pools, still spreading in the silence of the street.

23

*J*ANICE AND ABEL never dreamed that Marshall would take his side of the struggle to the churches. For a while he did not write, and Margaret said that he had not written to them either. Abel thought that Margaret had sent word to him to stop showing the horror of his situation. The letters that they had were cheering and dead; they were like the letters Margaret had written when she had first married and gone from their beautiful, safe new home to the wretched poverty of that shack with William. The sweltering weeks of summer rose and were gotten through somehow and other problems grew and flowered and died back with the summer. Abel had suddenly looked about him with new, stranger's eyes and decided that the neighborhood was beginning to show its age shabbily. They had the house painted and the porch fixed and when they realized that these repairs would take most of their savings, they raged and argued at the world and each other until the work was done and the house stood shining and strong in the center of the block like a good tooth in a rotting mouth. Then there had been a scandal flaring briefly in the papers when two children long in the Retarded Home were found to have been deaf all along and another scandal when a girl at the Deaf school was found to be pregnant. There were fitful attempts to form the Deaf community into some association which would have the power to speak for it in these and other matters, but the scandals faded and the thought died.

In August, a social worker at the Children's Hospital came to the church and asked for help in learning Sign. Her plea was interpreted movingly by the minister and she said that she had been to other places to get this help. Many people seemed interested when she told how deaf children coming to the hospital were frightened by the strange surroundings and machines. In their fear, they could not lip-read, especially from the mouths of strangers. Many were too young to read the words written to comfort or instruct them. There was a flurry of enthusiasm for a group of volunteer interpreters to go to the Court, the hospital and the welfare department when there was need, but when the group had been formed, these agencies refused the volunteers because of what they called "protection of confidentiality." Abel had given his name as a volunteer and at first he wanted to get a lawyer to make a fight of it, but interest soon waned and died; lawyers were expensive and no one wanted to fight for the privilege of doing a favor, so the project went no further.

In August the dope addicts came around with a petition and Janice and Abel signed it, thinking it was like the other one they had signed against the idea. The dopers had cleverly sent nice young people out with their petition instead of going themselves and showing their horror to the neighborhood. Later Margaret told them that the people with the petition were themselves the founders of the idea, the dopers. Janice shook her head, "That can't be—you didn't see them; they were nice young people. The real dopers must have been waiting behind the trees or in car while the young people went to the houses." There was a fuss about getting their names removed from the petition.

September began like a promise of peace. The hottest days were over and it seemed as though the world might stop its wildness and get back to its work, its school, its rhythm. Janice was at church the first Sunday in September, wearing a new fall hat she had bought, and although she knew it was early to do it, she was eager to put an end to a bad and troubled season. She had never liked to come early to church and always arranged to have last-minute reasons for keeping Abel from it, and now they went in and sat down, giving quick greetings to their friends just as the minister came forward to open the service.

He was new and very young, and they didn't know how long he would last. The Reverend Mr. Maartens had left twenty years ago after his wife died and since then there had been seven or eight of them, all young, none staying very long and one or two resenting the extra work that a Deaf community imposes on its Hearing members. The Deaf had withheld their feelings with this one. It was hard to begin to like a man who might leave even before he had gone a single liturgical cycle, advent to advent with them. This one seemed nice enough, but he was not of the Deaf; he had learned his Sign and not been raised in it. Abel noted that like all Hearing, it embarrassed him to use his face and body and so his Sign had no wit. He could never *be* Christ before Pilate and then Pilate before Christ, a thirty-second speech made with expression alone, drawn quickly and quickly erased without a single Sign. Hadn't the old pastor often done that? Now, Abel sometimes found himself dozing during the sermon.

He didn't even realize he had begun to doze this time, but a sudden stiffening at his side brought him up quickly and he looked at Janice. Was it time to go already? She was staring straight ahead, the little hat trembling 'I'm afraid, I'm afraid,' on top of her head.

"I'm glad that this young man called on *us* for help," the minister was saying. His Sign was satisfied, "and I am sure his grandparents, Mr. and Mrs. Abel Ryder, are very proud of him and his unselfish work. He says in his letter that the people with whom he is working need clothing and canned goods very desperately and, of course, money. He writes: Anything warm and durable, worn, perhaps, but still usable and in good repair would be a godsend to us this winter. Canned food or boxed food that will not spoil is especially needed." He put the letter down. "I think we might get up a special shipment. . . . I will put a big box in the church office and we can leave it there throughout this month. When you come to services or for Silent Bingo on Wednesday night, please remember to bring those clothes which would be useful and any extra canned goods from your shelves. I'm sure that the regular members of this church will also. In case you want to send money privately, I will leave the letter and address posted on the bulletin board.''

Janice had gone a dead white. Abel thought she was going to faint and so he held her elbow cupped in his hand and the two of them stared straight ahead, throwing their minds against all the useless ways of escape. Janice began to get up during Silent meditation, but he kept her, tightening the fingers on her elbow until he could feel to the meeting of the bones. Immediately after the final prayer, he enacted a quick charade, looking at his watch, feigning shock and the remembering of some important thing and pushing his wife before him to walk quickly from the church, faces full of the urgency of the errand on which they were going. They reached the back of the church seconds before the minister and Janice, no longer to be held, broke and ran.

Strangely, it was when he saw her running down the few steps and moving away down the street that Abel realized, felt, saw, the completeness of his love for her. Never had she looked so graceless, so ridiculous or so real. She was a large woman now; she had put on a great deal of weight since leaving work, but she didn't realize it and had kept to the little flowered hats she had always worn. This hat was perched up on her head like a hiccup, and beneath it, her face and body showed all of the forty-nine years of enduring fear, failure, the death of a child, poverty, changelessness, change, success, betrayal, her own imperfections and his also. He knew he had to catch up with her; she would fall off her little stilted shoes or faint and then there would be more shame than ever. He had spoken to the doctor about her fearfulness and shame, once, and the doctor had only said, "I would suggest counseling for her, but of course, for the Deaf . . ." So there was only himself.

He ran down the church steps and off down the street, catching up with her at the corner. They were both panting and gasping for breath, she half weeping and her hair already frayed out from its pins in gray wisps. The pain he saw in her face was almost more than he could look at. "Not the father alone——" Her hands did not need to catch breath. While she gasped for air, the words were flung from her fingers with stunning speed. "Both of them! She too! How could she? They took that boy, that fine, good boy when they had every money and learning, care, the world, every richness, every good thing and they *made a beggar of him!* They turned him to be a beggar and sniffle in the churches for the scraps in other people's closets! We can never go to church again. You know that. Never. It will be a disgrace to look at us. I want to go home and die in my house and never let her in again, my daughter, who made him a beggar!"

He knew he must try to calm her. If they could get to the Avenue, he would try to wave for a taxi to take them home. He looked up the street, yearning for some miracle to send a taxi cruising back on its way to the Avenue. People from church would soon be coming around the corner. "I don't know if it is so bad," he said, and the words were almost motionless, to soothe her, "it's for *them,* he is begging, not for himself. He's asking for the people down there, where he is."

"My hopes come true, then! Wonderful. Change the words on my grave if it says my grandson is a beggar. Say, Great Fame, Family Pride, he is a beggar's beggar!"

"Those Deaf who know, who are smart about the World won't laugh at us. They will understand that he is asking for these things the way a minister asks for money for the church, for the poor."

"He is down there making those black-people's riots, making trouble, and he is being a minister to a bunch of Deaf beggars!"

Deaf? She had said *Deaf* beggars. He was sure of it. "What?"

"I said he was being minister to black beggars."

"You said Deaf beggars."

"I said black beggars!" But the Signs were too different from each other. He knew that her hands had said 'deaf' whether she had wished to say it or not. "Come," he said. "Let's go before the people come."

But they had to forgive Margaret. They had to forgive her as soon as they reached home; their need for her was too constant a thing. Abel wondered if Marshall had written a letter to her church also. It was a richer congregation than his and Janice's and he asked Margaret when she came by on Wednesday to take him to the Social Security office. Janice was hiding in the bathroom. Abel greeted his daughter and asked her about the letter as casually as he could. Her eyes recoiled as if from too great a light. "How did you know?" And then, "Did your minister get one, too?" and then, "Oh, Lord!"

"Was it difficult for you?" he asked. "Are people saying bad things?"

"A few of them have been cruel. The ones I hated most were the pitying ones, the ones who acted as though he were some sort of Communist. . . . Oh—do you know that word, *Communist?*"

"Yes, I know it." And he smiled.

"I forget," Margaret said. "I keep forgetting that you— that you've changed," and she shook her head and then reached up unconsciously to check her hat. "Was there trouble for you?"

"Your mother," Abel said. "She was upset, a little bit afraid of what the people will say. She doesn't understand."

"Do you?"

"No, but I have been talking with some of the friends I have from Gallaudet. They read and understand things. I don't understand yet, but young people are trying to correct some of the evils in the world—what they think are evils."

"Was anyone ever so certain before just what should be done?"

"Well, we have one virtue, you and I, a virtue they do not use so much now."

"What is that?" Margaret asked.

"Loyalty."

"Oh, yes," Margaret said. "They use it a great deal, *our* loyalty; they depend on it."

They started out through the door. It had been raining and the air was sticky and unpleasant. As they went down the walk, Margaret fought the impulse to turn and look back at the house. When they were getting into the car she did glance quickly toward the two upstairs windows. Janice was caught in that glance, peering back, and Margaret lowered her head and ducked into the car before her mother could move or release the telltable twitch of curtain and step away into the equivocating darkness of the house. "Loyalty," Margaret murmured.

By the time they came out of the Social Security Office, they both felt tired. They had gone in, in mid-morning and it was now well past noon. They had waited on a succession of lines and filled out a succession of cards and applications and been directed and misdirected enough times to retain a slight sense of dizziness even out on the street. Margaret suggested that they have lunch at the new French restaurant that had just opened up near the Farmers' Market. It wasn't far from there to Page's where for this week only, the whole ground floor had been given over to an international display of crystal and glassware. Abel shook his head and said that he didn't want much to eat. He felt uncomfortable in large expensive restaurants. Janice might have fixed a lunch for them. She would be worried, since they hadn't expected to spend so much time . . .

"If we eat a sandwich somewhere quickly, won't you come and see the glass with me? I won't be getting back this way before next week and by that time it will be gone."

"Oh, all right, if it doesn't take long."

She had wanted to tell Abel that Marshall had his own heroics to warm him, but that she had wanted—needed—in this tiresome day in this ordinary week of buying school clothes, chauffering the children, shopping, cooking and cleaning, one soul-stilling, restful interlude of tranquility and beauty and spacious serenity. She was yearning for a peaceful and unhurried time of communion with something that was silent but not mute, for the discreet, muffled public place that wouldn't admit the suffering or embittered parts of everyone's life. The evenings at home were long now. William's anger at Marshall wasn't loud or violent; it was a low but constant undertone, like the half-heard vibration of some dangerous new appliance in the house. It was being kept at the low hum, awaiting Marshall's return and the first self-righteous word that he might utter. She thought she might be able to persuade her father to share this small moment of escape. As it was, they had a hamburger and cup of coffee in a crowded and a noisy place and with the lunch weighing greasily undigested, like bad memories, they drove down toward Page's.

Abel was nervous and a little dizzy because he was worried about Janice. They had been out far longer than he had expected and there was Janice, alone and still sick with shame, waiting in the house. He felt out of place anyway in the big downstown stores and he had tried to pull back from Margaret's invitation without having to tell her these things. He couldn't imagine why she wanted to take him to some store. To see glass. All that fragile glass, all that valuable, breakable glass was only waiting, perched on long glass shelves, to catch his sleeve in turning or be rattled to the edge by his unknowing step; to be brushed, pushed, tipped, rocked. There were a hundred scenes of humiliation and alarm waiting for him in such a place. She had pleaded and he had to sigh and give in. She owned the car, after all; he had to follow her.

It was another world, a haunting poem to silence; light without heat, movement held resting, rest that moved, facets that burned for a moment and then went black as one passed them only to have others, dark before, wake into radiances rimmed with a hair-thin rainbow. Of all the things that man does or makes, the art of glass seemed to Margaret to be the most beautiful. Everyone felt it. Few people spoke except in whispers of awe or delight. Margaret felt a powerful urge to speak with her father there, to share in their singular gift, words without the need to break the glowing surface of the silence. The bodies of men and women, angels, stars, flowers, danced in their worlds of crystal; visible winds blew across those worlds; the tides of seas ebbed and flowed soundlessly in the glass. Once he had asked her about the light. It must have been thirty years ago, maybe more, when she was very young. He had asked her if the sunlight made a sound. Wind did; that you couldn't see. Did sun? Did it hit the nailheads of the floor with a sound and warm over the bricks of the buildings next door with some other, gentler sound? She hadn't understood him then, and had laughed and said, "You don't *hear anything*. The sun doesn't make *any* noise," He had looked puzzled and said, "That's funny. I hear things in my head, things I think must be sounds. I always thought I heard that sound, the sun on things, on different things. And there's nothing, none at all?" She had shaken her head, lips pursued with the righteous absolute certainty of a first child. If only he would ask that question now—now when she, too, could feel the high, clear note when the single ray of sunlight broke its silence against an edge of crystal.

But Abel was impatient today, distracted by everything, distressed by the fragility of the glass and the closeness of too many strangers, so they didn't stay. Margaret straightened her hat and tried to make her face easy and pleasant, but there was a pursed, hard look of want around her mouth and for a moment, seeing it in the small mirror of her compact, she was ashamed.

He walked ahead of her quickly toward the car. She was being slowed by shop after shop that pulled her eye and made her turn for a minute toward each display. All the colors, textures and designs, all the profusion held her staring. There were rich warm furs in a dozen styles displayed so beautifully in the windows, handbags and hats and shoes, jewelry, in richness as austere as any poverty, fathering their mellow lights alone in their cases. She saw Abel's head losing itself in the crowd. She would have to hurry to catch up. Between two storefronts there was a tiny alley and blocking the entrance, a man was sitting on his coat. She nearly stumbled over his feet, sticking part way out onto the sidewalk. Her weight had been thrown forward and she came down heavily on her left foot, her arm out instinctively found the back of a woman's coat and hung to it for a moment. The woman turned. "Oh, I'm so sorry!" The woman nodded brusquely and was gone. Before her, the feet remained. She wanted them to belong to a drunk asleep in the alley, and so she turned and looked at him saying, "I beg your pardon, I'm sorry." But it wasn't the drunk. It was He. She had grown up and grown middle-aged, but he hadn't changed at all, not even his clothes, and he was here again with a bundle of cards this time, the manual alphabet and a sign: *"I Am Deaf."* The same hat with the same few coins as a lure. Then the sound of the light shattered the crystal. Margaret began to curse him. She used Signs she had never consciously learned, and Signs she knew and had tried to forget, the stunted, vulgar Sign of the untaught Deaf. For a minute the beggar's eye traveled appraisingly up and down, almost with relish, appreciating the details of her correct and tasteful exterior: a well-fed matron unacquainted with life's hard edges—she had given herself away. Then he smiled crookedly and answered with the single gesture universally used by Deaf and Hearing alike: the single finger, pugnaciously. There was nothing to do then but turn and walk on.

Abel saw his daughter coming toward him and for a minute he was frightened. The outfit looked the same, the studied look of her was the same. What was different was in her face, which she always wore in public with the same too-careful control. She looked, with all her neat perfection, like the fugitive of a bombed city.

"What?" he Signed unconsciously, as she came toward him. Her public self was fighting whatever had happened in the minute since he had last seen her walking and looking and stopping and walking again. She would not answer. The car was parked in a lot and they went in together, Abel to the car to wait and Margaret to pay the lot-attendant. He saw her at the little office fumbling in her purse for one thing and then another. It wasn't like her—his Margaret never seemed to be caught, to be vulnerable or even for a moment humanly off-poised with the ordinary discomforts of existence. His Margaret was safe, magically immune from the broken heel, the flat tire, the torn stocking, the drink upset, the sudden rain, the absence of nickels. It was harder to love such a person than it was to love someone like Janice, whose clothes were never, never right. But he did love his daughter, even though she was a little frightening sometimes, and now he was frightened in a new way, because when Margaret's face was not drawn smooth and blank to the world, who could know if a chair would hold or a car go, or the street lead him home as it had always done before? He thought pettishly; I'm too old to be given all this now. It's too late to have all these changes made in the people I need. Then he wondered what it could be that had changed her in a minute. Surely it wasn't longer than that. He had walked on ahead to keep her from stopping at every store and he had looked back now and then and seen the hat coming on along toward him, slowing a little bit when she was caught by some window, pausing, and then jouncing on toward him. Before he crossed the street he had looked again and seen her coming, no more than half a block away and he had crossed and gone up to the entrance of the lot to stand and wait and then she had come, changed.

She had finished paying and was coming toward the car, fighting more desperately now—rage or tears—he couldn't tell which. She got in and slammed the door so that every screw, bolt and gear remembered itself. Abel, seeking something that would make her be his Margaret again, said, "Why aren't you taking your other car, the new one that William got for you?"

"It's in the shop," she said stiffly, "to be fixed."

"What happened now, on the street to make you act so bad?"

"I met someone."

"Who?"

"A fit parent for a Saint."

24

*M*ARSHALL had decided that he wouldn't be going back to school. He had called them, collect to tell them. School was artificial, he said, the work he was now doing was real. William was quietly acid and Margaret, listening on the extension upstairs, said little. "Mother, you sound so sad. I wanted you to be happy, knowing that I'm doing work that counts, where I'm needed, that I don't have to live a hypocritical, dishonest life. I thought you would be happy about that."

"What a pity that with all those morals, your understanding should have improved so little," William said, and hung up. All that Maragret could say before she said good-bye was that she knew that he felt he was doing the right thing and that she hoped he would find fulfillment in it. The words sounded like something printed, and she thought crazily of herself sitting on the street holding a packet of cards printed with those words, a cap held out for money and the old tweed coat of the Deaf beggar. On the other side of the card might be the manual alphabet and the extra thing they always added, gobble-bobble-blobble to the less fortunate, blub-blub-blub to the disabled and handicapped. She hung up the phone and sat there crying.

And Marshall had written another letter. Janice and Abel stood dressed and ready to go to a meeting, holding out the letter he had written. Margaret knew it as she came into the house—something in the way they held themselves, in their closeness to each other, sleeves touching, a unity half attack, half defense, and she felt like the old dog that the boys used to tease back on Vandalia Street with its dented face and rickets-twisted legs. The days of that dog were full of shocks and deceptions, firecrackers, tearing bags of water. When it had been harried beyond its endurance, it had attacked itself and died, its teeth buried in its own leg. Here was a vision, a sharp memory of that forgotten dog thirty years later, looking up at her from a gutter that the mind had saved for some mysterious purpose of its own.

"Who is Society?" Abel asked. He was reading from the letter.

"I don't know," Margaret said. "I don't think he knows either."

"Well, it is dishonest," Abel said. "Marshall says it is corrupt." He spelled it elaborately.

"I know," Margaret said. "Marshall has always been too modest to include himself in his hardest judgments about Society."

"Well, if it is us, he thinks we lie and make evil wars and do evil things every day."

"I know that, too," Margaret said. "But the only serious lies I ever told were about him. I thought if he ever reconsidered and wanted to come back and maybe work with his father, I didn't want that way closed to him so I lied to a few people about his being down there." She did not mention that she had also lied to them.

"He said that William puts people out of work."

"I think William's work has given the world more good than evil, but no one really knows. It will take a hundred years to prove if automation has more good than evil in it for mankind, or more evil than good. There is no way of knowing now."

"What does Marshall want us to do?" Abel asked.

"I think he wants us to be guilty because of the poor. He wants us to be ashamed. He wants us to end poverty and despair."

Abel's eyes widened. He looked around him, at Janice and at Margaret. Then he smiled slowly. "Well," he said, in long, elegant Sign, "we did that."

"He wants it ended right now, for everyone."

"Then we can only do one thing," Abel said to Janice.

"I think I know," Janice said, and began to smile.

"It's like Sign," Abel said; "it's very much like Sign."

One by one, Abel, then Janice, then Margaret, then all together, they began to laugh.

The author wishes to express her gratitude for information, co-operation, and vital help extended by the following people and companies: Mr. and Mrs. Charles Billings, Mrs. Richard Russell, Louise Waller, Mr. and Mrs. A. R. Cheek, Mr. Bill Gray of *The Canyon Courier,* Mr. Frank Plaut, Mrs. Frank Plaut, Hershfeld Press, United Cigar Co., *Denver Post* "morgue."